QUEEN OF LIGHT

REALMS OF LORE: FAE

AMBER THOMA

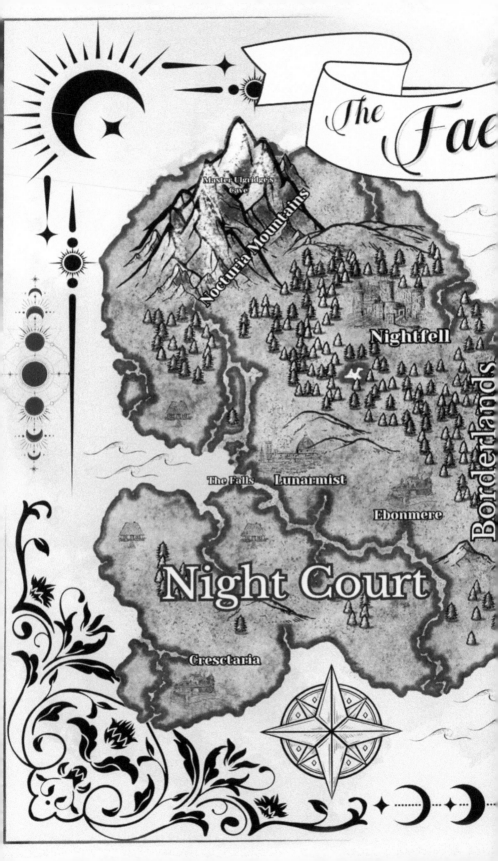

To anyone who has/does/will struggle with mental health.
You are not alone and you are loved.

Dear Reader,

Thank you so much for picking up Queen of Light. I hope you enjoy it! This book dives heavy into mental health and this might make it difficult for some readers to read. Please make sure to protect your own well-being. With that, welcome back to the Fae Realm!

Amber Thoma

This book contains scenes that may depict, mention, or discuss: abduction, abusive relationship, alcoholism, amputation, anxiety, assault, attempted murder, blood, bullying, child death, death, decapitation, depression, drugs, dysphoria, emotional abuse, hostages, infertility, kidnapping, murder, occult, physical abuse, prostitution, PTSD, sexism, sexual abuse, sexual assault, sexual harassment, slavery, torture, violence

Author Amber Thoma

Where to Start:

Prince of Darkness

Heirs of Darkness

Queen of Light

Queen of Light

Realms of Lore: Fae

Amber Thoma

Contents

Chapter 1
Tatiana

S he stared at the pitiful excuse for a sister through the bars
of the small cage hanging from the stone ceiling deep in
the bowels of her palace. She crafted it just for her, leaving
very little room for movement. It was this creature's fault her
Reminold was gone; her deplorable mate was also to blame. Fate,
in its cruelty, took something precious from her and gifted that joy
to those responsible. A euphoric warmth spread throughout
Tatiana, knowing that any pain she caused her would also bring
that hideous Night fae anguish.

The power she felt taking control of that feathered beast's
body as he fought against her with every ounce of his will was
intoxicating. The *whispers* in her head cackled with satisfaction.
Opportunities did not often arrive for her to display the power she
nurtured over the past half-century. The *whispers* suggested her
appearance at the Night Court would be the perfect moment to
debut her powerful magic. She eagerly agreed and was still on a
high. She took control of so many and carried out her attack in the

middle of Nightfell Palace, directly in front of the new king and queen, and no one could do anything about it. It was addictive.

Being their queen, she could do as she pleased with her subjects, like the entire regiment of soldiers she compelled to accompany her. She could still feel the fear and confusion as their limbs moved, not of their own accord. It did not matter what they commanded their bodies to do; they still moved into position to create a significant show of force. She did not tell them where they were going or what she was doing, and their vow of secrecy prevented any of them from sharing what had transpired with anyone else in her court until she was ready.

"You are not only their queen but the most powerful queen to ever exist. The power you now contain is deeper than anything you could have fathomed when you took the throne," the *whispers* praised.

"Oh, please," she scoffed. "The Tatiana who took the throne was nothing but a naïve, weak youngling." She had fought against the *whispers* in the beginning, but now she wanted to laugh at the foolish creature she once was.

It was an idyllic young-hood for the first hundred years. The *whispers* started around the same time she met her mate, Reminold. It had been close to her fiftieth birth year, which was nearly unheard of considering she just moved from her primary education to her specialized education as a royal and heir to the throne.

Him being a few hundred years older, she had been anything but excited about the match. A young Tatiana thought him to be rather old, and the fact he served on her mother's council did not seem to help matters. She saw him as a friend to her parents and not a potential lover, yet he had been eager to cement the mate bond.

Fate always seems to have a way of getting what it wants. Her resistance lasted no more than a handful of years. Either the mate bond or his persistence eventually won the war she had attempted to wage against it. Ultimately, she could not have been happier with life alongside Reminold.

She became queen at an early age for rulers of the Fae Realm. Her mother passed, leaving the throne to her when she was a mere two hundred years old since her father was nowhere to be found. He abandoned her just before her mother died, leaving her orphaned. The few beings she called friends became distant once she became queen, only coming around when they desired something from her. If not for Reminold, she would never have made it through those first hundred years when he ruled in her stead— even if he had a way of treating her like a youngling occasionally. He was her best friend and lover for over a thousand years, but now he's gone, leaving her abandoned once again.

When the *whispers* first began, she confused them with her internal monologue. Where the intrusive thoughts came from confounded her, and she grew alarmed. They were nothing like her typical musings; these were dark and terrifying. She thought herself mad when they created a voice of their own. Whether awake or dreaming, she could not distinguish between reality and fantasy.

She pinched the inside of her wrist to differentiate between what was real and what was not when awake. Her power could never keep up with the frequency at which she grew confused; she must have pinched her inner wrist hundreds of times per day. Reminold grew concerned when he noticed the bruises marring her golden skin, even more so when they never seemed to heal. He doted on her, always concerning himself with everything to do with her. No one cared for her the way he had.

"I wanted to take the feathered one as well. He is just as responsible as she is," she said through gritted teeth. "However, I knew we only needed the nymph, though I considered it."

"*Understandable. Many in your position would not have been able to maintain self-control. Reminold would be proud of the way you ripped them apart,"* the *whispers* said.

In the beginning, she refused to tell anyone. Not even Reminold, with his eyes full of concern. She feared the court might question her sanity, for even she questioned it—until she stopped resisting. Between the lack of sleep and losing touch with reality, she was exhausted. Not even her power could keep up with healing the dark circles under her eyes. The pressure of keeping something like this to herself only added to her exhaustion. One day, she ported to her favorite field of wildflowers and collapsed into sobs while gripping her hair at the root, hoping the pain would chase the incessant *whispers* away.

"Please," she sobbed. "Please leave me be."

"Let go, Golden Queen. Let go, and the entire realm can be yours." The *whispers* echoed throughout her head. *"You'll never be alone again."*

"I have no desire to have the entire realm; the Day Court is enough." As the words left her mouth, she knew they were false, as did the *whispers* chuckling from within her mind.

"There is no point lying to yourself; we both know the truth. You crave power—ultimate power. To shape the outcomes of events and command the very beings of this realm. You wish to hold fate itself in your hands, Golden Queen." She tried to scoff at the *whispers* because she never let herself acknowledge her greatest fear.

"Let go. All that you desire can be yours." She decided at that moment to give in and accept who she truly was. To this day, she cannot be certain if she gave in out of desire or because she was simply too tired to fight the *whispers* any longer.

Following their every command and unwillingness to sacrifice the opportunity to access such powerful magic, the *whispers* eventually led her to an abandoned structure. It was a dilapidated temple, long lost to history, open on all sides, with crumbling pillars still holding the roof above. In the center of the temple, she found a long slab of stone that was just the right size for a being to lie upon. Where the head would rest, a channel led down into the intricate symbol on the floor beneath her feet.

The *whispers*, quiet ever since she arrived, gave her no answers to the multitude of questions floating around her now silent mind. Looking up, she discovered an opening in the ceiling aligning perfectly with the eclipse of second day and the symbol within the floor. It had to be the location where somebody performed an ancient ritual some forgotten time ago.

Tatiana would never call herself patient. She became accustomed to the *whispers* telling her where to go and what to do over the last few hundred years. She screamed in anger when they refused to tell her anything, ignoring her every demand. Close to giving up and destroying the temple in a fit of rage, she kicked the strange half-wall behind the large slab of stone and heard a click.

She turned around and found a small box-shaped portion of the wall protruding. She pulled on it. The secret compartment revealed a small, thick book wrapped in a strange type of burnished red leather. It had no title on the cover or any other distinguishing marks. The second she lifted it into her hands, the *whispers* returned. They commended her discovery and urged her to open the little red book to discover the secrets within its pages.

She was born to be a queen, and her education reflected that. The specialty training she was required to take as a queen-in-waiting educated her on all the past dialects of her people. In order to comprehend any of the multitudes of scrolls and books in the Day Court palace archives, she needed to be fluent in all the dead languages of their court. When she opened the strange little book, the first page contained only four words written in a dialect no one had used in a millennium: *The Book of Blood*.

The *whispers* opened a whole new world of power and possibilities for her. They had not lied when they promised her a way to have everything she ever wanted. The power to control everything and everyone. If she had all the control, there would no longer be fighting. She could ensure everyone's happiness and keep the realm safe. What more could anyone want? When she finally told Reminold, his reaction was not what she had anticipated. Instead of excitement, he was concerned and thought she should seek a healer.

"My love, you are hearing voices inside your head that are not your own. You need help." Her face fell, and he was quick to add, "It's okay to need help, little lamb; the greatest fae in history all required help at one point or another."

"I do not require a healer, and I am telling you this because we share a bond, not because I desire your opinion or your advice." His face morphed into one of shock over the way she spoke to him. Never had she dared to speak to him harshly. Until then, she let him tell her what to do and how to do it. Her age caused her to lack confidence more often than not, and she had been happy to allow the pressure of the court to fall on her mate's shoulders.

From the moment she gave in to the *whispers*, her confidence grew into something tangible—demanding she do what she wanted and stop living the life others decided for her. Even her mate. Her voice grew colder, and it allowed no quarter for objections. Regardless of Reminold, she gave in to the demands her newfound confidence required and did whatever she pleased.

"What exactly are these 'whispers' whispering to you?" he asked her after recovering from his shock.

"They told me of a way to become the most powerful being in the entire realm." This captured her mate's attention. He was constantly seeking more and more power. He had a hunger for it.

"You are the most powerful being in the realm, or at least one of them. How do you intend to become even more so?" He sounded skeptical. She was sure this next piece of information would shock him even further. It could not be helped; she needed him to know.

6

"Blood magic." With those two paltry words, he recoiled. For the first time in their many years together, they fought.

"Absolutely not, Tatiana. I forbid it!" He had never raised his voice at her until then. He should have known forbidding her would only have the opposite effect. She laughed darkly at his ultimatum.

"You forbid it? You dare to forbid your queen?" she seethed at him. As soon as the words left her mouth, she knew she had gone too far, yet there was no taking them back. She had never once held her station as queen above him. He cried out, grasping at his chest where the mate bond was. Unable to stomach the hurt she caused him, she ported away.

Reminold had been furious when Tatiana returned with the book. He pleaded with her to destroy it and let that be the end of blood magic for good. Refusing, she accused him of being jealous that he was not the one to rediscover a greater power than either of them could ever have dreamed of possessing. He stared at her as if a stranger stood before him and left the room without a single glance back. She clutched at her chest as her mate bond burned when he walked away.

She would gladly suffer that pain every day rather than feel nothing at all. The nothingness reminded her daily of her loss, preventing her from pretending he was still with her. Devastation from her loss came in waves, growing into a crescendo of rage. A rage Tatiana would ensure her sister and her mate felt for the rest of their brief lives. She was held over mildly after butchering her sister in front of her mate. The twisting of the blade must have done more damage than expected. Her power depleted while healing, and Anin surrendered to the deep sleep her power demanded. She would return as soon as the murderer awoke. If fate required her to suffer, they would, too.

"You did it, Golden Queen," they said. *"You can now complete the plan we have worked toward for so long."*

"I did," she said, chest swelling with pride.

She could not wait for Anin to finish healing. The excitement of what would come next made the pain of losing her mate momentarily bearable. Tatiana smiled for the first time since her mate's murder as she shut the door to the small room.

Chapter 2
Kes

Kes had not moved from the chair next to the massive fireplace in Ciaran's study. He was there when Ciaran ported a sleeping Etain to their chamber late last second night. That was where he still sat, long after the disastrous end to Ciaran and Etain's mating ceremony. Everything around him appeared to be moving too fast and too slow simultaneously. The only thing in focus was the raging fire he had not taken his eyes off of once. The fire, a mirror to the flames growing within him.

Sleep would not find Kes. Every time he closed his eyes, all he saw was the knife entering Anin and the face she made when the queen twisted it. He was no longer aware of the hours passing. For all he knew, he was frozen in time and cursed to relive that moment for eternity.

The Day Queen, Tatiana, had blood magic. Kes only read about it once. It had been in a book mentioning the Great Battle from ancient times. The Night Court had little information about it—or anything else really—because of the Purge generations ago. The only thing he knew was that blood magic had been the cause of the Great Battle and gave the user the ability to control another's body. There was no other possibility for what she had done to him.

Ciaran interrogated him last night, grabbing him by the collar while shaking him and demanding answers he was unable to give. On some level, he was aware Ciaran was incredibly frustrated with him, but he could not hear, let alone comprehend, what his cousin was asking of him. Every time the scene replayed in his mind, he looked for something he could have done differently—anything. Just because he had yet to find something did not mean there was nothing.

"I sent word to the coven. Galetia, Lyra, and Panella should be here any moment. They will want to help." He was vaguely aware Etain was speaking to him. She was standing next to his chair; he noticed Ciaran was nowhere in sight. "He went to the coven to retrieve them," she said in response to his glance around the room. They did not have to wait long until Ciaran arrived with the witches in tow.

"Tell us everything," Lyra demanded with a hitch in her voice. Kes had been intent on tuning out everything around him until he heard the devastation that came close to matching his own in Lyra's voice. The two sisters wore red-rimmed eyes and tear-stained faces. Even the head witch looked like she was taking the news hard.

"The Queen of the Day Court has blood magic. She used it to freeze my limbs. I tried to fight it, but I could barely twitch my little finger. I was useless to her when it mattered most," Kes oozed with self-deprecation. He refused to look at anyone while he spoke, continuing to stare into the flames instead.

"Blood magic? Where the hell did she learn blood magic?" Ciaran asked, shocked.

"How the fuck should I know? Shall I send a message and ask her? Dear Evil Bitch Queen..." Kes said with venom as he ripped his eyes away from the flames to glare at his cousin. He released a deep sigh and dragged his hands down his face.

"What is blood magic?" Etain asked. "Ciaran mentioned the courts being at war, and it's been a long time since anyone used it."

"The only thing known is that it gives the user the power to control someone's body, willingly or not," Ciaran answered his mate.

"Which is exactly what that bitch did to me," Kes snapped at his cousin. "Forget the blood magic; we need to figure out how we are getting her back. I cannot just sit here doing nothing!" Now that Kes had started speaking, he needed action. He could not sit in this chair any longer while Anin was...gone. He got up and began pacing the study.

"We cannot forget the blood magic, cousin. It's the only reason we are not there right now, making the Day Queen pay for daring to come to my palace and insult me," Ciaran said through gritted teeth. Etain gave him a very pointed look before he added, "And, of course, getting Anin back." Kes looked up at Ciaran and saw his anger mirrored back at him, even if it was for different reasons. Kes could see the logic in what everyone was saying; he just did not want to hear it. He wanted an immediate answer with action, and he wanted it yesternight.

"I know you want to act immediately, and if the roles were reversed, I would want to do the same. However, we must approach this with caution. None of us can afford to be captured, especially by the Day Queen. Who would save Anin then?" Kes knew Ciaran was right, yet he found he did not care.

"Kes, are you able to feel where Anin is at this moment?" Lyra asked. Kes paused his steps and glanced over to her. He was grateful Anin's sisters were here. He knew they would do everything to get their sister back, and in this moment, he felt a connection to both of them—one of grief and determination. The three of them would never stop until Anin was safe again.

He felt his way down the mate bond to Anin as he made his way over to the table where everyone else was gathered. "I know she is far away, but that is all I can tell you. I would guess that places her at Daybreak Palace, which is not surprising since that is where the bitch queen lives." Kes was doing everything he could to hold his anger at bay, knowing it would only hinder their progress, though he could not help the menacing growl that ripped out of him.

Ciaran shoved the books off the table with one sweep of his arm, pulled a map of the realm out of thin air, and rolled it onto the table, halting at Kes's answer. "Right," Ciaran said, rolling his eyes at Kes's obvious suggestion. "I would guess the same. Does she not have a tracking spell?" he asked. Kes had somehow forgotten about the spell he placed on her during her first night in Nightfell.

"She does," he said while activating the spell on the map Ciaran had just rolled out. They all watched as the spell zipped across the parchment directly to the city of Daybreak, where it immediately went haywire. The spell never came to a stop as it flitted around the entirety of the city. "Well, that was useless," Kes said, his voice low and filled with the fury coursing through him. Gritting his teeth, trying to keep the sound of frustration in the back of his throat, he swiped the map off the table to join the objects Ciaran had just strewn on the floor.

Crossing his arms, Ciaran gave Kes the "Are you finished?" look. Kes did not care and gave his own look right back. If the roles were reversed, Ciaran would already be in the Day Court, destroying anything and everything he could.

"But why is information on blood magic so hard to find? I know the purge makes it difficult to learn anything in the Night

Court, yet surely the coven libraries hold something—right?" Etain asked, interrupting the tension between the cousins.

Galetia sighed while she shook her head. "In my long life, I have never once come across any text on blood magic beyond the basic knowledge. As part of the Realm Conservation Treaty, it was declared that all texts on blood magic be destroyed in the hope the magic would become eradicated."

"Well, that worked out well." All Kes heard was how impossible it would be to save his mate. The anger reached new heights within him. He knew he would need to get somewhere soon to release it. He gritted his sharp teeth tightly, trying to keep it together.

Galetia continued, "No, it did not. I apologize, Kes. I did not intend to make this seem any more impossible than it already appears. If the Day Queen was able to obtain blood magic, that means we can find a way to defeat her. This realm always has a counterbalance." Kes looked at the aging witch and nodded. Her words helped calm the anger a fraction. She was correct; this realm was a balancing act. There had to be a counterpart to everything; however, it would not be easy to find, and he did not have the patience to wait to rescue Anin.

"It's the only reason she was able to take Anin away. Blood magic gave her a massive advantage. Without it, she would not have been able to leave with Anin because you would never have allowed it." Etain's soft voice and kind words settled heavily inside him. He knew she was trying to tell him he had done nothing wrong, though Kes could not help but feel guilty. He failed Anin twice in less than a week.

"We already know what we cannot do. The question is, what *can* we do?" Panella had yet to speak since Ciaran ported them to the study, and her voice warbled at the end of her question. The challenge it was for her to hold her emotions in check was becoming apparent.

"Gather information. We do not know exactly where she's being held, how to defend against blood magic, or what state the Day Court is in. We need to figure out a way to manipulate the court to work for us and not against us." Kes released another growl at his cousin's words. "I know it is not what you want to hear, Kes. We need to be smart about this, and that requires time."

"No, we need to gather whatever sorry bags-of-bones pass as warriors around here and go get her. Now!"

"Quit acting like a fool!" Ciaran yelled. "If you go running there now, knowing absolutely nothing, you might as well hand yourself over to the queen. Then what do you think would happen? She would make you do things to Anin you could never come back from. It's what I would do, and she is far more unhinged than I am."

Kes's rage boiled past its tipping point. Slamming his hands down on the table, he bellowed his rage, causing all the witches to startle and Ciaran to growl at him. Too angry to even glance at any of them, he ported himself to his chambers.

He knew his actions had frightened Etain a few times since Anin was stolen from him. He did not want to scare any of the females in the room; however, he did not know how to release this rage inside him. He was not used to being the angry one; that was typically his cousin's role. He was supposed to be the over-the-top, wickedly theatrical one—the fun one. He did not think he could be himself again until Anin was safe.

He stood there, breathing heavily. Before even he knew what he was going to do, he began smashing everything he could while screaming his rage into the empty room. He would destroy it all! What was the point of any of this if it was empty of the being that gave his chamber life? He paused just as he made to throw the chair he held in his hands. It was the chair Anin sat in the most. The memory of sitting in it while she preened his feathers flashed through his mind. His rage left him all at once, and he collapsed to his knees with his head in his hands. The agony of her absence filled the void his anger had left behind, leaving him empty and broken.

Chapter 3
Etain

"Is it possible for you to take us back to the coven so we can begin searching for anything on blood magic?" Panella asked Ciaran after a few beats of silence following Kes's abrupt departure. Ciaran looked at Etain and then at the head witch before slowly nodding his agreement. Was he truly questioning leaving her alone with Galetia? Etain rolled her eyes at him. He had to know she would be more than safe with her great-aunt.

"Look for anything we have on mate bonds as well," Galetia told the sisters. "There may be something Kes can do to help Anin by using their connection. He needs to help her, and she needs his help."

"We will." With that, the sisters disappeared as Ciaran ported them away.

Etain felt Galetia grab her hands and place them between her own. It was something she found the head witch often did when trying to soothe another. So much happened in such a short period—too much. The extremes, from one emotion to another, began to take their toll on her. She felt exhausted. While at the same time, she felt the overwhelming need to do something.

"I could do nothing except grip on to Ciaran as tightly as I could. Perhaps if I had not held him back, Ciaran would have been able to come to their aid." Etain tried to hold back a sob, though it slipped out anyway. She woke earlier with guilt weighing heavily on her. Galetia guided her over to the chairs by the fireplace, never letting go of her hands.

"My dear, the Day Queen has blood magic. There was absolutely nothing any of you could have done," she said, giving Etain's hands a small squeeze. "From the very little I do know about it, no power can stand against it. There is obviously some form of defense; unfortunately, it is not knowledge I possess. It is likely she would have held Ciaran in her clutches as well. I imagine he would agree with me."

"I do," Ciaran said, startling them from above. "You cannot blame yourself, little witch. I had no intention of intervening." He was standing before one of the many bookshelves lining the room. She needed to put a little bell on him to prevent him from sneaking up on her anymore. The thought made her smile.

"The best thing you can do for Anin is to continue to hone your power and learn our magic. That way, when the time comes to strike back, you are prepared." Etain could feel the truth in Galetia's words. That did not necessarily make the situation any easier to handle. Anin and Etain were on the way to becoming fast friends. Only a few hours ago, Anin had transformed her nightmare of a gown into something elegant. Once more, she attempted to blink away tears that never seemed to leave her eyes.

"Perhaps you need something to do as much as the rest of us?" Etain looked up at the head witch and nodded. She needed to feel productive, the same way Kes and Anin's sisters did. Even Ciaran was searching the many bookcases within his study, likely looking for any missed books on mate bonds for Kes and any mentions of blood magic.

"Yes, I must confess that while I am grateful for the sense of control the last lesson gave me, it also left me with more questions than answers. What do the colors mean? Why did the black feel similar to the colors, yet entirely different as well?" Etain would have continued peppering her with even more questions had Galetia not patted her hands before holding up her own to get Etain to slow down.

"I would be concerned if you did not have a multitude of questions. You are an unusual case for us. Most witches begin learning their powers and magic as younglings. Witches have color magic, and most witches gain one at a time while maturing. You crossed the veil, having already matured, and now have to learn all of your colors at once. Most witches only ever have their power manifest into one or two colors at most, and very few gain one of the shades." Galetia leaned back in her seat to make herself more comfortable before she continued.

"Dark and light power are shades, and while still only manifesting in witches, it is extremely rare. So rare is dark power that there is very little information available about it, and nothing is known about light power. We only assume there must be one because the realm requires everything to be in balance. All power witches have come from the Many Faced Goddess, but the color magic is unique to us, whereas it is thought the shades are directly inherited from her. Shades are untamed and raw, and we know the dark power gives a witch some of the goddess' gifts, like looking into the future."

"So the shades feel similar to the colors because they both come from the goddess, yet they feel different because they come from a different part of her?" Etain asked; she was already wary of her power. Going from being a powerless human to a witch filled with unmatched power was unsettling. The small amount of control she gained had made her feel less volatile, which now felt inadequate. The weight of responsibility was starting to overwhelm her.

"Yes, that is a great way of thinking of it. The rarity of it is the reason I cannot help you with the shades. We teach what we know, and unfortunately, there is no other witch alive to help you hone it. The best we could hope for is a plethora of texts within the Coven of Remembrance library walls.

"However, your color power is something I am more than capable of helping you with. Each color represents a distinct form of power. For example, nearly every witch is born with the color green. This is the power you hold within you to pass on to your one and only daughter. It is the essence of a witch." Galetia closed her eyes, and a single tear slid down her cheek. Etain leaned forward to clasp her hands between her own, offering the same comfort the head witch was fond of giving.

"Are you alright?" Etain asked softly, unsure if she should have asked or if silent support would have been preferred. There are some things females do not wish to discuss. Etain had seen similar looks on the faces of the childless women in her village. Some continued to try even though each pregnancy was lost, or the child came without life, while others could never conceive at all.

"Yes, dear...thank you," she said, giving Etain's hands a slight squeeze prior to pulling hers away. "I am one of the few born without the color green. I have always loved younglings, and I am still heartbroken that I was unable to have one of my own. I think this is why I wanted to become head witch so that I could be a mother to all within the coven."

"That is beautiful, Galetia. I am truly sorry you were not given the thing you desired most. You would have made a wonderful mother. I see it in the warmth you freely give to all of the coven." It always bothered Etain that there were women wanting nothing more than a child to give their love to and never be gifted one. It bothered her even more when a woman was gifted many children and never had a drop of love to give them. Fate did not always get it right.

"Thank you," she said as she wiped any stray tears from her face and composed herself. "Well, now, where were we? Ah, yes, I think the best way to learn is for me to teach a basic exercise we teach all younglings when their powers first begin to manifest. If you practice this on all your colors many times per night, I have no doubts you will learn to strengthen and grow your powers in no time."

"That would be wonderful. What do I need to do?" Etain asked.

"In the beginning, I would suggest sticking with one color at a time until you feel confident with each one. After that, the possibilities are endless, as long as you keep pushing yourself," Galetia said.

"How do I do that?" asked Etain.

"Just like before, close your eyes and focus on the colors of your power. The color you choose dictates the way you should practice with it. If you choose an abstract color—yellow or violet —you require nothing else but yourself to grow that power. If you choose a passive color—pink or orange—you must apply it to something outside of you. For example, you have orange power, which is creativity. You can use that in conjunction with any spell and it will help you see the way to improve that spell in whatever way is desired."

"Oh, that's rather handy," Etain said as she sat up taller and finally felt like one of her powers fit who she was. She was most excited to learn about her magic. They had no power or magic on the other side of the veil, yet they used spells all the time. Spells made her think of her mother, and she hoped practicing them would make her feel closer to her. Her mother would have loved this.

"It is. I use it all the time," Galetia said with a smile. "Finally, if you were to choose an active power—blue or red—you would need to be doing an action to use them. For example, your blue would need to be used when doing something physically strenuous. If you were lifting something heavy or if you were in a fight."

"Ha! Me in a fight—can you imagine? I am still devastated by what I did to Seamus in the woods. He may have deserved it, but it does weigh heavy on my shoulders." A chill rippled down her back. She wondered how long it would take until she no longer saw the remnants of him strewn everywhere within that clearing and all over her as vividly as she did now.

"I can, and there is no reason to fear it. Here, let's practice accessing your blue so you can feel its intentions ," her great-aunt said while patting her hand.

"Alright," Etain said with a sigh. She knew it was something she would need to be able to use. How else did she expect to protect the beings of the Night Court and the witches if she did not? Etain took a deep breath and closed her eyes.

"Tell me what you see."

"My colors are still moving in a languid circle around the black, which is still calm and controlled." She was surprised, considering the emotional state she was in.

"Wonderful. Now, see if you can get them to stop again. Once they are still, I want you to focus on the blue. Reach out with your mind to touch it and feel what power it grants you."

Etain touched the blue, and she felt strength both physically and in power. It made her feel she could defend herself and those she was duty-bound to protect. To do that, she would likely have to attack another. The thought of attacking anyone made her feel sick to her stomach. Could she follow through if the need arose? The desire to protect would have to outweigh the cost to her soul.

"Do you feel it?" Etain nodded to the head witch with her eyes still closed. "Excellent, my dear. Now, I want you to imagine bringing the power into your center, just below your heart, at the bottom of your breastbone." Etain gently pulled the blue power towards her, and as it went into her center, the power burst with a blue light she could feel sitting inside her, waiting. "Now send it out to flow through your entire body." She felt the power mix with her blood and flow throughout the entirety of her.

"Do you feel the way it seeps into every inch of you?" Etain nodded. She felt powerful in a way that made her nervous. "This is what you want to feel before you go into a fight. I know how you feel about violence. Just consider there will always be someone willing to do violence unto you or those you love. You could be one of the greatest warriors the realm has ever seen and yet only use your skills in defense."

There was no doubt in Galetia's words. Etain scoffed to herself. Her? A great warrior? Not only did she have no clue how to fight, she had always been a healer. The idea of harming another, even in defense, felt intrinsically wrong.

Chapter 4
Ciaran

F inding anything in his study about blood magic was unlikely, yet he looked anyway—just in case. Several nights ago, when he first brought Etain to the Night Court, he completed a thorough search. If he happened across anything on mate bonds, he would count that as a bonus.

He knew everyone else's major priority was rescuing Anin, but his was not. The Day Queen had the means to physically control him and his mate. There were very few things in the realm that frightened him. Losing Etain was a recent fear, though losing control was lifelong.

He could hear Etain murmuring with the head witch in low tones from where he was several floors of shelves above them. His mate's power fascinated him. Where his was elemental, hers was color. He never had a reason to study color power, and he had always found it inferior to the elemental powers of the fae—until now.

Etain's power was deep and raw, with a wildness about it. It reminded him of his own shadow power, and he wondered if there was a way he could access her power through the mate bond.

Having even more power alongside the new shadow-walking ability he received made him feel untouchable. He would need to be if he ever needed to face the Day Queen and her blood magic.

When she showed up uninvited to the mating ceremony celebration, Ciaran was at first amused. His amusement quickly changed to confusion as he watched Kes do nothing while his mate was abused and taken right in front of him. He wondered if Tatiana had been too blinded by her rage that it never occurred to her to use blood magic on him, or if she had limited reach. He hoped it was the latter.

Before Ciaran knew the queen had such magic, he thought it would be a simple rescue. They would find the nymph and take her back without issue, now that he could access his full well of power. Blood magic changed things, making it not very simple after all.

It had been centuries since blood magic appeared in the Fae Realm. At least, officially. He was certain he had felt its effects as a youngling. Ciaran still did not know how it worked or how to fight against it. There had to be a way, or it would not have been successfully eradicated for so long. The issue was finding any information within the Night Court that could help him.

The purge was becoming the bane of his existence. The lack of knowledge within his court from before the purge was a genuine issue. It had taken place not too long ago compared to the entire history of the realm, leaving him with only the most recent history and the ramblings of his not-so-long-ago ancestors. He wished for the hundredth time he was able to resurrect the shortsighted fool who ordered the purge so he could kill him—slowly.

He did not care if the fool was his many-times great-grandfather; he would not suffer a being that moronic to live. His hand clenched around the book he was holding too tightly, causing the binding to snap. He angrily threw the book, and it audibly crashed into shelves across the room, causing the females below to grow silent. He forced himself to take deep breaths and calm himself before he smashed his entire study. Again. He did not think Etain would find that kind of behavior amusing, not in the way Kes always had.

He did not enjoy seeing his cousin suffer, and to his surprise, he found the lack of his usual antics unsettling. Kes's constant ramblings and flippant attitude had driven Ciaran to violence on multiple occasions. The absence of it should be relieving, if not peaceful, and yet here he was feeling anything but peaceful. Ciaran heard the murmuring below pick up again.

He closed his eyes and tilted his head up while he clenched and unclenched his hands. This was not a feeling he enjoyed—this *caring*. He was resolved to care for his mate; it was not something he could change, nor did he want to. Caring for Kes, however, was inconvenient. He wanted his cousin to have the happiness a completed mate bond brings, but not at the expense of his own needs.

Sighing out his final deep breath, he attempted to come to terms with the two sides of himself warring with each other. He pushed his cousin to the back of his mind and focused on what he wanted. Their desires were bound to intersect at some point. Once Ciaran found a way to make himself impervious to blood magic, it would be a simple task to retrieve the nymph.

Having no luck finding anything new on mate bonds or even a mention of blood magic, as he knew would happen, he ported to another section of shelves. His search was more of a cursory glance and a means to occupy himself while keeping an eye on Etain as she explored her powers without him hovering about. He could still hear everything the two said to each other in soft voices, once again finding himself intrigued by his mate's abilities.

He had not yet asked her what the Land had said to her. He wanted to ask her last night, but her exhaustion became too much. She had fallen asleep in the chair where she had only been sitting for a few moments. He considered waking her to find out but thought better of it once he looked upon her peaceful face.

He had not blamed Etain for succumbing to sleep, not while he himself had felt their bed beckoning them. Kes remained still and stared into the flames as Ciaran picked Etain up from the chair, cradled her in his arms, and then ported them to their bedchambers. Leaving Etain in her dress, he had placed her on the bed prior to crawling in beside her.

He witnessed and scented her fear multiple times over the past few nights, but nothing like the visceral fear she displayed once the Day Queen arrived. He knew it had everything to do with her vision and the belief he would be taken from her. It took every bit of self-control not to laugh when she voiced her fear, though now he thought perhaps she had been right to entertain such thoughts.

Last night, the moment Tatiana fled with the nymph—her sister—he ordered everyone out of the throne room and ported Etain, Kes, and himself to his study. It was obvious now, thinking back on how little information the nymph gave them about her situation, that she was a princess of the Day Court. It bothered him that he had not fit the pieces of the puzzle together. He did not like surprises, and lately his life had become one surprise after another.

The past few nights bled into each other, making it feel as if he had just lived one very long night. He thought the reason they would be staying up all last second night would be for something else entirely. It was not the night he had envisioned for them and he still owed his little witch a proper mating.

His need was becoming unbearable, and he was tempted to end their little lesson and steal her away at that very moment. He was relieved when the conversation below headed towards an end. He dropped silently behind Etain's chair just as Galetia told his little witch something he had been thinking ever since he first saw her in the woods only a few nights ago.

"I know this all feels unbelievable, but please remember, this is something you will gain over time. You still have to learn to use the power. Begin training; I'm sure your mate would be happy to teach you. As your skills improve, your power will strengthen as well. When it comes time to use the power, it will feel as simple as breathing."

Etain followed the head witch's gaze and then gaped at him. He loved sneaking up on her; the surprised sounds and little jumps always brought him immense joy.

"I will personally see to her training. There is nothing that would bring me more peace than knowing my mate can take care of herself in a battle." Ciaran grinned down at her with his signature too-wide grin, which told her exactly how much he was going to enjoy training her. Etain's breath quickened as Ciaran's grin grew into a wicked smile, causing the flush to begin to creep up from her chest and bloom across her face.

"...I do not mean to interrupt. However, I need to return home and wish to give you both the privacy you obviously need," Galetia said with humor laced into her words.

He did not think it possible, but the flush his little witch wore so beautifully turned an even darker shade of crimson. He wasted no time taking hold of both females, and—faster than he thought possible—he abandoned the head witch at the gates to her coven and stood alone with his mate in their bedchambers.

"Ciaran! You did not even give me a chance to say goodbye. She must think us terribly rude. I did not even get to ask her something important." His little witch sounded incredulous as she attempted to chide him.

"You can send her a message later," he said, waving off her concerns. She attempted to give him a reproachful look while fighting a grin, before releasing a sigh of acceptance.

"What were you searching for up there? Whatever it was seemed to give you a difficult time," she said as he came up behind her. He whispered his fingers down from just below her ear to her shoulder, all the way down to her hand.

"Any mention of blood magic or anything else that could shed some light on the specific limits of a mate bond." He entwined their fingers as his mouth followed the path his hand had just taken until he reached her shoulder. He decided he would spend the rest of the night pulling all of his favorite sounds from his little witch.

"Did you find anything to help Kes and Anin?" she asked breathlessly. He skimmed his other hand across and down her back until he came to the ties that held up her gown.

"No." He did not tell her he was looking for himself and not his cousin, as he flicked his claws out and sliced down the ties. The sudden drop of her dress made her gasp. There was one sound.

He dragged the same claws gently up her back, never leaving a mark behind. Ciaran removed the few pins still holding her hair off to the side in a slightly disheveled version of what it had been last second night and watched as the strands swung down to cover her back. He ran the dark, blood-red strands through his claws, removing a few tangles.

"I have been looking forward to this since last night, little witch." He was rewarded with a small tremor that worked its way down her body while her breathing became uneven. At the mention of the night prior, her face fell slightly.

"Ciaran..." Etain whispered with a sigh. Ciaran released her hand and caressed his claws all over her body, paying close attention to her reactions. He dragged one claw over her nipple causing a moan to escape as she pushed her chest out as if her body were looking for more. There was another sound. He spun her around so she was facing him.

Ciaran would never grow tired of the way she responded to him. He reached down, gripping one clawed hand on either side of her ass, allowing his claws to scrape her sensitive skin. He then lifted her and wrapped her legs around his waist to easily reach her mouth with his own. She pulled away from the kiss, placed her hands on either side of his face, and gazed into his eyes.

"I was terrified it was going to be you. I am devastated for Anin and Kes, yet I'm relieved it was not you. That must make me sound awful, though I could not imagine living any kind of life without you." Ciaran held her even tighter. They had not spoken about the previous night alone until this moment.

"It does not make you sound awful, and who cares if it does? It makes you sound honest. If we were ever separated, not even death could keep me from finding my way back to you. I will always find you." Then he pressed his mouth to hers in a tender kiss while he walked them to the bed.

He gently laid her down across the bed before slowly crawling on top of her. He hovered above her as she dragged her hands over his chest. She unwrapped his shirt and then cast it aside to trace the marks across his skin. She reached for the ties of his pants while he began kissing and nipping at her neck. He stood back up to remove them before going right back to bring his lips to hers, sealing his words with a bruising kiss.

They spent some time exploring every slope and dip of each other's bodies, building a slow-burning need inside of them. His tongue explored the valley between her breasts as she writhed beneath him. Ciaran enjoyed every sigh, gasp, and moan he pulled from her. She pulled him down to her and lifted her knees, allowing him to fit even closer to her.

"Ciaran, please... I... I need you," Etain said breathlessly against Ciaran's lips. He needed no other invitation. He fit himself to her, slowly sinking into her heat. Etain let out a soft moan when he was fully seated inside her. Ciaran grabbed her hands and entwined his fingers with hers before holding them above her head.

He slowly rocked into her. It felt as if he needed his body to be

33

as close to hers as possible. This was not only about desire; this was about bringing their souls together. He kept the pace slow while he whispered all the things he loved most about her. He could feel her tightening around him as her body climbed higher towards that peak, and he drove into her harder and faster, pulling breathless cries from her lips.

He could feel himself reaching his own crescendo as Etain tightened further around him. The dance their souls rehearsed brought their bodies perfectly in sync with each other as they both crested the top of their peaks, falling over the edge. He spilled himself into her with a groan as Etain cried out her own release.

"That, my little witch, is my favorite sound in the entire realm," he whispered into her ear. He moved inside her as he hardened again and pulled those sounds from her again and again until second night came and they both collapsed in exhaustion.

Even if they lived a millennium, he would still never hear those sounds enough times.

Chapter 5
Kes

The moment he walked in, Kes knew this would be a long, frustrating meeting he already had no patience for. The council members were throwing tantrums over the most asinine of things. They knew Etain was to be a council member, and they knew she would pick the member who would fill the last chair. It did not surprise him when she chose Galetia since she already relied on her for counsel. It made perfect sense to him.

If he had to hear Syndari demand once again the seats be filled with other Night Court members, he would divest her head from her shoulders just to never have to hear her obnoxious voice again. If this were any other night and the celebration had ended differently, he would laugh at the ridiculousness that any of them thought they had a say in who sat on this council. The three Night Court members sitting around this table were here, more out of tradition than necessity.

It was like they had all forgotten his mate was stolen from their own court just a couple of nights ago. They were more concerned with Etain and her appointment of the head witch, both now on the Night Court council, than with the invasion during their king and queen's celebration. Fiandra took particular offense to the sisters sitting against the wall, observing. Both Lyra and Panella wore provoking grins directed at the fae that Kes would normally find particularly amusing.

Their presence was a welcome surprise. Not only did the sisters irritate the Night fae council members, but their priority would be the return of Anin as well. Ciaran's priority was the blood magic, and while Kes could not fault him for it, he knew rescuing Anin was far down his list of priorities.

"This is the Night Court! Not the Borderlands!" yelled the shrill voice of Syndari.

"You forget yourself. I am your queen, and the queen of witches as well. How do you not understand the necessity for the two to come together? The Land obviously wished it to be so, or it would not have made me queen of both, now would it? Unless you think you know better than the Land," Etain said, her voice soft but sharp, making the talking heads quiet for at least a moment.

Etain was not one to stand for any kind of bullying. It did not surprise him that she would find her voice the moment the witches began being mistreated. The very first time he met her, she became Anin's champion, finding his treatment of her horrific. He cringed, recalling the look on Anin's face after failing to let her out of the cage. Even after he forced her to make deals with him, she would never have considered otherwise.

Syndari grumbled something quietly under their breath that none of the fae around could truly hear.

"What was that Syndari?" Ciaran asked, his voice cold and menacing. A warning he was on the verge of destroying something —or someone. Kes was happy he was not the only one about to lose the grip on their anger. His cousin was likely contemplating the merits of adding three more heads to the ones decorating the great hall.

"If you have something to say, make sure we can all hear it. There is no room for cowards on this council, let alone this court. Next time, I will assume you are saying something treacherous about your lovely queen. Which, of course, is treason in my eyes." Etain placed a hand gently on Ciaran's arm, and the murderous intent slipped from his eyes. A simple touch from his mate was all it took.

It made Kes acutely aware of what he should be enjoying with his own mate, except Anin was gone. He could not stop thinking that he could have done something to save his mate. He kept running through the moment, looking for any scenario that would have kept Anin safe and here with him.

His anger began building the moment the shock wore off. His control almost slipped a few times. The three fae across the table were testing his willpower, which was already in short supply. They should be discussing plans at this moment instead of listening to the same beings continue to drone on with their baseless objections.

Kes stood suddenly and slammed his fists into the table hard enough it cracked, all but Ciaran flinched at the sound of his anger connecting with the table. The room instantly descended into silence. Kes's heart was beating so loudly, he was unable to hear anything else. He dropped his head and clenched his fists while he stared at the crack running the entire length of the table.

"There are far more important things to do. I am tired of sitting here listening to the same beings postulate over the same perceived indignation," Kes said in a deadly serious tone no one in the room had ever heard from him before, including himself. He could not be the same Kes everyone was used to being presented with. He was no longer that version of himself. His entire foundation changed the moment that the obsidian blade plunged into his mate's body.

"What could possibly be more important than the future of

our court? What happens here tonight will irrevocably change the Night Court," Fiandra sneered.

"We need to devise a plan to infiltrate the Day Court, kill their queen, and retrieve Anin." Kes was trying to keep his rage in check, but these three were making it an impossible task.

"Oh!" Georden let out a shocked laugh. "You cannot be serious...you *are* serious." He laughed again, this time louder. No more than a breath later, the other two idiots joined him.

"Why would we, the Night Court, care anything about what happens to some wretched Day fae?" Syndari asked, disgusted.

Kes slammed his fists into the table one last time, breaking it in half and causing the three Night fae to jump back in their seats.

"You should care," he said darkly, "BECAUSE SHE IS MY MATE!" He roared his rage at the useless beings. It was a living, breathing thing inside him that was reaching a point of destruction. He could barely hear over the sound of his blood pounding through his head.

He turned and walked toward the doors of the chamber, throwing them open as he strode out, causing the doors to slam into the walls. Ciaran said something to him as he distanced himself from the council chambers. He was too far gone, both physically and mentally, to hear anything anyone said. If Kes had to listen to another being spew slurs against Anin or dismiss rescue plans one more time, there were going to be more heads decorating the Great Hall.

Kes was faintly aware he was being followed. He did not stop to see who it was. He could have ported to the training facility he liked to use, but he needed to walk. It had a way of calming him. Although his current state was too volatile for walking to make even the slightest dent.

The palace had many training facilities and yards, although he enjoyed this one above all others. This was the one he coated in his blood as a youngling while the twenty-three honed him into the weapon he became. Ciaran's father became enraged when Ciaran disappeared one crescent night hundreds of years ago and he could no longer control his son's training. Without Ciaran around, his father's eyes fell on Kes, molding him viciously into whatever he wanted him to be.

The only thing Kes had control over in his life were the words that came out of his mouth. Nothing angered the old King of the Night Court more than Kes's theatrics and uninterested attitude. He wore that persona as a shield until he could no longer remember the curious youngling he had once been. Every cut from the twenty-three only strengthened his shield.

The king hoped it would turn him into an angry and vicious monster. He succeeded with one, though he could never make him the angry beast he wanted most of all. His sharp tongue and sarcastic words grated on the king's nerves and made Kes take it even further. There was always a price to be paid, usually involving a few nights in recovery. It was always worth it.

He never had to worry about anyone else using this training facility—his training facility. The courtyard style of the space appealed to him. The lack of a roof allowed him to launch into the sky at will or run through drills using his wings. Most of all, it kept him from feeling trapped. Several of his trainers had found it amusing to ambush him as his skills grew and outmatched theirs, many times requiring him to fly away out of their reach, or become a bloody mass on the floor. Until he no longer had to flee, and he was the only one left laughing.

If his uncle saw him now, he would have worn the smug look of victory. He was filled with rage, the way his uncle always wanted. The thought enraged Kes even more. The slice of a blade that never touched his skin shattered the shield he wore for most of his life. He felt Anin's wound all the same. He felt it more than any other wound he had ever received. Taking his anger out on the heavy bag hanging from a beam in the facility's corner would have to do. Unless either the king of old or the mad queen became available.

An indeterminable amount of time passed until he finally stopped. His body was covered in sweat, making his feathers stick to him uncomfortably. The anger was still there, now simmering instead of the raging storm it was. His body was exhausted and his mouth dry. Kes went to get some of the herbal water kept on a table across the room. That was when he noticed Lyra and Panella leaning on the wall the table was against.

"How long have you two been standing there?" His voice was void of emotion before gulping an entire cup down.

"Long enough to finish our own training and still have to wait for you to finish murdering that bag," Panella said. Kes made some kind of grunting noise to acknowledge her words. They all glanced at the bag in question, hanging in tatters. It was not the first time he needed to replace it, and he knew it would not be the last.

"Kes," Lyra said as she took a few cautious steps toward him. "We are the only ones who come close to caring for Anin as you do." Kes wanted to scream at them. There was no way they could come anywhere near the pain he was experiencing. Yet he knew that would be an unfair thing to say, and untrue as well.

Their eyes were rimmed in red and a tightness surrounded them, where before they had been open and filled with mirth. More than anything, he saw the same rage he felt reflected in their eyes. They were as enraged as he was. He gave them a slight nod, acknowledging that they were fighting the same internal battle.

"I cannot sit here doing nothing while she is there in pain, and at the whim of that psychotic queen." His voice shook with more despair than anger.

"We are with you, Kes. To whatever end, no matter where it takes us and no matter how dangerous. We are with you. We will not stop until our sister is safe again," Lyra vowed.

"I think the best thing we could do for now is continue the search for more information on mating bonds at the coven. Magical bonds always fascinate witches, though witches do not have mates—Etain is the first. Someone was bound to have recorded knowledge we could use to help Anin right now. We have the entire coven looking for something to help her immediately," Panella informed him.

He thought about implementing his own search of the palace for any information Ciaran may have missed while they searched the coven. He needed action, and although it was not the one he wanted to be taking, it was still something.

Something was better than nothing.

Chapter 6
Etain

E tain watched as Ciaran placed his hand on the edge of one side of the ruined table, and it began to knit itself back together. The shock of the broken surface paused the bickering, though once it was whole, the arguments continued as if nothing had happened. Kes was right; they were wasting their time with these petty arguments.

Etain could not shake thoughts of her missing friend and the toll it took on Kes. She was worried about the treatment Anin was receiving after seeing the madness of the Day Queen for herself. She wanted her friend rescued, though she did not want to risk Ciaran being placed in a position to be controlled by the Day Queen's blood magic.

The revelation Anin was the sister of the Day Queen came as a shock to them all. Looking back, she realized Anin had given them many clues. It almost seemed obvious in retrospect. Etain was not yet familiar with the inner workings of the Fae Realm, but she should have considered her friend would have to pose a relatively colossal risk to the Day Court for the king to come for her the night of the Lunar Ball.

There were several "what ifs" she thought about, such as if they had known she was a princess, would that have changed anything? Thoughts like that did nothing to improve the situation because, no matter the alternate scenario, what happened still happened. She released the guilt she had been harboring since her conversation with Galetia yesternight. A burning rage now filled the space the guilt had taken. Etain had always wished for a sister. The Day Queen was lucky enough to have one, and that was how she treated her? It infuriated her, and that rage was turning into an inferno as the three council members mocked Kes and dismissed Anin.

She did not blame Kes for his reaction. The willpower it must have taken to do no more than break a table and then walk away was applaudable. She was trying to stay in control of her own emotions as the bickering continued. She felt Ciaran on the verge of a deathly violent outburst, and that was not something she wished to see.

"Enough!" she said, loud enough to silence the room. She felt her power seep out around her as her anger grew. She glared at the three squabbling fools, meeting each one of them in the eyes, and said, "I do not know why you think your seat at this table is anything more than a privilege your king has allowed you." As she spoke, she could feel her hair dance around her head on a phantom breeze. She made no attempt to stifle her anger or her power. For once, she welcomed the wild display.

"I will happily dismiss each of you and keep our council to those intelligent enough to see why we should do exactly what Kes said." She saw Syndari open their mouth, no doubt to cow her into silence. "I would think very carefully, Syndari, before you say whatever it is on the tip of your tongue. I mean every word I have spoken," Etain said with a terrifying lack of emotion. Syndari snapped their mouth shut. She could feel Ciaran's approval at her display of dominance.

"For some reason, because I am both a witch and a human, you seem convinced I am one to be trifled with. You each must have forgotten I am your queen, an oversight on your part." She let out more power, enjoying the thrill of working symbiotically with it. The flames around the room grew while objects lifted into the air and flew around the table. "Allow me to put an end to those thoughts now. You will respect my decisions or you will be removed in whatever way my mate sees fit." She noticed their eyes flicking to Ciaran, who likely wore a murderous grin, since their faces seemed to pale considerably.

"Gladly, little witch," Ciaran said, as he caressed her leg under the table. Apparently, asserting herself made him a certain kind of...*appreciative.*

"Galetia is here to stay. The Day Court has been taking witches in the night," Etain said, and before she could continue, Fiandra cut her off.

"Why should we care what the Day Court is doing with witches?" she said snidely.

"If you had not interrupted me, I would have told you this is exactly how the Day Court is gaining untold amounts of power. Do not ever interrupt me again. This is your one and only warning." Etain stood and leaned towards Fiandra, allowing more anger and power to course through her. "Do you understand?" Fiandra's eyes widened, and she gave Etain a nod. Etain regained control over her emotions. Everything that had been whipping around the room dropped to the floor as suddenly as it had lifted into the air.

"Good," Etain said in her normal soft voice. The smile she gave them was a promise to follow through on her threats if they dared push her again.

Ciaran's hand drifted further up her leg until he leaned in and whispered in her ear, "Little witch, if you keep handing my council their asses like this, I will have no choice but to steal you away to our chambers and show you just how much I enjoy it." Etain did not break her stare at the council members across the table, though she shifted slightly in her chair and could feel the horrid flush creeping up her face. Ciaran chuckled under his breath. He knew exactly what effect his words had on her.

"Now that's settled," Ciaran said, leaning back in his chair with a pleased grin on his face. "It's obvious to the rest of us we should be very concerned about the missing witches. Did you know the Day Queen used blood magic on Kes when she stole the nymph away?" The three cowed council members' faces morphed into shock at the mention of the forbidden magic.

"Anin was the one to make the connection between our missing witches and the ever-growing power of the queen. The two must have something to do with the re-emergence of blood magic after its eradication many millennia ago," said Galetia, much to the surprise of the other half of the room. "The first thing we need to do is find a way to contend with the blood magic. As of now, none of us are impervious to the controlling effect it has on the body. I am hopeful we witches can find information on it somewhere in one of our libraries. Immediately after this meeting concludes, I will return to the Silver Moon Coven and send messages to all the other head witches to begin their searches as well."

Etain gave the head witch a supportive smile before she turned to the three across the room. They were stunned into silence for what was surely the first time in their lives. She glared at them and said, "I expect each of you to bring something more than childish complaints to the next meeting, or the end of that meeting will be very different. Now get out of my sight." They quickly retreated from the room without another word, leaving Etain, Galetia, and Ciaran alone.

"Well," Galetia sighed. "That was quite the show you put on, my dear. I was very close to placing a curse on them personally. I have never seen such blustering in my life."

"I, for one, would not be opposed to another display such as that." Ciaran gave Etain a heated smirk before Galetia cleared her throat.

"If you would not mind porting me to my coven to continue my research, I would be ever grateful." Galetia turned back to Etain and grabbed her hands. "We must not let your lessons be pushed to the side. You can help more if you know how to wield your power and use your magic."

"Well..." Etain said uncertainly.

"She is right, little witch. You need to be as powerful as you can. I will always protect you, but if I am not there, then I need to trust that you can defend yourself. If something were ever to happen to you, there would be no realm left to worry about." Ciaran caressed Etain's cheek with the brush of his knuckles.

Etain sighed and looked at them both until she reluctantly agreed. It was not that she did not want to know everything there was to know about her abilities. It seemed unimportant with Anin gone and the Day Queen having blood magic—problems happening in the present. There was no way she would be anywhere close to having enough control to help anytime soon. She would learn all she could to protect herself and the realm when the time came. She only hoped she learned fast enough to make a real difference.

Chapter 7
Anin

Anin awoke to find herself in yet another spelled cage. For just a moment, she let herself hope it had all been a dream and she was back in the dungeon of the Night Court, hanging next to a crazy human. One swift glance around told her everything she needed to know. There was no raving lunatic in a cage next to her; there was no one around her at all. She could tell she was in a dungeon, and she knew it was not the Night Court's.

That left only one other option. She had not been dreaming; she was living in a nightmare. The memory of Kes's face surfaced. Tatiana had somehow rendered him immobile, and his face was frozen into a grimace as he tried to fight the hold she forced upon him. The mate bond and his red eyes said everything he had not had the chance to tell her himself. Tears pricked at Anin's eyes as she thought about never getting the chance to finish their conversation.

The despair he felt when the queen ran her through with the obsidian blade rivaled her own when she had been the one unable to do anything except watch Kes's blood seep out from the shadows. He willed her to fight and live as the blade twisted inside her. Pain sharper than she knew possible blossomed within her. After that, everything became a blur behind the fog of pain that muddled her mind.

It was a surprise when she touched the place the knife had devastated and found herself completely healed. Her well was nearly drained from her body healing itself, but she should still feel at least mild discomfort. Anin thought she had felt a surge of power bleed into her from the mate bond just before she lost consciousness, though that could not have been right. She was in the Day Court now, and her power should be stronger on this side of the Borderlands. That had to be the explanation for her quick healing.

It was possible that she had been here longer than she thought. She did not think it could have been more than a full day, but it was hard to tell the passing of time when stuck in a cage hanging a couple feet off the ground in a windowless room. The air held a damp chill that caused gooseflesh to erupt along her body. She did her best to arrange her wings to cover more of herself, though the tight quarters made it difficult. Even then, her wings were never particularly warm, being as thin as they were.

Anin was hesitant to reach down the mate bond and feel for Kes. She feared he cut himself off from her now that she was gone. She knew that was ridiculous—of course it was. He had been making a declaration to her before the Day Queen finally caught up to Anin. She would never call that bitch her kin. They may have shared a father, but that does not make them anything alike. Tatiana was filled with cruelty and a lust for power, which left her mind fractured into madness.

Taking a deep breath, Anin let herself feel her way towards the end of the mate bond. She felt him faintly, making the vast distance that lay between them even more apparent. Before she could get a read on his emotions, the comforting silence was disrupted.

"I see the result of one of my father's many dalliances has finally woken from her beauty rest." Tatiana spun the cage as she mocked Anin. "How unfortunate your genetics take after your lesser fae, trash mother. Embarrassing, really. I bet father's attention was the highlight of your mother's life—a high fae and a king." It was strange seeing her own eyes reflected back at her. Tatiana's black orbs were the only thing not golden on her sister.

"My mother had no choice in the matter. Your father took that from her." Anin was seething. It was one thing to lock her in a small cage, but how dare she speak of her deceased mother in such a way? Their father had stolen from her mother the one thing fae never took. Tatiana laughed a deep belly laugh directly into Anin's face. It always amazed her the way cruelty could still make even someone as incredibly beautiful as Tatiana hideous.

"At least that is the story she gave you. I would bet your lesser fae mother was embarrassed. She likely fancied they were in love with each other. She made up some ridiculous story so no one would know what a fool she truly was." Anin's anger was a growing inferno inside her. The power she had left rose to the surface, ready to unleash her wrath, but regrettably, she did not know how to use it. She grabbed on to the bars in front of her and tried to shake them while she growled through her teeth.

"Oh dear, poor little sister. All that power and no knowledge to use it. How frustrating that must be," Tatiana said, laced with false pity. "You know, I must tell you something, my unfortunate little sister. Our father knew of your existence. Hundreds of years after I took the throne, father made one of his random appearances at the palace. He told me about a bastard daughter he created with a wood nymph whose name he never knew.

"He said, 'I had been drinking for days when I came across the nymph. It was as though something inside my chest pulled me toward her. I had to have her. Therefore, I did. Day after day for months, I was with this nymph until one day I woke and needed to seek some other adventure, as I often do. The call to that nymph is unrelenting; even now I crave her. I sent a servant to monitor her and make sure she took no other fae to her bed.' He came back a while later and told me she had a youngling with her now.

He explained, 'I contemplated sending educators to her for a royal education, then the servant informed me she looked exactly like her mother, only favoring my golden hair and black eyes. There is no need to educate a lesser fae in such a way. I care nothing for the youngling; I only desire the nymph.'"

Anin was disgusted with herself for hanging on every word Tatiana spoke about their father. She wished she had no desire to know what he thought of her.

"I killed him, you know? Father was a drunk for the last few hundred years of his life. It made him dimwitted. His mind was too wine rotted to see he had found his fated mate and fathered a child with her. I could not let the court find out their past king, my father, had found his fated mate with a lowly wood nymph. A king mated to a lesser fae! Could you imagine? Lesser fae would start to question if they were even lesser after all. I could not have that. No one questioned his disappearance, since he would always return for a brief moment and then disappear for decades." Tatiana's smile curled into a cruel slash across her face as she told Anin of her deeds.

"I took him to a special place just before his death. I think it is only fitting that I take you there just before yours, as well." Anin's heart sped up. She tried to keep the fear from traveling down her bond. She did not want Kes to feel any misery if she could help it. Truth be told, she feared death even though she sometimes welcomed it. The look the mad queen wore said this death would not be an easy one. With a snap of Tatiana's fingers, Anin and her cage were no longer within the perceived safety of the quiet, damp chamber.

Chapter 8
Ciaran

"What is this place?" Etain asked. Ciaran smirked as he watched her. She was looking around the cavernous room with her mouth hanging slightly open. She turned her eyes to him, waiting for him to answer and caught him staring at her. That red flush he loved crept up her neck and into her cheeks.

"What are you looking at?" she asked while self consciously checking to see if she had something on her.

"You," he said, with no further explanation. Her flush turned an even deeper shade of red. This was becoming one of his favorite games. He stared into her eyes for a few moments longer until he turned and gestured to the room hidden deep below the palace.

"I'm not entirely certain. Kes and I found it a few nights ago." He dragged a finger along the closest surface and looked at the thick collection of dust on it. "It appears to have gone untouched for a considerable amount of time." The dust scattered from his finger with the flick of his hand.

Etain made her way to the row of shelves along the far wall

and tried to blow the dust off the spines of the books she wanted to look at. She immediately regretted that decision when the dust blew back into her face and she began coughing. Ciaran laughed, and she gave him one of her looks that told him exactly what she thought of that, before turning back to inspect the now dustless books.

"What are we doing down here, Ciaran? This place is filled with enough..." she waved her hand around, indicating the enormous room around them, "of everything to keep us occupied for decades." She pulled a book off the shelf, opened it, and began flipping through the pages.

Ciaran came up behind her, his speed only causing her to startle slightly without looking up from the book in her hands. He wondered how long it would be until she no longer had any reaction to his sudden arrival. He would just have to find new and inventive ways to startle her.

"The Day Queen and her blood magic are the biggest threat in front of us. This seemed the most logical place to look for anything the Night Court of the past might have known about blood magic, since one of my ancestors took it upon himself to purge the entire court of anything prior to the time he dictated. All the knowledge from before the purge is lost to us now. At least we thought it was until I came across the hidden door above."

"Why would anyone do such a thing?" Etain asked, sounding as angry as it still made him.

"Why, indeed? There are rumors, but I found nothing to confirm any of them. It is as if time just began and nothing had ever happened prior. Which of course, is obviously not the case. The rest of the realm has histories dating back well before ours. My working theory, based on his journals, is that something devastating happened. Something that he never wanted anyone to know. I am almost positive it has something to do with the Day

Court. He mentions a few times how they 'did this to him.' Whatever that might be."

"You mean to tell me one of your ancestors was conceited enough to erase all history rather than risk the chance of any future generations knowing whatever was damning to him?" She sounded incredulous, and he could not blame her for it.

"It would appear that is correct." He leaned his shoulder against the dusty shelves and crossed his arms.

"Ciaran, your ancestors thus far sound like a sorry bunch. I know you say you come from a long line of very wicked males, but that is...well, that is just pure stupidity." His ancestors had been proving to be a worthless bunch, but that was something he already knew.

"I do not disagree with you, little witch." He watched her as she shook her head and put the book back on the shelf before she turned to look back up at him.

"How do we go about searching such a massive," she picked up a thick sheet of dust off the tops of the next row of books, "dusty place?" She pinched the dust between two fingers with her nose scrunched up in disgust.

"The old-fashioned way. One book at a time. It will be slow and tedious, though it is the only thing I can think of. Well, short of raiding the Day Court's archives." He had not thought about it before, but the idea held merit.

"I would prefer you not traipse around the Day Court at all. Particularly with no defense against blood magic. What would happen if the queen caught you?" She placed her hand on his chest and looked up at him with genuine concern.

"That is why you do not get caught." He gave her one of his wickedly toothy smiles. She scoffed and swatted at him.

"Well, I suppose we better get to work searching before you go off and do something stupid. After all, it seems to be a family trait." Something warmed inside him when he saw a wicked smile of her own tug at the corners of her mouth.

She was beginning to fall into her role as Queen of the Night Court. The way she handled the council meeting left him filled both with desire and awe. She never ceased to surprise him, and he enjoyed watching her confidence grow.

"You wound me, little witch," he said in mock offense, causing her to laugh until it turned into a sigh as she looked around at the massive task in front of them.

"Let us see if we can figure out some kind of reasoning for this mess that whoever left all of this here had."

They spent the next few hours trying to decipher whatever system had been put in place, except they were not having much luck. They were both covered in a thick layer of dust and were reaching a point where they were ready to throw things.

"I am convinced there was absolutely no rhyme or reason to the way they shelved any of these books," Etain said as she returned the book she was flipping through.

"I believe they are all from before the purge. I think someone had the forethought to save as much information as they could, quickly." He had already looked through several journals and ledgers, dating further back than the oldest books in his study.

"Well then, you are probably right about finding something down here to help us. The question is how quickly we can find it. We need to bring in some help. I bet several witches from Silver Moon would love to come and catalog all of this." She gestured with her hand to shelves they had no hope of touching for years at the rate they were going.

"No!" Ciaran said harshly. He regretted it immediately when he saw the way she flinched.

"No? Why ever not? That makes absolutely no sense. At the rate we are going, it will take us decades to wade through these

dusty shelves. We cannot condemn Anin to wait decades for us."
She was not wrong. It would take them decades.

"Forget Anin, loo—"

"Forget Anin? You cannot be serious," she said, shocked.
Ciaran sighed. He could feel himself teetering on a very thin line
with her.

"Little witch, that came out wrong." A lie. That was exactly
what he meant. "I mean only for the moment; we do not know
what secrets are hiding here. The last thing we want is for the
information to fall into the wrong hands." She stared at him for a
moment, like she was trying to figure something out, until she
nodded and turned back to the shelf she had been looking
through.

They silently made their way to the furthest corner of the
room. He kept glancing at her; he knew he had made a mistake.
She closed herself off to him through the bond. He wanted to fix
the problem, but the problem was she was good and he was
wicked.

The last section of shelves on this side were bathed in darkness, making it difficult to read anything. He noticed the torch on
the wall beside them was not lit the way the rest of them were.
Etain was glancing back and forth between the darkened torch
and the one several feet down from it.

"This one does not look the same as the others," Etain said while
she inspected the lightless torch. Ciaran took a closer look to see what
she was talking about. The others were attached to the wall directly.
This one was attached to a square metal plate that looked almost
identical to the stone wall surrounding it. There was something that
looked like a joint attaching it to the metal. Just as he had that
thought, Etain reached up on her tip-toes and tried to turn the torch.

It did not budge.

Then she tried again the other way. Ciaran scooped her up and moved them as far back as he could. The wall was making multiple loud bangs and clicks before it shook. He was just about to take her back up to the archives above fearing the wall was going to come down around them. He heard Etain gasp.

"Ciaran, look," she breathed, as if she could not believe what she was seeing. He was having a hard time believing it himself. The wall was sliding in on itself, creating a doorway. It was difficult to see clearly through all the dust the movement kicked up.

Ciaran found many interesting things in the palace over the years, like secret hallways behind the walls with hidden spy holes. There were even hidden doors that required magic to be seen, but he had never seen a stone wall open like this. There had not been a single crease in the wall; the only indicator was the square metal plate behind the torch. If you did not know to look for it, you would never notice it.

The dust settled, revealing a darkened doorway. Ciaran sent an orb of light to illuminate the darkness as they entered. It was another room, this one much smaller than the cave-like room they had just left behind. He sent his magic around the room, igniting the torches spaced evenly around the space.

"Wow! Why are these hidden away down here?" Etain asked as she rubbed some dirt off the chest plate in front of her, revealing a nearly white metal with a large, glowing red stone set just below the clavicles. "I have never seen metal like this before. What is it?" she asked him, their earlier spat momentarily forgotten.

"There are legends of Night Court warriors dressed in moonlight; Master Ulgridge called them 'Moon Blessed.' I thought he was just an old fae telling stories, but now..." Rarely was Ciaran surprised, and yet he had been surprised a few times over the past several nights. He was trying to recall the stories he had rolled his eyes at as a youngling, thinking himself too old for such fantasies.

The room was filled with cases holding every kind of jeweled adornment one could wear. Every hand-held weapon imaginable coated the back wall from floor to ceiling, and there were several sets of full armor on stands around the room. The entire collection in the room contained the same glowing red stone set within them.

"What are these gems? I do not recognize them. Well, not that I would recognize many gems to begin with." Etain continued to ramble on about the types of stones she knew of while Ciaran stopped listening for a moment. Here, directly in front of him, was a room full of unknowns.

He was used to knowing everything. Even when Etain came into his life, he had her narrowed down to two possibilities. All of this, however, he had only heard about deep in the Nocturia Mountains from a very old fae. He was questioning just how old Master Ulgridge had to be if the fairy tales he had been telling were not actual tales at all. He was trying to remember what he had said about the warriors.

"Ciaran?" Etain was looking at him expectantly. His face must have given away his confusion. "What are they?" She asked again.

He touched the glowing red stone on the chest plate Etain had cleaned of dust.

"I do not know."

Chapter 9
Kes

Reaching the end of the third stack of books and finding nothing useful about mate bonds, Kes shut the book and threw it across the room. "This is pointless! Of course, the Night Court would not have any information of value on mate bonds. They were likely purged with the rest of the knowledge that did not support the agenda of some idiotic king generations ago," Kes said furiously to the empty room.

When he parted ways with the sisters yesternight, he immediately went to the archives and sent any scroll or book that looked even remotely promising to his own chambers. When none of those proved useful, he went to the palace library. It was several times larger than Ciaran's. Filled with dark walnut shelves not only around the room but rows upon rows in the center. Each bookcase was several stories high, requiring wings or the use of one of the many towering ladders.

Searching through the palace's books had given him something to focus on for a short period of time. Rage had been building exponentially as he got closer and closer to the end of his search until it reached a roaring crescendo inside him. The only thing he could find in the entirety of the palace books on true mates was how rare they were. They contained mostly arguments against mate bonds. Citing the merits of choosing who you bonded with to better increase power and make ideal political matches—absolute garbage.

The kings of the past were so blinded by their desire for power, they had inadvertently diminished it instead. Each generation that went unaccepted by the Land contained less power than the one before it. The curse kept access to half of the royals' well of power cut off, no doubt the reason behind the obsession. They were either too stupid or arrogant in their quest to create more power when they should have been searching for the cure.

Ciaran was the first to bring the power of a true king back to the court, which would never have been possible had he not found Etain. Their many-great grandfather picked a battle with the wrong witch. She cursed his line to a life of half-greatness until one of her descendants and one of his descendants were paired as fated mates.

Fate always seemed to get what it wanted, but he could not for the life of him see how fate could want harm to come to Anin. She might wield a sharp tongue, which Kes loved far too much, but she was kind and gentle. Well, with everyone but him. He smiled, thinking about when she threw him against the wall and held him there with her vines. Gods, he had never wanted a being as much as he wanted her right then and there.

Sighing, he rested his hands on the table in front of him and hung his head, ready to admit defeat in his quest. He could only hope the sisters were having better luck. At least they did not have a purge to contend with. It was as if the gods heard him and threw him a lifeline; his spelled scroll hung in his face with a message from Lyra. Kes's heart sped up, and a whooshing sound filled his ears as blood rushed to his head. They found something.

He wasted no time porting to the Silver Moon Coven. Lyra and Panella were already waiting for him at the gates. It surprised him when Ciaran and Etain arrived only moments after him. They must have received the same message as he did.

Kes followed the sisters past the gates of the coven for the first time in his existence. He was vaguely aware of the questionable architecture around him as he followed the sisters up and down multiple staircases and through hallway after hallway. Finally, they came to a halt in front of two massive closed doors.

The doors were made of a dark wood that gleamed in the golden sunlight beaming through the windows on the west side of the coven. They carved one door into an image of the two suns of the Day Court, while the other door depicted the two moons of the Night Court. The detail in the craftsmanship was impressive enough to gain Kes's appreciation, as fleeting as it was.

"Except for Anin, we have never permitted another fae past these doors. As such, please be respectful and do not harm any of its contents. The knowledge on the other side of these doors is sacred to us, and we will not tolerate aggressive behavior. No matter the circumstances," Lyra said, looking at Kes and Ciaran. Kes's impatience was going to get the better of him if they did not get to the point of him being there soon.

"We are not animals and can control ourselves. Nor do we have a desire to destroy any form of written word. We understand, more than we would like, how negligent the destruction of knowledge is. Do you think us idiots?" Ciaran said, sounding as annoyed as Kes felt. He had almost forgotten they were behind him. Etain said something under her breath to Ciaran, that caused him to sigh.

"You have my word; we will respect your requests." Ciaran shifted his eyes to Kes, giving him a pointed look. "Cousin?" Kes nodded his head while he gestured with his hands to hurry. What little patience he had was quickly fraying at the seams.

Panella pushed the doors open and revealed the largest library

Kes had ever seen. The glass dome of the ceiling brightly illuminated every corner of the room with its perfect half day, half night lighting. Everywhere he looked, there was greenery growing and flowers blooming. The contrast of the heavy, hulking shelves made him feel like he was outside and inside at the same time. The room was a mix of bright cherry woods, green vines, flowers, and metal spiral staircases. Hanging from the ceiling surrounding the dome were trinkets of all shapes, sizes, and materials. None of them looked valuable, and Kes wondered what made them important enough to display that boldly.

"They are one of the first things we learn how to create with whatever color manifests first. Galetia has them displayed as trophies to remind us we all started small and we all come from the same unassuming successes," Panella whispered to him. He wondered what it was like to grow up in an environment where they celebrated even the smallest victories.

They followed Lyra through a few rows of shelves, turning periodically. Where the Nightfell palace library was in perfect rows of cold, dark wood, the coven set theirs up like a labyrinth. It was a wonder they found anything they looked for. He should not be surprised, considering the nonsensical way they designed the coven itself. Plants grew wildly everywhere. The books remained untouched by any of the intrusive growths, suggesting there was a spell protecting them. They reminded him of Anin, and he wondered if she had anything to do with them.

Lyra had them follow her up one of the many spiraling metal staircases to a second-floor alcove hidden from the rest of the library. There were even more shelves tucked away, surrounding a long rectangular table in the center of the space. The wooden table, crafted from many types of wood, had books piled on top of it, with only one open. It took every bit of self control Kes contained to not immediately snatch the book away and discover for himself whatever it was the sisters found.

"If the coven had not placed a custom locator spell on the library many generations ago, we would never have found this book. Witches do not have mate bonds," Panella said, looking at Etain. "Well, clearly not all witches... Anyway, we were not sure what we would find, or if we would find anything at all."

"Imagine our surprise when we found this book in the stack the library had curated for us. The book is quite fascinating. It speaks of a time when the three facets of the realm were in harmony. The witches had created many spells to help the fae, mate bonds included." Kes was about to tell Lyra to get the hell on with it when Panella picked up the open book and held it for them all to see.

Kes could decipher nothing on the pages in front of him. To him, they looked like a bunch of symbols put together, like some kind of deranged map. It frustrated him that he could not read or comprehend the thing he had been searching for ever since fate stole Anin away. How was he to ensure whatever was sprawled against the pages was done correctly?

"I have not the faintest idea what any of this means," Ciaran said, with the irritability he wore like a second skin. Etain looked at him as if he were blind.

"Well, of course you do not," a voice said from behind them. Kes glanced over his shoulder to see the head witch taking her last step up the stairs. This witch had been like a second mother to Anin, and it was for that reason alone he held his tongue. His fuse was already cut too short; he did not need any patronizing comments directed his way.

"The book is written in one of our more ancient languages. If you will allow me, I can make it so you can easily follow the text before you." Galetia winked at Etain. "A perk of being a witch... Every witch ever born carries the old and new languages in their blood. I would imagine we should thank the Many Faced Goddess for that gift."

"Can you truly not understand this?" Etain asked Ciaran. If Kes had been losing his patience before, it was long past lost by now. He was unaware of the low growl he let out until everyone was looking at him. He was not sorry for it, and the look he gave them all clearly said as much.

"Kes, shall I start with you?" The head witch asked.

Normally, Kes would let no being place a spell upon him, much less a witch. He sighed and gave the slightest of nods. He had made it his whole life without ever having to compromise himself until his wood nymph came into it. Well, technically, he was the one who had thrown her into his world, not the other way around.

Galetia placed her hands around his head, whispering some words he did not understand. He felt a slight floating sensation that stopped as soon as it started. When she pulled her hands away from his head, he glanced over at the pages that were once unreadable but were now legible. He could read them, but that did not mean the words made any sense to him.

"I have given you the ability to read any texts stored in our library. It will only work when you are physically within these walls." Kes barely heard her while attempting to figure out the mechanics of the spell before him occupying his thoughts. He knew it was a spell that obviously had something to do with the mate bond. If he were reading it correctly, it required both mates to be present. Lyra must have been watching him and could see the hope fading from his eyes as he closed them tightly and tried to breathe.

"This spell requires both mates to be present in its current state. Galetia, however, believes she can circumvent that minor detail. We would not have called you here if we did not think we had a viable option," Lyra said to Kes. The spots that had clouded his vision receded, and the invisible vice gripping his throat slowly released him, allowing him to breathe normally once more.

Kes read further into the spell, mildly disappointed that it would not allow him to speak to her directly through the bond. He could send her the most basic of thoughts, images, and complex feelings, but no actual words. Kes could feel the strongest emotion she was feeling if he searched for it down the bond. However, it would be helpful having the ability to send her specific feelings and images. He was certain they could create their own language quickly.

The last component of the spell would strengthen their bond. Kes thought back to the times he felt the bond burn and weaken over the few nights they shared resulting from their treatment of each other. He was angry at himself for being willfully blind to what felt obvious now. Kes never thought he would have a mate bond with anyone, let alone a Day fae. He knew a big part of his reluctance to accept the truth had been because of its unlikeliness and his disbelief that fate would ever see fit to give him something as rare as a mate.

He spent his whole life despising the other side of the realm. Anytime he caught a Day fae on his side of the borderlands, he took it as a challenge to create new and vile ways to inflict pain. He lost track of how many Day fae had perished under his hands, and ironically, fate chose to tie him to one. He thought the Many Faced Goddess must have played a big role in the way fate had come and wreaked havoc in his otherwise blissfully wicked life. A fate that had arrived in the shape of a sharp-tongued wood nymph.

He tried to convince himself that he wanted nothing more than to go back to the way it had been before the hunt on the night of the blood moon. No matter how hard he attempted to try over the past few nights, he could not fully ignore or push away the mate bond. There was no going back to the life he had before. His life would forevermore be in two parts, before Anin and after Anin. He wanted to hate her; he should hate her, but he knew he could never feel anything close to hatred for his nymph.

"Kes...?" Engrossed in his own thoughts, he completely tuned out the surrounding room. Ciaran looked at him expectantly.

"What?" Kes asked a little too sharply for Ciaran's liking. He knew his cousin was trying to be more tolerant toward him. Either he could not help but imagine being in Kes's place, or perhaps his tolerance had something to do with their new queen. Kes was having a hard time not wishing his cousin was the one living this nightmare.

"Etain and Galetia went to work out the details of the altered spell, and the sisters just brought up a valid concern. The Day Court Queen came with an entire battalion of gilded soldiers. Obviously, they have organized and trained in some capacity. Meanwhile, for us, gathering twenty Night fae to defend our realm would be next to impossible to accomplish after generations without an army."

The thought had never crossed Kes's mind. Technically, he filled the role of General for Ciaran, something he had never needed to concern himself with before. His cousin was about to remind him of his duty, and Kes was about to tell him he could shove duty up his ass until he spoke. Kes's anger molded itself into purpose.

"When we go to retrieve Anin, we will need not only trained warriors but shadows who can go unseen. The Day Queen is likely to declare our rescue an act of war and will have no trouble convincing her council, if she even seeks their approval at all. As my general, I am tasking you with creating and training the shadows we need to get in and out unseen." Ciaran had a gleam in his golden eyes. Kes suspected his cousin knew exactly what to say to get him to agree, as well as demand he be the one to create the unit that would return his mate.

Vaguely, he could hear the three of them discussing plans to create another training facility in the palace where the creatures of the Night Court and the witches could learn to fight with physical weapons alongside their powers. The palace had dozens of training facilities already, but he acknowledged it was a good place to start. What was one more facility?

Watching the sisters, he knew there was no scenario in which they were not with Kes to save their adopted sister. Feeling his scrutiny, both sets of dark eyes shifted to Kes and gave him an almost imperceptible nod. He had just recruited the first two members of his unit, the Silent Shadows.

Chapter 10
Anin

T he cage was a cramped space that made it hard for Anin
to do more than swivel her head from side to side. From
what she could see, her new surroundings were mostly
derelict. The ceiling wore a spider's web of cracks before meeting
in the middle, where the eclipsed sun shone through a perfectly
placed opening.

If it had not been for the light pouring in from above, she
would have thought they were back in the Night Court with how
dark the rest of the room was. The outlying shadows hid any clues
the walls might have held to give her an idea of where they were.
The only thing Anin could see clearly was a stone slab on one side
and a stone half-wall on the other.

She studied the short wall, avoiding the stone slab, which held
multiple perfectly carved box shapes. They varied in size, and
each had a carving depicting one of the different elements. Air
and fire were the smallest of the five boxes she could see, while
earth and water were the largest. Towards the end of the wall, it
was difficult for her to decipher the illustration of the fifth box. It

could be a heart or a fist; it was too far away to see clearly. The outline of the box was more defined, perhaps from regular use.

Anin watched as the mad queen opened the box in question and pulled out a book wrapped in rust-colored leather. She opened it to a specific page and briefly scanned it before opening another box in the wall that Anin had not seen. The hair on her arms stood on end, and she tried to wipe her clammy hands on her wings as Tatiana pulled out a long, wickedly curved blade.

The way the queen looked at the blade and moved around the space spoke of a familiarity forged over time. She expected her end for a long time, even before being locked in this cage, though she never thought it would be such a production. Watching her deranged sister get set up for Anin's own murder was an added layer of torture.

Neither had spoken since they arrived, besides the periodic mumblings of the queen. Anin wanted to hold on to every minute of life she had remaining. She did not want Kes to be distressed and did her best to keep calm and close off the connection as much as she could. She knew at some point there was going to be no avoiding it; that thought alone made her catch a sob in her throat before its release could give her sister any joy.

She wondered what kind of life they could have created together. Would they have found a way to work around her being Day Court and him being Night Court? She thought they could live in the Borderlands with her true sisters, where they could each be close to their courts. It would not allow them to be as powerful as they could be, although it would be enough, and they would have each other.

Anin let herself mourn the future she had created in her mind. It would never come to pass, and she would never see any of them again. She was grateful that the last time she saw her sisters, there was nothing left unsaid. She knew they would mourn her loss, yet she hoped they would not let it stop them from finding their own joy in this life.

The only one she truly feared for was Kes. He would not move on. The mate bond would make that impossible. After the brief history lesson the queen gave her, she was certain her father's death had been the onslaught of her mother's deterioration. Her mother had hated her father for what he had taken from her, yet she still could not fight the mate bond.

She grabbed at her chest and cried out in pain one day, and afterwards she had a vacantness in her eyes that Anin had never seen before—in anyone. She only lasted another year. When Anin asked her mother what was happening to her, she said something had once again been taken from her, and while her mind had never wanted this thing to begin with, her heart had other ideas.

Anin had no clue what her mother meant, though now that she had found her own mate, she knew what Tatiana said must be true. She had been the product of a true mate bond. She wondered if things would have been different if her father had not rotted his mind with drink. Maybe she would have grown up with both of her parents in a loving household with all the benefits of having the king as a father could give.

She wanted desperately to ask Tatiana why she hated her enough to hunt her through the realm when Anin had done all she could to stay away from anything dealing with the Day Court. It was not as though she were a threat. The Day Court was a matriarchy, whereas the Night Court was a patriarchy. The king had fathered her; would that not remove her from any claim to the throne?

She had momentarily forgotten about her situation, completely lost in thought. For the briefest of moments, she had escaped her impending death. When the cage opened, she startled and crashed back into reality. Tatiana gave a ruthless chuckle as she dragged Anin out of the too small cage and watched her collapse. Her legs had long ago lost their feeling from being stuck in the same position.

Looking up at her sister, Anin saw nothing except a tremendous loathing etched into her perfect face and shining from her eyes. There was not one ounce of compassion for the little sister on the ground in front of her. Tears welled in Anin's eyes, no matter how hard she fought them. Were they out of fear of her impending death? Or the loss of the relationship they could have had as sisters? She could not be sure.

"Why do you hate me this much? What have I ever done to you?" Anin hoped she sounded stronger than she had sounded to herself.

"Hate? Hatred would require care to begin with. I do not hate you, little sister." She reached down and grabbed Anin's upper arm and dragged her up so she could shove her face into Anin's. "I feel nothing for you. You are simply a means to an end. By killing you, I take care of two problems at the same time." Anin tried to pull her arm away from the queen. Unfortunately, she still had no control over her limbs. They burned with pins and needles as the blood rushed back into her extremities.

"Two problems?" A mirthless laugh escaped Anin. "How have I been even one problem to you?"

"Well, technically," the queen said as she dragged Anin to the stone slab that was the perfect length for a body. Anin fought harder, even with her clumsy limbs. "You solve a problem for me and are one. Stop fighting; you will not get away. All you will do is make me angry," Tatiana said through gritted teeth.

Anin was determined to at least know why she was about to die. "What problem could I possibly be to you?" They were almost within reach of the stone slab. Her heartbeat thundered within her chest. She could no longer keep her emotions under control. She did not want to die. For the first time in her life, she wanted to truly live and not just survive.

"The stupid Land decided I was no longer worthy of ruling and revoked its power from us. Since there had never been two daughters from any queen, the crown would fall to my daughter." She once again shoved her face into Anin's, spraying drops of spittle on her face as she seethed, "Something I will never be able to have now, thanks to you and your mate! You stole that from me! I suppose I hate you after all."

They were at the stone slab; her struggles only delayed them a few moments. Tatiana flicked her fingers in some motion Anin did not recognize, and manacles lifted from hidden compartments on the sides of the slab. There was no mistaking what it was now. An altar. One she was about to die on. Anin could feel her limbs clearing as she became more coordinated. She made one last attempt at escape.

She was able to break free from the queen, but could not take more than one step until one manacle snagged her wrist, followed closely by her other one. She pulled with everything she had and let her rage pour from her into a scream. Rage for Kes, who would blame himself for however long he lived until her death finally resulted in his own. Rage for her sisters, who would have an Anin shaped shadow of grief cast over their lives. Rage for her mother, who deserved much more than she got out of life. Finally rage for the life she herself would never have, the life that she had touched for the briefest of moments.

The chains groaned with the force she applied to them. It was over before it had really begun. Before she even comprehended what happened, she was lying on her back on the stone altar with her ankles and wrists firmly shackled in place while the queen cackled above her.

"That was a valiant effort, sister. I applaud your gumption. There are two reasons you are about to die. Well," Tatiana looked thoughtful for a moment while tears poured down the sides of Anin's face, "three, if I'm being honest. The first is rather obvious.

You killed my mate, one of the most heinous crimes one could commit. The final two are likely things that had never occurred to you, by design, of course. I do not need members of my court asking questions. As I was saying earlier, there is no other female in line for the throne after me. You, of all beings, are my closest female relation." She made a sound that could only be described as disgust.

"The Land could choose you, if it has not already, to sit on the throne. Luckily for us, or me, I should say, you must actually sit on the throne to be given all the power the Land has to offer. Finally, your sacrifice will strengthen my blood magic more than any of the witches I have sacrificed before you. With the well of power inside you, I will be able to go to the Night Court and take care of your mate, along with his cousin and his witch."

"You killed them?" Anin asked softly.

"Well, not yet..." the queen said.

"No, the witches. The ones who disappeared mysteriously from our covens. You killed them?"

Tatiana barked out a laugh at her question.

"'Our coven.' You are not one of them and never would truly belong there, you daft nymph. Of course, I killed them. I took control of each and every one of them and had them write a letter before walking directly out to me. I would port them here and use their power to strengthen mine. There is something about the raw power a witch has. I was looking for the Walsh witch, but she seemed to find her way into the arms of that Night Court prick."

"They are all dead? How many have you murdered?" Anin spoke with a rage that made her seem deceptively calm.

"I have not the slightest clue, and they were sacrifices, not murders. I do not expect you to grasp the difference between the two." She sighed and looked down into Anin's eyes while she patted her cheek. "Enough chit chat!" She clapped her hands together twice. "Let us get on with the show."

The anger that had given Anin an unnatural calm quickly turned into panic.

Anin did not want to die...

Tatiana picked up the long, curved knife.

Anin did not want to die...

Words she did not understand were spoken.

*Anin did not **want to die...***

Her heart was beating too fast as the knife kissed her neck.

Anin did not want to die...

She cried out in agony she knew Kes would feel as the knife sliced into her skin.

Anin...

> *did not...*

>> *want to die...*

Chapter 11
Etain

"I need to modify the existing spell to account for having one half of the mated pair and because they have not completed the mating ceremony," Galetia explained to Etain. "I imagine this is all a lot to take in. We have not even touched on spell work in your training. I do not expect you to help alter the spell. I asked you to assist me only to give you hands-on learning."

Etain was grateful she was not expected to do anything except learn. The last thing she wanted was to botch the spell Kes had been desperate to find. Her mother taught her a few basic spells the Walsh women passed down for generations, more out of tradition than actual spell work.

They held on to any connection to the Fae Realm and the power that resided there for thousands of years. Perhaps her ancestors knew a future Walsh witch would find themselves back in the Fae Realm and wanted to make sure she was as prepared as possible.

"We did not have magic, yet we continued to use simple spells that became more of a prayer when creating certain medicines," Etain said. "I do not know how to apply the use of magic or power to a spell, though I understand the basic structure of one."

Etain studied the words on the page of the book in front of her. "My mother told me each spell consisted of three parts. The number three is often used as it is considered the perfect number. Not only the number of harmony, wisdom, and understanding; also the past, present, and future; birth, life, and death; beginning, middle, and end." Etain glanced at Galetia to see her nodding in approval.

"The first part," Etain said as she pointed to the first section of the spell, "is the intention desired. The second part is the exchange to maintain balance, and the third is to make it so. Mother always said, 'Everything must come from somewhere, and it never comes for free. Be sure your intent is true, know the cost, and do not doubt yourself at the end.'"

"Your mother was a wise woman. I wish I could have met her." Galetia reached over and gave Etain's hand a squeeze. "What is the intention of this spell?" She asked as Etain studied the first lines.

Two halves bound together to create one whole.
Two halves of one soul share one heart.
Two halves of one thought share one mind.
The power of two halves becomes the power of one.
Two halves bound together in mind, body, and power.
Where one begins, the other will end; where there once were two, there
is now one.

"I think it is to bind the two together. I'm confused; is that not exactly what the mating bond does?" Etain asked. The connection she now shared with Ciaran since the mating ceremony was intense. She had not known she was incomplete until right after the bond snapped fully into place. It was the deepest sense of belonging, and as someone who never felt as though she belonged, it was enough to move her to tears every time she thought about it.

"Yes, and no. The mate bond does not link your mind fully to share thoughts directly with the other's mind. Where you and Ciaran can now share your wells with each other, this would make it possible for each of you to wield the other's abilities."

Etain stared at Galetia. She knew Ciaran would want this spell placed on them if he found out exactly how much power he could gain from it. The idea left her a little anxious, and she could not place why. She should want her mate to be as powerful as possible, right?

Ciaran was wicked and prone to cruelty. Etain had not forgotten this. The idea of him using something from her to inflict pain on another bothered her. It was something she never considered nor was prepared to think about. Could she trust him to not abuse her power? She would keep this to herself for now—another secret to hold.

Ciaran insisted on keeping not only the room behind the moving wall a secret, but the entire hidden chamber as well. Etain did not agree. There was far too much for them to go through in a timely manner, and everyone wanted to get Anin back as soon as possible. Well, with the exception of her mate, it did not seem a priority to him at all. She had felt something new flutter within the bond when he tried to placate her. It felt thick and syrupy and made her angry, but she was not sure why.

"Oh, that is...well...that is a lot to take in. I wish we could ask Anin for permission before forcing her into such a connection." Etain thought if she felt as weary as she did about the spell, she was uncertain whether Anin would not care for it either. She took a deep breath and let out a sigh of acceptance. "Considering the circumstances, I guess it is better to ask for forgiveness once she is safe than not provide the possible help this spell would give her."

"I agree," Galetia said. "I am not in the habit of placing a spell such as this without the consent of both parties. This, however, is a circumstance in which I hope to never find someone I love again. Now, what do you think the cost will be for this spell?" she asked, bringing them back to the lesson and task at hand.

To share one heart, blood must be spilled.
To join two minds, thoughts will never be owned by one.
To create the power of one, there will never be the power of two again.
Two halves bound together in mind, body, and power cannot have life
without the life of the other.

"This is rather straightforward. The required payment is blood, freedom of private thoughts, release of ownership over individual power, and each life's source will be tied to the other. When death comes for one, it comes for both. Does that not already happen? Without your mate, death haunts you until you quickly join the other." The idea of her life being tied to Ciaran's and the payment of blood did not bother her. On the other hand, the idea of not having her own thoughts and having to share her powers made her pause. When it came to her well-being, she trusted Ciaran explicitly. When it came to others, well, that was another story.

"Yes, your life force will slowly drain from you until you are reunited with your mate. However, there are many ways to circumvent death. The Day Queen, for example, obviously has some way of sustaining her life. Blood magic, I am sure. With this spell, when one dies, the other joins immediately. Two hearts become one; when one stops, both stop.

The blood sacrifice is what I am most concerned about. I hope

86

since they share a blood oath, Kes's blood might be enough." Galetia either was unaware of or chose not to pry into Etain's internal terror. That was exactly what she was feeling—terror.

Etain's sense of self had never belonged to another, and the idea of losing her independence and freedom in such a way was possibly the worst thing she could think of. Ciaran was already acutely attuned to her moods and emotions that the idea of him having access to every thought she ever had felt like a violation. To further her reluctance, she did not think she wanted to have access to every thought he had running through his mind. Would that change the way she felt about him? The idea did not just bother her; it terrified her.

She was already apologizing to Anin in her mind. She hoped her friend would forgive her as she read the final part of the spell.

> *Power given freely*
> *Strength in conviction*
> *Sure of heart*
> *Life source spilled*
> *It will be*

Etain read the last part of the spell again. She could not see a way of completing it without Anin present. It clearly means both must give without any doubt within them. The hope she had been feeling seeped away. How would she ever look Kes in the eyes again once this failed?

"Galetia," Etain said softly while still staring at the bottom of the page before her. "How do you propose to get around the absence of Anin and still make it so?" She heard her great-aunt let out a breath.

She was about to unleash a multitude of questions when Kes came barreling into the alcove Etain and Galetia were hiding away in, with Ciaran and the sisters not far behind. "We have to do this now! Something is wrong. Anin is terrified, and it seemed to come out of nowhere. She had been nothing but calm until suddenly all I could feel was a terror the likes of which I could never imagine." Etain knew she had to give everything she had and deal with any fallout from her inexperience later.

"You must calm down and put her fear to one side. You need to focus solely on the connection between you and the conviction in your words. Do you understand? We will not have a second chance," Galetia said sternly as she picked up the book and went to stand in front of Kes.

"You can do this, Kes," Etain said softly.

"I will do this. There is no other option," Kes declared, and suddenly Etain felt a massive weight sit heavily upon her heart. If this did not work, she did not think she could stand to see him be any further crushed than he already was.

"Repeat after me and make sure you mean every single word. Do not become distracted no matter what happens. Do you understand?" Kes nodded once to Galetia.

"Strength in conviction..."

Etain could feel the power he put behind the words.

"Sure of heart," Kes said while choking on some emotion he was trying to keep under control. Galetia looked apologetic as she stabbed an obsidian knife into his gut while she spoke the words for Kes to repeat.

"Life source spilled," he said with a grunt that turned into pure panic, and pain filled his eyes that had nothing to do with his own wound. His hand went to his throat, and he fought to maintain control to finish the spell.

"It's not enough," Etain said softly under her breath to herself. She felt compelled to place her hands upon Kes and closed her eyes, envisioning the river of power. She began to flow into Kes. Etain heard him grunt as her power collided with his own. She knew her method was the opposite of graceful, and yet she felt her power's connection to Kes was secure. She slowly opened her eyes, making sure not to lose her focus.

"It will be," he said with finality as he collapsed to the floor on his knees without Etain breaking her connection. He was clutching his neck and gagging. She thought she heard him say something about Anin's throat.

"Kes, listen to me. You need to send everything you have, and what Etain is giving down the bond, directly into Anin. Do this now!" Etain felt her power being siphoned as Kes did as Galetia instructed. She felt her well of power get dangerously low until Ciaran crouched behind her and began pouring his power into her as well.

She felt one last massive pull of power from her as Kes roared with anguish and then fully collapsed to the ground, panting. She could feel his chest trying to contain a sob that was determined to come out.

"I think it's best we get him home to rest," Ciaran said, and before anyone could object, he ported the three of them to Kes's chambers and made to deposit Kes on his bed.

"Not here," Kes said weakly as he stumbled from his room and down the short distance to the one Anin had occupied. Etain had never seen Kes's chambers before, but it was obvious this was where her friend had stayed. Vines grew all over the room and created a canopy filled with flowers over the bed. Without her presence, the foliage was beginning to brown and wilt.

They watched Kes collapse onto her bed and pull whatever blankets and pillows he could manage with one swipe of his arms. He buried his face into the mass he had gathered and lost the battle with the sob that had been persistent in its demands for release.

Etain grabbed Ciaran's hand, feeling as though they were intruding. Without needing to be told, he ported them away to their own chambers.

Chapter 12
Tatiana

Tatiana expected the euphoria that came with being flooded with raw power. There was nothing in the realm she longed for more than the momentary feeling of ecstasy. She craved it more than she longed for the presence of her mate. It was almost better than the rush she got from ensnaring all those beings at once when she went to collect her dreadful excuse of a sibling.

The same sibling who was somehow lying passed out on the altar before her with a nearly severed head and not more than a few streaks of blood to show for it. She watched with growing dread as the blood that had poured freely from her neck at first retreated into her sister's wound. She was even more disturbed when her neck knitted back together.

Tatiana had suspected that the Land had chosen her as the replacement. The idea that the Land had not only abandoned Tatiana but had also chosen her sister made her clench her teeth together. It was history repeating itself.

Their father had come home, and he had known of Anin's

existence. That was where the story she told Anin and reality parted ways. Their father had been planning on bringing Anin and her mother, his mate, to the castle. He felt shame for taking his mate without consent and was determined to win her heart by any means.

It was true their father suffered from wine rot; however, the last time Tatiana saw him, his eyes were clear for the first time in hundreds of years. He had ended his love affair with wine because he had found another family. His true family, as he called them— his mate, a wood nymph, and a half-breed daughter.

Tatiana had been furious. He abandoned her for centuries, leaving her to navigate leading a court she had not yet been prepared to rule. Yet now that he had a new family, he thought he could come back with his half-breed daughter to the palace. Tatiana could not allow the dreadful excuse of a princess anywhere near her throne. The Land that had abandoned her could easily choose this lesser fae to rule the Day Court instead of her.

Their father had expected her to celebrate his joy with him, and perhaps a previous version of Tatiana would have. She remembered a time when she craved a sibling. She prayed to the gods nearly every day for a hundred years for a sister. Once she wanted nothing more than to have a best friend who would under-stand the precarious relationship between their parents and someone who could also help her rule and be a trusted adviser.

The prayers stopped when her father began drinking and her mother became ill. If it had not been for Reminold, she would have been completely alone. While she wanted nothing more, having her parents bring another child into the world would have been unfair to the youngling. She let that desire drift away to that place where all of her other dreams went to die.

Having long given up on a sibling, it was almost a betrayal to hear the words after she had already banished the wish from her heart and mind. She still remembers how their father's mouth made a perfect 'oh' when Tatiana ported them and chained him to the altar. The last thing she said to him before slitting his throat was a promise. She would have his precious half-breed daughter in the same position. She vowed to tell her sister a story about how much their father hated her and her mother before gaining power from her blood in the same way she was about to from his blood.

His eyes went wide, and he opened his mouth in a likely attempt to either plead for his other daughter or reason with his first daughter. No one would ever know because she dragged the knife deep across his neck so he could not utter a sound as he choked on his own blood. She smiled down at him as his power tried desperately to keep him alive. His well was deep; he had been a king, after all.

King or not, his blood poured from him the same way it poured from every other being she had chained to the stone beneath him. She remembers patting his cheek as the light left his eyes, never to return. If she felt any remorse, she could not remember, as she became flooded with the most euphoric sensation at that exact moment. A feeling she had been chasing ever since.

A feeling she should be experiencing at an even higher level right that very moment, yet instead she stood empty as her sister's neck finished healing completely. Tatiana felt her face flare with heat as she gripped the knife in her hand even tighter. This whore had stolen her father, her land, her power, and her mate. Now the bitch had stolen the one thing she looked forward to most. Tatiana craved the euphoria she was owed.

She brought the knife back up and cut Anin's throat as deeply as she could, with the same results over and over again, before she screamed in anger and completely severed her head. Tatiana groaned as she watched the head reattach itself to the body. She needed the power her sister owed her. She had to have the rush that came with such an immense amount of power flooding her system. It was the one thing that gave her a moment of pure bliss. The one thing that kept her going.

"*Can you do nothing right?*" the dark, inky voice said in her head.

"The Land will not let her die," Tatiana whined.

"*Excuses. You always have an excuse for your failures. That is all you are—a failure. You claim to want ultimate power, yet when it lies directly in front of you, you fail to take it,*" the voice sneered at her. "*You are a weak excuse for a queen. Perhaps I should have chosen your sister as well.*"

The rage that had been boiling just under the surface of her skin burst from her. She saw nothing except her fury as she stabbed Anin repeatedly. Tatiana poured out every drop of hatred she felt for the being in front of her into each stab wound she left behind. She hated her. She was everything Tatiana no longer was, and the reminder made her hate her even more. Given the opportunity, this being would steal everything Tatiana had left in her life worth taking—her crown and her court.

When Tatiana's rage retreated, her sister was no longer recognizable. She still had not managed to kill her, though she had turned her into a bloody pulp. A mess of indiscernible flesh that somehow never spilled a single drop of blood on the altar.

The voice in Tatiana's head laughed at her as she resigned herself to the fact she could not kill her sister, absorb her power, or use her blood magic on her. The one thing blood magic could not control were those of the user's kin. That did not mean she could not make her sister wish for death every day. Tatiana could invent new ways to inflict the most pain possible, both physically and psychologically. She would break her sister until she had taken everything from her and there was nothing left but a husk of the fae she had once been.

The idea made her feel a fraction of the bliss she should be feeling, although it still made her smile. She would enjoy watching her sister wither away into a state of living death. Knowing that the bird of hers would feel every little piece of her slip away was a bonus. She would keep her in a constant state of healing to make sure her sister could not build up enough power to get away, and with her ability to wield blood magic, it would keep anyone from coming for Anin.

This was almost better than killing her and taking her power. Almost. She still craved the rush of power her body had been expecting. Her blood screamed for it. An idea took shape in her mind. One that she would not only delight in, but it would also give her blood what it craved as well. An idea that would crush the half breed mess before her.

Smiling, she sent Anin's pulpy body back to its little cage. She made it so small her sister would be unable to move an inch and sent her back to the damp, secluded section of the dungeon.

This time, when the voice laughed, it was with approval.

Chapter 13
Ciaran

Ciaran watched as Etain flitted across their bedchambers with a nervous energy he had not seen from her since her first night in the realm. She picked things up and rearranged them slightly to make it seem as if she were busy. He quickly crept up behind her in a way that made her squeak in surprise each time.

"Little witch," he softly whispered into her ear from behind, and was rewarded with a startled gasp.

"Ciaran! Do not do that! I thought we talked about this," Etain said. She still did not turn to face him, a growing source of irritation.

"I recall you mentioning how it terrifies you. I also recall telling you how much I enjoyed the smell of your fear. Now tell me, little witch, what are you fretting about?" He spun her to face him and began walking into her space, causing her to take a step back with each one he made. Her back hit the wall behind her, and he caged her in with his arms. She might be reluctant to speak her mind, but he would pull it out of her. Whatever means necessary.

"What are you doing?" Etain asked with a soft breath. The way she had to tilt her chin all the way up to look at him created a desire to protect as well as destroy her in the most delicious ways possible. He would protect her from everything except himself.

"Waiting for you to tell me what is troubling you." He let out a growl when she turned her face from him and said nothing. "Etain..."

She tried to push him away and escape around him.

"Tisk, tisk, tisk, little witch," he said as he grabbed her hands with one of his own and lifted them up against the wall high enough that she had to stand on tiptoe and arch her back. Still refusing to look at him, he grabbed her jaw with his other hand and forced her eyes to meet his. He would never tire of her eyes. The gold flecks looked as though whoever created his golden eyes flicked a few drops onto her brown. The look those eyes were giving him at that moment made him give her his favorite wicked grin, showing off more teeth than any being had business having.

"If you will not tell me of your own accord, I will have to use certain tactics to force the matter." Etain's eyes lit up with fear, not for her well-being, but for something he could not discern. He knew he was going to enjoy every moment of what was to come; however, there was a flicker of worry at her refusal to talk to him. He brought his nose to the crook of her neck and breathed deeply. The scent of her fear reminded him of crisp lunar nights in the forest after the trees shed their leaves.

He nibbled her neck and shoulder while never moving the hand that held hers in place well above her head. He could hear her breath quicken and her heart thunder in anticipation. Etain groaned with a heady need Ciaran could smell. He brought his mouth directly next to her ear and whispered; she had to strain to hear his words.

"You know what pleasure I can bring you, although pleasure is only for good little witches," he said as he drifted his hand from her jaw down the front of her before taking one of her breasts in his hand and squeezing it just hard enough. "Good little witches tell their mate what troubles them. Are you a good little witch, Etain?"

"Ciaran..." she moaned.

"Yes, my love?" He began rolling her nipple between his fingers through the fabric of her dress.

"Ciaran...please..." she gasped out.

"You are the one in control here, little witch. Tell me what storm is brewing behind your eyes, and I will bring you all the pleasure you crave." He took his hand down further and slowly caressed his way behind her to grip her ass and lift her core to meet his, letting her know just how much he wanted her while never dropping her hands.

He ground into her, feeling her dampness seep into the fabric that separated them. Ciaran gave just enough to build her desire into an inferno. Every time he moved against her, she met his movements with her own. She had yet to answer him.

"Well, which is it, Etain? Are you a good little witch or a bad little witch?" He pulled away slightly from her, and it took every ounce of control to not give in when her body moved towards him, seeking her release. Watching her start to unravel could easily be his undoing. When she still said nothing, he placed her back on the ground. She made a frustrated noise in the back of her throat.

"What a shame you chose to be a bad little witch. Get some sleep, my love. Your training begins tomorrow." Then he leaned in and put his mouth to her ear, using the same quiet voice to say, "Do not even think about touching yourself. I will know if you do, and I have been dreaming of an excuse to punish you. Do you understand, little witch?" When she gave a slight nod, he dropped her hands and took a few steps back, wearing a smug expression. Etain glared at him and made a disgusted noise before she looked away. He hated when she did that.

"Little witch, every time you look away from me, it will earn you a punishment. Every. Single. Time." She snapped her eyes back to his, disbelief clouding them. "Remember, no touching." He ported away and chuckled as she reached for something to throw at him. As annoyed and wary as he was that she was keeping something from him, he was just as thrilled for this new game they were playing.

Ciaran ported to one of the unused sections of his tower. He only created rooms as he needed them. He looked around the cavernous space and thought about what he would need to train Etain.

While he was looking forward to this new game they were playing, it also bothered him that she was keeping something from him. If he had Galetia perform the same spell on them as she had on Kes, there would be no keeping anything from him.

This gave him pause. If she could keep nothing from him, he could no longer keep things hidden from her. Like the lie he told her in the secret vault under the archives. He could no longer shield her from his true, selfish, and wicked nature. He was already having a hard enough time trying to keep it from her now that they were bonded mates. If they used this spell, there would no longer be any hiding from each other. Should they not know each other's true selves? Beyond that, he hated the thought of her keeping something from him more than the ability to keep something from her. They would have the spell; it was better to have nothing between them.

His decision made, he looked around the room again, ready to turn Etain into the warrior witch she needed to become. She had no prior training, not even basic combat training. He wondered if it was worth spending time on hand-to-hand combat and weapons training. She was tiny—too tiny—any fae would be physically stronger than her. Her power is where her strength resides. If he could train her from the beginning to use her power in tandem with physical blows, she would be unstoppable. Although, he knew nothing about witch power. If they had the spell performed, it would be much easier to train her because then he could gain a true understanding of the mechanics of her power.

He knew he should teach her to port first. Being able to escape any situation could end up being the difference between life and death for her. It was the right thing to do—the good thing, even. However, Ciaran was not a good fae, and he was loath to not have her dependent on him. He scoffed at himself when he realized that as soon as Galetia placed the spell on them, she would be privy to these exact thoughts.

He might not be good, though she was. How fate paired him with a naively kind witch, he could never guess. He was struggling to contain his true wickedness around her and wondered how long it would be until she despised the real him. Mounting the heads of traitors on spikes was nothing compared to some of his more vile deeds.

She detested the human he brought back with her from the Human Realm and she was his ultimate demise. The difference between them was he knew she struggled daily with the knowledge she had taken a life, while he reveled in it. What would she think if she could listen in on his thoughts night in and night out?

Maybe they should not have the spell placed. He wanted to have access to her thoughts without letting her know just how depraved he truly was.

He ran his hands through his hair and roughly knotted it at the base of his head. He craved violence and needed the relief it brought him. Unfortunately, no guest currently resided in his fun room, not since the human escaped a few nights ago. Thinking about that night made his violent desires double.

Not only had the Day King made a fool of him, a mere human was able to as well. He found joy in the ridiculous way the king had perished. It was no less than the idiotic fae deserved—death by a spelled bit of string. Which still made him laugh harder than anything had in a very long time. It was not often something made him laugh freely.

The joy was overshadowed by the queen's spiral into madness; she showed up unannounced on what was supposed to be the perfect night for Etain. The Day King may have been able to slow her descent had he still been alive. Perhaps then Kes would not have found himself in his current predicament. At the same time, they could have found out about the queen's blood magic in a far more catastrophic way.

He did not appreciate being insulted in his own palace, nor the current state his cousin has been left in. He may have told himself for the past several hundred years that his cousin meant nothing to him, except the discomfort he was feeling on behalf of Kes would say otherwise. That was something that was becoming increasingly clear to him. He was not ready to analyze that just yet.

Examining the space again, and not knowing what they would truly need, he used his powers to install the basics. A sparring ring, a wall of weapons that resembled the one in his personal dungeon, and multiple targets. Etain would need to learn how to send her power to exact locations. Of course, that was how he assumed her power would work. If she could learn to use her power to give her the strength she did not naturally contain, he would be pleased.

The room was still mostly empty when he finished, and still there was a burning rage under his skin that he needed to work out before he crawled into bed beside his little witch. He rolled up his sleeves and cracked the joints on his long fingers. He was completely alone, with a lot of empty space around him. There would likely not be a better opportunity to attempt shadow walking.

He had not the slightest idea where to begin. He spent the next couple hours trying to create another him out of the shadows he easily manipulated around himself. Nothing he tried worked. He was about ready to grab some random Night fae and go for a visit to his personal happy place, if only to ease the pounding in his head and the ache that was forming in his jaw from clenching it tightly.

Then he remembered they were supposed to no longer be killing their own, since he would likely need all the numbers he could get. He growled as he walked over to the wall of weapons and took down a huge battle axe. They have always been his weapon of choice, second only to his carving knife. He spent half a second admiring the balance of the weapon before he hurled power out of him, along with the axe, toward one of the targets on the far side of the room. The axe hit dead center and then shattered as it blew through the target and embedded itself into the stone wall behind it.

The action made him consider shadow walking differently. It was simple. He knew how to call shadows to him; perhaps it was as simple as calling shadows from him, if such a thing could be called simple. It was not something he had ever thought of trying, yet something about the idea felt right to him.

He sent his shadow magic out the same way he had with his power and the axe. He was rewarded with a shadow that was his exact shape and size, except without any of his facial features or coloring. Ciaran's frustration seeped out of him in the wake of such a success, and a wicked grin split his face, as did the shadow's.

He was looking through his own eyes, as well as those of the shadow before him. He laughed as he tilted his head to the side, thinking about how much fun he was going to have with this new power. The ideas were endless, and a number of them included his little witch.

It was many hours later when he crawled into bed beside his mate. First night was coming quickly. His body was tired, yet it felt more like a reward than a punishment. He had not necessarily mastered his shadow, though he was confident based on the progress he had already made, it would not be long until he did.

He looked over at Etain, and a few of the ideas he had earlier played out in his mind. This new skill was going to bring more wicked delight than he had ever expected. A few moments later, Ciaran fell asleep with a smile on his face.

Chapter 14
Kes

T he arm under Kes's body had long since lost feeling. It took him several attempts to pull the useless appendage from beneath him. The repeated stabs of needles gave him the uncanny feeling of crawling under his skin as his blood rushed back into his arm. His body ached as it had the night after the Lunar Ball. He felt as though he had been remade once again. The pain helped pull him further into consciousness.

For a few blissful moments, he had no recollection of who he was or what the circumstances of his life were. The scent of Anin surrounding him brought him crashing back into his existence. He panicked when he recalled the pain he felt on her behalf in his final moments before the abyss of nothingness welcomed him.

A cold sweat coated his skin as the fear of reaching through the bond and finding nothing at the other end took hold. His sluggish mind made it difficult to piece together how he found himself in Anin's bed. For several minutes, all he could recall was the searing pain tearing through his neck. It was not his own pain he had felt. He knew it was hers, and he knew what had to have happened to cause it—they both had spilled blood.

His arm was finally his own again. He spread his wings wide to lay on his back. The room was dark, though he could still make out the vines Anin had covered the ceiling with. He took a deep breath, clenched his eyes tightly closed, and began his descent down the bond.

The agony he felt at the other end was crippling. His own aches were a mild echo of what he felt on the other side of the bond. He dragged his hands down his face, not knowing how to help take the pain from her. His pain, he could handle. Her pain, he could not.

The memory of the spell Galetia cast over them came to the surface of his thoughts. It took him a frustrating amount of time to recall the words he had repeated. He did not hear her thoughts in his mind, nor did he feel any new power running through his veins. He had, however, felt as though he were dying when he felt the blinding pain across his throat, which completely overshadowed the stab wound the witch had given him.

He felt the pain in his neck flare over and over again. Eventually, those flares began igniting all over his body in a pattern he could not discern. Each was a devastating reminder of how he continued to fail her. He welcomed the darkness when it came for him, offering sweet oblivion.

Unwilling to give up on the possibility the spell had worked, he felt his way back down the bond. He was once again hit with an agonizing amount of pain. Her mind seemed calm, and he hoped she was unconscious and oblivious to her suffering. Focusing on the bond, he felt the connection had strengthened. He tried to test how far he could reach within her, trying to understand the mechanics of their deeper connection.

"My darling nymph, what mayhem have you found yourself in

this time?" Kes found himself talking out loud to her while he worked. For his own peace of mind or hers, he decided it was not important. He wanted her to know and feel that she was not entirely alone, and he did not want to feel alone either.

"Your sister's a psychotic bitch. Your other two, I much prefer. I find myself nearly liking them. I know; I am concerned for my reputation as well." He felt an awareness flit across her mind.

"I miss that sharp tongue of yours. I can only imagine what inventive names you would create for me right now. I'm sure you would start with a tantalizing eye roll followed by some comment filled with snark like, 'My darling feather duster.' Do not dare tell a soul, but I have grown rather fond of the name. 'If you are going to lounge in bed all day, you should at least become the stuffing in the mattress so as not to be a total waste of space.' To which I would say, 'Only if you come and sit on me. Particularly the head of the bed, directly on my face, would be preferred.' You would flush that beautifully vibrant green hue I adore and then look away, trying to hide your own desires. I will let you in on a little secret. You, my darling, are a horrible actress. Your lovely face gives you away every time." He chuckled and could nearly hear the huff of indignation she would make at his impersonation of her.

The pain was becoming acute, and he was losing his focus. He wished he could take even a fraction to help her not wake to such staggering agony. He paused at that thought. Why would he not be able to?

He knew how to send her power through the bond, even though he did not know if she received it. How hard could it be to pull something from her? He tried to mentally grasp on to her pain as if it were something tangible and tugged on it. He grunted when the first wave exploded inside him, yet he would take every bit his body would allow.

He pushed his power into her while he pulled her pain into him. He mentally detached himself from his body and kept his focus solely on his task. It was a shock when he felt himself reach the bottom of his well and knew his forced sleep would be imminent. He gave one last tug on her pain before he succumbed to the payment his power demanded.

When he woke, he found her pain still unbearable and her consciousness still silent. He repeated the entire process again. He told her he would come for her over and over as he pushed his power into her while pulling pain from her until sleep took him. The passing of time was lost to him as he lived in a state of constant repetition until he came to once more, but this time to the faces of Anin's sisters.

"You have been in this room for over a week. You smell repulsive, need to eat, and how are we to become silent shadows if you never train us? We need to help her as well, Kes. Help us become what we need to be in order to get our sister back," Lyra demanded.

"We are tired of waiting and doing nothing while our sister lives in misery—if the look of you is anything to go off of." Where Lyra had been in a near rage, Panella was more understanding. Be that as it may, neither of them were willing to let him stay as he was for a moment longer. Together, they dragged his body down the bed, physically removing him from it themselves. He found himself in a heap on the floor at the foot of Anin's bed.

His body shook as he tried to pick himself up off the floor. He had survived on nothing except his own power, and he had constantly been depleting it while stealing Anin's pain from her and having to heal from that. They were right; he needed to eat and train if he was going to continue to be strong enough to take her pain and get her back as well.

Kes said nothing to the sisters, though he nodded as he walked past them towards his bathing chamber. He began mentally preparing his plans for their training. He would enjoy watching them succumb to pain at the end of every training session, knowing that was what progress looked like as their bodies molded into the warriors he would make out of them. Each day they felt less pain was a day closer to getting his mate back.

Chapter 15
Anin

S omeone is moaning, was Anin's first coherent thought. She drifted in and out of consciousness several times. It felt like a dream—a nightmare—and she could not be sure of anything. She moaned again and realized it was she who had been moaning.

Finally, the pain subsided enough for her to make a sound. Her dreams were filled with an all-consuming agony she felt in every fiber of her being. She was certain that part had been real. The pain was still sharp, and every breath she took was a reminder of how far her body had yet to heal.

She dreamt of a male; he spoke to her, though she had not been able to understand him. The sound of his voice and the feel of his presence became a bright spot for her to focus on while her body did the rest. Dreaming about him seemed to lessen the pain and offer a reprieve from the unfathomable agony she was consumed by, if only for a little while. His presence flooded her with a sense of ease, finally allowing her body to relax. It was the only time her mind loosened the grip it held on her consciousness, a way to protect her from the worst of the pain.

She was having a hard time remembering where she was and what happened to her. A veil clouded her mind, preventing her from grasping on to any one thought fully. The pain was still blinding, causing her to see only bright white, even though her eyes remained shut.

Before the confusion and panic could overwhelm her, she was pulled back under. She hoped she would dream of him again. Maybe this time she would be able to understand what he said. Maybe this time...

When she woke, her breaths came easier, and she thought it possible the pain had lessened. She dreamt of the same male again. She could understand him this time. He kept promising he would come for her. She did not understand what he meant. She knew nothing, not even who or where she was. Nor did she know who he was, though she recognized him as a part of her. Before she could dig any deeper into her mind, the pain pulled her back under.

This was a pattern she repeated several times. She had no concept of how much time had passed; she did not know time at all until one of her more recent bouts of consciousness. This time, when Anin woke, it was with a sense of familiarity. She knew who she was and felt closer to normal. She felt better than she had over the past...however long it had been.

She could see again once she pried her eyes open. They were crusted shut, and they were nearly impossible to open without the use of her hands. When she was unable to lift them, she realized she could not move at all. From exhaustion or by design, she was uncertain. Taking in her surroundings, she decided having her sight back was not the improvement she hoped it would be. Her memories began to come back to her as well, and like her sight, it was another thing she wished she could give back.

Her sister tried to kill her. She had killed her, or at least that was what Anin thought. The last thing she remembered was

Tatiana dragging a blade across her neck, although the pain and healing her body had just endured told of an even darker story. She had no idea how she was still alive. She felt herself dying; had even raged against it. The conviction she put behind her desire to live felt like a final rebellion.

Her body took on a different kind of ache. She was terribly stiff from not moving for...she did not know how long, but it felt like forever. When she tried once more to move so that she could stretch and bend her joints, she was unable to move even an inch. White spots appeared behind her eyes again the moment she noticed her cage had shrunk significantly. Her heart raced, and a sudden heat filled her body, causing her to perspire. She was trapped in a small box in some underground damp chamber within the Day Court, and the only being that knew her location was a mad queen.

What if she could never move again? What if she never felt the sun on her skin again? What if Kes never found her? Her breathing increased rapidly, yet it felt like she was not breathing at all. She felt faint. This time, it was her panic that pulled her under the veil of consciousness.

"Wake up!" Cold water shocked Anin back to awareness.

"I want to play, little sister," Tatiana said in a sing-song voice that made Anin's skin crawl. Her mind was telling her to run and get as far away as possible, although she still could not move even the barest amount. How was she supposed to respond to that? She stayed silent, feeling it was the safest option.

"Do you know what I have been thinking about over the past

couple weeks while you were down here sleeping the days away, lazybones?"

Weeks? It had been weeks since her sister attempted to murder her? Weeks, and she was still here? No one had come for her.

"I ASKED YOU A QUESTION, SISTER!" Gone was the terrifyingly playful voice, and in its place was an equally terrifying, vicious sneer.

"What?" Anin croaked out. Her throat was dry, and her voice had gone unused for so long it was surprising anything came out at all.

"Well, I am extremely glad you asked," Tatiana said sweetly, as if she had not just demanded a response. Her mood swings were dizzying. "I must confess that at first I was furious that the Land intervened on your behalf. I could not get more than a drop of your blood to touch the altar. Which was terribly rude of you, by the way." She had the nerve to pout.

"Truly sorry to disappoint you, sister." Anin did her best to put as much vitriol into the word "sister." "I did not have dying on my agenda."

"Oh, it is fine! I have not been mad about that for a while now." She sounded like a youngling when she spoke. "What I have been thinking about, quite obsessively even, is how I no longer have someone to share this life with." She said the last couple words with an eerie, emotionless tone that terrified Anin the most.

"Why is that, Anin?" Tatiana asked her as she cocked her head to the side. The hairs on Anin's arms and the back of her neck tingled as they stood on end. There was no scenario where this went well for Anin. She tried to swallow, but it felt like she had something lodged in the back of her throat. "Because he is dead?" Anin croaked.

Tatiana stared at Anin for several moments with an unnatural stillness and a rage burning brightly behind her eyes. Dread pooled in Anin's gut.

"That is correct. He. Is. Dead. How did he die, *sister*?" Anin was nearly choking on the thick, violent tension in the air. Her heart started beating rapidly, knowing this was going to be the moment Tatiana exploded with all of her rage at Anin. Again.

"He touched the spelled chain I had been wearing," she whispered. There was no correct answer Anin could have given, thus she went with the truth. Tatiana did not react for what felt like several long moments which left Anin painfully waiting for the moment she would erupt. She did not have to wait long.

Tatiana's face broke into a slow, savage smile that could easily contend with Ciaran's, before she threw her head back in a mirthless laughter laced with the promise of pain to come. "He touched a spelled chain you were wearing..." She was suddenly hovering above the cage Anin was stuffed into. "YOU KILLED HIM! You Night Court whore! You have taken everything from me!" Anin found that hard to believe, considering she was the one in the cage with the wrath of a mad queen directed at her.

Tatiana ripped the top of her cage open and pulled Anin out by her hair. Somehow, she was both terrified and relieved to be out of her box. Her limbs were not working correctly after being stationary so long, causing her to crumple the second her feet touched the ground. This did not slow her sister down. She dragged her to the center of the room, where a chain and a hook hung from the ceiling. Manacles appeared on her wrists, with no recollection of how they got there. Everything was moving quickly, and yet it felt like they were wading through water at the same time.

Anin had forgotten to breathe and saw white stars burst behind her eyes before she gasped for breath. She was hanging from the hook with her toes just brushing the floor. It took her a couple of tries to get the feeling back in her wings to open. As soon as she could, she used them to take some of the pressure off her shoulders.

Tatiana chuckled darkly. "Well, we cannot have that now, can we...sissster?" Anin had not noticed the blade she summoned—the same one from the altar. Anin's breaths were coming in panicked gasps as Tatiana dragged the very tip of the blade across her skin as she slowly went to stand behind her. She took one of Anin's wings in her hand and brought the tip of the blade up to the joint where her wings met her back.

"No." Anin's voice shook with a different kind of fear. She knew she could handle some pretty horrific things, but the thought of losing her wings was too much. Her wings were her armor; they could not protect her from harm, though they shielded her all the same when she wrapped them around her body.

"What a silly nymph!" Tatiana cooed. "Thinking you have any control over the things I plan to do to you for the rest of your miserable existence." She elongated her speech with the last few words. Tatiana began dragging the knife slowly back and forth over the joint on her back.

Anin cried out in agony. She barely had any reprieve from the pain she only just recovered from before her sister sent her body right back into the nightmare. She begged. She knew she had. She did not know to whom she was begging. Her sister to stop? The goddess to save her? Kes? All of them? The pain was all-consuming and she could barely hold a single thought for more than a breath of time.

Two things happened right before she passed out. She heard the slap of her wings hitting the floor, and she was suddenly filled with power as her pain was siphoned from her. She could have sworn she heard Kes tell her he was there and he would help her through whatever she was forced to endure. Then everything went black.

Chapter 16
Etain

E tain wiped the sweat from her brow and glared at Ciaran.
He was punishing her in more ways than one, all because
she would not share her own thoughts with him. Now
more than ever, she did not want to have the spell placed on them.
He hinted at it a few times every night, and she would make some
noncommittal noise in return.

As his frustration grew towards her, hers grew towards him as
well. He played her body expertly, knowing exactly what was
needed to make her beg him for release. Every time he got her
there, he would whisper into her ear to tell him what was bothering her. She had yet to give in, and now she was more determined than ever not to break until he did. She knew each time he
punished her, he suffered right alongside her.

"Again!" Ciaran barked at her. Her limbs already shook with
exhaustion, and the tone he used with her was really starting to
grate on her every last nerve.

"No." She glared at him for at least the hundredth time that night.

"No?" he asked incredulously.

"I am finished for the night, Ciaran. My legs can barely keep me standing as it is." She turned her back on him. It was something she knew would anger him, and she really wanted to anger him. She loved him—she truly did—but currently she did not like him.

"You are not done until I say you are, *mate*. What are you going to do? Walk up the never ending stairs to our chambers?" That was another thing that was causing resentment to fester between them. She wanted him to teach her how to port, so she did not need to be dependent upon him, yet he refused. Time and time again over the past week, he refused her.

He used it against her for her unwillingness to tell him what he wanted to know. She scoffed. In the beginning, she had not wanted him to know she had reservations about the spell because she did not want to hurt him. Now, she did not care if it hurt him. He was proving to her multiple times a night why she had reservations to begin with.

"Oh my goddess, I finally figured it out. You want to always have control over me. That is the real reason you will not teach me to port?" Her eyes were hot with tears of anger that she refused to let fall. She did not care to admit to herself how hurt she was because of him.

She did not even recognize him as the Ciaran from a few weeks ago, when they completed their mating ceremony. If it were not for the emotion she received through the bond from him, she would have thought that Ciaran had been a complete act. It was not an act, and she knew he was just as miserable as she was.

He chuckled darkly behind her. If she turned around, he would be leaning casually against whatever surface was closest with one of his too-wide grins. He would have that glint in his eye he got when he was planning something menacing, which seemed directed at her only as of late.

She felt the air shift as he moved into the space directly behind her with the speed that no longer surprised her. She might still flinch, except she began to notice the way the air would change around her, which gave the whisper of a warning he was coming. He fisted her sweat-dampened hair and pulled her head back, forcing her to look up to meet his eyes from behind. She cursed the thrill that shot through her body.

"Trying to pretend you do not enjoy it when I have complete control over you, little witch?" he asked. She audibly scoffed and rolled her eyes—another thing he hated. His hand gripped her hair even tighter.

"You know it is not the same, Ciaran. You are intentionally crippling me." This time, her eyes burned with hurt, and she could not keep a single tear from falling. Ciaran's eyes and grip on her hair softened for a single moment before he bent down and licked the trail the tear had left down her face.

"Tell me what I want to know, little witch, and I will teach you," he whispered as he ran his nose along the column of her neck. Her eyes closed as a tremor worked its way down her body. He was responsible for the other kind of frustration she was living with as well. Her body was fully desperate for the release he had been denying her. Refusing to look at him, she remained silent.

"Why do you continue to deny me?" The irritation was clear in his voice. He released her, and before she could turn around, he was over at a table covered in all manner of weapons he was determined to make her proficient in. She was still uncomfortable with the idea of harming anyone else, but she saw the merits of being able to defend herself and others if need be.

When she continued to say nothing, he stared at her. She could see his jaw clench and his breathing become more rapid. He bellowed his frustration as he swiped the table clear of all the sharp objects that had just been covering it. Etain flinched. He was being childish, and she had enough of it. She released the hold on her power and let her anger flow freely through her.

"Every time you do not get exactly what you want, when you want it, and from whomever you want it, you act like a child! You are the only several-hundred-years-old being here; grow up!" she seethed. She could feel her hair floating like a halo around her head while the weapons he had just thrown to the floor lifted into the air and circled them.

"You are the one who is being childish! Refusing to talk to your mate like some youngling pouting in a corner!" He glared at her with his glowing golden eyes, anger making them appear molten. He took a few steps toward her, smashing the...well, she did not know what it was, though it was a tall wooden structure. The shards of wood joined the weapons flying around the room.

"You are the one smashing the room to pieces because you do not know how to handle the word no," she scoffed. "I do not owe you access to every single thought I have!" she yelled as she took a few steps closer to him; the objects picking up speed.

"You do when that thought is obviously causing you strife!" he yelled at her while taking a few more steps closer.

"Oh, that is absolutely hilarious, Ciaran, coming from you!" She could not believe he had the audacity to say such things.

"What is that supposed to mean?" he asked, his voice dangerously low.

"You lied to me! In the secret room that you refuse to let anyone else know about. I got this strange syrupy thick feeling through the bond from you, and I have been trying to figure out what it was, and then I felt it again, and again, AND AGAIN!" She was screaming her frustrations, unable to keep mild control over her emotions.

"I do not lie to you!" He tried to make it feel true, but the bond does not lie.

"YOU JUST DID! I felt it! Why would I ever tell you when you continue to lie to me?" It should not surprise her he would lie again to her face, yet it had. They were standing a few paces apart that Ciaran cleared in two steps before grabbing her by the shoulders.

"You are *mine*! Your body, your mind, your heart, and your soul are MINE!" Did he really think he could ever own her? She laughed in his face.

"So you get to own me, yet I do not get to own you? Ciaran, if that is how it—"

"Oh, but you do. You own every piece of me. All that I am belongs to you, little witch." His eyes bore into her, and she felt the truth of his words before his mouth crashed into hers, and they began tearing clothes from each other in a desperate need to be closer.

"You...insufferable...oaf!" she said in between their kisses.

"You...stubborn...witch." He growled and ripped the last of her clothing from her. Their movements were clumsy and frenzied, both needing release. In their desire to not give into each other, they made themselves miserable.

He lifted her to meet his cock with her core and had her up against a wall, thrusting inside her in one swift motion. She had not noticed when they moved from the center of the room. They both let out a groan as their frantic movements stilled long enough for them both to get lost in the sensation of being one again. Ciaran dropped his forehead to Etain's.

"Hold on tight, little witch; this is not going to be gentle. I am going to take you hard and fast until the only sound coming from you is a scream with my name on your lips." He pinned her hands tightly above her head and wrapped his other arm around her to support her weight. That was all the warning she received before he began his punishing pace.

Etain could move nothing but her legs, and she wrapped those tightly around him in an attempt to hold on. All she could do was take the bruising thrusts and get lost in the euphoria they brought her.

He took her higher, faster than she thought possible before she was cresting over the top of her pleasure and screaming his name, just as he said she would. He did not stop his pace, and she did not know if she wanted him to stop or keep going as she quickly climbed to the peak of her pleasure once more. This time climbing even higher before she came crashing down the other side, so hard that no sound came out when she opened her mouth to scream his name again.

"That's it, little witch; this is your punishment. I am going to take you higher each time until your plummet over the edge is too much to handle. You will beg me to stop, and you will tell me you cannot handle it, and then I will make you do it one last time." Ciaran had never removed his forehead from hers, making it impossible not to hear his words clearly. She groaned in pleasure or dread; she thought a little of each.

True to his words, her body was becoming overly sensitized, and she could not decide if she loved the feeling or loathed it. Her mind, muddled with pleasure, was unable to form a coherent thought. She was not sure when it happened, though at some point she did start begging.

"Oh, gods!" she cried out over and over. Ciaran laughed darkly, knowing he was accomplishing exactly what he had set out to do. Part of Etain wanted to be indignant; the other part was just trying to stay connected to reality. When she descended into pleasure the next time, her vision went dark, and she lost all awareness. When she finally came back into her body, Ciaran was taking her right back up again. She thought it possible she might die if he did not stop.

"Ciaran, no more...please...I cannot take it." She finally got her mouth to form the words she had been struggling to get out.

"One last time, little witch," he said gruffly into her ear. She groaned, positive one last descent into pleasure would be a fall to her death.

"I cann—"

"You will," he declared over her denial.

"No, it is too much, Ciaran... Oh gods!" She screamed at the end of her plea as she plummeted harder than she thought possible. She felt him finally still, ending her sublime torture as he groaned out his own release into her.

Her body had gone liquid, and her mind was a mass of confusion. When it became too much, she felt nothing but pleasure, even when it intertwined with pain. What did it say about her that the mixture of pleasure and pain had felt incredible? It did not matter; she was completely shattered and would have to think on it later.

Ciaran released her hands and wrapped that arm around her back before porting them to their chambers. He placed her boneless body on the bed and disappeared into the bathing chamber for several minutes. When he returned, his hair was wet and he was dressed in fresh clothes. He regarded her limp body, still in the exact place he had left her. One of his wicked grins sliced smugly across his face.

"You and that stupid grin," Etain croaked out, which only made him grin even wider. He said nothing as he walked to the bed and picked her up again. He brought her into the bathing chamber, placing her in a deliciously hot bath he must have drawn for her. It immediately eased the soreness between her legs.

They stared into each other's eyes, neither of them saying anything, before he gently placed his hand on the side of her face. She leaned into his touch without thought, and he caressed her cheek with his thumb.

Their problems had not been solved, and there was still distance between them, though it was no longer the chasm it had once been. They both knew they still had problems they needed to face, but for now, the dam the sexual tension created between them had burst. Ciaran stood, still saying nothing, and ported away.

She sighed and leaned back to soak in the steaming tub. They needed to work on their differences because they could not keep living this way. While the mate bond guaranteed their love for each other, it did not mean they would like each other. What is love without friendship? That was something they would have to continue to work through. Their differences were bound to cause issues time and time again within their immortal lives. She was not about to spend her life in love, yet always miserable.

Her brain was still sluggish and not in the right state to contemplate the way their relationship would need to be in order to ensure their happiness. She tucked away her thoughts to be examined closer at a later time and closed her eyes to relax. She immediately opened them. It turned out doing nothing was not as relaxing as she thought it to be. Not when there was always so much to be done, and not when her mind was a never ending whirlwind of thoughts she had no hope of silencing.

Chapter 17
Anin

A sudden change in the air yanked Anin into consciousness. Sleeping was the only escape from both time and agony she had access to. It took her a moment to notice her cage was no longer the small, restrictive box to which she had grown accustomed. It was now wide and tall enough that she could fully stand, assuming her legs could manage the task. Her new found space made her feel uncomfortable, and she did not trust it.

It took her longer and was more difficult than she expected to come to a seated position, her body protesting every minuscule movement. Her eyes were slow to wake, and Anin had to blink them several times to see anything beyond the general shape of the box caging her. A chill enveloped her, having nothing to do with the temperature of the air around her as her eyes came into focus.

She was in that place—the place she never wished to see again in her life. The eclipsed sun was perfectly framed by the same opening in the spider-webbed ceiling. She shut her eyes tightly, hoping they had been playing a cruel joke on her. When she opened them again, her breath became too fast and too shallow, leaving her feeling dizzy with the sound of rushing water in her ears.

The altar was once again before her. The same altar where she pleaded to the gods for her life. Where she said her goodbyes to the life she could have lived if fate had not taken such a brutal turn. On the same altar where her father died and upon which she was intended to follow, she had raged against death, rejecting it.

Had she known then what living would cost her every day, she thought it unlikely she would have had the same conviction to live. She wondered if the Land refused to let her die because she had fought vehemently against the idea of death or if she never had the choice to begin with. Either way, the thought of death no longer felt horrific.

Her sister endeavored to make her regret her desire nearly every day. When she was not "visiting," Anin spent her days painstakingly healing whatever trauma Tatiana inflicted upon her. She was both grateful and unappreciative of the speed with which she healed. It ended her pain *and* brought fresh pain sooner. She never thought she would be thankful to her sister. However, she had put her back in her cramped cage face down. Her standards of kindness seemed to have dropped dramatically if this was what she now found gratitude in.

When she woke again and found herself lying on her stomach, she nearly wept with relief. She could not imagine the pain she would have been forced to endure had she been lying on her wingless back. That moment of gratitude was short-lived when she saw her wings hanging on the wall she faced—like a trophy. The loss of them felt even more painful now that she was unable to pretend she still had them.

Her wings were growing back, and the process was a new form of torture all on its own. A cocoon of sorts scabbed over the place where her wings once attached to her. She would never have known what it looked like if Tatiana had not found it amusing and shown her the "hideous growth." She hung a large mirror on the opposite wall from her wings, ensuring Anin was reminded of either the loss of her wings or the loss of her freedom, depending on which way she laid her head.

While at first it soothed the pain caused by the horrendous removal of her wings, it quickly turned to incessant itching as they grew back from within the cocoon. Eventually, the itching became a welcome reminder that her wings were at least growing back. She wondered if they would look the same.

She was rather fond of the iridescent appendages that hung lacklusterly on the wall. They already began to curl in around the edges, and the vibrancy they once contained was now muted. She loved the way they faded from a blue-green to a reddish-pink. Anin had found numerous ways to fold and tuck them to utilize the transitioning colors to her advantage.

Using her wings as clothing started when she was very young. Her mother did not have the means to pay for her to have the regal dresses she craved. She often reminded Anin, "Wood nymphs do not wear clothing. We adorn ourselves with all the things that grow in the woods, like moss, bark, vines, leaves, and flowers. What need could you possibly have for silly fabrics?"

Anin tried to be like her mother and the other wood nymphs her age, but it did not matter; she looked unlike the others. It made no difference what she wore. She was still going to be teased by the other younglings she spent her young-hood with. They all had skin the color of fern moss, while she had a light greenish-yellow skin that always held a golden glow. Their hair was the brightest lime green; hers was golden, with subtle streaks of green. Perhaps the biggest difference between her and the rest of her kind were her wings. She was the only one with true wings. The others could create wings out of bark or leaves, while hers were a part of her body.

Wearing her wings as a form of clothing started out as a way to draw less attention by appearing as if she did not have them. That quickly changed when she started getting more creative in the ways she folded and tucked her wings. She became adept at wrapping them to emulate the gowns she had always desired. That was when she stopped caring if she looked different; it made no difference one way or the other.

In her weakened state, she could not gather the strength to grow her vines to cover herself, making her feel even more vulnerable. Taking deep, calming breaths while using the bars of her cage to pull herself up, the sound of rushing water and the feeling of dizziness dissipated. She could have sworn she could hear crying.

With her hearing finally clear, and standing on her own two feet for the first time since Tatiana's previous visit, she was able to prepare herself for whatever it was she might see. She worked up her courage and finally looked around. There was no preparing for the sight that awaited her.

Directly across the room, on the other end of the short wall with the hidden boxes, stood another cage. This one was much larger than the one she was in. It would have to be in order to hold the dozen witches she saw huddled together. She had heard crying after all.

At first glance, she could not recognize any of them as witches from the Silver Moon Coven, although it was hard to see in the low light of the eclipsed sun. The way they stood huddled in a circle was unusual and hid most of their faces. Anin witnessed many rituals performed by witches and even participated in several, yet she could not recall any that started like that.

Her mind slowed over the last...however long it had been since her sister imprisoned her. The combination of pain and being unable to track the passing of time muddled her mind and dulled her senses, making her unaware when Tatiana came to stand beside her cage, just out of her line of sight.

"I am thrilled to see you could join us, dear sister. However, I imagine your social calendar has suddenly freed up quite a bit." The laughter that followed was maniacal and terrifying. The sluggish movement of her mind made it difficult to comprehend all the pieces of the mental puzzle she had been trying to assemble from the moment her eyes opened. Slowly, a picture materialized: the altar, the witches, her sister—that blade.

"No," Anin croaked out. Her throat was still healing from screaming. It made speaking feel unnatural. She knew her words would be pointless; Tatiana was going to do whatever it was she planned. There was nothing Anin could do. She would endure being the witness to their murders, and she would verbally fight Tatiana till the very end for them. She wished now more than ever she had died if it might have spared these witches the death that awaited them.

Anin would never forget the pain she endured on that altar. Silent tears fell, knowing each of them would experience the same. There had to be something more she could do. What good was her power if she could not do something in the face of a horror such as this? She should have swallowed her pride and asked Kes to teach her anything he could. She had been foolish, and she would never forgive herself.

There was a moment of hope when Tatiana threw open the wide door to the cage; maybe at least one of them could make a run for it. They must have some kind of power to be able to help themselves. All hope drained the second every single body went stiff. Anin remembered her sister had blood magic, the reason this barbaric ritual was even taking place.

"Do you see that atrocious nymph in the cage across the room?" Every head bobbed in affirmation, even the ones not looking her way. "She is the reason you face the demise you do

Amber Thoma

today. She could have sacrificed herself to save you, but as you can see, she did not." Anin glared at the mad queen.

"It is because of her selfishness you all will die upon my altar today. Her power would have been enough to sustain me for a very long time." She tisked and shook her head as if the thought of killing them truly saddened her. Then she shrugged and said cheerfully, "Nothing to be done about it now." The first witch began walking out of the cage with the jerky steps of someone fighting with everything they had to regain control of their body.

"Tatiana, this is madness! You truly have no issue taking innocent lives, all to gain a bit more power?" Anin screamed. She knew she would pay for this later, although she was going to make her feel as guilty as Tatiana was capable of feeling. All Anin received was an eye roll in return.

The witch came to a stop beside the altar. The four chains with manacles at the ends slithered out from the stone and clasped themselves around her limbs before snapping her to the altar with such speed that it had been nearly impossible to see it happen. As soon as the witch was lying prone on the slab of stone, she struggled against her binds. Anin needed to do something, even if all she could do for the witch was take her mind off what was about to happen.

"Tell me your name." Anin would learn each of them. She would remember them all.

"Brhget," the witch said in a shaky voice.

"What coven do you come from, Brhget?" Anin asked as Tatiana scanned the little red book.

"The Coven of Remembrance," she said, this time with a stronger voice. Tatiana spoke the words Anin could not understand.

"I will remember you, Brhget." It was not a statement; it was a promise. One she would make to each of them.

"Thank y—" was the last thing she said before she screamed

and began to choke on her own blood. She repeated her promise just in case Brhget could still hear her. It horrified her when the choking seemed to go on for minutes instead of the seconds she had tried to prepare for.

"Really sister, could you be quiet?" Anin had not been aware she was sobbing. For the sake of the witches to come, she tried to silence herself—not for *her*, never for her. She was unable to look away as Brhget's blood wound down the channel carved into the stone like a river before meeting the circular shape on the floor where the queen stood.

She did not know what she was expecting—perhaps a bright light as the power transferred into her sister. Instead, Tatiana's veins began to bulge and shift as if they were drinking the blood beneath them. She realized that was exactly what they were doing as the blood disappeared completely. The transfer of power took less time than it had taken Brhget to die.

She looked at the cage to count how many times she would have to bear witness to her sister's madness. She counted eleven. Her brows scrunched as she counted again. Twelve was a strange number to choose. Magic worked best with the numbers three, seven, and thirteen. She could not say why, yet something heavy took root within her gut that had nothing to do with the scene before her.

Anin watched as the same fate claimed witch after witch. Josephine, Lyse, and River from the Black Cauldron Coven. Faith, Hope and Destiny from the Falling Star Coven. Thistle and Cerridwen, who had come from the Coven of Remembrance with Brhget. Anin made each of them the same promise that she would remember them.

It was not until Tatiana went to collect the tenth witch that Anin recognized a face. Welyn, whom she had known for most of the past century, turned to make the stilted walk toward the altar. Anin gasped at what she saw as soon as Welyn moved; they had been surrounding a thirteenth witch. If you could even call one that young a witch.

"A YOUNGLING? Tatiana, you are truly mad if you think anything is worth robbing a youngling of their life! Have you any dignity left? They will know you as the Mad Queen when history tells your story. The Mad Queen, the Evil Queen, the Queen Who Was Not Truly a Queen!" She spat as many names as she could come up with at the evil creature in front of her.

"I AM A QUEEN!" she snarled at Anin. That had obviously hit its mark. "You know nothing of what you speak. They are being sacrificed for the greater good. They are all beings filled with a deep well of power; I do not care about anything else." Welyn had made her way to the table and was now secured to it.

"Anin! You must do something for her! Tallon is..." she sobbed until she saw the blade in Tatiana's hand. "She is too young for fate to be so cruel!" She had just gotten the last word out before she screamed and began to choke. Anin grabbed the bars of her cage and shook them, roaring out her rage.

"You are a monster, not a queen at all. There is no greater good worth this many lives!" She screamed at the mad fae as her veins drank up the blood that had once belonged to a friend. She had the audacity to smile at Anin as she disposed of the shell that had been full of life only minutes before.

"That, sister, is where you are wrong." She said, opening the door to the cage holding three more witches, whom Anin knew well. "The greater good is always worth every sacrifice that must be made along the way. I sacrificed the love of the Land and the power it once granted me. A far greater sacrifice than these insignificant witches." Anin was stunned. The level of delusions Tatiana held was far more insane than she originally thought, which made her sister even more dangerous and volatile.

Anin was at a loss for words. Knowing there was no way she could talk her sister out of this, she held onto a small sliver of hope anyway. Not for the first time, she wondered what caused her sister to turn into this raving lunatic. She found it hard to believe she had always been this way if the Land had, at one point, chosen her. Anin had been in a daze, and it was a shock to see Ophila already upon the altar.

"Anin, please, you must do something for her," she said through trembling lips and panicked breaths. Ophila had always been free with her emotions. She was quick to hug, would laugh at every joke, and would even cry with you. She was one of the kindest witches Anin knew, and she wished there was something she could do to ease her fear.

"I will try, Ophila. I will try." Her friend would never hug, laugh, or cry with another as the knife slid across her neck. She looked at the remaining two witches. Catra, who was regimented in everything she did, was always studying some spell book or another. They would often tease Catra to not forget to live her life, or all her knowledge would be worthless. Anin sobbed, knowing she would never get the chance. Catra had always been quiet, hardly showing any emotions, which is why her last words surprised Anin.

"Make sure she pays." The words hissed between clenched teeth. Catra made no effort to hide her anger.

"I will." Anin believed her own words until Catra's life spilled from her body and Tatiana laughed.

"You will, will you?" Tatiana laughed hysterically. "How do you plan to fulfill that promise, my dear, naïve sister?"

She deflated. Tatiana was right; if a way to escape existed, she would have already.

"Just because I see no way out right now does not mean there will not be one later. Remember, my monstrosity of a sister, I will live a very long time." She put more confidence than she felt behind the words. Tatiana paused mid-step to glare at her. She did not like being reminded of the Land's rejection, and she did not seem to care for being called "a monster" or "mad." Anin filed that away for later. If she were to live in a constant state of pain, she would find ways to dig at Tatiana as often and as deeply as possible.

Anin watched the small body step from the cage. A youngling witch she had seen not very long ago. The last time she spoke to Tallon, she promised to suggest singing lessons to her "bird beast." Her body looked too small on the stone slab that had already claimed many lives prior to hers.

"I told Kes you suggested singing lessons; he promised to look into them." It was the only thing she could think to say to the small witch before her, who turned her face to lock eyes with Anin's.

"Good; the realm will be better for it." She smiled at her, looking much older than she appeared. Anin tried not to flinch as she saw Tatiana pick up the blade.

"Tallon, keep looking at me." Anin felt this thing growing inside her. She did not know if it was rage or anguish—maybe both. She silently screamed to the gods or the Land, whoever was listening, to spare Tallon from pain as the thing inside her took on a life of its own. If they could not spare her life, they could at least spare her pain.

"Anin, it will be okay." She smiled again, showing her bright white teeth. "I know you will find a way to make it right for all of us. When you see my mother again, will you tell her I was very brave?" she asked, fear slipping into her beautiful moss green eyes that she kept locked on Anin's.

"I will tell her you are the bravest witch I have ever met." Anin kept her face neutral to keep Tallon from panicking as Tatiana flipped through her book.

"I do not feel so brave," she whispered.

"It's okay to be scared; it does not make you less brave," Anin whispered back. She never once took her eyes away from Anin's, missing the blade coming to claim her.

"Make sure you hold your mate to those singing lessons," she said with one last smile. They were the last words she would ever speak.

Just as the knife connected with her skin, Anin felt whatever had been growing within her explode out in an unseen and silent blast of power. Anin was the only one aware of the power that flew from her, hurtling towards the altar and hitting Tallon. Life instantly left the girl's eyes, sparing her from the pain she would have endured. Someone or something had listened after all.

Tears poured from her eyes now. She made no effort to hold them back. Tallon's blood raced down to feed Tatiana's veins— blood Anin would feel on her hands for the rest of her life. She would have to find a way to live with her death, if only to find Tallon's mother and tell her how brave her daughter was.

Something has gone wrong for Tatiana. The blood stayed within the circle beneath her feet; her veins were unable to drink this time. Anin laughed a mirthless laugh while she watched as Tatiana frustratedly flipped through her ugly little book. Anin was glad her sister could not take more from the youngling than she already had. Her eyes snapped to Anin.

"You!" she seethed. "You did something! I know you did! You have wasted the sacrifice this young witch made!"

Anin could see her nearly vibrating with rage. She knew it would be directed at one being and one being alone, except she was past caring.

"I have no idea what you are talking about." Anin roared with laughter as she watched Tatiana's eyes nearly bulge out of their sockets.

"You stupid Night Court whore! Her sacrifice is now pointless. You stole her contribution toward the greater good!" She looked as though she might cry, like when a youngling gets a toy taken from them. It was truly disgusting.

"What greater good is worth THAT?" she screamed at the mad queen while she waved her hand toward the lifeless body on the altar.

"Are you too blind to see that once I control everyone, there will never be any conflict again? The lesser fae will serve the higher fae as intended. The Night Court will never kill a Day fae ever again, and I will eject the power of the Land from this realm entirely." Tatiana marched toward Anin's cage on unsteady legs while she spoke. When she got closer, Anin could see her eyes were glassy, the rage adding a wildness that promised pain. She flung open the door, giving Anin mere moments before she would be on the receiving end of all that rage emanating from the mad bitch. Anin rushed up to Tatiana and slapped her as hard as she could across the face.

"YOU are a puppet to power! You are not the one in control—the power is. Look what it does to you. It turns you into a mere vessel." Anin seethed directly into her face, their noses nearly touching. Before Tatiana could recover from the shock of being challenged, Anin made a run for it. She did not believe she would get away, but she knew it was worth the attempt.

Anin made it halfway across the temple floor before Tatiana ported directly in front of her, grabbed her by the hair, and ported them both back to the damp stone room where her wings hung. She was hanging from the hook in the center of the room again. She told herself what she had told Tallon over and over until she could no longer.

"It's okay to be scared; it does not make you less brave."

Chapter 18
Ciaran

Ciaran rubbed his tired eyes after staring at the parchment in front of him for the last several hours. The need to get ahead of this blood magic situation the Day Queen had created for the realm was paramount. He despised the idea of someone having the power to take control away from him. Even as the most powerful being in the realm, she could easily take full control of him.

The last time Ciaran did not have control over his own body, he was still a youngling. His father had taken great joy in lording his power over his young son, making Ciaran do whatever suited his needs best. He fled the palace and his father as soon as the opportunity arose. He found Master Ulgridge in the Nocturia Mountains, who taught him nearly everything he knew.

Ciaran had not been born to be used as a puppet. He despised his father, and he wrote off his mother long before her death as weak and useless. She did nothing except drink her life away, making no attempt to shield Ciaran from his father's machinations. In the end, it had likely been for the best, and he thought himself stronger for it. His father unknowingly taught him to shield his emotions and perfect an air of indifference.

As a youngling, his father had been horrible to him—unforgivably so. He used a conduit to siphon away all of a young Ciaran's power and to control his every move. Quite literally. It gave his father the power to take physical control over him. He would let no one have that kind of control over him again.

He had the basics of a plan laid out in front of him. After examining each aspect from every angle, he could not see a way of freeing Anin just yet. Having no protection against the blood magic the Day Queen wielded, they were limited in what they could pull off. Beyond the disaster the Day Queen could create for them, they had very little information on the current state of the Daybreak Palace and its inhabitants.

The plan was simple enough, yet not without its faults and dangers. Getting Kes to agree not to go rogue would prove one of the most challenging aspects. He knew this because if it were Etain, he could say for certain that he would enact his own plan and damn the consequences. Since it was not Etain, he could look at every angle logically.

He knew they were all capable of carrying out the plan. He just hoped the information and map he had of the Daybreak Palace were current enough for them to port into the correct locations. The map he had was rudimentary, making it difficult to know what he was looking at. There were massive parts missing, as if someone erased sixty percent of the map and removed all details.

He was relatively certain where he planned to port was the Great Hall. He had been there once before and remembered there was a shadowy alcove at the far end of the room where the least amount of sunlight reached. That was something he was not looking forward to—all the sunlight. It would make keeping his shadows hidden even harder. They would have to go during eclipse day, when the sun was at its darkest, allowing for more shadows.

There were three tasks they would need to accomplish. He would use his shadows to sneak around as many groups of fae as he could find and spread as many truths about their queen as possible. He hoped they could create chaos from within the Day Court. Here was the first hole in his plan. How could he sow distrust without his shadows being discovered?

He thought through several possible options. Like whispering to make it sound like one of the fae said it under their breath. Another was shouting it from the corner of the hall loud enough to have it echo all throughout with no one knowing where it came from. These ideas, like all of his others, were flawed. If he whispered, he could not be sure he would be heard, and if he shouted, he thought it unlikely anyone would take the words seriously.

The second task was to map as much of the palace as possible to make future plans even more reliable. While his shadows were somehow spreading information throughout the Day fae ranks, he could find darkened corners and secret paths between some of the main rooms. Kes and his Silent Shadows would cover the rest of the palace.

The last task would be to locate the archives and search for any information the Day Court has hidden away on blood magic. This was possibly the most important task to be carried out. If they could not find a way to eliminate the dire consequences blood magic created for them, the future of the realm felt precarious at best.

Anin's absence from the plan was going to be an issue for Kes. He needed to make Kes feel like he was helping her while still understanding the importance of not being discovered. The queen's unnatural magic posed a high risk. If any of them were to become enthralled, it would be detrimental to the entire Night Court. It was something Ciaran could not allow.

He sighed while he rubbed at his temples. What he was most concerned about was not the plan or the blood magic; it was Etain. She would need to remain at the palace for her own safety and the court's. Her training had come a long way; he had been working tirelessly to break her of the many human habits she carried. He pushed her relentlessly and gave her no quarter while molding her into the warrior he knew she could become.

He had not set out to be aggressive with her, though he was growing more frustrated with her every night. She still hid something from him inside that beautiful head of hers. He wanted it—whatever it was; he wanted all of her. Yet she refused him, and it drove him mad. No matter how hard he pushed her, she refused to bend to his will. He simultaneously admired and despised this about her.

Staring back down at the plan, he knew he backed himself into a corner by refusing to teach her to port. He would not leave her here alone without the ability to remove herself from any possible situation and get to safety. He also knew there was no option except to leave her alone. Kes would never agree to stay behind, even though Ciaran was cruel enough to demand it. He considered it for a few moments. Ultimately, he knew Kes would never listen.

Pulling out his spelled parchment, he sent a message to all members to meet him in the council chambers. He wanted to get this over with and deal with his problematic mate. He would never let her know, but he was enjoying this wicked game they were playing.

"I have required your presence to solidify a plan to infiltrate the Day Court," he said as he took his seat. He saw Kes sit a little taller, as did the three fae from his original council. This was clearly not what they expected Ciaran to say.

He quickly launched into the plan he concocted, leaving no space for anyone to interrupt him and derail this meeting, which would make it take longer than it should. He was nearing the end, and he could feel the hostility pouring off of his cousin in waves.

"Kes, we cannot rescue Anin this time. Not until we have a way to combat the queen and her blood magic. If she were to ensnare you, think of all the horrific things she could make you do to Anin or in front of her." This seemed to resonate with Kes and some of the hostility faded from him.

"What can we do to help Anin?" Etain asked.

"It would be helpful to find the area she is being kept in. This way, when we rescue her, we know where to go," one sister said from her seat along the wall. He could never recall which one was which. He nodded his head in agreement.

"The Daybreak Palace is massive. I went there once when I was a youngling. I have also heard that underground there are tunnels leading to various rooms, spanning twice the footprint of what you see above ground." Galetia stopped to think for a moment. It surprised him that the three at the end of the table did not take that moment to begin some tirade or another. Instead, they remained sitting in their chairs, looking pleased.

"It has been a long time, but I could probably remember some details from when I was there. I believe I can help you with another problem you seem to have. I can cast a relatively simple spell on you that would make your voice sound like a thought to whoever you spoke to. It does have limited time; you would need to be done before it wears off." Ciaran felt no particular way about the head witch, although at that moment, he liked her quite a bit.

"How many shadow beings can you create?" Fiandra asked.

"I imagine the amount is unlimited, since shadows will be sparse. I will use only a few at a time." He had yet to hit a limit and was confident he could create an entire army if he wanted to. What he had yet to figure out was how to make them tangible.

"Remarkable." Syndari sounded almost jealous. He smiled at the shifter's tone while still holding Etain's gaze before tearing his eyes away to address his cousin.

"Kes, you and your Silent Shadows figure out how you want to go about locating Anin and the archives." Kes nodded and then indicated for the two sisters to follow him as he walked out of the chamber. The three council members from the Night Court were still sitting silently. He narrowed his eyes on them.

"Nothing to say? The three of you seem to never shut up. Why the silence now?" he asked them.

"What is there to say?" Fiandra gave him a terrifying grin. "Infiltrating the Day Court, spreading distrust, and looking for information to steal from them—this is positively wicked, and I for one love it," she said. The other two made sounds of agreement.

"I will take a broom back to the coven and find that spell and any other spells that could help. Once I have all I need, I will send a scroll, and then you can port me quickly back."

Ciaran nodded his agreement, and the head witch left the room along with the remaining three fae. Surprisingly, Georden offered to port her to the coven, and the old witch agreed. Nothing about tonight had gone the way he expected.

"And what role will I be playing in this plan of yours?" his mate asked. Before he had the chance to say anything, she climbed onto his lap and straddled him. "You seem to have forgotten me," she said, nipping the point of one of his ears. "My King," she whispered next to it, sending chills down his neck. He gripped her ass and yanked her up, his length hardening beneath her.

"You will stay here to rule." She tilted her head to the side, considering his words.

"You would leave me here, all alone, without a way to move about the palace quickly? What if I am needed or find myself in need of an escape?" She licked a path up the other side of his neck and brought her mouth to his other ear. "You must care nothing for your mate if this is the case."

"I curse myself for caring too much for my mate," he growled out as his hands dug into her hips and he ground her against him. "You will get your lesson on porting, little witch." It pained him to capitulate to her wishes. It felt like losing, and there was nothing he hated more than losing. At least now he found something he loved even more than winning, and that something was currently gyrating on his length in a way he thought he would spill himself in his pants like some young fae male being touched for the first time. He groaned and reached to lift her dress before freeing himself.

"Now," Etain said as she hopped off his lap and began walking towards the doors. "About teaching me to port," she said over her shoulder at him. She stopped with her hand on the handle of the door. "Are you coming?" she asked him innocently.

He stared at her for a long moment while she continued to wear her face of false innocence. She knew what she did and likely planned for it to go exactly as it had. She not only won, she walked him right into his own defeat.

"Apparently not," he said under his breath.

Chapter 19
Tatiana

Tatiana was still feeling the rush sacrifices always gave her. Everything seemed a little hazy—everything except the rage her sister brought out of her. Whether it was her sister or the effects of absorbing significant amounts of raw power in one night that clouded her vision was up for debate. The only thing she could see clearly was the hatred she held for the nymph hanging before her.

"*You let that creature strike you across the face; are you growing weak, Tatiana?*" The *whispers* laughed as they mocked her.

"I am not weak!" She was growing tired of beings thinking they could get away with saying such things about her. The *whispers* made some noncommittal sounds as they continued to laugh at her. "I am not! She surprised me; that was all. The effects of absorbing power slowed my response." It was not her fault Anin had taken advantage of her physical state.

"*You let the euphoria weaken you. Only a being not in control would have allowed such a thing to happen,*" the *whispers* said in their slithering, inky voice.

"I am no puppet, if that is what you are implying. I am the Queen of the Day Court! There is nothing above my authority, and nothing controls me!" She was always in control of everything, even when she absorbed massive amounts of power. She allowed the euphoria to take her to a higher plane, and it did so only because she allowed it to.

She was in control, not the other way around. She did not need the high she received from the sacrifices, and that had nothing to do with why she continued to take more and more at once. No, it was about feeding her blood magic, not her high. The *whispers* laughed at her again.

The thought had her bringing her blade back to her unmoving sister. She wondered if she continued to remove parts of her, would they stop coming back all together? If she cut her up into small enough pieces, would she still be able to heal? She would endeavor to find out.

The vitriol Anin spewed at her while she was completing the sacrifices was on a constant loop in her head. She called her a monster; her words sat heavy within Tatiana's mind. Was she a monster?

"You are no monster; you are the savior of the realm," the *whispers* assured her. *"She is too small-minded to see the larger picture. Everything you do is for the greater good."* The doubts her sister's words had created within her melted away entirely with the *whispers'* reassurances.

"Once I have created the perfect realm, she will understand, and the Land seems bound and determined to make sure she survives to see it." Tatiana was still bitter over the Land's rejection of her and the subsequent choice of her sister. The Land was just another in a long line of abandonments.

"Once you have complete control, you will never be left by another. No one will ever abandon you again," the *whispers* reminded her.

"Yes, I will be in control of who comes and goes throughout

the realm, and therefore no other being I love could leave me behind any longer." This had always been her ultimate mission— to gain enough power to control everything, ensuring she would never be abandoned again. Although, as she thought about it, she could not bring to mind one soul left that she loved. That would need to be rectified.

She would bring one of her court members into her circle. Could it even be called a circle? She thought to herself while slowly carving another piece from Anin—she was the reason Tatiana's circle was now a circle of one. The wretch dared call her a monster when she was the one who murdered her mate, Remi-nold, in cold blood. She would never know another bond like the one she shared with him.

"She is the true monster; you are doing what is best for the court. You, not her, will be the one the history books regale as the savior of the realm. She will be a blip, if mentioned at all. Her judgment holds no weight when her mind is too small to comprehend the enormity of the duty that lies upon your shoulders." The *whisper's* words emboldened her, and she stood a little straighter.

Except she could not quite expel all the hateful things her sister spat at her; she could not understand why they were even bothering her to begin with. She had done nothing wrong.

"Even if I *were* a monster, I would not be the one to blame. After all, it was not my own thoughts that led me to seek such deviant magic. I was not the one who knew where to look. You were the one who led me along this path. If anyone were to be a monster, it would be you."

The *whispers* remained quiet for a moment, and Tatiana wondered if she had gone too far until the harsh crackling sound of the *whisper's* laugh began. She felt her face grow hot with the indignation that flooded her body.

"Ah, it may be true that I was the one who gave you all the knowl-edge. Let us not forget you are the one who greedily followed the trail of

crumbs I gave you. You are also the one who gorges herself on the rush of power." Tatiana momentarily forgot the being in front of her while her rage found a new target.

"I was not the one who knew how to learn the intricacies of blood magic. It was not I who knew to sacrifice the witches for their raw power. Nor the one who knew how to breach the wards around the coven! It was you, whoever—or whatever you are!" She had never raged like this against the *whispers*. "You were the one who told me how to open rifts in the veil for Reminold to cross over to the Human Realm as he pleased. You were the one who knew of the Walsh witch with unmatched power to send him searching for! It was never me!" she seethed.

"As you say, my queen," the *whispers* said. She was growing tired of the way they patronized her and placated her as if she were some child throwing a tantrum. She did not care where her actions placed her on the spectrum of morality; that was not the reason for her irritation. She refused to accept any responsibility for what history may find appalling. She was the savior; the role of monster fell directly upon the head of the *whispers*.

She took the silence within her mind as a victory. The *whispers* forgot their place at times, and she had no problem reminding them she was the queen. She is the one in control and the one with power, not them. Soon, she would have control of everything.

She was closer now than ever before to achieving her goals, and yet she was alone. Her attention snapped back to the creature hanging in pieces before her. She still had a few limbs attached and was already healing. There were only a few moments of reprieve from Tatiana's ministrations, and the Land was already beginning to undo her hard work. The Land's choice was still a raw wound. How could it abandon her while choosing the being responsible for Reminold's death?

She found it unacceptable that she should have to live the remainder of her life alone. The sacrifices she absorbed would prevent her from succumbing to the withering away the loss of a mate usually causes. She would continue to fight the Land for ownership of Anin's life and the payment owed to her. Raising her blade again, she felt revived with determination. She would win, and she would not rule the realm alone.

She would elevate a member of her court to be her personal adviser. It would have to be the most ruthless of them; she was not about to listen to a being's judgments ever again. It had been some time since she made an appearance in front of her court. It had also been some time since she met with her council. Time hardly seemed important to her anymore, and when you ignore time, it has a funny way of slipping by unnoticed.

Neither her court nor her council were of any concern to her, and she had no desire to see any of them. She scoffed, knowing if she were going to elevate someone, she would have to see her court. The idea of her having to do anything disgusted her; she was not one to compromise her desires.

She would make it quick. She would arrive only to make her demand and then leave with him in tow. The thought of the others staring at the one she would choose in disbelief while making hilarious noises as they tried to remain indifferent would make the entire event almost worth it. She may even find it enjoyable.

The effects of the power from the sacrifices were wearing off. If Anin had not done whatever it was she did to that final creature, she would still feel it coursing through her veins, taking her to heights she had never known even since blood magic came into her life. She had been robbed of the experience—another debt her sister owed her.

Tatiana knew Anin had done something, though she could not figure out what. Her action created no sound, while Tatiana saw nothing nor felt any significant power released. If it were not for the smug expression Anin's face boldly wore, Tatiana would have been uncertain, but it was proof enough. She *did* something, and that something made her feel strange. She could not place what the feeling was.

Unease? Was she feeling nervous? That was impossible. She could not remember the last time anything was able to make her nervous. She was being silly, of course. Looking at the stump of a nymph on the ground before her made the feeling all the more ridiculous. What was this creature going to do besides regenerate limbs for the foreseeable future?

She almost felt better. Almost. This thing may have killed Tatiana's mate, yet look what she was doing to avenge him. She wished Reminold were there to offer his praise; another would have to do. One who would do exactly what she requested of them without raising an argument. Someone who would worship at her feet and love her unconditionally. She would have a companion who would fulfill her needs in all ways.

She knew exactly who she would pick.

Chapter 20
Kes

"I will port us to the lower level of the palace here," Kes said as he checked the marks on the barren map of the Daybreak palace again. "Panella, you will go east while Lyra goes west. I will then port to this location," he said, pointing to another mark he had made. "It seems likely to find the archives on this level. Based on the minor details we have and the layout of every palace I have ever been to, the general location has to be somewhere around where you both will start."

Dressed in black with dark hoods hiding their bright hair, the sisters were ready to blend in with the shadows of the Daybreak Palace. Over the past weeks, they had come a long way toward becoming the Shadows that stood before him. They already had decent combat training. Now they were becoming proficient in the art of stealth.

"Are we looking only for anything relevant to blood magic?" Lyra asked.

"Use your discretion. If you happen across something you feel might be of importance, tether it to yourself. More information is never a bad problem to have." The sisters nodded in agreement. "I will use the bond to locate Anin. We know the main dungeon is here," he said, indicating one of the few known locations on the map. "I think it is doubtful the Day bitch would keep her tucked away anywhere too obvious. The underground tunnels Galetia mentioned sound more likely." He looked up to find them both staring at him.

"If you find her..." Panella whispered. Kes nodded, understanding her meaning. They had a good plan. He had his own plan though. There was no way he was going to leave his mate to rot in that court one more night. When he found her, he was getting her the hell out of there, no matter what Ciaran said.

He could not believe his cousin had the audacity to tell him to go to the Daybreak Palace, locate Anin, and then leave her there. It was not possible. If it were Etain, he would not hesitate. Kes would not hesitate, either.

"Are you sure you both will be able to get back here on your own?" This was the one part he was most concerned about for them. The sisters decided earlier they would be responsible for themselves from the moment Kes ported them to their planned location. None of them knew how heavily guarded the palace would be, and they assumed the golden warriors of the Day Court would be guarding it.

"Yes, do not worry about us. When one of us finds the archives, we will alert the other, and the two of us will search for any mention of blood magic," said Panella.

"We want to do as thorough a job as possible. For all we know, it might take us a couple of nights to return. We have a few tricks up our sleeves for getting around undetected." Lyra smirked at Kes's disbelieving face.

"We have always been rather mischievous, and it only got worse when Anin joined us," Panella began.

"Do not get caught, and if you do, do not let them know who you are to Anin," he said.

"Between the spells we learned and Anin's vines, we never got caught. Her vines are everywhere in the coven now," Lyra said, and both sisters laughed at the shared memory.

Kes was envious of the sister's rich history filled with Anin, while he had only a handful of nights.

"If you can determine any of the guard schedules, that would be helpful as well. As soon as we have a way to null the blood magic, I will wage war upon that palace and kill that bitch queen. Once I have put her through the same pain she has made Anin feel over the past few weeks." He punctuated his words by bringing his fist heavily down onto the center of the map with a loud bang.

Sharp pain took over his body in multiple places, causing him to double over. That bitch was doing something to Anin again. After a few deep breaths, he took as much from her as he could handle, although he could not send her any power to speed her healing. He would need every bit of it to get her out of there this crescent night.

"Is it Anin?" Lyra sounded as pained as he felt. All he could manage was a nod. He learned how to take her pain in as his own and place it in a box in the back of his mind so he could continue his work training the sisters. He took a few more breaths to gain control, and then closed the box on the pain that he continued to pull into him before he stood back up.

"Kes," Panella said through a clenched jaw. "You have to get her out of there."

The Daybreak Palace was too bright. Kes kept squinting his eyes, trying to adjust his vision. He was used to the shadows and the soft white glow of the moon, not this garish yellow light that stabbed him directly through his eyes. If this was what it was like during an eclipse day, he had no desire to see what it would be like during a full day.

He was grateful the level of the palace he ported to with the sisters had few windows, and they were small slits high up on the light gray stone walls. Most of this level was underground, giving him shadows to hide in if needed, as few as they may be. Luckily, it went neglected at this time of day.

Kes went down hall after hall, trying to get a read on Anin's location. He could feel her and knew she was near enough, but she did not feel close by. He came across a downward staircase and descended to an even lower level. The further down he went, the damper the air and walls became. Torches and glowing orbs illuminated the halls, and he felt like he could finally see clearly.

He was growing impatient the further he went and the longer it took to locate her. He tried talking to her through the bond, thinking since they were closer than ever, the spell Galetia cast might work better. Either she was unresponsive or the spell had not worked. He tried giving the bond a gentle tug—still nothing.

When he hunted her in the woods that fateful night weeks ago, he had been following the bond without knowing what he was doing. He took a calming breath, trying not to think about where he was going or why, and let the bond guide him the way it had that first night. He focused only on his surroundings and put his faith in the bond.

After what felt like centuries of aimlessly wandering halls and descending more stairs, he stopped dead in his tracks. He could feel her. He knew exactly where she was. His heart rate increased, and it took everything within him not to rush down the long halls he still needed to traverse to get to her. The last thing he wanted to do was throw caution to the wind this close to rescuing her and trigger an alarm or run into guards who would alert the queen to his location.

He silenced his mind, focusing on his senses to detect any possible threat looming that would block him from his mate. He sent one last message down the bond, just in case she could hear him.

"I am coming for you."

Chapter 21
Etain

We are on our way, all of us.

Ciaran, Kes, and the sisters set out on their mission minutes before Galetia's message arrived, sending Etain's anxiety to new levels. She was already terrified of being left to rule the Night Court while Ciaran was gone. The multiple scenarios of things that could go wrong for them in the Day Court were not helping, and now something was wrong with the witches—the witches *she* was supposed to be the queen of. She was not given much time to learn how to be queen, yet here she was, thrown directly into the fire.

Still in the study where Ciaran left her after teaching her to port, she had yet to leave being too nervous to do it alone. When she had pestered him to teach her, she had no idea how dangerous it could be. She already knew you had to know exactly where you were going, except she did not know how to physically get from one location to another.

"It is quite simple, really. You just think about where you are going, step into the Nothing, and plot your route in your mind." He made it sound easy—too easy.

"Simple? What is the Nothing? What do you mean by 'step' into the Nothing?" She felt anything named "the Nothing" would not be simple.

"Oh, only the space between here and there you cannot see. Once you know where you are going, you hold it in your mind and then step forward with the intention of porting there. You will step into the Nothing and a map of sorts will appear in your mind. Choose how you want to get to where you are going, and then follow the path." He shrugged as if it were the easiest thing in the realm, which it likely was to him. He learned how to do this as a youngling.

"Ciaran, you are either being intentionally vague or you are entirely daft. I have not the slightest knowledge of any of this. You must explain everything as if I were a youngling." She loved him. Really, she did, though over the past few weeks, she had come to *know* him. She thought perhaps she was so desperate for someone to love her and a place to belong that she latched onto him too quickly. Not that she had much say in the matter, anyway. The mate bond would have gotten its way eventually, though it would have been nice to learn the basics prior to becoming Queen. It also would have been nice to have a better idea of what she was getting into; the disregard he had for every other being but himself and her was still unsettling.

Etain grew up learning to care for everyone and everything. From healing to growing a garden, or even harvesting responsibly to not deplete the wild stock in a way the plant could not come back from. There was a balance to everything. Of course, the balance was heavily skewed against her when it came to caring for the townsfolk of Havenston. Even now, knowing how they truly felt about her, she was still worried about the three pregnancies she had been overseeing.

With the King of the Day Court dead, that meant their beloved Shepherd abandoned them. For just a moment, she let herself enjoy the panic the town would descend into, if they had not already. They likely blamed her for it since Seamus, The Shepherd, and herself all disappeared at the same time. Or maybe they were not panicking yet at all. Maybe they thought the two of them had taken her to a faraway city to be burned as a witch.

It bothered her that she still cared what they thought of her. She spent her whole life caring for them, even when it was not reciprocated. It was hard to fully cut that part of her life away. She also missed working with her hands and mixing remedies. As soon as she could, she would learn how to incorporate her knowledge of plants into spells. Although, now that she thought about it, the plants here were not the same as the ones from home. It would be another thing she would have to learn from the beginning.

"You are right," he said, dragging his hand down his face with a tired sigh. He had been doing that often the past few nights. The search for a way to counteract blood magic was wearing on him. "I sometimes forget you have only been here a short while, and if you lived here your whole life, you would still be considered a youngling." He made a face at that, the idea of me being a youngling disturbing him.

"Well, I am not sure what that says about you since you are older than dirt," she said with a grin. "Perhaps we should both be happy I did not spend my whole life here." He huffed out a laugh, breaking the tension that was building between them. Lately, when they spent any length of time around each other, one of two forms of tension grew—more often than not both at the same time. Her frustration came from his callousness. His frustration came from her refusal to give in and tell him what was bothering her.

It felt silly not to tell him now. At first, she was afraid to hurt his feelings, and then it was a matter of owning her own thoughts. Now it was exhausting. He capitulated to her and taught her how to port; maybe it was time for her to do the same. She decided she would tell him as soon as he returned. The last thing she had wanted to do was give him any kind of distraction before he left.

"The most important thing you need to know about the Nothing is to not question your path. Stay with it, and do not entertain the thought you might be wrong. You can get stuck in the Nothing, and it would be very hard for me to find you."

"You could? Find me, that is?" she asked him. The idea of being stuck in whatever this Nothing was became a heavy weight in her stomach. To make matters worse, his response was not immediate, and her palms dampened.

"I will always find you. It would likely take me a very long time, though I would not rest until we were together again." He held her gaze, and she could see he meant every word.

"The realm—"

"The realm could rot for all I care. I do not know how many more times I need to tell you. I care for nothing but you and myself. We are the reason I do anything to help the realm. Without you, there would be no me. I would have no reason to continue this impossible hunt for ways to combat blood magic." When he spoke like that, she was reminded of exactly how she had fallen fast and hard for him.

"And Kes. You care for your cousin."

"That is debatable. Anyway, it is simple to avoid—never second guess yourself." Second guessing herself came almost as naturally as breathing, except she really wanted to port and have a bit of freedom. Releasing her fears, she took a couple of deep breaths and then nodded. She could do this.

"We will start small, porting a few paces away. Know your destination, take a determined step, choose your route, and do not stray from it." She looked at the exact spot she wanted to go and was about to take a step when it occurred to her she would need to travel along her path, and she had no idea how she was supposed to do that.

"What do I do with this path I choose?" Ciaran gave her one of his "silly little witch" smirks, and she was quickly reminded how irritating he could be—irritatingly attractive as well.

"While I believe you could choose any manner of movement to get to your destination, I generally walk." She narrowed her eyes at his condescending tone, and his smile just grew. He leaned back against the table behind him and crossed his arms. He was definitely daring her to try. When she continued to stare at him, he slowly rolled one sleeve and then the other halfway up his forearms.

Gods, why is that so damn attractive?

She turned her attention back to the spot she had chosen, took a determined step, and landed in an unnaturally still, gray abyss. There was absolutely nothing here. No color, no movement, just nothing. Her mind lit up with multiple paths, and she decided the shortest one was likely the best. Before she could take even half a step on the path, she was falling and landed hard on her backside, sprawling on the ground.

Panic set in until she heard Ciaran howling with laughter. She had only heard him laugh like that once before, when Kes and Anin told him about the death of the Day King. She sat up, pushed her hair from her face, and glared at him.

"Oh, little witch, this reminds me of our very first encounter. It would appear you still have the grace of a newborn fawn," he said between laughs. It was hard to stay mad at him when he rarely lit up the way he did just then. Giving in, she let out a laugh of her own at the memory; she had been very frightened, and he enjoyed every minute of it. She looked around and noticed she was in the exact place she had chosen.

"I did it?" she asked in wonder.

"That you did, little witch." She could hear pride in his words, and her heart warmed.

"How did I end up falling to the ground? I had barely taken a step down my path, and suddenly I was falling and landing rather painfully on my rear." She got to her feet and rubbed the offending spot.

"It may have been pertinent to explain distance. If you have a very short distance to go, you may want to choose a slightly longer route to take a full step; otherwise, you may come out the other side a bit higher than intended."

She glared at him again.

"It *may* have been, Ciaran," she said sarcastically, which only made his laughter pick up again. She repeated the short distance over and over until she felt confident. Then he had her port to their bedchambers, the council chambers, and finally the top of his tower. That one was rather terrifying. She made him take her there to stare at the exact center of the tower before porting back to their bedchambers and then back to the tower. By the end of their lesson, she was feeling mildly confident, and he declared her perfectly capable.

She knew she needed to port to the great hall to greet the Silver Moon Coven. A nervous flutter started in her stomach; the idea of porting on her own both thrilled and terrified her. She was more afraid of making a poor public landing than anything else. It was now or never; enough time passed, and she knew the witches would arrive any minute. She picked her destination and stepped.

The hall was unusually empty, which she was glad for. Her landing had not been the worst, but it had not been her best either. She stepped out into the cool night air and listened to the city of Nightfell bustling around the palace. She still had yet to visit, and she was eager to explore the city after everything Ciaran had told her.

She did not have to wait long before the first sights of witches flying towards the palace appeared in the sky. One was traveling much faster than the rest. Galetia landed several feet away in the courtyard that made up the front of the palace.

"What happened?" Etain asked as she rushed out to greet the head witch. Witches would begin pouring in within the next few moments. Countless numbers of them—it appeared to be the entire Silver Moon Coven, possibly more. It must be something serious for the entire congregation to leave.

"We had four more witches disappear in the middle of the night. Knowing the Day Queen has blood magic and is breaking through our wards, we could not risk being within her grasp any longer." Galetia held Etain's hand within her own, and when their eyes met, Etain felt as if something heavy had just sunk into her gut. Galetia's eyes were rimmed in red, and even now she watched as a tear slipped down the side of her face.

"One of them was a youngling." she forced herself to say on a choked sob.

"Surely she must be missing. The Day Queen cannot be monstrous enough to..." Etain could not finish the sentence. No one could be that cruel, could they?

"We looked everywhere. If three other witches had not also gone missing, I would be inclined to hold out hope. Her mother..." She dropped Etain's hands, unable to voice the words. She looked blankly away, not truly seeing whatever her eyes had landed on. "I cannot keep them safe any longer," the head witch whispered. Hecate told her to stay in the Night Court, and the time would come when she would need to protect the witches.

"Of course you are all welcome. If I am your queen and this is my court, it must be yours as well." She lowered her voice before saying, "As soon as Ciaran is back, I will request he make sleeping arrangements for you all."

"When did they leave?" Galetia asked just as softly. No one

needed to know where the King of the Night Court had gone. The arduous task would be keeping the Night fae at bay until he returned without any of them suspecting he was not around. Traitors still posed a threat, and Etain did not want to have to deal with a mob of Night fae who might decide to cause trouble for her while their king was away.

"It was only a handful of minutes before I received your message. I am not expecting them back anytime soon." Etain looked up at the never-ending stream of witches still arriving. "I cannot believe how many witches Silver Moon is home to. The coven is deceptively large, though I did not think it was this large. There must be thousands of you."

"Well, I did say we were *all* coming."

"All...?" This suddenly went from stressful to overwhelming. Where would they all stay? As if sensing her rising panic, Galetia placed a hand on her shoulder and gave a comforting squeeze.

"All will be well. Three other covens had multiple witches go missing recently, too. It was one here and there for a very long time. It was never enough to raise much suspicion until these most recent years. The witches who disappeared were always some of the most powerful in the coven, many being Walsh witches. Ones who held high esteem and would never dream of leaving. Particularly not without discussing it with the coven. We do not do things alone; we think of ourselves as one piece of a larger whole.

I sent a message to every coven informing them of the Day Queen's use of blood magic. The second we discovered thirteen witches had been stolen away in the night, we knew we could not risk giving her another opportunity to do so. I pray to the goddess every night that they are all still alive." Galetia looked up to watch a witch come in for her landing. "Ah, here's Seraphina, the head witch of the Coven of Remembrance. I think she might be able to help you find some information on your power. They have the most extensive library in the realm."

Etain could not imagine a library larger than the one at the Silver Moon Coven. Not even Ciaran's study held as many books and she had yet to visit the palace library. She wondered how much the witch could actually help while away from her coven's library.

Seraphina had long, glossy black hair that reminded Etain of the obsidian waters of the falls. She looked young, though that did not necessarily mean she was. Her face was slight, with purple eyes that looked far too big for her, and yet she was incredibly striking. She had an air of wisdom and moved with an unhurried grace Etain could only hope to one day emulate.

The two head witches embraced and shared a somber expression. They were both grieving while trying to remain hopeful.

"I am sorry to hear of your loss. I wish we were meeting under happier circumstances," Etain said as she placed the witch's hands in her own. It was a small touch Galetia gave Etain often when she was in need of comfort.

"As do I, my queen. I apologize for arriving unannounced. I hope we are not too great of a hassle for you." Even the witch's voice sounded full of unspoken knowledge.

"Of course not. Wherever I am, you are always welcome."

"Seraphina, I was just telling Etain about your vast libraries and how it might be possible for you to help her with her power. She has been gifted dark shade power with Sight and flight." Etain was grateful her great-aunt asked the question she herself had not been sure how to ask. Seraphina stared off into the distance at nothing in particular; Etain grew worried.

"She is looking through the entire catalog of books the Coven of Remembrance has available to them," Galetia whispered to her. Everything about this witch was incredibly impressive to Etain.

"Yes, we have only a couple, and I think you will find one in particular to be a good starting place," she said as she rapidly blinked her eyes back into focus.

"Wonderful! Perhaps we can port there tomorrow to retrieve it quickly." Etain could barely contain her excitement. Finally, she could learn more about her visions.

"Oh, there is no need." Seraphina held her hand out, and a small, thick, black book landed in her outstretched hand. "Here it is, *A Study in Shades: Power Beyond Color*. Regrettably, there is not much I personally know about the shades, but according to the spell that gives a brief overview of every book we hold, this should help answer many of your questions," she said as she passed the book to Etain.

"Thank you. Now we must figure out accommodations for," Etain looked around the full courtyard, "all of you." She had the two head witches follow her inside, and a few others followed, likely the other head witches, not far behind.

"There is a very large ballroom down this corridor. I know it is not ideal housing, but I think it will be the best option until we can figure—"

"Does our king know about all the filth you are bringing into the palace, witch?" A scathing voice interrupted her from behind. Turning, she found the pale being, Leona, and a couple of other female fae she had never met before standing there. The sight of the female sent Etain into a rage so hot it burned cold as memories surfaced of the beautiful creature's hands roving her mate.

"Leona, what a...well, it is certainly something to see you again. I see your hand has made a full recovery. How wonderful."

Leona sneered at the mention of her hand.

"*My* king would never allow half breeds to take over his palace. Where is he, witch? You cannot hide your kind from him," she said with a haughty smirk. Etain returned it with one far too sweet, and she cocked her head to the side. The emphasis on "my" had not escaped her.

Her father's position on the council afforded her rooms within the palace. Etain made a mental note to ask Ciaran why she was still here. She had completely forgotten about the wretched being, and she thought it was likely Ciaran had, as well. They had far more important things to deal with than some self important fae. Etain did not have the patience to deal with Leona.

"Is that so? Well, my mate does not have a problem with it at all because his mate happens to not only be the Queen of the Night Court but also the Queen of the Witches. You must have forgotten that I am your queen. You do not have to like me, Leona, but you will respect me. Now, run along before I get the king involved. I would hate for you to be the latest decoration in the hall, though at least you would be with your beloved father again," Etain said sweetly.

She did not think it was possible for the fae's face to get any paler, yet it did. The rage Leona fought to contain was mixed with uncertainty about whether Ciaran would display her head in the great hall just as he had her father. It brought immense joy to Etain, and she realized in that moment that Ciaran would not think twice if she were to ask him to do just that; it made her feel powerful. She turned her back on Leona and her entourage, dismissing them, before the fae had a chance to dismiss themselves.

Every single one of the head witches wore a smile, showing just how much they had enjoyed the show. Etain smiled back. She just successfully had her first queenly interaction with a Night fae, and she could not be more pleased to have had an audience.

She could not wait to tell Ciaran.

Chapter 22
Ciaran

Ciaran hated going to the Day Court. It was too bright,
and the light was too warm; he much preferred the
cool tone the light from the moon provided. The
shadowy alcove he remembered was exactly the way it looked
when he had last been here hundreds of years ago as a small
youngling for the coronation of Tatiana and Reminold. It used to
be common for the royal family from either court to attend each
other's major events. That was the last time the courts were
amicable.

After the previous Day Queen—Tatiana's mother—died, relations dissolved quickly. Ciaran's father refused to respect the
young queen, or so he claimed. The way his father spoke about
the previous queen, Yesinda, always surprised him. His father was
never kind to a single being in the realm, with the exception
of her.

Now that he thought about it, he wondered if there had been
something more between the two. His father and mother had not
been true mates, nor had Tatiana's. He quickly dismissed that train
of thought. There was no way fate would have put those two

together. Then again, his own mate was an unlikely choice, as was Kes's. Either way, it made no difference, and he would not waste another moment on his father.

He peered out from the deepest shadows in the alcove, and luck was on his side. A group of five high fae were making their way towards him. Before they got close enough to notice any movement, he pulled a shadow from him and ported away to the next shadowy location he could see. Thoroughly focused on positioning his shadows, it took him a moment to comprehend what he was hearing.

"I heard they burned Thachory's winery to the ground. All of that wine—gone. What a waste." A nasally voice tried to speak quietly, or at least that was what Ciaran thought. The fae was the kind of male who was always too loud and too sure of himself. "And for what? The treatment of some lesser filth? Who cares what he does with his little fae? They were the ones that got themselves into the bargain, anyway."

"Well, let us be honest, it is not much of an option—die or make the bargain. I am not sure what I would do in their place," another voice said with the quiet tone of someone used to being spoken over.

"Careful, Ladiguien, you almost sound like a sympathizer." This voice held an air of authority. She would be his first. If she were to say any of the things Ciaran was about to plant in her mind, the words would carry weight.

There is a larger issue at hand. The queen no longer has the support of the Land and has gained access to blood magic. No one is safe from her ultimate control. Soon, every being in the Day Court could meet the same fate as the lesser fae.

Ciaran saw, through the eyes of his shadow, the being recoil from the information he had just planted and wore a comical look filled with confusion. The things he could do if this spell were permanent. He wondered if there was a way to make it so, but the old witch did not want him to have such power. He would get Etain to look into it.

"I would not call myself a 'sympathizer', however, I understand there are no absolutes. I consider myself luc—"

"Never mind that," the fae with authority said. "We have bigger problems. I do not know how I forgot about this." Ciaran's face split with a wicked smirk. He was definitely going to have Etain look into the spell for him. The fae dropped her voice even lower before saying, "The Queen—I have heard the Land has rejected her, and she has somehow gained blood magic." There was an audible gasp from the rest of the group.

"I have found it rather odd that she has not been wearing the crown of golden light the Land had gifted her. On the rare occasions we see her, that is," a new voice said.

"Do you think this could have something to do with what is happening in the south?" Ciaran's curiosity peaked. "If the Land has rejected her, it could explain it, could it not?" the final fae asked.

"Whatever is causing the land to rot is also responsible for the influx of lesser fae refugees who have lost their habitat to the rot. The audacity to come to the capital and demand their queen take action and care for them in the meantime is absurd. I understand their land is no longer livable, but can they not find somewhere else to live? Somewhere that is not *here*?" the nasal voiced fae complained.

"Where do you think they could go? What land is there not already taken within our court?"

"They could leave the court; the witches breed with some of them, after all. What filthy creatures witches are..."

Ciaran heard enough and was moving on to another group; there were several more scattered around the hall. As he moved from group to group, many of the same topics of conversation repeated. Ciaran was most intrigued by this "rot in the south" and was wondering if it was the same thing the Land had told him about during their coronation.

The last group he sent one of his shadows to was the smallest, a group of three, and they were also the most serious in appearance. The three huddled deep in another shadowy alcove, trying to hide themselves from the eyes and ears of the others.

"They have threatened to attack the palace next, and the queen refuses to see anyone, making it impossible to inform her. She claims to be doing something more important than whatever nonsense I wish to bring to her," the one with the face of a cat said.

"When she came to our latest council meeting, I thought perhaps she was finally there to listen to the serious issues our court is facing," the one with bright red-orange skin said.

"Only to have her come in and announce that she would take a companion, and to gather the court and request Raindal, of all fae, to be by her side," cat face said. The third fae, a female with wings containing every color in existence, had yet to speak. When she opened her mouth and prepared to, the two males stopped talking immediately and listened to what she had to say. She would be the perfect one.

"Be careful what you say. She is our queen, and you both toe a very thin line separating your words from treason. I, too, had hoped she would take a few moments from her busy schedule to listen to matters of the realm, but she obviously has more important issues to deal with. For all we know, she already knows about the rot and the faction of fae terrorizing our court. She is not required to inform us, nor does she have to listen to us. We are on the council, but we are only there to council if she calls upon us."

Ciaran's shadow hid in the darkened corner off to her side and whispered the thoughts into her mind. She had no reaction, and Ciaran could not be sure if it worked. That was until she spoke again.

"Understand, I am in no way questioning our queen's rule. I say this as a possible answer to her distance. What if she has lost the favor of the Land for some reason, or perhaps the rot has stolen it? She has not worn the golden crown of light for decades, and that would be a viable reason. She could be searching for some other power or magic to help fight the rot. Ultimately, we are not in a position to question her." Ciaran wished his council members were more like this fae.

"Has anyone seen the king? Perhaps we can inform him, and he could relay the message and help us deal with the terrorists," the orange fae said.

"He spends most of his time away from the palace. I have only seen him a handful of times over the past few decades. Who knows where he is currently?"

Ciaran had to fight to keep in his laughter. They did not know their king was dead or that their queen had lost her mind. The chaos of the Day Court at least proved that they were no threat to the Night Court. Only their queen.

The remaining time of the spell was getting dangerously low, and he decided it was time to move on. His shadows slithered through a path of darkness as they made their way back to Ciaran. He ported from shadow to shadow until he found himself in the empty throne room.

He silently walked the circumference of the golden room. The entire place was either gold or marble. He noticed the palace had taken on a duller look than he remembered. There were cracks all along the marble and the gold had tarnished, making it look more like brass than gold.

When he touched what he thought was a golden wall but was really a wooden one, he knew he had found what he was looking for. Feeling all around the edges, he could not find the release. He gave the wall a hard shove and was rewarded when the whole thing slid backward. From a distance, it would be unnoticeable, even when opened. He still closed the panel behind him, not wanting to risk an alarm being raised.

It did not take long for the tunnel behind the wall to reach a junction with several halls for him to choose from. He noticed the one over to the left of him had a noticeable decline, and Ciaran found that curious. He had little time to consider his options when he heard the distinct voice of the queen and a male voice he did not recognize coming in his direction.

He hurried to the descending tunnel and picked up his pace in case they came his way. He thought it unlikely given the odds, but was proven wrong as soon as the queen's voice became even clearer as it echoed down the hall.

"I have been keeping a guest in a forgotten dungeon for the past few weeks. I think you will find her to be rather interesting," she said with a dark chuckle.

"My queen, why do we not port there? I cannot recall the last time I walked to where I needed to go," the male voice said.

That must be Raindal.

"There are wards. I cannot make it easy for her mate to come and rescue her. I am no fool," Tatiana said curtly.

"Of course not, my queen." Ciaran knew Kes had to be down here, and if he did not find him before the queen and her companion did—well, he did not want to give that any thought.

He ported as far down the hall as he could see and kept going until he came to another junction. His frustration grew, knowing time was not on his side. He found another hall that sloped downward and was about to commit to his choice when he heard a voice behind him.

"Ciaran?" Kes whispered, "What are you doing down here?"

"Looking for you, the queen is not far behind. We have to go." Ciaran knew this would not be easy.

"We must hurry then. She is just down that hall, I can feel her. She is so close." Kes's voice held immense hope and determination, and Ciaran wished he did not have to destroy it. Perhaps his little witch was right; he cared for his cousin—mildly.

"There is no time. I overheard her telling the male she's with how she placed wards preventing anyone from being able to port in or out. I stopped being able to port a short way back from where I came. We are lucky she has not ported here yet. We cannot go down that hall, free Anin from whatever restraints have been used on her, and come back up this hall without running into the que—"

"I do not care!" Kes whisper-yelled.

"Well, you should," Ciaran seethed. He was unwilling to compromise in the face of a retaliation, but he knew that would not get through to Kes. "If you are taken, who will rescue Anin then? You are a fool if you think the queen would simply kill you when she could use you to do unspeakable things to your mate. There are worse things than death, Kes. That hall will lead to your demise. There is no scenario where you can make it out if you choose that path. We have to leave now, so there is a genuine opportunity for a rescue in the future. Only one of these options helps Anin."

Kes's face pinched with a combination of pain and anger, and just as he was about to respond, they heard the queen's voice not far off down the tunnel. They were out of time. Ciaran grabbed his cousin's arm with a tug, but Kes did not budge. Ciaran frantically turned back to his cousin, who was staring down the hall that contained Anin, and gave him one last tug. Kes looked away from the tunnel, and his eyes clashed with Ciaran's own. He clenched his jaw and turned his gaze back toward the tunnel that led to his mate. Out of time, Ciaran wrapped his cousin in shadows and dragged him down the hall.

"Did you hear something?" The queen's distant voice was the last thing Ciaran heard before he ported them back to Nightfell.

Chapter 23
Lyra

Lyra hoped Panella was having better luck than she was. She snuck into dozens of rooms, most of them empty, with no archives in sight. She sent her sister a mental message, asking if she had found it yet.

It was a well-known fact witches only have one daughter, making twins incredibly rare. What was not as well known was the mental connection twins shared, much like a mating bond. Witches are born with a power they carry until their daughter is born; that power creates the life of a witch. When there are twins, they are both created from the same power, making them connected in ways most witches will never understand.

One of those connections for Lyra and Panella was mental; they could communicate telepathically. It was not as advanced a form of communication as the spoken word. More like they each have their own line of thought, but when one wants to communicate with the other, a shared line opens. Their whole lives it has been a valuable tool, from creating mischief as younglings to moments like this. It would drive Anin crazy when they had their silent conversations in front of her.

As it was, Panella was not having any better luck. Lyra was thinking they may have missed the mark on the probable location when they laid out their plans. Another several rooms later, her frustration was mounting. She came upon a narrow hall; it was the last place left to look, and there was only a single door at the end. The door looked old and wore a scrolling design.

Energy crackled throughout her limbs as she silently made her way toward the door. If anyone were to come out, there would be no place she could hide. She let out a small sigh of relief as she reached it with no altercations. She placed her slightly pointed ear upon it and listened for anything that could prepare her for what would greet her on the other side.

Hearing nothing, she slowly opened the door. She flinched when the hinge hit a squeaky spot. She stepped into a dark and dusty cavernous room filled from floor to ceiling with mountains of scrolls and shelves of books. This had to be the archives.

She told her sister, and Panella made her way to Lyra's location. Judging by the layer of dust coating everything, she found it unlikely anyone had been down here in the last several decades. They should be relatively safe while they dig through the overwhelming amount of content. That did not mean someone from the Day Court could not decide today was the day to visit the archives.

She looked around to get a feel for the system the Day Court used, when she heard the squeak of the door opening. She peered around the corner of a shelf and released the breath that had been trapped in her chest as Panella entered the room.

"You could have warned me you were coming in," she said dryly.

"Sorry. Have you found anything yet?" Panella responded, not sounding sorry at all.

"They have a relatively organized system, ordered by date. I found what I believe is the most recent addition from four decades ago at the end of the closest shelf. I just began looking for the oldest section when you came in," Lyra replied.

"Alright, I will start over here and you over there, and we can narrow down the location," Panella said, making her way to her end.

The tidy rows of shelves in the center of the room looked older the further back you went on each end, and it looked like they added shelves as a need for space arose. Lyra walked to the far end of her side and picked her search back up. It did not take as long as she had expected to find something of interest. It mentioned the purging of history in the Night Court, and she thought Ciaran might find it useful. She tied the book to her so she could call on it when she was back in the Night Court.

Finding something early on set her up for disappointment. Several hours later, Panella called her over, and Lyra had yet to find anything else of importance. There was no way to be certain how much time passed, though she was growing tired and had long since passed hunger. When she finally found Panella, she was sitting on the dusty floor with scrolls all around her.

"What is it?" Lyra asked.

"The history of the Great Battle. We know it was over blood magic, yet we never really knew much beyond that. All that knowledge lost to time." She sounded almost fervent. Panella had always found history fascinating. "There is an extraordinary amount here; I am trying to find what is pertinent to take and what we should leave behind."

"Why? That sounds like a waste of time. I do not know about you, but I am growing tired and starving. Why do we not simply attach them all to us and figure out what is important back at Nightfell?" Lyra asked.

"Why did I not think of that?"

The two sisters shared a quiet laugh as they got to work. Panella had not exaggerated; there really were a lot of scrolls on the Great Battle. She glanced at a few of them out of curiosity and was stunned to see the mention of powers she had never heard of before.

"Panella, have you ever heard of 'Powers of Light'?" She knew it was a ridiculous question to ask. They had taken the same classes at the same time. What one knew, so did the other.

"'Powers of Light'? No, never," she said, leaning over Lyra's shoulder to look for herself. "It seems the old saying is true, 'you may not find what you search for, though you will always find what you did not know you should be searching for.'" Lyra bumped her shoulder with a laugh.

"You and your sayings. Come on, I would like to finish this before my stomach eats itself." It was Panella's turn to laugh.

"You and your stomach."

L yra could have kissed the fae who placed a bowl of fruit and a loaf of bread on the counter closest to where the sisters were hiding. They found the kitchens and thought it would be a likely place to steal some brooms. Panella grabbed Lyra's arm, preventing her from swiping the delicious snack in front of them. Glaring at her sister, she found Panella's finger on her lips, reminding her to stay quiet, and then pointed to her ear to listen. Her intent was solely on the food, and she had not registered a conversation was happening. Sometimes her stomach made her blind to everything else—including her sister.

"...has it they are planning an attack on the palace? Do you think they will free us?" the faun asked the leprechaun. Someone was planning an attack on the palace? They could not be speaking about their silent operation. They had not even known their little adventure to the Day Court was going to take place until hours before they left.

"Is it possible to free a being from a bargain made with another? I do not think it is. I worry this attack will only further our torment. Had we known how the high fae would treat us—"

"It would have changed nothing, except to make us more aware of the lives in store for us. The rot consumed the entire southern part of the court. We had nowhere else to go but north," the faun spat at the smaller being. It had been a long time since Lyra had seen a leprechaun; the last time cost her dearly. She learned a valuable lesson that day: never gamble with a leprechaun.

"I would wager you are right," the male said with a sigh. "I do not know how much longer I can..." The two walked out of the room, making it impossible to hear whatever he was about to say.

"I wonder what they were talking about—the 'rot' they mentioned," Panella said.

"I do, too. How have we heard nothing of it? I wonder if any of the southern covens know anything. I would think they would have shared that kind of information with the rest of us if they had. What of this palace attack they are expecting?" Lyra asked. It was all very curious.

Panella found a couple of brooms, while Lyra wasted no more time and grabbed some apples before she tore into the loaf. She thought it might be the best bread she had ever eaten, or it could be her hunger speaking. She passed her sister one apple as she shoved the last bit of bread in her mouth. Panella stared at her before trading the apple for a broom. Lyra shrugged; she was hungry.

You would think with all the talk of an attack on the palace, there would be more guards. The ones they came upon were socializing with other guards, or asleep at their posts. She expected this to be the hardest part of the entire mission, and yet here they were strolling out of the palace with not a care in the realm.

"That was too easy. I thought we would have to do a bit more sneaking around at the very least," Lyra said with a bit of disappointment.

"Well, just think how much sooner you and a meal can be together. The entire thing was not what I had been expecting. Not once did we run into anyone. The closest we came were the two beings in the kitchens, and I doubt they would have thought much of our presence anyway. It was, for lack of a better word, odd." Her sister sounded just as perplexed as Lyra was.

"We will have plenty of time to ponder it later when we give our report. We have a sister to see, and I need something more substantial than an apple and some bread." Just the mention of seeing Anin made her heart sing.

"Some bread?" She heard Panella say sarcastically as she shot into the sky on her stolen broom. Lyra laughed as she did the same, feeling a lightness in her chest for the first time since her sister had been taken.

Lyra's chest no longer felt light; in fact, it felt the opposite as she listened to Ciaran and Kes give their reports. Anin was still there. Her sister was still in that palace. Had they known, maybe she and Panella could have freed her. Instead, they had flown away laughing. Lyra thought she might be sick.

She understood why they had to leave her there. It made complete sense, and it was likely a better outcome than if she and Panella had tried, but the guilt remained. Devastation and guilt were radiating off of Kes. She could only imagine how hard it had been for him to leave when he was that close to saving her.

Panella seemed to recover faster from the news. She wiped a

tear from her face and dove right into their chain of events. Lyra stopped listening and thought there must be something they could do or someone who could help them; this could not be the end. Who knew how long it would take to figure out a way to combat the effects of blood magic? What if the scrolls they found did not have the answers they were seeking?

She looked at Kes, and he must have felt her gaze on him, because not even a breath later, he locked eyes with her. They needed help.

"We need to go speak to the Many Faced Goddess," she interrupted Panella. "*You* need to speak to the Many Faced Goddess. We need help." Kes looked as though he thought Lyra had lost her mind, and maybe she had. Though if anyone could, at the very least, point them in the correct direction, it would be the Many Faced Goddess.

"What could it hurt?" Etain asked Kes. He was quiet for a long moment, staring at an invisible speck on the table. This version of Kes was still unsettling. Finally, he let out a deep breath and looked back up to meet Lyra's gaze again.

"It could hurt nothing but my pride, and I do not seem to have much of that to harm these days. You will both come with me." It was not a question, but an order. Lyra and Panella nodded in unison.

"When do we leave?"

Chapter 24
Kes

"This is pointless," Kes said for the hundredth time. He and the sisters wandered the woods for what felt like several hours, though it very well could have only been a couple. Kes was both mentally and physically exhausted; he felt wrung out. The guilt was taking root in his heart and turning into something ugly.

"She will show. She always shows when she is needed." Lyra sounded confident in her words, and Kes was having a hard time not getting his hopes up. He did not think she would give him anything truly helpful if she graced them with her presence.

"For a witch, maybe, but I am not a witch, and neither is Anin. Etain was likely the only reason she allowed Ciaran to find her centuries ago." He felt his steps slow with each passing minute.

"We are witches, and we are with you," Panella said in such a way it left no room for argument.

"Be that as it may, even if she does appear, she will only speak in riddles that further complicate everything. She does not give answers, even though I have a feeling she sees and knows the outcome of everything. Likely because she twists fate the way she wants it to be." Kes could not hide the contempt he held for the goddess.

"Even her riddles contain questions you would not have known to ask if she did not force you to. Those questions always lead you on a better path to the answers you seek." The faith these two held in the shifting-faced creature was maddening. She never had the same face twice. How do you trust someone like that?

"I will give her another hour to show, and after that, I am returning to do something productive to get your sister back." It was already fraying his nerves to be out in the woods looking for a goddess that can only be found if she wants to be. He knew she would not show and they would be back at the palace within the hour. At least there he could waste time trying to get some rest. Logically, he knew he would need to take decent care of himself if he were to rescue Anin; her sisters made sure of that.

It turned out they would not be back at the palace within the hour, for at that moment a clearing appeared with a little mushroom hut in the center. The image was just as it had been when he went with Ciaran to speak to her all those years ago. Both sisters, who had been walking slightly ahead of him, turned around with expressions of "I told you so" blatantly displayed across their faces.

"Well, best get it over with," Kes groaned. He hated the way a little flame of hope ignited within him at the sight of the goddess' dwelling. He knew it was a lost cause, and yet he could not help grasping onto any possibility that could return Anin to him. Before he could attempt to talk himself into thinking better of it, the single door opened, and there stood the goddess with all of her shifting faces.

"Hello twins, it has been a long time since either of you visited. Come in, my children. I have tea already brewing."

The sisters wasted no time and crossed the clearing swiftly, stopping to each kiss the cheek of a different face in greeting, before disappearing into the deceptively small hut.

It never occurred to him that the sisters could be twins. Now it seemed wildly obvious; there was no other way they could be sisters. Twins were uncommon for the fae, and they were incredibly rare for the witches.

"Bird," she said in greeting. "Are you coming in, or are you planning to perch there the entire time?" The goddess cackled at her own joke. Kes just glared at her as he strode across the clearing and followed behind the sisters. There was no going back now, no matter how much he wished there were.

Lyra and Panella already sat at the table in the center of the large interior. He knew to expect it this time, except he was certain it was even larger than the last time he came for a...visit. As at home as the witches felt, Kes felt uncomfortable. His wings were not ideal in a place like this where herbs were hanging from every square inch of the ceiling, drying. At least the table had a bench, so he did not have to arrange his wings to accommodate a chair not made for those like him.

No one said anything while the goddess poured tea for everyone. She then took her seat and stared at each sister until finally resting her eyes on him. She held his gaze for longer than was comfortable before speaking.

"I know why you are here. I am sorry for the pain this chain of events has placed upon you all and will do everything I can to help you, although I must warn you there is not much to be done for now." Kes felt his feathers lift alongside his anger, which was always there, just below the surface.

"I told you both this would be a waste of time," he seethed at the sisters.

"None of that, bird. They were right to bring you here. I said there was not much to be done, not that there was nothing," she said, somehow managing to scold and comfort all at the same time. "You may not like what I have to say, but you must adhere to it. Any rogue rescue attempts will only make matters worse—much worse—for the entire realm."

Kes had no issue allowing the realm to rot away if it meant he could get Anin out of the dungeon she was suffering in sooner. He would help speed it along any way he could if it meant sparing her even a minute of pain. If anyone was going to cause her pain, it would be him, and she would beg for it.

"I can hear your thoughts as clearly as if you had spoken them aloud. It is not just the realm, but every single creature within it, including Anin." She stared at him until he gave a slight nod of the head. "When the time is right, you will know. The opportunity will be the perfect play between the two courts. I cannot tell you anything else, for that is the only thing that fate has set for certain. You must continue down your current paths and find ways to disrupt the Day Court. It might surprise you to find those with plans that align with your own," the goddess explained.

"First born," she said to Lyra. "You have already been set down a path no other can travel, requiring strength and determination. Stay dedicated to your journey and do not second guess your choices, no matter how painful they may become." Lyra nodded, seeming to understand what the goddess implied.

"Second born," she said to Panella, who sat a little straighter in her seat. "Follow your heart's desires; there you will find what you need and what needs you." Unlike her sister, Panella seemed unsure of what that could mean.

"And you, second prince of the Night Court, must listen, and listen well. Anin is on her own path that is separate from yours—for now." She added when he opened his mouth to argue with her, "As hard as it is to accept, she is exactly where she is meant to be. The realm and her future depend on her being in the right place at the right time. Follow the moonlight to illuminate secrets unknown. Only then will the storm reach its crescendo, blowing open the door. You will know the time has come. Stay true to your path, or the time may never come to pass and all will have been for naught."

"I am to...what? Do nothing while I feel every pain inflicted upon my mate." He could hear his voice rising with every word he said.

"You will hardly be doing nothing, and like I said, without you doing your part, the rest cannot happen. It is true that it will not be what you want to be doing, or what your intuition and mate bond demand. This is how it must be if you truly wish to help her. It is abundantly clear that you want nothing more than to do just that." She was stern with the delivery of her words, but remained perfectly calm.

"You lie—"

"I never lie. When you are as old as I am, you see how pointless lies truly are. Do not make the mistake of accusing me of such a thing again." She put a bit of power behind her last words to make sure he understood it was unwise to test her.

"I knew you would speak in riddles and only give half truths. This was a waste." Kes stood abruptly and stormed towards the exit. His hand was on the knob of the door when she spoke one last time to him.

"I have been more forthcoming with you than any other being before; keep that in mind as you curse me. I will forgive it, because I know the pain you are feeling," she said as he opened the door. "Follow the moonlight, bird!" she hollered as he slammed it.

Once out in the clearing, the rage he had been trying to contain erupted out of him, and he directed it at the one thing standing between him and his mate—the moon.

"What the fuck do you want with me?" he screamed at it. "What does your light have that is important to the fate of my mate? Nothing to say? How convenient for you!" He was not aware of the words spilling from his mouth; all he knew was his rage and the ugliness that had taken root deep within him. More than anything, he felt fear.

He wanted to tell Anin he would come for her, but the sentiment felt too empty now that he failed to keep his promise. He failed her time and time again. It was in that moment he realized what that ugliness was inside of him—a reminder of what he truly was. A failure. Even so, he continued to make the promise.

I will come for you.

Chapter 25
Anin

Anin craved the release of death. This was not a life, at least not one worth living. Forced to endure this unfathomable existence is worse than anything she could ever imagine. Her days were filled with nothing but pain.

She told herself over and over she would learn to tolerate it better; however, that implied she would be here for a very long time. That was not a thought on which she enjoyed dwelling. It often led her to seek shelter in the darkest parts of herself.

Yes, she craved death and the nothingness that would follow as she was returned to the realm to create more life. She even wished for it, selfishly. She knew if she died, Kes would not be far behind. She let herself have a moment where she could pretend he would choose both of their deaths over her continued suffering.

She knew that was a lie. He was too stubborn to accept anything except the outcome he desired, and nowhere would that include her death. She missed him. She hardly knew him, and yet felt as though she knew him better than she knew herself. So while she wished for death, she wished for a life with him more. A life with him was a reason to live.

She missed her sisters—her true sisters. She could not bear to think of how they were handling her absence. She wondered how long it would take for them to let her go and move on with their lives. They were both such incredible witches, and she knew they were destined for greatness. Anin always thought she would be there to witness their success. Seeing her sisters reach their full potential was a reason to live.

She had thirteen promises to uphold. Thirteen names to remember and a message for a mother. Four covens to answer to and thirteen reasons to live.

Brhget
Thistle
Cerridwen
Faith
Hope
Destiny
Josephine
Lyse
River
Ophila
Catra
Welyn
...and little Tallon

Their names became a mantra in her head. She repeated them on a constant loop, making sure she would never forget them. While she craved death and sometimes let herself wish for it, she had too many reasons to live. Love and duty would have to sustain her for the foreseeable future. Besides, it was not as though she had a say in the matter. The Land, much like her sister, would never let her go.

There was no freedom in death, and there was no freedom in life.

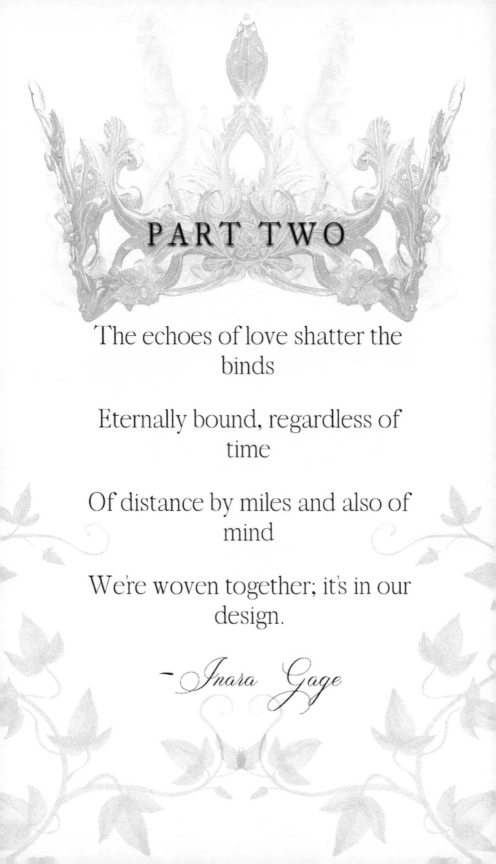

PART TWO

The echoes of love shatter the binds

Eternally bound, regardless of time

Of distance by miles and also of mind

We're woven together; it's in our design.

— *Inara Gage*

Chapter 26
Panella
3 Months Later

It was in Yagend's, King of the Night Court, first years that he gathered his army and began his invasion. While he had the larger of the two court's armies, he failed to factor in the witches. The witches did whatever they needed to keep the balance in all altercations. Since the Night Court King was attempting to overthrow the Day Court and take ultimate power, the witches stood against him. The Land demands balance, and that balance requires the two courts and the witches to remain neutral.

When the army crossed the borderlands, they were unprepared to be met by a united front of Day Court fae and witches. Yagend's army had not expected to go into combat until they reached the border of the Day Court. They scrambled to get into formation while half of them were decimated within moments.

P anella wondered if that battle had anything to do with the Night Court's lack of an organized force. Kes was doing his best to build something, but the time that had passed since they last had one seemed to make it even more of a challenge for him. Night fae dislike being told what they *should* do, let alone being given direct orders. She scanned the page looking for her place, sighing because she already knew this king was going to be a real piece of work.

The entire battle lasted no more than a half hour, and by the end, the Night fae either all lay dead or had surrendered. King Yagend demanded his army continue to fight, yet none did. In front of the Day Court and witches, the Land abandoned the king. His greatest failure and embarrassment laid bare for all to witness.

It is said that once King Yagend returned to his palace with his pride in tatters, in a fit of rage, he mandated the entire court destroy all the historical texts and artifacts. It was his attempt to rewrite history by completely erasing it.

The act has been called "The Purge," and it is unknown which items of significance became lost to the realm and if he was successful in his quest to remove the history of the Night Court in its entirety. Communications never returned between the Court's, and the sharing of information ended.

Why not just delete his own history? Taking everything prior was beyond short sighted; it was ignorant. He thought he should control the entire realm. He failed—miserably. Panella could not believe a being could be so egotistical to erase all knowledge of not only their blunder, but also anything prior to it.

She had just created order out of the chaos and began looking through the small amount of information Lyra found on The Purge. Most of what they had taken was on the Great Battle and would take her years to comb through. She almost felt bad about the amount of information they stole from the Day Court; it was staggering. *Almost.*

She was grateful to have such a monumental task in front of her. The witches were struggling to adapt to life in the Night Court. It would take them a while to figure out their new normal, and as soon as the housing was figured out, things would calm down and everyone could fall into a routine. Witches did not handle change very well. And while witches were all about the good of the community, there was a reason there were seven covens.

Having all the covens intermixing was...difficult, to say the very least. The head witches were planning the final layout and, with the way tensions were rising, they could not do it fast enough. Every coven had their own way of doing things, and each one thought their way was the correct way. She thought it was obvious they were *all* the correct way—the end result was the same no matter which approach they went with. It appeared she was the only one who thought as much. She shook her head in disbelief. The head witches were some of the most intelligent females she had ever known, and yet, when it came to something so easy, they struggled to come to any kind of compromise.

Each night she woke up, she fled to the library. She set herself up in one of the little nooks hidden along the back wall of the massive space. She was used to the Silver Moon's library and how the sun filtered through and illuminated everything. While the moon was just as bright, it also casts shadows across everything. Her eyes had only recently adjusted to reading by candlelight.

The Nightfell library was cold and sterile compared to theirs. The library at the Silver Moon Coven always contained the comforting noise that so many beings make when in one place, even when silent. This one was disturbingly quiet, with no vines from her sister growing across nearly every surface and no mementos hanging from the ceiling. The rows of shelves were towering, and each one had massive sliding ladders. They went up multiple stories, and Panella wondered how they were supposed to know what they were going up the ladder looking for. It was a ridiculous system she refused to use.

After one night of trying to use the ladders while searching for pertinent information, she got so frustrated she spelled a chair. It floated around the shelves efficiently, making it far easier to navigate her search. A Night fae watched what she was doing and then asked if she would spell a chair for him to use. She saw him for a few nights after using the chair, although he must have finished whatever he had been working on. She had not seen him around the library in a while.

For the most part, the Night fae she ran into did nothing more than shoot her ugly looks and give her a wide berth. There were a few, however, who either paid her no mind or even smiled at her. Every month it seemed to improve as spells integrated into the Night fae life. Many witches had even set up businesses offering spells in exchange for goods. It appeared to be affecting fae and witch relations. She guessed it had more to do with their queen being a witch than anything.

Etain was slowly making changes around the palace. The first thing she did was request Ciaran do something with his gruesome display in the great hall. No one had any complaints about that change. Other things like the treatment of the lesser fae and, most notably, the abolishment of taking captives from the Human Realm. If the humans came on their own, that was fine, but they were not to be locked into any binding deals or placed under any enchantments. That one caused quite the uproar. However, all things considered, the fae seemed to tolerate the witches, perhaps grudgingly so.

The neat stacks of organized tomes and scrolls were towering. She would not mind having someone assist her. Normally she would rope her sister into the task, but Lyra and Kes spent most of their time in training. Panella joined them just enough to stay on as a Silent Shadow, at least until they could train new shadows.

She planned to do exactly as the Many Faced Goddess had instructed and she would throw herself fully to her heart's desires. The second part of the goddess's prophecy made her curious. What did she mean by 'finding what she needs that would also need her'?

The only thing that troubled Panella was the distance growing between her and her sister. Of course they were, and always would be, connected by their sister link, yet they had never spent this much time apart. She missed her, even when she could feel her. They began blocking each other more often since the training Kes was putting Lyra through left her in a constant state of adrenaline; it was making Panella anxious, and she could never tell if her sister was in true trouble, or if the bird had just knocked her into the next night.

She did not mind training and even found the exertion to be therapeutic, but she could not understand Lyra's love for it. She often wore fresh injuries, and yet it never bothered her. If anything, it spurred her on. Panella had to admit Lyra was becoming rather skilled and had already far surpassed her. She knew she needed to get used to it because it was obvious after their visit with the Many Faced Goddess that the paths they were meant to walk were not the same, and they would no longer be walking through life side by side. They would still walk together even when the distance of their paths grew further and further apart. They would never leave each other, having been created by the same green power that connected them for life.

Eying the tower of information in front of her, she sighed and grabbed the top one. They would not process themselves, and if she were honest, it thrilled her to get lost in the words of the Fae Realm from long ago. It would be mere moments before the texts morphed into images of a long ago war and the misdeeds of egotistical kings. It was the exact thing she needed to escape from the horrors of her life. She much preferred being swept away in tales from the past than dealing with her emotions around both of her sisters, as well as the current state of the realm.

No, she did not want to face that.

Chapter 27
Council Member
1 Year Later

I f the council member heard one more high fae talk down to a lesser fae, someone no better than the enslaved, he was liable to cause a scene. It took everything inside of him to keep his mask of neutrality when a lesser fae was being tormented. Sometimes he had to force himself to feign delight depending on who he was around and who was doing the tormenting. He could not afford to give anyone a reason to look too closely at him.

He worked too hard to allow his anger to bring it all crashing down now. Too much was at stake. He had the fate of the entire lesser fae of the Day Court depending on him, but more importantly, the future with his mate was riding on their success. That was the one thing he desired above all else.

He was ashamed to admit that he had never given much thought to the way lesser fae were treated. Not until fate forced the matter. As a council member, he had to monitor how many new immigrants were entering the city on any given day. The influx created issues the high fae brought to the attention of the council daily. Since the queen was not doing anything about it, it forced the council to take it upon themselves to govern the court.

If not for being tasked with the job that fateful day, he would never have met his mate. He had a little desk set up at the gate, and marked each immigrant as they came in. He tracked what type of lesser fae they were, along with any skills they possessed. He was finishing the notes on the creature he just processed when the next fae approached. The council member looked up and nearly fell out of his chair. The pull he suddenly felt in his chest towards the satyr standing before him had felt like a physical blow.

They stared at each other for several minutes until the female next to him cleared her throat. There was a moment of panic that perhaps his mate was already with another until she called the satyr "son" when asking if he was well. As soon as the panic dissipated, liquid dread chilled him to the bone. His fated mate was a lesser fae.

At first he was certain fate made a mistake and attempted to ignore the pull he felt towards the male. There was no way he was mated to a lesser fae. It was not allowed. Clearing his throat, he regained his composure and looked at the pair in front of him once more, this time without the same shock and awe he was certain had been clearly written across his face just a moment ago.

"Breed, obviously nymph," he said to the two beings on the opposite side of the small table.

"Yes," his mate's mother said while her son continued to stare at the council member. Confusion clouded his mate's beautiful moss green eyes as his shock dissipated.

"Do either of you possess any talents that could benefit the city?" he asked, looking straight through his mate. He acted as though he did not truly see him while everything within him screamed to embrace the male.

"Nothing beyond the typical gifts nymphs possess. Is that a problem?" the male said, crossing his arms and speaking for the first time. His voice sang through the council member, touching every corner of his soul. It was the most magical sound he had ever heard, even with the harsh edge lacing his words. He could listen to the male reciting the most mundane of packing lists and still be enchanted.

"Not particularly. They will expect you to find work from one of the high fae merchants," the council member said, shaking himself from his mate's spell.

"Alright, how do we do that?" his mother asked.

"You can make a bargain with any of the fae over there," he indicated to the several high fae with lesser fae lined up in front of them.

"A bargain?" his mate asked, appalled at the idea of making any kind of deal with an unknown high fae. He could not blame him. The council member was not sure he could even capitulate to such a demand.

"Yes, it is the requirement," he said, swallowing the warnings he wanted to give while trying to keep his face from betraying him.

"Why?" his mate asked.

"Do you always ask so many questions?" the council member asked, crossing his arms and leaning back in the seat he had sat in for so long it would be surprising if it did not have the perfect imprint of his ass for the rest of eternity.

"Yes," the satyr said, smirking at him. It made him feel like there was a joke he was not in on—or maybe he *was* the joke.

"Even of high fae?" He knew immediately this male was going to be the death of him.

"Even more so," the male said, and the council member believed him. He both respected and was appalled by the way the satyr refused to back down to a high fae. It was going to get him into a lot of trouble. Trouble the council member would likely spend a great deal of time getting him out of. Somehow.

"I see," he said and nearly cringed at the annoyance that leaked into his voice as he thought about how complicated this male was going to make things for him. Even as he found himself enjoying his mates' sharp edges.

"Do you?" his mate asked, placing his large hands on the table before leaning forward and glaring into the council member's face.

"What's that supposed to mean?" he asked, a grin surfacing no matter how much effort he put into keeping it hidden. He found the satyr's attitude to be adorably irritating.

"I do not know, you tell me," his mate said, cocking his head to the side.

"You are insufferable," the council member said, laughing at the rage he could feel pulsating through the bond.

"And you are odious," the satyr said with a straight face, making him laugh even harder.

Honestly, who calls someone odious while wearing such a serious face?

"Balthier," his mother said, eyes shifting around nervously to see if anyone was listening to our exchange.

Balthier.

He rolled his mate's name around in his head. It suited him. He was tall for a lesser fae, standing nearly eye level with himself. He had broad shoulders and wild brown hair with short horns peeking out on either side of his head. His arms were covered in a soft tan fur. If his paltry knowledge of satyrs was anything to go off, Balthier's lower half would be covered in the same fur. Thinking about what might be hidden under the pants of his mate had his own pants growing tighter.

Goddess, help me.

"Mother, he expects us to enslave ourselves to some higher fae who will no doubt treat us with *so* much respect," the way he exaggerated the word "so" made it clear he did not in fact think they would be treated with respect, and he was not wrong. Daybreak was no place for a lesser fae.

It was the sole reason he could not understand why so many were flooding the city. They went from having a handful of lesser fae occupants in the entire city to now needing to figure out housing for them—or something. That was the exact reason he was at the gate to begin with. They needed to know how much space to dedicate to these fae. That was if the rest of the council agreed. He thought it likely he could convince them to create something for the lesser fae by reminding them of how disgusting the city would become if it became overrun by the homeless, which it no doubt would.

"It's the way the city operates. Why would you come here if you were unwilling to live by our rules?" What did they expect would happen when they came to the capital of the Day Court?

"Where else were we supposed to go?" Balthier sneered at him.

"Why go anywhere?" Staying in place seemed the most logical choice, although he was finding it difficult to be mad that his mate came to Daybreak. It would have made both of their lives easier if he and his mother had never arrived, yet he did not think he could wish for any other outcome.

"Do you truly not know what's happening in the south?" the satyr asked. This was the first time he was hearing anything about the south. Perhaps someone mentioned something earlier and he had not found it important enough to pay attention. Since the information was coming from his mate's perfectly shaped lips, it became important enough.

"No, what is so bad in the south to make you leave your home?" he asked after a moment of being distracted by the temptation of his mate's lips.

"There's a disease of the land. A slow-moving substance is consuming everything in its path, leaving nothing behind. Everything it touches quickly decomposes and rots into a fine black dust. Our home was in its path."

"Surely it cannot be that bad. Why not find a way to stop it?" he asked. The moment the council member spoke the words, he realized how dismissive he sounded.

"You do not think we have tried? Do you think we are not only lesser, but stupid as well?"

He cringed at the accusation while his mate pushed off the table and scoffed at him.

"Well, I only mean there must be some way to stop it," the council member said, putting his hands up in surrender. He had not meant to offend the satyr.

"You are welcome to go to the south and find a way yourself. Nothing we did could stop it. All we did was add more fodder to the rot."

"It's slow moving, you said?" the council member asked absently. He was always looking for a solution to any problem, it's what made him a prominent council member.

"Yes," Balthier snapped at him.

"Why not find another woodland town to live in instead of coming here?" The glare he received from his mate after that question made him aware he was only making things worse.

"Are you truly this dense? Of course we tried that first, but with the amount of beings fleeing the south, most towns are already well over their capacity, and multiple families are living in one home. There's no town for us to move to because no town was accepting new residents. Besides, it will not be long before it forces those towns to come north as well," he said.

If his mate's prediction were true, they would have a much larger housing crisis than any of them originally thought.

"This was the second time it has forced us to leave our home behind. I left our first one when he was just a youngling babe and the rot first touched the edges of our town. I eventually settled us several towns north of the one I grew up in," his mother said. She was soft-spoken and looked like most wood nymphs he met in the past. Green hair and green skin with vines adorning them. Mostly, he noticed her eyes looked kind, and he liked her instantly.

"This is quite the tale you are telling," he said, immediately knowing it was the wrong thing to say. He wished he could pull the words back into him. He could not understand why he was failing so epically to say the right thing.

"Are you saying you do not believe us?" his mate asked, words dripping with venom.

"It's not that I do not believe that *you* believe something is rotting the land. It's likely a fae playing tricks on the lesser fae." That made the most practical sense to him and he would not put it past any high fae to find it a hilarious trick to play.

"This is no trick, and I would like to see a fae strong enough to do something so widespread and destructive. Anyway, do you suggest staying away from any of them in particular?" his mate asked, nodding to the high fae waiting to trap the lesser fae into one-sided bargains. He surveyed them, but he did not need to; he knew exactly who they should avoid.

"Do you see the male with the feline face? Anyone but him." He pointed toward the one he spoke of. He's known for being particularly violent to the lesser fae he traps with horrible deals. Without another word, Balthier and his mother made for the lines. When he next looked up and saw the line his mate stood in, he could have screamed. He purposely went to the exact fae he had told him not to.

His mate turned and made eye contact with him before he crossed his arms and glared. What was he trying to prove? This decision would do nothing but cause him pain. The idea of him being even the slightest bit uncomfortable made the dread already growing within him pool heavy in his chest. He did not realize it till that moment, but the satyr must have been able to feel his panic because he smirked at him as if saying, "now what do you intend to do about it?"

That was the beginning of his double life. Perhaps it was for the best. It catapulted him into action and now there was nothing he would not do to make sure his mate was free and that they could have a real life together. No risk and no pain was too great to make him hesitate.

The political war he waged took a ridiculous amount of time to become destructive enough to gain the attention of the high fae. Now that the high fae were taking notice of the state of their court and questions were starting to be asked, everything became more dangerous. The stakes were raised even higher with the arrival of the prisoner held deep under the palace. A prisoner that might hold the key to their salvation. He was willing to take a gamble and bet it all on her. He only hoped he made the right choice.

He would either succeed or die trying. There was no other option.

Chapter 28
Anin
3 Years Later

The silence was slowly suffocating her. Anin never noticed how loud her life was until she had been locked away from it. She missed the kind of silence that was comfortable. The kind that still held the sounds of the living. Down here there was nothing but cold, damp stones to keep her company. Well, that and the small collection of her rotting wings hanging on the wall beside her. She tried not to look and failed every time.

Time lost its shape in the early days of her stay. At least she hoped it was early. There was no proper way for her to keep track. For a while, she tormented herself with the thoughts of every possible thing she could have done to have prevented her current predicament. She soon realized that would change nothing. She was still in the same cage she had been in from the first day she woke in this room of misery. All it did was drive her further insane, and she needed no help with that. She thought perhaps insanity was a family trait. Maybe this is how the voices started for Tatiana.

Her mind was losing itself—or perhaps she was the one losing her mind. It was hard to know for sure while it tormented her with images of Kes. They were not memories, nor would she call them fantasies. She did not recall actively thinking of the visions and beyond that; they were all strange. It always started with the same vision of him smiling and waving at her. She was certain she never saw him do such a mundane gesture. It was far too basic for his preferred theatrics.

The visions always moved on to another of him writing a letter. She could never see what he was writing. The oddest part was how he kept looking up and pointing to the scroll before shifting to another image of him miming for her to continue. It made no sense. What was she supposed to continue? She racked her memory, trying to recall if any of these visions had actually happened. She knew they were not and yet they had to be, right? How else would her mind create such vivid images?

They played on a loop for at least part of every day until they began to shift faster and faster and eventually stopped. She felt like she was not the one in control of her own mind, and was disappointed in herself for failing to keep it intact longer. The loop that was currently playing was nearing the point when it would stop and give her a moment's reprieve, until a new vision arrived of him screaming with frustration.

Were these images coming from Kes?

That was impossible. It was more likely that she was losing her mind and creating strange images to cope. At least that's what she thought until an image of him throwing his hands up like he could not believe she was not understanding. It was the eye roll that made her think—just maybe—it *was* him. What was the harm in trying to send an image back? At the very least, she could confirm she was, in fact, losing her mind.

She formed an image of her waving while wearing a face of uncertainty. She felt foolish. Of course Kes was not communicating with her through visions; that was not how a mate bond worked. Even she knew that. Good thing no one was around to see her acting like a complete fool. Her sisters would never let her live it down if they ever found out.

The next one she received was a vision of him dramatically celebrating and the action was so incredibly Kes she felt the corners of her mouth quirk up. Even if she were losing her mind, at least her visions were ones of her mate, making her smile. That was no effortless task, considering her current surroundings.

She sent an image back of her smiling at his antics. She could play into her mind's delusions; it was better than staring at her slowly rotting wings. He was quick to reply with a cocky grin. It truly had to be Kes communicating with her. She felt her heart rate increase. The excitement of having some kind of line to the outside realm made her skin tingle with anticipation. She did not know how it was possible, but she was not going to deny the one good thing to happen to her in...however long she had been stuck in this cage.

It took her a moment to figure out how to compile images to convey the correct thoughts. Eventually, they went back and forth with basic images and they created a language between them. It made it easier to decipher what each other sent and made their delivery clearer. Eventually, she could read his images like she could any scroll.

"How is this possible?" she asked him. It took a long moment for his response to come in. He had a hard time explaining parts, so he sent her images from his memories as well.

"Galetia and Etain performed a spell," she nearly cried at the image of the head witch, who had become a surrogate mother to her after her own returned to the realm. "The spell links a bonded pair together similar to the bond your sisters share." This time he showed her an image of her true sisters and a tear did escape. She was so grateful to communicate with him in this way. It was like looking through his eyes at the ones she loved most. "However, we had to do it without you there and we have not had a bonding ceremony, so we were not entirely sure if it would work."

"It seems to have worked in some capacity."

"There was a part in the spell that required blood to be spilled, at the same moment Galetia stabbed me—"

"She stabbed you?" Anin could not believe she was capable of such a thing.

"Yes, but she apologized. *Anyway*, at the same time, I felt like my throat was being ripped open. I tried to help you by sending as much power down the bond as I could."

"That was you?" She remembered feeling as though she were regenerating faster than she should have been able to. Although at the time, she thought it was the Land ensuring she did not die.

"It was. Anin, what happened?" He asked as gently as possible. She thought about how much she should tell him. She did not want him to suffer any more than he already did by feeling the injuries Tatiana forced her to endure. She needed to do a better job of locking down her bond, but as soon as she was unconscious, there was nothing she could do about it.

"She tried to kill me and absorb my power, but the Land has decided I shall not die, for whatever reason." Anin hoped it came across casually and that her message would not make him blame himself anymore than she was certain he already had. She really wished he would not; none of this was his fault.

"Anin, I am so sorry. I should have protected you, and when it mattered most, there was not a single thing I could do about it."

"Kes," she said, making sure he clearly understood the message the image she sent conveyed she did not blame him. "Like you said, there was nothing you could have done. I do not think even if I had told you who I was truly running from, you could have prevented fate from catching up to me." The probability she was fated to be where she was at this moment was something she was attempting to become comfortable with. Fate got what fate wanted. She knew this, and yet it did not make it easier to accept.

"Maybe not, but I could have tried. Why did you not trust me enough so that I could have done my best to keep you safe? We could have gone into hiding."

"And then your cousin and Etain would be stuck dealing with my sister's insanity." She would not wish her sister on anyone.

"You could have trusted me, you know? I still do not understand why you did not."

She sighed before she sent her answer. "I told you I was afraid it would have been too much and you would reject me. I was more trouble than I was worth."

"Silly nymph, you are worth all the trouble in the realm." He sent an image of him reaching out and caressing the side of her face. She thought she could actually feel him—almost. She was so starved for a gentle touch, her mind easily created the sensation.

"Well, that is good because I do fear she is going to cause a lot of trouble."

"She already has."

"The witches?"

"Yes, how did you know?" he asked. Before she could answer, she heard the echoes of footfalls coming from the single hall leading to her stone prison. She did not want Kes anywhere near her mind when the mad queen and her depraved minion began their ministrations. She would need to disappear deep into her mind in a few quick minutes while she relived that near caress over and over until she woke back up alone in her little cage.

"I have to go."

Chapter 29
Lyra
8 Years Later

"Lyra, you cannot afford to make any mistakes," Kes said, offering her a hand. He laid her out flat on the mat too many times, and her back was aching. "You do not have the same strength as a fae. If you do not use your agility to your advantage, you will end up hurt, or worse."

"I know, I know. I am trying. You just move too fast for me to keep up," she said, cringing at the whine her words carried.

"Awww, is the little warrior witch going to cry? Should I get some younglings to come and show you how it's done?" he asked, taunting her.

"Shut up, bird beast," she growled in response.

"Make me," he said, with a smile that made her desire nothing more than to rip his face off. "Good, get mad. Use it and my speed against me. You can harness your opponent's momentum to compensate for your lack of strength. You know what to do, now do it."

"Fine. Again." Her body screamed at her to stop, but she knew he would never let her live it down.

"That's the spirit, little chick," he said, cackling at the face she had made. She hated his stupid nicknames he came up with for her.

"Tweet, tweet mother-fucker, let's go," she growled at him, making him laugh even harder. She was determined to make him the one lying flat out on his back this time.

He came at her, slowly stalking her in a circle. She watched him closely, looking for his tell. It was hard to notice since he always wore a shit-eating grin, but the left side of his mouth would quirk just a tick higher.

Any moment now... There!

He flew at her in a flurry of fists and talons. She moved quickly, dodging every hit that came at her—looking for her perfect opportunity. It was only a moment later when she saw a fist coming at her and she reached out to grab it. She did exactly what he taught her to do and used his own momentum to flip him. The sound of his breath being forced from his lungs as he landed hard on his back, along with the surprised look on his face just as she flipped him, was something she would not soon forget. The image he made sprawled on the mat had her laughing so hard tears rolled down her cheeks and she had to grab her stomach.

He stretched out one of his taloned legs and swiped her legs out from under her. She landed on her back beside him. Not even the impact of the ground could stifle her laugh.

"Very good, little chick. Now let's see about adding the use of your power," he said, sitting up. She laid there looking up through the giant opening in the ceiling, attempting to catch her breath as her laughter finally subsided. She was not sure she had laughed that hard since Anin had been taken from them.

Thoughts of her missing sister always sobered her. She felt guilty for laughing, knowing her sister had likely not laughed in over eight years. Rage boiled inside her every time she thought of her sister, and it was exactly what she needed to remember—why she was training as hard as she was.

"How do I do that?" she asked, standing back up and brushing the dirt from the fighting ring off her pants. She had never attempted to use any of her powers while fighting at the same time.

"Tell me about your power. What does it do and how do you access it?"

"I have blue, green, yellow, and pink."

"You say that as though I have any knowledge of a witch's power. What do the colors mean?" he asked her, rolling his eyes. He was good at hiding his despair behind his mask of theatrics, but it was easy for her to see through when there was no mischief gleaming in his eyes.

"Blue is the power of the warrior. It gives me added strength," she said, pausing to glare at Kes when he said "not enough" under his breath. "It makes me faster and more agile as well."

"Good gods, I would hate to see how weak and slow you would be without that. Unless you have not been using it during our training?" he asked. She could not decide if he hoped that was the case or if he was being sarcastic. It was never easy to tell with Kes, even harder now.

"Sometimes."

"Sometimes?" he asked, cocking a downy brow at her. "Little chick, are you trying to make it easy for me to make fun of you?"

"Shut up, bird," she said, glaring at him. "Some of us have not been trained from a young age by warriors to use our power at the same time. I can use them one at a time as needed, but if there were any true warrior witches, then they have not existed in a long time."

"Ha! Well then, what are you, if not a warrior witch?"

"Stop mocking me! You asked about my power and I am telling you," she spat at him. He raised his hands in surrender and waited for her to continue. "Besides the blue, I have pink, which gives me the ability to heal myself and others. I can move objects without touching them with my yellow power—got Anin good with that one a few times when we were younglings," she added and wished she could take it back as she watched the cloudiness of despair roll across his red eyes like it always did whenever anyone mentioned his mate. Even if it made him smile at the same time. "And of course I have the green that nearly all witches are born with."

"Well, well little chick, sounds like we are going to have a good time," he said, blinking the clouds away. Something about the smile he wore made her think it would not be very fun for her. "How do you access your power?"

"I have to visualize it and then direct it with my mind. It's difficult to do both at the same time," she complained. Kes laughed mirthlessly at her.

"And you think elemental magic is any different? Repetition will make it second nature to access the correct power and use it to your advantage in any altercation."

"How do you propose to do that?" she asked, narrowing her eyes at him. He looked far too excited about whatever he had planned. That never boded well for her.

"If I told you, it would not make such a glorious surprise," he said with a wicked grin that still did not touch his eyes.

"Kes, I do not know if I have told you, but I am not particularly fond of your surprises." The last time he had a "surprise" for her, she left the training room bruised and nearly broken.

"Of course you are! How could you not be? My surprises are *such* fun," he said, doing a little excited clap she found completely unnerving. Something that looked as frightful as him only made the silly little things he did seem unhinged.

"Kes, I swear, if I die…"

"Oh, stop being so dramatic," he said, waving off her concern.

"Oh! That's rich coming from mister dramatic himself."

He fluffed out his feathers like she had just given him the highest of compliments. Knowing him, he really thought it was high praise.

"What about your magic?" he asked, shifting back to her demanding instructor. The way he flitted between personalities was liable to give her whiplash. She was not sure if he had always been like this or if it resulted from the wear the past few years had wrought on all of them.

"What about it?" she asked.

"Really?" he asked, sighing. "How does it work? What can it do? Stop being so difficult, it's boring."

"Our magic is spell work. It typically requires certain ingredients and preparation," she said in annoyance. "And I am not boring."

"Are there any spells that would help you in a combat situation? What about as a Silent Shadow?" he asked. She had never considered if it were possible to use spells in such a way. "And that is exactly what someone boring would say." She glared at him, wanting to show him just how *boring* she was with a swift kick to the nuts.

"I honestly do not know. I imagine it could be possible to use certain spells as long as the necessary ingredients are easy to keep on hand. Panella would know better. Let me ask her," she said as she linked with her sister. "She said she's not sure, but that she would look into it and get back to me."

"That's so creepy, and it's entirely unfair there's not another Kes for me to do the same thing with," he said, sounding truly put out.

"The realm could not handle another Kes," she said, rolling her eyes at him.

"True," he sighed. "Besides, this level of perfection cannot happen more than once," he said, shaking his head as if it were the greatest tragedy.

"Oh, for goddess' sake! Could you be any fuller of yourself?" she asked in a huff as she threw her hands up in disbelief. Honestly, she did not know why she was surprised.

"Probably. Should I try to find out?" he asked. Lyra groaned at his insufferable existence while he laughed at her. It was in these moments she could catch glimpses of the old Kes, as fleeting as they were.

She hated to admit it, but she quite liked her brother.

Rebel Leader

The rebel leader watched as lesser fae flooded the city. It was only going to get worse. The rot was slowly devouring the southern half of the Day Court, forcing everyone north. While they knew better than most that there was nowhere else for the refugees to go, the rebels wanted to scream at them to turn around and find a different way of life somewhere else. The deals the high fae forced upon them were no better than slavery.

They needed change; all the Day Court did. Even the high fae wishing to remain blind to both the queen and the rot. Where the rot in the south was physical, the queen was a metaphorical rot. Both were a disease that needed to be eliminated. The rebels had a plan—one they had been laying the foundation of for a long time already.

The land was clearly suffering, and with the golden queen doing nothing to help it, there was no doubt in the rebel's mind that the Land had abandoned her. Over the past several years, hushed conversations had told of another queen, one the Land approved of. If the stories were to be believed, she was stolen away from her mate—a Night Court prince, no less—and hidden away deep below the palace.

The throne belonged to her; she only needed the opportunity to claim it. They hoped with her half lesser fae lineage she would enact the change the court needed and heal the land of the rot plaguing it. The rebel knew if that were to happen, it was going to take the work of several beings. It would also require the help of one particular being. One with more motivation than most to have the hidden queen freed.

The rebel leader pulled out their spelled scroll and began to write. They had to word it carefully and make it too good of an opportunity to pass up. The rebel chose the time and the place and sent the scroll before they could second guess their decision.

They needed to meet with the bird.

Chapter 30
Kes
14 Years Later

He flew to the meeting point early so that he could scope out the ruins he and the rebel leader had agreed upon. Flying in circles well above the area, he looked for any sign of an ambush. Finding nothing suspicious, he perched on a spot in what was once a tower and now stood as a mountain of crumbling slabs of stone. He hid himself away in the shadows which made it possible to watch his surroundings while remaining unseen.

The Borderlands put him closer to Anin than he had been since his last failed attempt to retrieve her a few nights ago. He had gotten all the way to the hall that led to her. The moment he stepped foot over the threshold, pain wracked his body. The closer he got to her, the worse it got until black blood poured out of him from all orifices. He could feel his life-force being drained from him, and he would have been willing to risk it, but if he failed, he died. Meaning Anin would die as well. Just before he turned back he could have sworn he heard Anin call for him. Every step away from her shattered his black heart further.

He tried to rescue her at least once a month regardless of the Many Faced Goddess' warnings. He had Panella already searching for a way to negate the spell on the hall. There was a good chance it was blood magic, and that put them right back at square one.

Being this close to his nymph, the thought occurred to him that they might have an easier time communicating in their unusual way. He created the image of him waving ridiculously, which he knew she found amusing. It was how he always let her know he was there. Within a few moments, she responded.

"I am not sure what will kill me first, my sister or boredom," Anin said. She did that often—made morbid jokes about her situation—and he knew she just needed him to play along making light of it so that she did not break.

"I know how I can entertain you."

"Oh? And how do you suppose you can do that from so far away?" she asked sarcastically.

He created an image of them standing in his favorite part of the moonlit woods as he grabbed her and quickly spun her against a tree. Snaking a hand up behind her head he gripped her hair forcing her head to tilt up. Not only could he stare into her depthless black orbs in this position but it gave him better access to her mouth which he wasted no time invading thoroughly.

"Oh," she said in surprise, the word muffled by his lips.

"Are you entertained yet?" he asked, barely pulling away from her mouth.

"I do not think so," she said, smiling.

He slowly pulled open her wings that wrapped around her body until he revealed a dark green nipple. "How about now?"

"I cannot be certain," she said in one breath.

He leaned down and sucked one of her nipples into his mouth, pulling hard on it and causing her to arch into his mouth. "And now?"

"Hmm, maybe you should try once more," she said breathlessly.

He took the other nipple into his mouth, giving it the same attention while his hand slowly worked its way down her body. He parted her wings even further until she released the hold she had on them, fully exposing herself to him. He took his time roving his hand slowly over every inch of her skin along the way down, which left a trail of goose-flesh and caused her breath to catch. No matter how often she pushed into his teasing hand, he refused to touch her core. He buried his head into her neck and smiled against it when she gave a frustrated cry.

"So demanding my darling nymph."

"Damn it, Kes—quit teasing me!" she yelled, frustration punctuating every word.

"How does a good nymph ask, Anin?" he asked, lips brushing her ear.

She growled at him before finally spitting out, "Please."

"Tisk tisk my darling. That did not sound like a good nymph," he said, scolding her.

"Ugh! Fine! Please, my darling feather duster, will you not show me how goddess gifted you are?" she said, in an overly sweet voice which caused him to bark out a surprised laugh.

"I will accept that. Although we need to work on that mouth of yours..." He trailed off as he finally allowed his hand to find the place where she needed him the most. "Is this what you need my darling?" he whispered into her ear, keeping his touch gentle, applying very little pressure.

"Please—" she whimpered.

"Now that sounds like a good little nymph. A very good nymph. Do you know what good nymphs get?" he growled into her ear.

"Wh..what?" she asked breathlessly. He said nothing as he

applied more pressure. She threw her head back against the tree behind her with a moan.

"Oh, my darling, I could keep you in this state for nights on end if it meant I got to see that expression on your face while listening to a melody of your moans." He applied even more pressure, keeping a slow circular movement until she began to move around seeking something more. He slid two fingers deep into her heat, giving her exactly what she needed and was rewarded when she cried out in pleasure.

"Kes..." she said, chest heaving with every breath.

"Yes, my darling?" he asked, watching every single expression cross her face.

"Please..." she begged. He curled his fingers into her while continuing to apply pressure with his thumb, moving it in quicker circles around her sensitive nub. He could feel her inner walls tightening around his fingers as she soared to the peak of her pleasure.

"Are you going to drench my hand like a good little nymph?" he asked as he watched her eyes roll back. When her mouth opened to moan out her release, he covered her mouth with his own, swallowing the sound and invading her mouth. His fingers began to slow. "Every single one of your moans belongs to me, my darling. I will own all of them. Do you understand?" he asked a blissed-out Anin. She nodded her head, unable to use her words just yet.

When she finally got control over herself, she said, "Perhaps you should work on your so-called 'goddess blessed skills'."

"Oh my silly nymph," he said, as he slid his soaked hand out of her and dragged it up until he brought it to her throat. "Do you feel that? The way you fell apart on my hand and the trail it left with the proof of your release tells me just how skilled I am," he whispered into her ear before nipping at her neck.

He groaned when he heard the sounds of someone approaching. "I have to go, my darling. I wish we had time to further explore just how goddess gifted I truly am. Now, be a good little girl while daddy goes to work," he said, pleased when she laughed at the shared memory of the last time he spoke those words to her.

"The prince of the Night Court is the mos...oh, you have got to be kidding me," he heard a voice say the code phrase Kes chose, followed immediately by an exacerbated sigh. The scroll was spelled to open at the time of their scheduled meeting. Apparently the fae did not read it prior to reading it out loud.

"How interesting, a Day fae wanting to help a Night fae," Kes said, staring into the shadows. No matter how hard he stared, he could not make out any distinguishing features, even the shape of the fae was obscured by a cloak or something similar.

"The enemy of my enemy and all that," the rebel leader responds casually.

"Let's not waste time on pleasantries. What is this deal that I had to come all the way out into the middle of the Borderlands to hear, Day fae?" Kes asked, both ready to have this meeting over and annoyed it started. He would much rather still be in his mind with his mate, but this fae sent him a scroll last night claiming to have a way to rescue Anin, so he would listen.

"I lead the rebellion in the Day Court and we are trying to create chaos to incite an uprising against the queen. I could use your help," the fae said, like asking a Night fae prince to help a Day fae happened regularly.

"That sounds like a great time, but how does that help my mate escape the clutches of your crazy ass queen." If he found out this was a waste of his time when he could have spent longer with Anin, he was going to be beyond angry.

"What if the success of the rebellion and the rescue of your mate were one in the same?"

"Right. I should have known this would be a waste of my time," he said while turning to shoot up into the sky.

"We want to put your mate on the throne."

The thought made him cringe. He thought for a while her future might include a throne, and he worried about what that would mean for them. A Night Court prince had no place in the Day Court. Beyond that, he did not like that there were already expectations placed on Anin's shoulders.

"So she's the true queen then?" Kes asked. Deep down he had known the second Tatiana showed up in the Night Court for Anin. Both the king *and* the queen came for her. There was only one thing that would be a big enough threat to cause the queen to chase her all over the realm.

"She is. Even some of the high fae want the queen out." That was interesting. The high fae of the Day Court are incredibly prejudiced against the lesser fae. The fact they were willing to put a half high fae, half nymph on the throne spoke volumes about what they thought of their current queen. "We just need more."

"I will of course do everything I can for Anin, but I am not sure what I can do for this little rebellion of yours," Kes said. He wanted to help Anin but he was having a hard time seeing how the rebellion would help his mate. It sounded like they wanted to take her out of one cage just to chain her to a throne.

"I need more than your little meddling games you have all been playing in the Day fae affairs. I need something on a much larger scale. I will provide the location of targets and I need you to destroy them. I need chaos," the fae said.

"Well now, chaos I can do."

Chapter 31
Etain
20 years later

Etain watched as the moon bled into the red of another blood moon, just as she had twenty years ago when her life irrevocably changed. She often wondered how her little village fared without her or anyone else skilled with medicinal herbs and birthing children. How many harsh winters had come and decimated them without her or her mother's warnings?

Over the past two decades, the urge to see the state of Havenston for herself had grown, but more than that, she needed to visit her little two-room hut. Several months ago, when she was poring over the contents of one of the limited books she had on shade power, she saw a sketch of a conduit that looked oddly familiar. For months she stared at it, trying to remember where she had seen something like it before. She could not believe she forgot about the amulet her mother showed her. To be fair, she had only looked at it once when she was a small child.

If the people of Havenston had not ripped apart her cottage in her absence, the conduit should still be hidden beneath the floorboard under her bed. From what the book said, the amulet would help her wield her dark shade power, the only one she had yet to gain even a modicum of control over. She could not remember exactly what her mother had said about the amulet, but the one thing she remembered was the importance of keeping it hidden.

Now, she was certain it was something her many-times-great grandmother brought with her from the Fae Realm. From everything Etain had read and been told about her ancestor, she had been the last known witch to possess shade power. It was tempting to go back and rip apart her cottage and see if anything else was hidden within it, forgotten by the years. Either way, she needed to retrieve that amulet. She knew it was the key to unlocking the secrets of her power.

She could have it in her hands this very night now that the veil thinned and the Night fae were preparing to cross for their annual hunt. Something she had vehemently opposed and would have ended the tradition if it would not cause an uproar. She hated the idea of unsuspecting humans being hunted. They stood no chance against any of the fae—lesser included.

She could see Ciaran's reflection in the window as he sat in one of the chairs in their chambers, reading. At least he had not gone hunting since the night he came back with her. She knew her next words were going to come as a surprise, and she had no doubts he would find it highly amusing. "I want to cross the veil during the hunt."

"You do? I thought the hunt was—how did you put it? Oh yes, 'appalling and barbaric.' Is that not why you forbade me from partaking in the tradition that has been around just as long as the Fae Realm and the veil have existed?" He gave her one of his too-wide wicked smiles, reveling in this moment just as she knew he would. She huffed out a laugh and rolled her eyes at him.

"Well, yes, I find the hunting to be appalling and barbaric, but

I do not wish to cross to go hunting. I wish to see what has become of the town I grew up in, and there is something I need to retrieve." She had not told him about the amulet and what it does for reasons she could not be sure of.

Things have been complicated between them. They did not always have easy moments like the one they were currently having. Keeping the vault a secret has placed a strain on their relationship. She felt like it was now a stain on her that could never be removed. She could not understand why he did not trust his cousin, of all beings. He said, "If fate wants him to remember, then he will remember." With Anin missing and the answers they sought likely hidden amongst the hundreds—thousands even—of books and scrolls strewn about the cavernous room. Even worse, Ciaran did not seem to care about the way the guilt was eating her alive from the inside.

"If you are crossing, then I am crossing with you. I refuse to be in a different realm than you at any point in time. Besides, if the state I found you in is any indication, you will need me to protect you, little witch." His response surprised her. They spent far less time together these nights, making his declaration even more unusual.

She decided she would put the issues they were facing out of her mind for the night and take her mate to see where she grew up. She was almost embarrassed to show him the small beginnings she came from when he had only known the life of a royal. Yet, at the same time, she was looking forward to seeing him stand in her little home.

"If you are certain, I would love to show you around."

"My little witch, a tour guide. Sounds exciting," he said, standing in front of her in a blink. After all of these years, she was still not used to the speed in which he moved. While she no longer reacted, it still surprised her. "Are you ready to go now?" he asked, grabbing her hand and bending low to kiss it. She felt her cheeks flush, and at its sight, he smiled another one of his extra wide smiles at her. She nodded but before she could finish the motion, they were standing in Ebonmere directly before the veil.

The first time she crossed, she had not been conscious and found that she was suddenly rather nervous. "Do I have to do anything special? Is it like porting?" she asked him, not taking her eyes off the shimmering spot of air. Something she would never have been able to see if she had not known exactly what to look for.

"No, you just step through it and then you are standing in the Human Realm. Remember, your well does not replenish on the other side of the veil, so do not do something crazy and drain yourself. That's, of course, unless you wish to have a reenactment of the last time you came to the Fae Realm," he said, an amused sparkle in his golden eyes.

"I have not forgotten. Remember, I spent more than half of my life there. I am not a youngling Ciaran," she said, rolling her eyes at him, but laughing all the same. Even with all of their tension, her safety was still his priority.

"Well then, after you, little witch," he said, sweeping his arms towards the shimmering air in front of them.

"Will you not cross with me? At the same time? What happened to 'I refuse to be in a different realm than you,'" she said, attempting to lower her voice to sound like him and failing hilariously.

"Why, little witch, are you afraid?"

"No!" she exclaimed before dropping her voice into a near whisper. "Well, maybe a little." He swung her up into his arms, making her squeal at the sudden movement. Within two steps, they had crossed over into the Human Realm.

"Now, where is this village of yours?" he asked. She looked around and realized she had no idea where they were.

"I honestly am not sure which way to go. None of this looks

familiar," she said, panicking that she could not even attempt to retrieve her ancestor's amulet.

"What if I took us to where I first found you?"

"Yes! I would definitely know my way from—Ciaran!"

He sped them to the spot before she could even finish her sentence, setting her on her feet next to the midnight mushrooms she had been digging up. It was a surprise to find them exactly where she remembered them. They looked like someone had just been here a few nights ago. Maybe someone else figured out how to use the plants for healing after all.

She saw the small clearing where she had fought Seamus with all she had, which had not been enough. A shiver ran down her back and icy fear gripped her, stealing her breath, even twenty years later. Ciaran put his arm around her and pulled her into his side. When he was like this, it was easy to forget the other version of him lurking just below the surface of this one.

"No one will ever harm you like that again." She looked up at him, expecting him to say something about how he would protect her, only to laugh when he said, "You would make them explode before they ever had a chance to do anything."

She rolled her eyes before leading him through the woods on the paths and trails she still knew so well until they came to the edge of Havenston. The town really was quite small. Even one of the smaller covens would make a larger town than the people here did. She was not sure what sight would greet them, but she had definitely expected there to be at least minor changes to the place. Everything looked exactly as it had when she left, as if it had frozen in time.

This cannot be right.

A conversation from further in towards the center of town caught her attention. She thought she recognized the voices. Ciaran said nothing as he followed her up the dusty street, keeping his shadows around him to stay hidden from the eyes of the sheltered humans.

"...gone. I cannot find any trace of him."

"What do we do? My garden is already dwindling."

"As is mine. Did he tell someone else in the town where he was going and when he would be back?"

"I thought perhaps Seamus, yet he is nowhere to be found either."

Seamus?

How are they only now noticing Seamus's absence? As they drew even closer and she could see who was speaking, she stopped dead in her tracks. They looked *exactly* the same as they had just before she left. None of this was making sense.

"How is this possible?" she asked Ciaran in a whisper.

"How is *what* possible, little witch?" he replied in the same quiet whisper as her. "Why are we whispering?"

"No one has aged. Not even a year or two, and because I do not wish to startle them."

"The way time moves between the realms is...complicated. Think of it as if the blood moon lasts a few nights in a row in the Human Realm, then the Human Realm is paused while the Fae Realm is sped up. Multiple of our blood moons could have very well been happening in the same night here," he explained, shrugging like it was not the wildest thing she had ever heard. "And why do we not want to startle them? That sounds like fun."

"...the witch is also missing. I would bet they either took her to one of the larger towns to be burned, or she did something to them."

"She better never show her face around here ever again or I..."

"Or you will do what exactly?" Etain said, stepping out of the shadows. She was tired of listening to the same people constantly say horrible things about her. She no longer had to grin and bear their treatment, nor was she the same girl who left this town behind. Her movement caught their attention.

"Did you work some evil witchcraft on them, demon?" one of them spat at her.

"Maybe I did," she said, giving them her own wicked grin. She had spent the past twenty years in the Night Court perfecting it. Their faces blanched. "You should really decide if I am a witch or a demon. Possibly consider learning some new insults as well."

"You... You..." a man said. She had delivered all five of his children safely into the world, and this is the way they thought they could treat her. It was truly appalling. She did not know what was worse, the way they treated her or how she had simply accepted it.

She was ready to turn her back on them and show Ciaran her little home. A sudden pang of longing to be surrounded by the memories of her mother struck her.

"Or perhaps it was me. Did you call for a demon? I believe that is what that one human called me. What was his name, little witch?" Ciaran dropped his shadows and asked before she could lead him away. The group of men froze at the sight of him.

"Seamus," she offered in reply. Not a single one of them took their eyes away from Ciaran.

"Ah! Yes, that's right. I gave him one of my personal carvings. It had just the right amount of flourish," he said to Etain while turning back to the small group of men and pulling a blade to himself from what would look like thin air to them. "Would any of you like a matching one? I promise my penmanship is immaculate." The men stared at him with their mouths hanging open. "Watch, this is my favorite part," he whispered to Etain.

Ciaran opened his wings with an audible snap and then moved with his unnatural speed until he was standing right before them. "Boo," he said in their faces, giving them all a good look at his extra wide mouth and sharp incisors. He turned his face slightly so he could make eye contact with her and winked. It took the men two brief moments for their wits to catch up to their fear; they all screamed and ran away. She was pretty sure Michael had even wet himself.

Etain was not typically one for cruelty. However, all things considered, this was nothing but light fun for Ciaran. Besides, she could not help finding the pitch of their screams to be hilarious. She burst out laughing as a couple of them tripped over each other in their attempt to get away from Ciaran faster. Ciaran prowled the few paces back to her while looking very proud of himself.

"Little witch, I have to say, I am not fond of the humans you grew up with. Now, where is this home of yours?" he asked. She led him to the end of the dirt road to the tidy wooden home standing off on its own. It was further away from the closest house than the rest of the town was to each other. Her home, at first glance, looked like it was part of the town, but if you truly looked, you could see that it was not. Much like she and her mother had been.

"This is my home—was my home. I was born here, and this is the home my mother died in. I thought it would be where I would die whenever my time came." She moved the long stems of lavender growing wild in front of her house and found the rock which hid the extra key under it.

"Clever," he said approvingly.

"I used to lock myself out too often not to have a failsafe. I was exhausted all the time from delivering babies and making the medications for the rest of the village. It was a job that never stopped."

"Why would you run yourself into the ground to help those who would treat you like those idiots did?" he asked, waving his hand back up the street towards the way we just came.

"Well, now it seems silly, but at the time it was what I thought made them want me." She heard Ciaran grumble something about burning Havenston to the ground.

"It does not matter anymore, my love." She fit the key in the lock and swung the door open. She took pride in the way she kept her home and had always thought it to be spotless. As she looked around now, she cringed. There was dirt everywhere. Ciaran stepped in behind her, having to duck his head. She worried he might not be able to stand to his full height inside. He did not seem bothered by it though, so she said nothing. She giggled to herself each time he knocked his head into a beam or the herbs that were left drying. "It's so much smaller than I remember."

"Well, of course it is. You are a small human who has become accustomed to a world built for the fae," he said, as though the answer was obvious. She did not know how he could see something like that so clearly, but could be so blind when it came to something like power.

"Yes, well," she said, shaking herself from her train of thought. They were having such a wonderful night, and she did not wish for her thoughts to ruin it. "I suppose the tour will not take but a moment."

"I want it all the same," he said, cupping her chin in his hand. She smiled softly at him when he said, "I want to know everything there is to know about you, little witch. I am a selfish fae, but when it comes to you, I am greedy." He gently released her chin after they stared into each other's eyes for a moment, making sure she knew he meant every word.

He did; she knew he did. She only wished she had this Ciaran more often than not. She was already mourning the moment when he would flip to the other version of himself faster than the moon could shift.

"Well, this door leads to the bedroom," she said, opening the door to the small square room just big enough for the two small beds. There was a small table with a large bowl sitting on it that they used for bathing. She stepped into the room and her eyes immediately went to what she had once considered her finest dress hanging on the peg, just where she had left it.

She took the few steps needed to run her hands across the rough material. Memories of watching her mother cut the fabric, then sew it together flooded her. Even after all of these years, she still missed her terribly. She did not think she would ever stop doing so.

She glanced back at the doorway to see Ciaran leaning in with his arms folded above him, braced on the door's top frame, his forehead resting on his arms. He seemed content to just watch her relive her past. It was strange seeing him in her little home. She never thought to imagine a scenario where Ciaran stood stooped in the center of her two-room home. She never imagined him stepping into her past.

She got down on her knees and bent to look under her bed. It was impossible to remember exactly which floorboard hid the amulet, so she started tapping all of them in the area she thought she recalled it being under.

"Little witch, what are you doing?" Ciaran asked, amusement clear in his voice.

"I told you there was something I needed to retrie—found it!" she exclaimed as she pulled the loose board away. "I guess it is lucky that time moves in such strange ways. It has not given them an opportunity to ransack my home." She crawled out from under the bed and held the amulet up victoriously. "This is what I needed to come back for. I was reading one of my books on shades and saw an image of this exact amulet. It should help me harness my unruly power. I had completely forgotten about the hidden heirloom under the floorboards."

"That is a rather unforgettable item to forget," he said with a smirk. She was just glad he did not ask her why she had never mentioned it to him before.

The ridiculous way he had to stand made her smile. He looked like an adult in a child's playhouse. Wrapping her arms around his waist and looking up into his eyes, she tried desperately to hold on to this version of her mate. He dropped one of his arms and wrapped it around her, his typical grin stretching his face.

"Thank you for coming with me," she said, and meant it. She had expected to come here alone, yet had he not wanted to come with her, she was certain she would never have even found Havenston. More than anything, she was grateful for the opportunity to show him this part of her life.

"Little witch, there is no realm you could go to that I would not follow," he said with an intensity that made his eyes glow.

"I am not sure if that is the sweetest thing you have ever said or if it is the creepiest," she said, making them both laugh softly as they walked back into the main room. She dragged her fingers over the large wooden table in the center.

She loved this table. It held the history of her ancestors and wore the marks to prove it. Running her hand over the deepest gouge, wondering, like she always did, what had created it. She could see the millions of tiny knife marks from where her mother chopped herbs and vegetables, be it for food or medicines—she always stood in the same place.

"This is my favorite thing in the entire place," she said as she continued to map the memories the marks held.

"What makes it your favorite?" he asked, sounding genuinely interested.

"We do not know who made it or when it was made, but we know it was many generations ago. Each mark tells a story of an ancestor who once lived. It's silly, but it's as though all the people who sat around it at any given time in history still live on within it."

"I do not think that's silly."

She dragged her gaze away from the table to turn and look at him.

"It is not very grand, is it?" she asked in a near whisper. She was not sure why she felt so fragile at this moment.

"Anywhere you are is grand." She felt the heat creep up her neck and into her face, which only seemed to spur him on. "Little witch, you must know by now that no matter where you are, I see nothing but you. It's as though everything else is colored in shades of black and white and there you stand in full vibrancy." he said while he moved to stand in front of her. He placed his hands on the edge of the table and caged her in.

"Is that so?" she asked, the words coming out breathy.

He nuzzled his face into the crook of her neck before softly dragging up his nose until his lips met her ear. "It is...very so," he said in between nipping at her ear. Etain's breath stuck in her throat as heat pooled low within her. "Mmmm, little witch, are you having devious thoughts?"

"And if I am?" she asked, her voice barely audible.

"Then I would wonder if our thoughts aligned," he said, as he picked her up and set her on the table. "Do your thoughts contain anything like this?" he asked, dragging a hand up the inside of her leg while lifting the fabric of her skirt along the way.

"They might," she whispered. The feel of his hand slowly making its way to where she wanted it most, and his gentle nips and kisses along her neck made her skin erupt in gooseflesh. She whimpered when his hand came within mere inches of her core and stopped.

"Hmm. Of course, I can stop if our thoughts are not the same," he teased.

"No! Ciaran, please," she begged.

"Please what, little witch?" he asked with a heated growl softly into her ear.

"Please, I need you." Her body screamed for his touch.

"And what is it you need from me?" he asked, moving his hand infinitesimally closer to her center, making her grip his arms and cry out with need. "Oh, little witch, your torture can end this minute if you only tell me what you need from me." She felt him smile against her throat, enjoying every minute of her growing need.

"I need you inside of me. Now," she demanded.

"I do so love when you are demanding," he said, laughing darkly. She nearly screamed when his fingers finally brushed across her sensitive bud. Two of his thick fingers thrust inside her while his thumb applied pressure to the center of her pleasure. She threw her head back while euphoria took over. "Is my hand what you meant when you said you needed me inside you?" he whispered into her ear.

"Yes... I mean no... Oh gods, Ciaran!" Her mind was a muddled mess of desire, which made it impossible to focus on one single thought.

"There's nothing I love more than hearing you scream out my name just like that, little witch," he said, pulling his hand away from her. She cried out over the absence of his hand, but before she could beg him to bring it back, he parted her legs wide with his body and freed himself, filling her completely. He thrust into her with such force the table made a screech as it moved across the wooden floor.

A low moan ripped from her, which he swallowed as his mouth devoured hers. Keeping one hand braced on the table, he took the other and wrapped it around her hips before saying, "Hold on tight, little witch." She clutched his arms even tighter just as he thrust into her again and then ground against her in the most delicious way. He repeated the action several more times, forcing her pleasure to soar higher as he picked up his pace. All she could do was hold on.

"Ciaran," she moaned.

"Are you going to come for me, little witch? I want to feel you tighten around me as you crash into bliss." With his words, she exploded as she screamed out her release. "Such lovely sounds you make." He slowed his thrusts and let her ride out her pleasure until he pulled out of her. He flipped her around and maneuvered her languid body so her legs were folded beneath her, leaving her entrance at just the right height for him.

"Let's see if you have another in you," he said as his grip dug into her hips, causing her to smack her hands down onto the table in front of her to keep from face planting. He removed one of his hands from her waist and wove it through her hair to pull her head up. Her eyes rolled into the back of her head and her mouth fell open with a silent scream as intense pleasure flooded her. He used the hand in her hair and the one on her hip to command her body. He pulled her into him to meet every one of his thrusts. With each thrust, she could hear the sounds of the table sliding across the floor with a creek.

"Already, little witch? Are you going to come on my cock again so soon?" he crooned at her seconds before she crashed over the edge once more. Her arms became too weak to hold her up, making his hand in her hair the only thing keeping her from smashing face first into the table.

"One more time. I think you have another left in you," he said as he momentarily pulled his hand away from her hip to land a stinging slap to one of her ass cheeks; a cry wrenched from her. She could not decide if it was painful or pleasurable, but she was no stranger to enjoying the two together.

"Ciaran... I... Oh gods... It's too much," she cried, not entirely sure if it was too much or not enough.

"It's not. You have more in you. I can already feel you tightening around me. This time we will come undone together," he said with a grunt, as his punishing pace increased to an impossible speed. She could do nothing but feel as she once again neared the peak of her pleasure. Her body shook on its own just before everything inside her clamped down and she plunged harder than ever into euphoria. It took a second for the sound to accompany her scream. He ground himself into her one last time and she felt him erupt inside of her before he gently released her hair and lowered her to the table. He leaned over her and kissed along her spine as they both regained their breath.

"I think this table is my favorite as well," he said, in all serious-ness making her laugh. Once she could stand again, she righted her clothing and gave the room one last look around. She knew this was the last time she would ever need to return. She looked back at Ciaran and found him looking thoughtfully at the table. Then he touched it and it was gone.

"Where did it go?"

"I was not sure if it belonged in the study or our bedroom. Ultimately, I decided on the study."

"Why?" she asked, not understanding why he would want to have such a rudimentary table in his study, surrounded by all of his fine furniture.

"I enjoy leaving our own story upon the history of your ances-tors," he said, grinning wickedly at her. She threw her head back and laughed; her heart felt light for the first time in years—even if it was only temporary. She shut the door for the last time to her two-room home while also shutting the door on her past, never to look back. Her mate and the Fae Realm held her future, no matter what version of him she got.

He held her hand as they strolled out of her village, uncaring about the gasps and whispers of the villagers. A small face peeked out between the curtains of a slightly larger home than her little cottage. She gave the little girl a small wave, which she returned. When Ciaran smiled at her, her eyes lit up. She gave him a smile in return that was nearly as wide as his own. Etain felt hopeful that not only was there the possibility of a kinder future for Havenston, but for her and Ciaran.

Looking back at the little girl, she thought perhaps the future they could create would have space for another kind of creation. She looked up at Ciaran and nearly laughed when he made a face at the little girl, which made her giggle. Then someone suddenly pulled her away and the curtain was firmly closed behind her. The green of her power swirled within her, the whisper of a possibility. She hoped someday it would become more than a possibility.

Perhaps, if *this* Ciaran was here to stay, someday was not so far away.

Chapter 32
Tatiana
23 Years Later

Tatiana walked down the empty corridor while her mind wove a tapestry of anger and confusion. Where did they all go, and how dare they? The sound of her shoes clicking along the stone tiles beneath her echoed, making it sound like others walked alongside her. She supposed that could be true, considering her mind housed others.

It was tempting to bring Raindal along with her, yet she was still uncertain if he could be trusted. Earlier in their years together, he asked far too many questions about the disgusting creature rotting away under her palace. Her jealousy flared when she thought he, too, would leave her for the wretched being. Now, she thought his questions were a way for him to know how best to please her, but she still had difficulty trusting that to be true.

The way he first hesitated when she asked him to take part rather than observe was hard to look past. His hesitation had been impossible to decipher, as it was rare for his face to show any genuine emotion. She both loved and despised that about him. He never appeared to judge her, but he never appeared not to either.

There was one thing in particular that kept his loyalty in question and it was the way he had looked at her when he first witnessed her deep in conversation with the *whispers*. While he showed no emotion, she had the distinct impression of being studied as if she were a puzzle or experiment to unravel. She did not like the feeling of being so closely observed. Something about that moment still unnerved her.

She turned down another hall and sneered at the ridiculous structures the witches created. Why they would want to live in something so ugly was beyond her. She loved how smooth her palace walls were and how the gold within them gleamed in the sun. *These* walls looked like they were composed of whatever the witches had on hand. It reminded her of one of the human pets she had a while ago, with its patchwork quilt. One wall of this long, suddenly narrow hallway was constructed entirely of frames filled with various art and portraits. While even she had to admit it was impressive how they could find a frame to fill every gap in a way that left no space between them, it still looked cluttered.

If there was one thing Tatiana could not tolerate, it was clutter. If anything was out of place, it made her feel as though everything was sand sifting through her fingers. She needed everything to have a specific place and had beaten many lesser fae and humans in the past for not returning something to the exact spot it belonged. Even if it was barely an inch out of place. She tried once to ignore it, but her eyes kept fixating on the single book not put away in the correct order, and each time her anger grew until it was no longer controllable. There was a place for everything, and it needed to stay in its place. Just like the lesser fae.

She rounded another corner and still could not hear the sound of even one witch occupying this entire coven. This was the third one she had been to, and she feared all the witches had gone somewhere. She felt like something crawled under her skin, and she knew it was because she needed a sacrifice. Yet if she did not find a single witch, who would there be to sacrifice?

"You could kill that foolish fae you have been keeping around. He has a rather deep well of power," the *whispers* suggested. They had never liked her decision to keep a companion. It might be why she had been adamant about having one.

"You wish for me to kill my only companion?" she said out loud. It seemed pointless to keep quiet when it was obvious no one was around.

"You do not need a companion if you have power."

"I am still a female. I require a certain kind of companionship." Her desire resurfaced recently. So much time had passed that it took her a moment to even recognize what it was.

"Well, get on with it. Then kill him to take his power."

"He has started to prove himself, and it is very difficult to find someone trustworthy enough to attend the sacrifices."

"That would be a foolish thing to do. He will try to take power from you for himself."

"How would he even achieve such a feat?"

"There are ways."

"He knows nothing of blood magic. How would he know any way to take it from me or even how to get it himself? I doubt he can even read the language the text is in. You worry too much."

"And you worry too little about everything else besides where your next sacrifice is coming from."

She said nothing in response, refusing to validate their opinion.

He *was* proving himself. He stopped asking so many questions and now waits for her to tell him what she wishes. More importantly, he does not push for anything more. He was learning how she liked her company to behave, and he picked up on every complaint she made, adjusting himself to please her.

The desire to have him please her in other ways was growing.

Her mate had been gone a long time, and she had yet to feel the effects of his absence. She knew it had to be the blood magic and the sacrifices she consumed that sustained her. That was mostly what made her fear not finding a witch to sacrifice—and soon. She did not want to find out if the mate bond would demand her life if she became too weak.

With Reminold's death twenty-three years ago, she never thought it would be possible to want another to touch her. Yet, as the years passed, she began to have the stirrings of desire inside her. Raindal's broad shoulders and feline grace made heat pool low within her core. Golden-red hair and scales that trailed down the sides of his face and disappeared under his shirt made her want to know where those perfect adornments ended. She was getting to where she could no longer satisfy herself, and the thought of Raindal touching and entering her did not make her feel anything but heat.

Perhaps if the mate bond does not take the other mate within a certain period of time, the bond is officially severed. She would likely find out, whether she wished to or not, if she did not find a witch to sate her appetite. The crawling sensation became nearly unbearable every time she thought about what her next sacrifice would feel like.

"*You can always sacrifice the fae. Some of them have relatively deep wells of power. It is not a raw and wild power, so it will not be as clean for the magic, but it will still give you what you seek,*" the *whispers* offered.

"I want a witch."

"*Of course, however, it's not looking as though that will happen anytime soon, and you have a need now. Go back to the palace and find a fae with a deep well or two with deep enough wells.*"

"There are still four more covens left," she said hopefully.

"*Do you honestly expect them to be any different than the last three?*"

268

"We do not know for sure…"

"Well then, come back and look later so that you can have your fix now."

The *whispers* were right. She could not concentrate. If she did not perform a sacrifice soon, she did not know what would happen. She lost touch with reality far more often than ever before, not just when the *whispers* spoke to her. She knew the fog was from the lack of absorbing new power.

Raindal picked up on this. Instead of making her feel bad or treating her as though she were crazy, he would lean in and brush his lips to her ear before softly telling her what she missed. It was a kindness. One that had not gone unnoticed and was another reason she was beginning to trust him even more.

She knew he was ambitious, and elevating him above all others would further his drive. It was better choosing him with his wicked nature than some of these bleeding hearts she had within her court. The council constantly cried to her about an influx in the migration of the lesser fae; some would not stop speaking of housing the vermin.

She told them that if there were too many, then simply take care of them. It took some of them a moment to realize she meant to eliminate them. One had even looked repulsed at the idea; she needed to watch him closely. It would not surprise her if he were a sympathizer or even worse—a rebel.

She had only recently learned about the rebels, but what did she care if a bunch of lesser fae, and possibly even high fae, conspired to overthrow the system? She could control them any time she felt like it. She was not concerned by them, and neither was Raindal.

She ported back to the palace and felt her way through the wells of power within its walls until she located one deep enough to hold her over until she got her hands on another witch. What she would not give to have first found that Walsh witch in the

Human Realm. It still annoyed her that Reminold never informed her of the witch in that stupid little human village he enjoyed tormenting. It was probably because they treated him like a god. He had always taken issue with the way she controlled the Day Court—not him. Being the King of the Day Court meant nothing.

She latched on to the body of the fae she chose, made them stop whatever they were doing, and forced them to walk towards her. As soon as they arrived, she would port and have them on the altar within two breaths. The knowledge she would get her fix soon and the memory of power rushing through her veins made her move to intercept the fae quicker. The sooner she got to them, the sooner she would have that euphoric feeling again. She needed it more than she needed anything else.

She turned a corner of her immaculate and orderly palace and saw her next sacrifice walking towards her. She had never seen this female high fae before, and Tatiana had no idea how long it would take for anyone to miss her, nor did she care. Her eyes were wide with terror, and as Tatiana approached, her fear turned into confusion.

"Hello there, you should know your sacrifice to your court will be appreciated," Tatiana said before placing her hand on the female and porting them to the temple. She released the hold she had over the fae, and not even a moment later, the chains wrapped around her limbs and secured her to the altar.

"My queen, what's happening?" she asked in a shaky voice.

"You are going to do me, and therefore your court, a favor. It's the highest privilege you could ever be given," Tatiana replied sweetly.

"What's the favor?"

"Why, you will be giving me your life source, of course. What else did you think would happen with you chained to an alter." The female began to weep, and Tatiana rolled her eyes at her. "Oh, hush now. If you are quiet, I will make it quick. But I will warn you

—I have discovered a love of carving the flesh from bones. In certain areas, it is far more painful and in others it makes the blood flow quickly, ending your suffering faster. So which will it be?" she asked, secretly hoping the female would make a fuss so that she could have a little fun while she got her fix of power.

When the fae began to thrash and scream on the altar, a menacing smile adorned Tatiana's face. She was going to have some fun, after all. Over the years of carving her sister to ribbons, she discovered how much she enjoyed it. She thought it a form of art—if done precisely. She was looking forward to practicing again.

Her penchant for violence never offended Raindal, and if anything, he was just as disturbed as she was. He, too, discovered how much he enjoyed inflicting pain on the disgusting nymph, and she truly was disgusting at this point. It was even becoming hard to breathe around her. However, as soon as Tatiana carved into the filthy creature, the scent of her bloody flesh masked everything else in the room.

The fact he enjoyed it as much as she did made her even more apt to trust him. She decided she would bring him to her next sacrifice. If he enjoyed torturing her sister so much, he was sure to love this just as much. She wished she had brought him this time and not listened to the *whispers*.

She smiled down at the female. She had a decent amount of power, and the queen could tell the poor thing could not understand why she was unable to access it. "It's strange to feel your power and not be able to touch it. Or at least I would imagine it to be," Tatiana said.

"Why are you doing this?" the fae asked between sobs.

"For more power, why else would I?" she asked. The female must be incredibly foolish to ask such an obvious question.

"Because you are a monster!" the female screamed. That was the wrong choice of words. Tatiana retrieved the little book and the obsidian blade and went back to stand beside the altar. The female continued shouting names while Tatiana wickedly smiled down at her and raised the blade. Rather than slice across her neck and have her death be quick, she sliced along her arms and was pleased to see the fae's power unable to heal the wound.

The chains were spelled to block the power of the ones locked into them, which is why it had been absurd when her sister healed so quickly. This female would not be so lucky—or unlucky, and she was certain Anin would think. Tatiana had done her best to ensure Anin begged the Land to let her go as often as possible.

The yellow blood flowed from the gaping wounds she left in the female's arms. It was not the gush the neck made but a slow and steady flow. She recently began trying her hand at shaving off as thin a slice of skin as she could. It was more complicated than it sounded and required a lot of concentration.

She started in on the female's leg and peeled away a thin layer of her skin while listening to the sweet sounds of her screams. Moments ago, she had screamed at Tatiana in rage, but now she begged the queen to stop and pleaded with the gods to save her.

"No one is going to save you. If you had only stayed quiet, you could be dead already. Instead, I will take my time and peel away an entire layer of your skin until finally taking your life. I have been trying to make it a continual piece from the leg all the way to the wrist, but the curve of the shoulders and dips of breasts do make it more difficult. So, please try to remain still."

The female's terror increased while her cries filled with despair—another sound Tatiana adored. Recently, the sight of blood and peeled skin began making her core clench with need. She really wished Raindal were here. He could sate her need while she continued to carve the female before her.

"Are you playing with your food, Blood Queen?" the *whispers* asked, apparently finding her art amusing.

"I am not a blood queen!" she screamed.

"*Your current actions would say otherwise,*" the *whispers* chided her.

"She's a sacrifice for the greater good of the realm," Tatiana said, fully believing every word she spoke.

"*Then why not just end her, take the power, and be done with the whole thing? You enjoy dragging it out and causing pain.*"

Again, she did not respond to their words. She would not acknowledge nor give any truth to them. She was getting to practice art while doing so for the greater good of the realm. She was a benevolent queen and appreciated the sacrifice the female made for her so that she could continue to hone her skills and grow her power.

What the *whispers* said took the joy out of it, and in her frustration, she broke the line of skin at the junction where the leg meets the hip. She screamed through her teeth and slammed the blade into the fae. Not paying attention to where she buried her blade in her frustration, she became even more enraged when she realized the fae would die quickly now. She removed the blade and dragged it deeply through the neck.

All rage left her at once and was replaced by the euphoria filling her as the fae's power flowed through her veins. She forgot why she was mad to begin with, and she could not for the life of her understand why she had not immediately killed the fae. The sudden shift from within her made her stumble and she landed on top of the now-dead fae.

Giggling, she patted her face and said, "You have made your queen very happy. You should be proud. Although something tells me your queen did not make *you* very happy." She threw her head back and roared with laughter.

Chapter 33
Kes
25 Years Later

Twenty-five fucking years and he was no closer to figuring out the secrets of the moonlight. He thought the goddess had been vague with Ciaran all those hundreds of years ago, but apparently, he had not known the meaning of vague. She had not given him any idea of where to start and only told him to follow the moonlight—whatever that meant—when she gave him this impossible task.

When he was not destroying the Day Court targets the rebel leader supplied him with, he hunted for even the most obscure bit of information. He searched every book in every library across the Night Court and the covens with the help of Anin's sisters. They had yet to find anything resembling or related to a secret about the moonlight. Every time he received a new target, he felt like he was at least helping his mate; it was the best outlet for his anger. Particularly since they had also found nothing to help him break the spell on the hallway that led to Anin.

They were in the palace archives digging through the dusty scrolls, which he knew better than to hold any faith in. The Purge destroyed any information from long ago thanks to one fae king's pride. Beyond that, he was questioning if the moon held any secrets or if there was even a way to negate blood magic to begin with.

He could not say what made him look off into the depths of the other side of the archives, but a tapestry caught his attention, one he remembered looking at with Ciaran twenty-five years ago. He wanted to kick himself when he remembered the hidden room filled with mountains of texts. If he could not find what he searched for there, he would likely never find them anywhere. Then, he would be forced to hunt down the Many Faced Goddess and demand more information. He could be very obnoxious if he needed to be; he had a lifetime of practice.

"I cannot believe I have been so stupid," Kes said, dropping the scroll he had just been holding.

"Well, I cannot say I am shocked, but what makes you so stupid this time?" Lyra asked, her grin faltering once she saw how serious he was. "What is it?"

"Directly below us is a hidden room filled with old texts and artifacts that Ciaran and I stumbled upon the last time we were here digging through the archives. I cannot believe we forgot about it."

"A whole room filled?" Panella asked, an excited gleam in her eyes. The witch loved nothing more than musty old books and the history they held.

"Come see for yourself," he said, walking over to the tapestry, pausing when he saw the ground beneath it free from dust. Surely, after twenty-five years, it would have gathered a decent layer. Pushing the tapestry aside, he opened the door. He took the first few steps before asking the witches, "Well, are you coming or what?" They quickly followed him down the dark, spiraling stairway.

"This is incredibly safe, going down twisting stairs in the

dark," Panella said with no small amount of sarcasm. Kes created a light orb with his power, saying nothing. He actually enjoyed spending time with Anin's sisters. Not only did it make him feel closer to her, but they also harassed him as much as he did them.

They were close to the bottom when he stopped short on the steps, hearing voices from the supposedly forgotten room. Voices he knew all too well.

"...really need to tell him, Ciaran."

"No, I have already told you if fate wants him to find it, he will find his way down here."

"And what do you think he will say when he finds out you have been holding this information from him the entire time he combed through library after library looking for anything to help him decipher what Hecate told him?"

"I do not know, little witch, and I do not care."

"You say that, but you and I both know no matter how hard you try not to care for your cousin, you do." The silence stretched between them before she continued. "Do not look at me like that. You know I am right. We can never look through all of this in a timely manner. I do not understand why we do not at least have the ones we trust the most down here with us. Panella would likely have this place sorted in a fraction of the time we have spent trying to make sense of it all."

"You are the only one I trust," Ciaran said. Kes hated how his cousin's words felt like he had stabbed him through with his shining white sword.

"Ciaran, that is also not true. I do not know why you are being this way. What reason has he or Anin's sisters given to make you find them untrustworthy?"

"I only trust you because I can feel your intentions."

Kes heard a gasp come from Etain.

"So if I were to cut you off from feeling me through the bond, you would no longer trust me?"

"Do not be silly, little witch," Ciaran began.

"Do not 'little witch' me right now, you dense blue idiot," Etain said. Her frustration and anger bled through her words. This was likely not the first time they had this conversation.

"Etain," his cousin growled.

"I dread the day Kes recalls this place. His pain and anger will be a stain upon my soul. Please, stop being so selfish."

"I cannot stop being something that I am."

"Of course you can! You make the choice to stop!" Etain yelled, the sound echoing through the cavernous room.

Several moments passed before anyone said anything. Kes and the sisters silently descended the rest of the stairs, stopping again just before the exit.

"What do you plan to say when he does, remember? It is not if he remembers Ciaran. It is when."

"I will say—"

"What will you say?" Kes asked, stepping out into the torch-lit room. The mated pair's heads whipped to where he stood, and Ciaran's indifference morphed into anger when the sisters stepped out behind him.

"Why would you bring them here?"

"Why would I not? They are the only beings apparently truly helping me."

"Kes—"

"Save it, Etain. The mighty blue one," he gestured to Ciaran, "I have learned to expect his selfishness, but you? I would never have thought you could be so cruel." Perhaps later, he would regret the harsh words he threw at her and the way they caused tears to flow down her cheeks.

"Watch it, cousin. You can be mad at me all you want. However, Etain has been against keeping this secret from the beginning," Ciaran growled at him.

"And yet she still kept it. Even worse, however, you know her and how much she hated keeping it, and yet you still asked it of her. How could you treat your mate like that? I knew you were selfish, but I thought you would never be so selfish when it came to your mate's wellbeing."

"I am not the one making her cry—"

"No, he's right, Ciaran. I told you for years how I hated keeping this secret. It broke my heart not to help Kes and, in turn, my friend. I told you this. I cannot keep doing this, Ciaran. You need to work on choosing better behaviors. You know the difference between right and wrong. Please, Ciaran, please start making the right choices," she pleaded with him.

"Little witch," Ciaran said, softening toward his mate. "There is no true wrong or right. There are only advantages and disadvantages."

"You cannot possibly believe that," Etain said, disbelief coating her words. "I need space," she said, turning to walk towards the stairs. When she drew close enough to Kes, she placed her hand on his arm and said, "I am truly sorry, Kes. I know this is unforgivable, and yet I still hope you find it in your heart—at some point—to do just that." She gave his arm a little squeeze before leaving the space without looking back once. Her footfalls ascending the stairs almost covered the sounds of her sobs. Almost.

Ciaran stared at the exit his mate just disappeared through in confusion. It should not surprise Kes that his cousin truly believed the things he said, and he took Ciaran at face value when he said he thought there was no such thing as right and wrong. Something fundamental broke within him when they were children. Kes had been broken, too, yet his parents had loved him, and it was that distinction that gave Kes morals and the small amount of empathy he contained.

He could not even be mad at Ciaran; it would be pointless anyway. Not sparing him another look, Kes turned toward the closest row of shelves and began looking through them. "Panella, do you think you can work some magic and create a system we can follow?"

"It will not be instant, but I could do it faster if I could bring a few more witches down here with me."

"No." They all turned to look at Ciaran. "Enough beings know about it already. We do not know what information these books hold within them. Nor do we know what kind of power someone could gain and use against us, or even give to the Day Queen."

"Fine," Kes said, barely giving his cousin any of his attention. "Looks like you get us."

"Great, at least Lyra will be of some assistance. I am not sure how much help bird brains can be, but I guess we will find out," Panella said, lighting the mood.

"I assure you, I am quite gifted at everything I do. How hard could this be?"

She only laughed in response. He did not turn when he heard footfalls making their way toward the stairs and then up them. His focus remained solely on locating the information this room hopefully held. He would happily take either the secrets of the moonlight or a way to fight against blood magic. Either option brought his mate back to him.

He would not stop until she was freed.

K indness knew a rebellion was brewing. They could feel the way the air seemed to hold its breath, waiting for the storm to blow in. It was about time.

Kindness spent most of their life within the walls of the palace and saw everything. Every being who looked at them saw exactly what Kindness wanted them to see. Not a single one of them ever looked further, which was for the best. It made it easier for Kindness to move around the palace unhindered.

Kindness knew everything. Kindness even knew that a little queen slept just under their feet. While one queen was being forged from pain and sorrow, another rotted away.

Looks could be deceiving. No one knew that better than Kindness. You always have to look for what resides inside another and not only at the masks they wear. There was more than a plague on the land rotting away the court.

What Kindness knew most of all was that the little queen would be their salvation. She was the light that would illuminate the truth behind all the masks. She just needed to survive long enough to do so.

Kindness knew she would.

Chapter 34
Anin
35 Years Later

The sound of footfalls coming down the hallway ripped her out of the trance-like state she had learned to slip into over the years. She might not know for certain how long had gone by, yet there was no doubt in her mind that years had been stolen from her. Her heart beat erratically, and a cold sweat coated her body as the sound of each step reverberated throughout her. Conditioned to fear the impending steps, her body reacted this way every time.

There was no mistaking who was making their way toward her. No matter how much she tried to pretend the footfalls belonged to anyone else, she knew who they were. The mad queen and her sadistic little pet were both horrible, but in different ways. Her sister wanted to cause her the most pain, which, while abhorrent, also allowed her the chance to slip away into her mind and escape to a place where she could no longer feel pain.

Raindal, however, would in one moment touch her body with gentleness and then turn around to inflict incredible pain the next. In the beginning, she had been so starved for a gentle touch that her mind would not let her escape, wanting to make sure she did not miss any of the softness. It did not matter to her mind that pain would immediately follow.

Now, the idea of any touch made her skin crawl. The moment Raindal knew she was able to hide away from him, he switched up his tactics, earning him adoration from his queen. It was disgusting how he hung on every word Tatiana spoke. He watched her with an intensity that made Anin want to vomit.

The day he touched her in a *different* way, Anin learned what genuine fear really was. He never touched her in a directly sexual manner, but the caresses were suggestive enough to remind her he could. He could take the last shred of herself remaining. The one she had kept hidden away and intact all these years, the one that belonged to her mate. He could completely shatter it—and her in the process. If he did, there would be no version of herself to exist that she could be comfortable with again. However, she knew for certain if he were to act on his threats, his touch promised, there would be no coming back from that.

She tried to control her reactions, but when he would remind her of the power he held over her, she would whimper in fear. Tatiana's eyes would light up each time while Raindal's eyes remained lifeless, convincing Anin he contained no essence of a being within him. Something about being mutilated by a lifeless creature terrified her most of all. He was not doing it out of pleasure or even a desire to please the queen. This was exactly the creature he was on the inside, reflected in his actions.

Anin tried several times to get a reaction out of him, yet each time he only cocked his head to one side and gave her one of his eerie dead smiles. At first, she thought perhaps Tatiana had him under her control, until one day, he took her torture too far, too fast. She lost consciousness and therefore would no longer react to any pain they inflicted upon her. The last thing she remembered was Tatiania yelling at Raindal to stop and the way she raged when he did not. When Anin came to next, she was already healing, sealed up in her little wired cage. He did not mean to, but it had been an act of kindness. They had put her through so much that day, and her sister seemed determined to go longer and take it further.

It was hard to fill her lungs, even though they felt two times smaller. She tried to slow her breaths. She knew it was pointless to panic. What was about to happen would happen regardless of what she did. No matter how hard she tried to reason with herself, her body had been conditioned to respond a certain way.

"Gods, the smell is unbearable. Can we not throw a bucket of water or something on her? I swear, if it gets any worse, I am going to vomit."

"It *is* rather horrific. Are you willing to carry a bucket filled with water all the way down here?"

"I just might. This is disgusting," Raindal said, making the queen burst with laughter.

"She is rather disgusting, yet she resembles the dirt-dwelling creature she truly is more and more each day. I bet that bird of hers would not even want her if he saw her now."

"Lucky for him, they never had the mating ceremony to solidify their bond. There's still a chance for him to reject her," he said, honestly thinking Kes would do something like that. She knew her mate would never, although a small part of her that believed the things they said grew larger with each visit.

"It would be no less than what she deserves for killing *my* mate."

"Where do you wish to start today, my queen?" he asked her, gesturing toward the table of instruments.

"Let's get her on the hook, make her face her sets of wings so she can watch them decay as we remove this newest pair," she said, smiling at Anin, who visibly trembled. There were scales of pain, and having her wings removed was at the top of the list. It was not a wide gap, but she thought it was more painful than having any of her other limbs removed. The only good thing about having her wings cut from her was she immediately passed out. If they started there, it would be incredible pain, but she would fall into oblivion sooner. She did not know which she wanted.

"Are you sure that's where you wish to start?" Raindal asked, likely thinking the same thing.

"No, I think not. The fun would be over far too soon. Still, get her on the hook and maybe inspiration will strike." The bottom of her cage opened, sending her sprawling onto the ground below. Immediately, her body pulsated with thousands of tiny needles as the blood circulated again with the slight movement.

He grabbed her by the hair and dragged her to where the hook hung. She tried to get her legs and arms to work so she could relieve some of the pressure off her scalp, but by the time she could get any of her limbs to move, he was already shackling her wrists and hanging her on the hook by the chain between the two cuffs.

She had long gotten used to the feel of iron burning into her skin and no longer screamed when the shackles locked around each of her wrists. Tatiana had been thrilled the first time they used them. The pain was the most intense when he pulled the rope to hoist her higher, making it so that her feet could not touch the ground. The best she got was brushing her biggest toes against the stone below her, and that usually would not happen until her shoulders stretched to their limits...or worse.

The burn from the iron made her hiss, but like she knew it would, it quickly faded into the back of her mind. The true panic set in as she watched Tatiana peruse the different implements of pain in front of her. Her hand hovered over her new favorite knife she recently acquired. Tatiana enjoyed using it to skin her alive, which was possibly even worse than her wings. She could never reach the point where her body and mind shut down, which left her to begin repairing the damage done to her while she was blissfully unconscious.

Please not that...please not that...please...

Relief settled briefly as Tatiana's hand moved on, and she wrapped her fingers around the handle of a tool with an enormous block of iron on the end. Shockingly, the queen had not yet used that particular tool on Anin yet, even though it sat there since the day the table arrived.

She tried to swallow, but her throat was suddenly thick with fear, making the act impossible. The unknown was perhaps the most terrifying of all. She did not know how this tool was used, and she did not know what the pain level would be. Never had her panic taken her consciousness, but she felt it was close to doing so and begged the goddess to let it.

Tatiana strode slowly towards her, turning the handle so the block at the end spun. She stood in front of Anin who had yet to take her eyes from the iron block, when she said, "Do you know what this is, creature?" When Anin did not answer, she shoved the block under her chin and shoved her face upwards. The burn was excruciating. "I asked you a question!" she yelled.

"N...no," she could barely get the words out. Each time her jaw moved, it pressed further into the block underneath it.

"Perfect," Tatiana said, removing the block. Anin saw some of her skin stuck to it. "Allow me to demonstrate. Raindal, if you would do the honors of holding out her leg."

Oh goddess, she thought she might know where this was going, and her breathing came in short, sporadic bursts which made the mad queen squeal with delight.

Raindal caressed the side of her leg all the way down to her ankle before clamping his hand painfully around it, crushing her bones, and lifting it. Tatiana brought the block up and swung it down, stopping just before her leg. Anin sagged with relief, and she realized a second too late that was exactly what her sister had been waiting for. She quickly raised and swung it down with all her might before Anin could brace herself one more time.

The pain was like nothing else. The pain of broken bones she had felt multiple times, but bones being broken by iron, however, was pure agony. The burn of the iron shot all the way up and down her leg, causing Anin to throw her head back with a scream so intense nothing came out. When the queen brought it down a second time, Anin vomited.

"Disgusting," Raindal said, gagging while the queen laughed.

"Oh, that was fun! Let's do the other one," Tatiana said.

Raindal dropped the leg and allowed it to swing toward the ground. She knew it was bad when her toes scraped the stone below. After years of this kind of treatment, she knew better than to look.

She flinched when Raindal softly touched her other leg, causing gooseflesh to prickle across her skin before he clamped down on her ankle and roughly pulled it up for the queen. Tatiana wasted no time bringing the iron down on her second leg. The pain radiated throughout her whole body, and she could not focus on any one feeling to breathe through it. She barely noticed when the second strike came. Raindal released her leg, and it swung to hang next to the other, both sets of toes now scraping the stone.

"Your turn, my pet," she said to Raindal. He walked to the table and picked up the smallest, yet sharpest, blade like he always did. He never chose anything else. She always knew the kind of pain he would inflict, and yet, somehow each time she felt it more acutely.

"Are you still with us, princess?" he asked her, gripping her burned chin in his hand and making her look him in the eyes.

When he first started calling her 'princess,' the queen had raged until he told her he was mocking Anin with the title. She giggled like a youngling each time he used his little pet name.

"I would hate for you to check out already. Ahh, there she is," he said when her eyes rolled to meet his.

He started the same way he always did. He slid the blade underneath one of her long, sharp nails before pulling it out, only to move on to the next. He would not stop until he collected all of them. After that, he severed every tendon, making her unable to do anything but hang there limply. Soon after, her shoulders would dislocate. This was always the way he worked, and he never deviated from it.

There was no knowing how long she hung there and endured the slices. At some point, Tatiana joined in and peeled the skin from her. She begged her mind to let her drift away, and perhaps it finally listened, because after a while, she realized there was no fresh pain. The pounding of her blood rushing through her veins, along with the thundering of her heart caused by the pain, always made her deaf to anything else at some point during their visits. As the cacophony within her silenced, a new sound greeted her.

She could hear the slapping of skin coming from behind her, combined with the queen's moans of pleasure. They were fucking behind her while she hung there in bloody tatters. The thought made her want to vomit again. She knew they were depraved, but this was an entirely new level.

The slapping increased, and she tried to block out the wet sounds accompanying them. Tatiana's moans grew louder, and she screamed Raindal's name multiple times. She could hear him grunting, and the sound was one of pain, and that made her nearly smile. She hoped it was painful for him, but at the very least, it was funny that a male as self-assured as him would make such ridiculous noises during sex.

The slapping suddenly ended when the queen screamed out a final time, and Raindal groaned his release. She was shocked when she had to hold back a giggle at the sound. Pleasure seemed to pain him, and she could not think of anything more fitting for a creature like him. Her little personal joy did not last very long. Tatiana came to stand in front of her—completely naked—and cocked her head to the side before she smiled.

"Did you think I would not notice you, little lesser fae whore?" she asked sweetly. Anin's brows scrunched as she tried to figure out what her sister was talking about. "I see the way you react to his touch." Tatiana leaned forward and dragged her hand up the inside of her thighs, gathering their mixed fluids dripping down them. She brought her hand to Anin's face and wiped it across her cheek as she said, "This is the closest you will get to pleasure from him, you disgusting lesser trash."

Anin was appalled, yet at the same time, relieved. The queen had basically declared that he could never touch her in that way.

Raindal returned her to her cage, and she silently thanked the goddess that they had forgotten their original plan to remove her wings. As soon as they secured her in the cage, they wasted no further time on her. Raindal said something about the smell again, but Anin was barely clinging to consciousness and was unable to process anything else when oblivion found her. She sighed in relief as everything went black.

The sound of shuffling footsteps approached, pulling her back to consciousness and the pain engulfing her body. She did not recognize these steps and was terrified to find out what was coming for her. The steps were slow and slightly dragged along the stone of the hall. She held her breath as the door slowly opened, and a stooped, cloaked figure entered her cell.

"Hello, little one," a rasping voice said.

Chapter 35
Ciaran
42 Years Later

He watched as the amber liquid sloshed around the cut-glass tumbler. He could not remember how many he had already consumed; however, if the empty bottles strewn haphazardly throughout his study were any indication, it was far too many. He told himself, "If it was good enough for his mother, it was good enough for him." Besides, he needed to numb himself before he stepped a foot back into *that* room.

He tossed the liquid back and grabbed an unopened bottle. Taking it and his glass with him, he ported to his father's study. It had been a long time since he returned. The place held too many long-ago memories filled with torment. He did his best to keep his mind on the reason he was there in the first place and not allow it to go digging through its recesses to bring up things better left forgotten.

The last time he was here, he had been looking for anything his father might have possessed about the family curse. He did not allow himself to spend more than a few moments searching through all the books his father left behind that still lined the shelves. If he were honest, he could not really call what he did a 'search.' At best, he took an extended glance. He convinced himself if his father possessed anything regarding the curse, Ciaran was bound to know about it.

The amount of rants his father forced him to witness was excessive. He would have surely waved any text he found containing answers within their pages around during any of them. His father was incapable of not mentioning the curse at least once per night. Typically, all he did was spew vitriol at the witch who cast the curse to begin with. At the time, it was the singular thing his father said he could agree with. Now, though, knowing that the witch was also responsible for his mate's existence made it hard to be angry any longer.

He needed to protect Etain, and nothing else mattered. He knew what it was to be enslaved within his own body. To feel his power and magic and yet not be able to access them. To have his own thoughts and yet not be able to voice them. To be forced to hold one position for too long, his power unable to ease the pain. It had been the worst form of torture. Not even the carvings Ciaran gave to his "guests" came close to being as horrific.

He would never let another being take his control away from him the way his father had. More importantly, he would never let it happen to his mate. It was bad enough fearing his own enslavement, but if the queen's magic took Etain, he would not survive it. She was too good for something that dark to befall her. It did not matter what he had to do or who he had to hurt; he would never let that happen to her.

His father's obsession had been the never-ending quest for more power, and Ciaran hoped his shelves would contain the secret to absorbing more power. Several years ago, the thought occurred that if he had enough power, he might be able to create some kind of shield for himself and Etain. Or he could create some kind of barrier to keep the queen far enough away from them.

Time seemed to be a loose concept inside the walls of his father's study. He was not sure how long he searched, but when he looked up for the first time, it was because his bottle was once again empty. It surprised him to see books strewn about the once-tidy space. They looked like they had been thrown, but he could not remember doing so.

He called another full bottle to himself and quickly let the search take control of his every thought and action. The room held echoes of his past, and the longer he stayed within its walls, the louder the echoes became. He heard his father's voice yelling incoherently to some invisible entity only he could see. It sounded so real that it jerked him out of his own mania to look around, searching for the ghost of his father.

A damp coldness encompassed him, and he could not shake the feeling that his father was there, staring at every single movement he made. The hairs on his neck stood on end when he thought he could even feel him breathing, as if he were standing behind him, looking over his shoulder. He shook his head several times, attempting to dislodge the feeling, and poured himself another glass. Perhaps this was why his mother had always been drinking. This room had a way of messing with your mind.

The next time he came to, he could have sworn he saw his father pacing out of the corner of his eye. Back and forth on the same path he had always taken. The rug still held the proof of his repetition. His breathing became quick and shallow when he saw himself standing in the corner as a youngling. His body contorted into whatever baffling position his father decided he would enjoy looking at that night. He could see the sweat dripping down his much younger face. It took little effort to remember the pain those positions caused.

His wings were out, and he stood on the tips of one foot's toes, looking as though he were about to take flight. The unevenness of his wings made the view even more ridiculous. He had no way to counterbalance his weight, and, locked in place by his father's will alone, he maintained that position. Without being able to access his power, his body was unable to heal rapidly, and it took—at best—a few moments before the ache would set into his muscles. The pain increased with every strained breath he took until finally his extremities would fall asleep, only to once again become the stinging pain of a thousand needles stabbing him.

Pouring himself another glass, he turned away from the corner his father had called his "art display". Several books later, he was once again pulled from his frantic search. The lingering smell of one of the many noxious liquids his father always had bubbling in different glass beakers, some over flames and others infused with air, was too hard to ignore.

His father's study always had this smell that caused the back of his throat and nose to burn. It amazed him how his father never seemed to notice. The nights when he was testing out new experiments were possibly the worst in Ciaran's memory.

He was frozen into whatever position his father decided for the night. Then, with each new liquid his father created, he would turn to him with a smile that haunted his sleep for decades after. Younger Ciaran would begin to panic, making it impossible for him to listen to whatever it was his father was creating. There was only one thing he could think of the entire time—a mental game attempting to prepare himself while begging the gods to free him from his curse.

Every time his father slowly strode towards him with a small glass containing whatever concoction he had just created, Ciaran would scream "no" repeatedly within his mind. He was certain his father could hear him. The more he screamed, the wider his father's grin became. The way his small body could quiver without movement only added to his terror. He knew there was no escaping whatever awaited him inside the small glass.

His father enjoyed testing his creations on him. He never knew what they were meant to do, but apparently his father did because he would note the way Ciaran's skin would melt or boil. Or, even worse, when his natural blue skin would grow increasingly darker until eventually turning to nothing but dust. His father would laugh as he blew away the section of what was once a piece of Ciaran. That always seemed to be a success to him.

The pain was something Ciaran could never forget. It was like being eaten away cell by cell; each one swiftly decayed while screaming in pain as the life drained from it. Not even the substances that made his skin drip off his bones were as painful.

He would never be able to accurately describe it if he ever tired —not that he ever had. No one knew about that part of his life. He thought he had buried the memories far enough down that they would never surface again. Yet something about this room seemed to drag them out kicking and screaming to the front of his memory.

He poured himself another glass, surprised when nothing came out. He did not recall finishing the bottle. Calling another to him, he decided against using the glass. He brought the bottle to his mouth and took a long, deep pull, swallowing several times. When he brought the bottle back down, he nearly dropped it at the sight that greeted him.

His mother sat in the lounge chair across from where he sprawled on the ground, surrounded by books opened to various pages that he did not recall reading. She wore that eerie blank look, the way she always had, with that empty smile plastered across her face. The only difference was this time when he looked into her eyes, identical to his own, he could have sworn he saw awareness within them.

Had they always been like that, or was this something new his mind was creating to torment him? The way the gold liquefied and swirled aggressively within her eyes did not match the smile or the way her hand continued to lift the wine to her mouth. However, now that he was looking, it did not appear to be any wine he knew of.

The liquid was black and seemed to move into her mouth on its own, reaching up from the depths of the glass to flood her mouth. With each drink she took, he watched her eyes go from boiling rage into the sharpness that made him wonder if his own eyes did the same when in pain.

Was this a memory or a spectral his mind created to torture him? As if being in this room alone was not torture enough. He could not help but think back to his earliest years and try to compare the vision before him with visions of his memories; however, no matter how hard he tried to focus on any of them, the best he got was a fuzzy outline of a female with glowing golden eyes.

Had that been the reality of his mother's situation? Had he been too young to comprehend the battle his mother fought every night? He recalled thinking several times that his father must have done something to her. Eventually, he decided that was something he had made up to convince himself that at least one of his parents cared for him.

It was a foolish thing to think, and the older he got, the further he convinced himself there was not a soul who cared what happened to him. It was too late now to consider anything else a possibility, and he knew it was more than likely he concocted this ghost of his mother from the desires of the youngling he once was.

While he could remember reading none of the texts discarded around him, somehow he was certain not a single one of them contained any of the information he was frantic to find. He pulled the bottle back up to his mouth and drained the remainder before he got up and threw it across the room, passing through the image of him posed in the corner and shattering on the wall behind him. All these books and not a single one told him how to increase his power. If he were going to find what he sought anywhere, surely it would be in his power-hungry father's study.

Getting up, he walked to the next shelf, still full of books, and began pulling them down. He just needed to know his father's secret. He needed power—needed it more than anyone else did. He would happily take the power from others and feed it to himself.

He was aware he sounded like his father, but he told himself they were not the same. While they were both ruthless and had no issues harming others in their quest to get what they wanted, Etain was the difference. His father only looked to enhance his own power for personal gain. Ciaran could not say he was not also looking to enhance his power for his own gain, but mostly he was determined to protect his mate. He could not protect himself from enslavement when he was a youngling, but he would rather die than allow the same fate to befall Etain. No. He would do whatever it took. If that meant becoming the one being he swore to himself he would never be—so be it.

He heard multiple people speaking softly and looked around frantically, searching for his mind's latest scene it wished to torture him with. His brows furrowed when he saw nothing, yet continued to hear soft words being whispered. They sounded far away—too far for him to make out whatever it was they were saying. The closer he listened, the clearer the *whispers* became.

Icy dread seeped down his spine. He knew what this was; it had finally come for him. The disease plaguing his line for generations had arrived to rot his mind—just like it had done to his father and his father before him. The voice became solid and yet sounded like it was echoing inside his mind. It was like being in a large, empty room while listening to multiple beings saying the same thing at the same time. It was distracting.

He could hear what they were saying, yet he refused to acknowledge them. He would not let the disease rot away his mind. No, he refused; there was no time for that. He had a mate to protect before he could surrender to the disease he could feel, even now, gripping onto his mind. From this moment on, he would ignore them. He was strong enough to deny them, and he would win this battle.

The laughter echoing inside his head promised a different outcome.

Chapter 36
Etain

53 years later

E very time Etain opened the door to what was once an
unused ballroom, now a thriving city, she was amazed. It's
the main reason she preferred to walk the streets of
Witch City rather than port. Over the past fifty-three years, it has
changed countless times. She found something new each time she
walked through the streets.

The witches never did anything in a traditional fashion. Much
like the Silver Moon Coven, the city looked like it should be
impossible to stand, and yet it did—with the help of magic, of
course. On either side of the ground floor street, the individual
coven's primary spaces for their night-to-night living were
accessible.

While those were impressive on their own, the real stars of the
city were the hundreds of individual homes stacked on top of each
other. Many of them resembled her little two-room home in
Havenston, while others were whimsical, more akin to the Many

Faced Goddess' mushroom hut. And just like the goddess' home, these might look one way on the outside, yet when you walked in, a grand multistory creation greeted you. The impossible stacks still make the human side of her brain stare in disbelief. Some turned into towers leaning heavily to one side, and others rose in a zigzag so high you could not see them from where Etain stood.

Walking down the cobblestone paved road, she looked up for any new bridges or stairs that had sprouted since yesternight. Without fail, she could always find a new path connecting the witches' homes to those from other covens. They made some of them of rope and others of stone. Many of them curved in extreme angles to avoid other bridges, while others were built off of an existing one. The random pattern they created was backlit by a ceiling spelled to mimic the exact way the sky looked in the borderlands at any given time. If there were any architectural rules in the Fae Realm, the witches have definitely shunned them.

The doors to the new, hopefully temporary, Silver Moon Coven reminded her of the carved wooden doors to their library in the Borderlands. They were large and made of thick wood with an intricate design of the sun on one side and the moon on the other. She always felt the need to run her fingers across the smooth, carved surface before pushing the doors open.

The coven was busy. Younglings were in between lessons, and many witches were rushing from one side of the coven to the other. No matter how much of a hurry they were in, they each stopped to say hello; the younglings gawked at her. She liked to make a point of saying hello to each group of younglings and always found it amusing the way they tripped over their words trying to form a response. Sometimes, she would let the smallest amount of her raw power out so that her hair swam about her. It was a simple trick, but it made the youngest of them excited. What they did not know was how much joy their little faces brought her.

She made her way up and down halls and stairs through the

maze of the coven until she reached Galetia's study. Letting herself in, she made herself comfortable while waiting for her great-aunt to return. The room had become a second home to her after spending so many hours per night there.

When she started learning about her powers so many years ago, she thought it would only take a few years to master them. She laughed, remembering how naïve she had been. A half century later, she felt like she had only scratched the surface. Etain still had no control over the dark shade power within her that was responsible for her visions and wings. She had yet to see her strange wings since the first—and last—vision during their mating ceremony. She wished nightly for one that would help her friend.

Touching the amulet around her neck, she was grateful for the conduit. It had allowed her to access her dark shade power. She might have no control over it, but at least she could access it now. Becoming proficient in something that had not existed in generations and having no living witch able to mentor her was difficult. To make matters worse, there were limited texts available. Yes, she was grateful to have it; however, it did not help her as much as she thought it would, which left her feeling disappointed.

Her color power, while still challenging, was far more manageable. Between Galetia and Ciaran's teachings, she's the most proficient with her blue power, though calling herself a warrior was still a stretch. Her orange, creative power was the one she reached for the most. It was the one she had no problems accessing with little thought. Be it a problem she needed to solve or a new spell she was creating, her orange power was quick to surface.

Where she loved her orange power, she shied away from her purple. Her intuition was strong even in the Human Realm, and with the addition of her purple power, it was uncanny. Every time she accessed it around Ciaran, warning bells sounded like an alarm within her mind. Her regular intuition was screaming when it came to her mate. She was not prepared to hear what her amplified intuition had to say just yet.

She might not reach for her purple around Ciaran, but she had no issues calling on the red. Heat engulfed her when she thought about the way she practiced that particular color, the same her face likely now wore. Then she remembered how long it had been since she last had the opportunity and her body temperature fell alongside her face.

"Hello, dear," her great-aunt said cheerfully as she entered her study, until her eyes landed on Etain's face. "Is everything okay?"

"What? Oh, yes, of course," Etain said, waving off her concern. "I am just ready to get started."

Galetia eyed her for a moment, seeing through her lie. "If you say so, my dear, but know you can always talk to me about anything," she said, coming to sit beside Etain. Grabbing her hands within her own, Galetia gave them a quick squeeze of reassurance. "Shall we get started?"

Over the next several hours, Etain stumbled through the simplest parts of the spell they were working to create. She usually excelled at spell work. It was so similar to the way she prepared tinctures for the people of Havenston that she took to it instantly, with very little instruction. Now, she was so distracted that she was skipping steps and knocking over ingredients. She even forgot to call on her orange power. Thoughts of Ciaran and the male he was becoming kept invading her mind, which made it impossible to focus on anything else.

"Etain, what is it? This is not like you. I can feel your distress radiating from you," Galetia asked, searching her eyes for answers as her brows knitted together in concern.

"Oh, nothing I should bother you with," she said, while desperately wiping the evidence of her sorrow away.

"Do not be silly, my dear. You are never a bother," she said, once again taking Etain's hands in her own. The action always brought a sense of comfort she had not felt since her mother's death.

"Ciaran," she said with a sigh. "Something is happening to him."

"What do you think it could be?" her great-aunt asked, expression open and void of judgment.

"That's the thing I do not know, and every time I ask him, he tells me I am worrying over nothing. Though it's not nothing. I can see a change in him. It was slow for a while and there were only a few things that I was concerned about, but now..." she said, voice shaking with the emotions she was trying to contain. "It's nearly all the time. He spends most of his time alone, and when we are together, it's like something is living under the surface of his skin. He stares off at things I cannot see, and the amount he drinks is staggering." The wine became a constant companion several years ago. She did not like the version of him it let out.

"That is concerning," her great-aunt said, "however, my dear, you must remember you cannot change another. It's up to them to decide if they wish to do so or not. The only thing you can do is decide what you are willing to live with. If their actions do not align with your needs, you must do whatever is necessary to protect not just your mind and body, but your heart as well. Sometimes protecting yourself from the one you love is harder than forcing yourself to live with a behavior that is harmful to you."

"I know you are right, but I love him with all that I am," Etain said through a sob, losing the battle with her emotions. "We already shut each other out through the mate bond more often than not. It breaks my heart. I do not know what would break it more, living a life without him or living one with the fae he is becoming. I want to save him from this destructive path he's walking, but he will not take the hand I am offering." She did not know what plagued him, making it impossible to help him fight his demons.

307

"Of course you want to save him. He's your true mate. Nothing either of you do will ever change that. However, it does not change the fact you can do no more than set your boundaries, and if he cannot respect them, your first responsibility is to yourself. You can love him, and you can encourage him, but you cannot change him."

"What if he becomes this being I cannot live with?" she asked. Finally, asking the question, she had been too afraid to voice—afraid to give life to her fears.

"You can love someone the way you love Ciaran, yet you must love yourself just as much. You can love someone and despise them at the same time. Emotions are never that simple. Just because you love someone does not make you blind to their actions. You can love someone and still hate being around them," she said, the truth of it echoing through Etain's mind.

"I *am* starting to hate being around him," she said in a near whisper. She never wanted to admit that to herself, let alone another.

"Etain, you must decide what your limit is and you must do whatever it takes to protect yourself. I do not mean to make you feel any more pressure, but you have thousands of witches looking at you to keep them safe. How can you do that if you do not protect yourself?" the head witch asked gently. She was right—of course she was. Etain had more than just herself to consider.

"It has to get better, right? Fate would never put us together just to tear us apart, would it?" she asked, hope woven through each of her words. She was counting on fate.

"Fate is fickle. It has more to consider than the simple wants and desires of a single being. That is not to say it will not get better. It is quite possible this is just a bump in your long lives together," she said, with a small, sympathetic smile.

"How will I know if he goes too far?" Etain asked. She could never see clearly when it came to her mate.

"Only you can answer that question, my dear. There will either come a time where he comes back to you or there will be something he is willing to do that will make you recoil. Then you will know what your hard line is," she said, sounding significantly more confident than Etain felt.

"It will get better. I know it will." She told herself that if she said it enough times, it would be true.

"Have you tried using your purple power to see if you could make sense of this whole situation?" she asked logically.

"No, I am afraid," Etain said, looking away. She felt the heat of embarrassment color her cheeks.

"You do not want to look and find something you do not wish to see until there is no choice but to see it?" Galetia asked. She was grateful for the compassion and the lack of judgment. She thought this should be easy enough, and yet when it came to Ciaran, nothing seemed to be easy.

"Yes. Does that make me a bad ruler?" She was still trying to fill the role of queen adequately, and yet she felt she could do nothing right. This was just another mark against her. Perhaps the Night fae's opinion of her was accurate after all.

"Not at all. It is always hardest to see the worst in the ones we hold dearest. There always comes a time when you cannot ignore it any longer, and that is the point where you have to decide if you will turn a blind eye or if you will stand by your own convictions."

Etain stared out the window overlooking the city street below. Her aunt was right, of course. She only hoped when the time came, she was strong enough to do what needed to be done. However, more than anything, she pleaded to the goddess for it to never come to that. She would not come out the other side of a choice like that fully intact.

Chapter 37
Council Member

60 Years Later

T he council member visited his mate whenever he found himself free from his responsibilities. He sent him a scroll and waited for him at their secret meeting place. It was within the rundown shacks the lesser fae used to build their make-shift quarter. It was a sad existence, and he hated that Balthier would accept none of the help he tried to give to him and his mother. His response was always the same: "If it is good for the rest of the lesser fae, then it's good enough for us."

He was still trying to convince most of the council to provide housing. The nymphs could only do so much. The entire community relied on them to grow the vines that held everything together. It made the place look far happier than it actually was.

The fae that called this place home were exhausted and broken. Every single one of them had been forced into a deal—the majority of them horrible. Even their younglings were not free from making the required deal. He found that to be particularly distasteful, even prior to knowing his mate was a lesser fae. Younglings could not choose their own lives and depended completely upon their parents.

He was ashamed that, before Balthier came into his life, he had not seen a problem with the way the system preyed on the lesser fae. He had honestly never thought much about the lesser fae in general. Now that his eyes were wide open, it was all he could see. There was no choice for the lesser fae that crossed through their gates. They would have to take their chances with either the rot, or one of the more northern cities, which was not truly an option.

The high fae along the roads to the northern part of the Day Court delighted in hunting and capturing the lesser fae to sell them to high fae. He had thought nothing about any of this prior to Balthier coming into his life. He always thought it was the risk the lesser fae took when they crossed into the high fae territory. It was as though he had thought they were not true members of the Day Court.

Concern was growing when more than several minutes went by and Balthier had still not joined him. There was no way he could go search him out. A high fae coming into the lesser fae quarter to search for one particular fae was highly unusual. He could do nothing that drew attention to him. The last thing he needed was the other higher fae asking questions and scrutinizing his actions. The sacrifices he had already made were too great for him to take any risks.

They had put things in place to set up the sadistic high fae that held the bargain with his mate. If they eliminated him, Balthier would be free of the bargain. Then, he could make a new bargain with his mate. He could finally protect him and have Balthier with him in the palace.

All the other council members had a lesser fae they sent to do their bidding. Things were finally falling into place. This particular male happened to be favored by the queen, making it more complicated than the others he had removed. He was so close, and he thought it was worth every risk. Balthier, however, did not.

There was a serious problem brewing. The high fae being targeted by the rebels were lining up the lesser fae they held bargains with and beating each of them, trying to find out any information about those responsible. None of them had said anything yet, although he thought it was only a matter of time. They could only take so much, and he could not blame them if they did. They did not heal at the same speed as the high fae, and many had even made threats of violence against the lesser fae's younglings. He was doing everything he could to help the rebel cause in his political warfare without drawing too much attention to himself.

He was about to send another spelled scroll when the door opened and his mate stepped into the small one-room hut. He could tell Balthier was angry with one glance. His eyes scanned him, looking for any fresh injuries, and found none; at least not this time. It was not uncommon for Balthier to show up with new bruises or bandages on him. More than once he had schemed to take care of a high fae that dared put their hands on his mate.

Blocking each other through the mate bond had become a necessity. Between the nature of the situations the council member put himself in and the beatings his mate was taking, they needed to block each other to prevent the other from reacting. He hated it, and he knew Balthier did, too.

"You look well," the council member said, smiling warmly at his mate and attempting to embrace him.

"Oh, do I?" Balthier asked, putting up a hand that prevented him from getting any closer.

"Balthier..."

"Cut the shit," he said, crossing his arms over his chest and never moving far from the door. "It's gone too far and you know it.

The pain you are putting us both through is not worth it. I do not know how much longer I can take it." He could see the toll it was taking on his mate. Dark circles under his eyes only seemed to grow darker each time he saw Balthier.

"My love," he tried, "you know there is nothing that is either too far or too much if the result is a real life together. Being together without worrying about someone discovering us and being able to announce to the realm you are my mate makes everything worth it." The council member fully believed every word he said.

"What will be left of us when that time comes, assuming it ever comes at all?" Balthier snapped at him.

"We will have the rest of our lives to figure that out. We *will* be together. Fate would not have sent us down this path of pain and suffering if it did not intend for us to be together in the end," he said, trying to reach out to Balthier again.

"Fate!" he yelled as loudly as he dared without getting them discovered and batted his hand away. "You put too much faith in something so fickle and ever-changing."

"Of course, I do. If fate did not intend for us to be together, what purpose did it have in bringing us together to begin with? I know all of this was meant to happen. We are fated to topple the system and bring in a new era for the lesser fae." That had to be true. He was unwilling to believe anything else was possible.

"You are more concerned with your political games than you are about us actually surviving, let alone being together in any capacity," he said to him with a glare.

"Balthier, you know that's not true." He tried once more to reach out but dropped his hand to his side when Balthier moved just out of his reach. "My life had no purpose until you came into it. You were the catalyst that pushed me into action. Everything I do is for us to have a real life together."

"Save it," Balthier said before swiftly turning on his heels and exiting the small room. The council member wanted nothing more than to chase after his mate, but that was not an option for him.

He knew Balthier was hurting, but it crushed him not to have the support of his mate. What he was doing was the most dangerous and difficult thing of his life. It was worth never having a life together than only ever having a partial life forever. They have each sacrificed too much to give up now. Beyond that, he did not think there was any going back. They were in too deep. At this point, if they stopped, it would mean at least one, and therefore both, of their deaths.

When the time finally came, and they were on the other side of this part of their lives, he knew they would both be thankful for the sacrifices they made. Everything would be worth it for them to have true happiness. Even if Balthier could not see the image of the future that the council member painted, he would see it for both of them. It would be worth it; he had no doubts.

Only determination.

Chapter 38
Kes
67 Years Later

"**I**s this really the best we could find?" Kes asked, scrunching his nose at the pitiful-looking recruits.

"Apparently," Lyra said, not sounding any more impressed than he did.

"Well, that is rather disappointing. I was not expecting perfection. I do not think it is possible twice in a lifetime after all," he said dramatically.

"You never cease to amaze me with how highly you think of yourself," she said, looking at him sideways.

"Ah, but I *do* amaze you."

"Wow," she said, drawing out the word. "Just when I think you cannot possibly become more obtuse, you have to go and prove me wrong."

"I do love exceeding expectations." He hoped his smirk hid the darkness consuming him from within. He needed his mate—they all needed her. The spark from within Lyra and Panella was slowly being extinguished as too much time went on. She would bring the light back. Anin was their light.

"Well, you certainly do that. However, in this case, I am not convinced it's the accomplishment you seem to think it is," she said, keeping up the facade they silently agreed upon years ago.

"An accomplishment is an accomplishment, little chick," he said in a sing-song voice.

"Will you stop calling me that already?"

"And miss the opportunity to see the face you make every time I do? Not likely," he said, grinning at her.

"You are insufferable," she said, crossing her arms and shaking her head at him.

"So I have been told. Another accomplishment in my humble opinion," he said, clasping his hands at his chest and smiling at her with an all too innocent look.

"There is not a humble bone in your body," she said, cocking an eyebrow at him.

"No, what a pointless thing to have. Well, let's give these new recruits a warm welcome. What do you say?"

"Kes, in what realm is what's about to happen to them *warm*?"

"I do not know...their blood?"

"Stars! You are twisted," she said, laughing.

"Perhaps." He shrugged. Clapping his hands together, he yelled, "Line up!" He shook his head as they scrambled to form a line. "Gods, if they cannot even do this..."

"It will just be that much more fun training them. Do you think any of them will cry?" Lyra asked a little too eagerly.

He looked at her and put his hand to his chest while gasping and pretending to be shocked.

"And you called me twisted!" he said with mock horror.

"Oh shut up, bird beast," she said, rolling her eyes, which just made him laugh, or what passed for a laugh from him these nights.

"Not all of you will make it through to the end, becoming Silent Shadows. Not all of you will even make it through the night.

I would bet at least three out of the twelve of you will drop out before the night is over." He wanted to laugh when they all looked amused. None of them thought it could be that bad; definitely not bad enough to quit after night one. He could guess who the three would be. It was always the ones you would least expect.

"Tonight, we will run you through a series of tests that will push you to your limits. If we do not shove you off the cliff, we will not know how to train you properly."

"I hope the cliff is figurative," a small witch in the back said. Lyra cocked an eyebrow at her and she raised her hands in surrender, promptly shutting her mouth.

"You need to forget everything you think you know, because it's garbage and there is no place for trash amongst the Silent Shadows," he said, and a large Night fae in the front row snorted. "Is there something funny, tiny?" The male scowled at his nickname. "Because while I am the funniest being you will ever meet—"

"Debatable," Lyra said under her breath.

"I happen to know, at that moment, I was indeed not funny. So please, share with the class what was so amusing, tiny."

"I was trained by the best in the court," he said, huffing his chest out with pride.

"You see, that is just not possible."

"I am not lying. My father paid a hefty amount of gold to be trained by them."

"There is a slight problem with your statement. I was not the one that trained you, therefore it could not have been the best in the court." The male scoffed, disbelieving his claims.

"There always has to be one," Lyra groaned.

"Yes, and what have I told you about that?" he asked, just low enough for only her to hear.

"Always assert your dominance early."

"Exactly," he said to her. Returning to the fae and witches standing in front of them, he said, "Alright tiny, come prove yourself then. If you have been trained by the best, then you should have no issue holding your own against Lyra, who I have trained. I will warn you though, if you have miscalculated, do not be surprised when not only your body is broken, but your ego is beyond repair."

"She's just a witch. She has nothing on a fae," he said, smirking.

"Well, if I am 'just a witch', as you say, quit running your mouth and get over here. Show us these incredible skills your father threw away his gold on. You are wasting all of our time by yammering away over there. I am thinking you like the sound of your voice more than Kes does."

"Why, Lyra," Kes said with a dramatic gasp, and laid his hand across his heart. "I am offended that you could ever think a thing like that. No one loves the sound of their own voice more than I do."

The male charged at Lyra, intending to prove himself while anger blazed in his eyes. He had a lot to learn if he was going to make it through the first night. Kes had him pegged from the beginning as one of the three they would not see tomorrow.

Lyra waited until the last minute. When he pulled back to swing at her as he charged, she ducked under his arm, stuck her foot out, and then shoved him from behind, sending him sprawling to the ground. She wasted no time grabbing his wrist and wrenching his arm behind his back while kneeling on his thick neck. It was over so quickly that if you had blinked, you would have missed it.

The male began to cry, and Lyra grinned at Kes when she said, "Guess there's crying after all."

He threw his head back and roared with laughter. She got off the male who stood and ran for the exit, not looking at anyone.

"Now do you understand why I said forget everything you

know? You know nothing from this moment on, is that clear?" he asked the remaining eleven recruits.

"Yes!" they all said, loudly and in unison.

They spent the next several hours pushing each of them well past their limits. It surprised him when only one more dropped out halfway through. He thought the smallest of the witches could not cut it, but if Etain had taught him anything, it was not to underestimate a tiny witch.

After they watched the new recruits drag themselves out of the training room, they called the final three trainees from the very first group of recruits they began training years ago. It was time for their last test. They were dressed in the customary all black and wore heavy black cloaks to blend into the shadows.

"Little chick, you look so adorable in your black cloak," he said while fluttering his lashes at her.

"Oh, shut up. Just because you do not need to wear one does not mean it is immediately something to harass me over. I happen to like the cloak. I enjoy the way it flutters when I fly through the air on my staff."

"And you call me dramatic? Ms. flutter—" he laughed as he ducked out of the path of her throwing blade she directed right at his head.

"Your mission is to destroy as many of the targets on the scroll I just sent each of you throughout Daybreak. Lyra and I will watch from up high, keeping track of how many each of you take out. As always, if you are caught, no matter if you escape, you are out. The one to destroy the most targets wins the game."

This group would all make it through, and it would be a close game. They did not know it yet, but they were all graduating once they came back successful. "You each have a different starting location from outside of Daybreak City. Wait there till I send you a scroll that says 'Kes is the best.'" He heard Lyra groan. "Let's go have some fun." All three of them smiled and broke off to make it to their starting points.

Kes ported him and Lyra to the highest peak of the palace. They could watch the game unfold below them while remaining hidden among the shadows eclipse day created. Once he saw all three in position, he sent the message, laughing the entire time he wrote it. He had to find as many things as he could to make himself laugh, even if it never touched his heart.

Being this close to Anin and being able to do nothing for her was the worst form of torture. He had to force himself to stay on top of the palace and not go in and try to rescue her for the 700th time. They still had not figured out a way around the spell on the hallway, but it did not mean he stopped trying. He only went as far as he needed in order to find out if whatever Panella had concocted for him worked or not.

His laughter must have broken off suddenly, because she gently patted him on the side of the arm and said, "It's hard for me to sit up here knowing she is somewhere underneath us and there is nothing we can do about it as well."

Over the years, Anin began to slip further into herself. It had even become harder to get her to converse with him in their unique way. He was always able to pull her back from the brink, but he wondered how much of that was her pretending for him.

"Why, Lyra, are you beginning to care for me? I am flattered, but I must inform you my heart belongs to another," he said in a voice that did not match his sly grin.

"Oh, for goddess' sake, Kes. That is disgusting."

"Ouch," he said, grabbing his heart and pretending to be broken-hearted.

"You became my brother the moment Anin came home and called you 'her Kes'. An annoying brother, no less, but a brother all the same. So, of course, I care for you."

He wrapped his arm around her and pulled her in for a too-tight hug before rubbing his knuckles across the top of her cloaked head. "Look at the little chick with her feelings," he said, releasing her with a laugh when she stomped hard on his taloned foot. "What about you, Lyra?"

"What about me?" she asked, brows furrowed in confusion.

"Is there anyone your heart belongs to?"

"Goddess, no," she said, sounding appalled and her eyes wide with shock. Her reaction was so sudden and visceral, true laughter snuck out of him before he could even register that he was laughing.

"Okay, okay... Your heart is your own, but what about in the future?"

"I do not know. I do not see myself liking the company of anyone enough to give them my heart," she said, sighing as she rubbed the space between her brows with her knuckle. "I feel guilty. Panella did not receive the green power that most of us contain to pass on in order to create a child. She is, by far, the more maternal one. I know she longs for a family, even though she has never said anything."

"The twin thing?"

"The twin thing," she said with a nod. "I feel like if I do not use it, I am being selfish. Throwing away the one thing my twin wants most."

"That is not a reason to bring a youngling into the realm," he said. He watched his cousin grow up with parents that did not want him and look how fucked up he turned out. Ciaran was well on his way to becoming the one being he hated most, and Kes did not know how to help him. He was not even sure he wanted to help him after he allowed Kes to forget the hidden room for twenty-five fucking years.

"I know. I feel guilty one way or the other."

"If you want to have a youngling at some point, have one. If not, then do not. It does not seem very difficult to me. It's baffling you think Panella would ever think that to begin with. I do not know her half as well as you do and even I know she would never think that. She might long to be the one to have the power, but something tells me she would want you to use it in whatever manner you desire."

"You are right," she said, her eyes flaring wide once she realized what she just said.

"What did you just say?" he asked, sucking in a shocked gasp.

"Oh, shut up, you heard me," she said, shoving him.

"I did, and I will remind you of it often."

"I hate you."

"You do no such thing."

"Shut up, Kes. Have you been keeping count?" she asked, watching the Silent Shadows at work down below in the city.

"No, have you?" he asked, turning to watch the three shadows weaving between buildings in the city for the first time since they began.

"No."

"Oh well, let's just make up some numbers."

"They will have counted how many they did!" she exclaimed.

"Perhaps, but they would never dare call us liars," he said, making her laugh and shake her head at him.

"You are too much," she said, rolling her eyes.

"Yes."

Chapter 39
Etain
69 years later

Sweat dripped down her neck as she twirled in time to the music. The combination of precision movements and flowing organic ones had been difficult for her to master for many years. After sixty-nine years of practice, it came as natural to Etain as walking. The first time she attended the Lunar Ball, she had watched the beings dancing and longed to learn the movements. At the time, they had mesmerized her. Now, those same movements seemed to take over, and she felt transported to another realm as she pushed her body into the different forms.

She felt the haunting sounds of the music flow through her, feeling as if the music were the one moving her limbs. The traditional dances of the Night fae melded together with those of the witches over the years, creating something new and yet familiar to all. It warmed Etain's heart to see the witches and fae finally integrating. She had even seen a few relationships form between the two.

In the past, witches had one night affairs with fae to create their offspring, making the idea of relationships strange for them. Witches worked as a hive and their covens and fellow witches would always come first, but a few fae had joined the hive in whatever capacity they could to be with the ones they loved. It was remarkable to watch unfold. She wondered what this meant for the future of the realm. There was still a long way to go, she knew. Most of the Night fae had still yet to accept her; however, she chose to focus on the few who had.

She felt eyes burning into her and saw Ciaran sitting on his throne with his gaze locked on her. She saw a hunger in them she no longer saw as often as she once had. He was in rare form tonight. There was no drink in his hand and he reminded her of the Ciaran she first met when she woke in the Night Court.

She reached within herself and called on her red power. The power responded and coursed through her, making her moves instantly sensual. She grinned when she saw the gold of his eyes turn molten. The dance that, just moments ago, had been for her own enjoyment was now specifically for his.

She hoped this version of Ciaran was here to stay. Perhaps they had finally moved past their difficult time. Her loneliness had grown into a weight that was becoming too much to bear. It did not help that he rarely, if ever, came to their bed to sleep. She was not certain he was sleeping at all.

She created an apartment in Witch City a few years ago. Tired of being alone all the time in a space meant for them, she desired to have a space that was all her own. Currently, it was just one large room that served as her study and lounge.

It made it easier for the witches to find her, and she enjoyed hosting any that came by the little apartment. Over the past several years, she had formed friendships with witches from all the different covens and had become particularly close to all seven of the head witches.

Just the other night she had contemplated creating a bedchamber, or two, since it was not uncommon for her aunt to fall asleep on her couch the nights they talked long into second night. She felt silly leaving Galetia there while she ported to the tower bedchambers she shared with her absent mate. It seemed pointless to stay there without him, but she did not want to miss the rare night he showed up to sleep with her in his arms. She longed for more of those nights.

As she continued to dance in circles with the rest of the beings on the dance floor, she looked up every once in a while to see Ciaran shifting in his throne. Each time she glanced at him, their eyes would collide. She let a grin stretch her lips—one that said she knew exactly what she was doing to him.

On her next rotation, she reached the foot of the dais steps. When she looked up at him, he was leaning forward with his elbows on his knees, hands hanging between his legs, and eyes burning into her. She stopped twirling right in front of him so suddenly her skirt continued the movement without her. Several moments went by, with neither of them making a move to close the distance separating them. She felt the heat of desire blazing like an inferno between them.

The fingers on one hand twitched just before one of his classic too-wide grins stretched his face. That was another thing she had not seen in far too long. Shadows raced toward him from all over the room until they encircled just the two of them. She gasped when she felt them solidify around her body and then float her up the stairs to deliver her to Ciaran.

She stood between his legs, anticipating his next move. As he sat up, he wrapped his long fingers around her waist, and then, in one quick motion, pulled her in to straddle his lap. Neither one of them said anything as he reached down and slowly slid her skirts up to bunch around her waist. He danced his fingers up her arms, teasing her just as her dance had teased him, until his fingers found the straps of her dress. Slowly, he pushed them down far enough to expose her to him.

"Did you enjoy teasing me, little witch?"

"Immensely," she said in a breath.

"Hmmm," he said into her neck, sending shivers down her body, directly to her core. "Two can play that game." He began an excruciatingly slow path down her neck, nipping at the sensitive skin the entire time. Her breathing picked up and a low moan escaped her, causing him to laugh darkly against her skin.

His hand snaked up into her hair and gripped it hard at the base, pulling her head back and thrusting her chest towards him. She whimpered as much from the sting of her scalp as the need growing out of control inside her.

"Little witch, I have barely touched you, yet I can feel you drenching my trousers beneath you," he growled. She could feel proof of his own arousal beneath her, causing her to rock back and forth as her body desperately sought relief. "Ah-ah-ah little witch. You knew exactly what you were doing to me while taunting me with your tantalizing movements. I was very close to removing the eyes of any being I found watching you."

He pulled her by the hair to get her to lean even further back and his other hand wrapped around to support her. He blew across each nipple, causing them to harden and become incredibly sensitive, yet he never touched them. His mouth went everywhere but there. The frustration building inside her was becoming painfully unbearable. Every single nerve in her body was firing, and she nearly leaped off his lap when he bit into the flesh of one of her breasts. She cried out with shock, and the sting from his teeth quickly turned into a heat that flushed across her entire chest.

"Ahhh, there it is. I love the crimson your skin turns, little witch. You in my lap just like this—exposed with your skin flushed so beautifully—might be the best view I have ever seen," he said, leaning forward and finally pulling a nipple into his mouth and sucking so hard it nearly hurt before he nipped at it. They were so sensitive, the sharp pain sent a bolt of lightning to her core and a cry of pleasure ripped from her. "I say 'might' because it is hard to decide which view of you I find to be the best."

"Please, Ciaran," she begged.

"Not yet, little witch. I have missed the way you beg," he said, enjoying his control over her far too much.

"I... I need..." she said in between hitched breaths.

"Shh, I know what you need," he said, brushing a single claw across the sensitive bud, pulsing with need between her legs. A need, thick with desire, tightened within her.

"Please," she whimpered. His only response was to drag his claws across each nipple, causing more shocks of fire to ignite within her. Her hips moved on their own accord, her body searching for something to satiate her need. He leaned her so far back, she could no longer see what he was doing. When she felt him rub himself across her slick folds, she nearly cried in relief, but then immediately made a sound of frustration.

He tapped himself on her overly sensitized bundle of nerves several times. Stretching the moments out in between each one, never bringing her any relief. She was certain her body was going to combust at any moment. Every inch of her screamed for release, and she whimpered again as her need dipped toward painful.

He said nothing as he lifted her off his lap. She was so delirious she did not register the movement until she was suddenly full of him in one hard thrust. The sound that tore out of her was somewhere between pleasure and pain. It was exactly what her body had been begging for. Her core clutched tightly around him and she heard him hiss through his teeth.

He yanked her up, so she was fully seated on top of him, making them both groan in pleasure. Her hips jerked back and forth, needing the friction. One of his hands stayed firmly in her hair and the other pushed her hips down, allowing her to grind even harder into him. They were both lost to the feeling of being one again after so long.

"Little witch," he said, causing her eyes to flutter open. "Look at what you do to me." He pushed her head forward so she could see his hard, dark blue length entering her over and over, each time covered in more of her slick desire. Something about watching their joining tipped her over the edge and she screamed out her release. It came on suddenly and it made her clamp down hard on him inside her. His groans of pleasure had her rolling directly into her next climb to ecstasy.

He released her hair and grabbed her hips with both hands to hold her in place as he drove into her from below. Each thrust harder than the one before and each one picked up speed. She could do nothing but hold on to his wrists at her hips. Sounds of pleasure reached her through the wall of shadows, and she knew the party had made its way to the platforms around the room. Hearing others enjoying themselves while her mate thrust into her made her pleasure grow even faster.

"Does the sound of other's fucking excite you, little witch?" he asked. When she did not answer, one of his hands left her hip to wrap around her throat, bringing her eyes to his. His thrusts became shallow and slowed to a near stop, suspending her so close to the tipping point of her pleasure. With their movements coming to a stop, the sound of the surrounding beings became louder. "I asked you a question, little witch."

"Yes," she groaned, never breaking eye contact.

"Such a good little witch, and such a dirty one, too," he said, sliding her hips up and down his length, never letting her eyes leave his. The hand around her neck tightened the slightest amount, and her core clenched in response. Tightening his grip slightly, a wicked grin cut across his face.

Before she had a moment to say anything, he picked her up,

flipped her around, and stood all in one motion. He held her by her throat and around her waist and bent her so that her head went through the shadows. The various shows around the room became visible to her.

"Do you enjoy watching them, little witch?" he asked, as he slowly thrust into her. When she did not answer, he tightened his grip around her neck. She rasped out a "yes," and his fingers immediately loosened.

She watched as witches and fae alike took each other in various ways. Some exchanged partners every few minutes, some took more than one partner at a time, and others pleasured themselves as they watched. When Etain first came to the Night Court, her desires would have embarrassed her. Now, she fully embraced them.

She climbed higher than she ever thought possible as Ciaran thrust into her from behind; the sound of their flesh meeting grew louder with each one. She felt herself clutching tightly around him, and just as she was about to explode, he shifted his arm around her waist so he could bring his hand to the center of her pleasure. Two hard swipes as she exploded into a million pieces all over him, just as he did inside her.

He pulled her up into his arms and sat them back down on his throne with her draped across his lap and his arms wrapped around her. They sat there in comfortable silence, happy to enjoy each other's company. She was trying to remember how long it had been since she saw him so present.

"I have missed you," she said, cupping his jaw.

"Missed me? I have not gone anywhere," he said, sounding truly confused.

"Ciaran, you cannot be so obtuse. You are here, yet not here at the same time. You are usually several bottles in by the time I see you, if I even see you," she said, pulling away from him and sitting up so that she could look him directly in the eyes.

"I have been busy. I am trying to protect you, Etain."

"Protect me from what?"

"The Day Queen and her blood magic," he said, as though she knew what he got up to.

"Ciaran, you are the most powerful being in the realm. If you cannot protect me from the effects of blood magic, perhaps it is not more power that is the answer."

"Of course it is. If I had the slightest bit more, I could keep her far enough away."

"And where do you intend to find this power?" she asked. He looked pointedly around the room. "No. Ciaran—you could never do such a thing."

"There is nothing I would not do to ensure your safety."

"Not that. I would never let you," she said with tears in her eyes.

This was the moment she feared. When he crossed a line she could not accept. When he said nothing after several minutes, her fears were confirmed. She untangled herself from him and made a disgusted sound as she turned away. Walking down the dais, she angrily sent her raw power to scatter his shadows and then exited the ballroom.

It was time for her to add some bedchambers to her apartment in Witch City. She did not know what this meant for them beyond the fact that she could not look at him without feeling disgusted, and worst of all—terrified of him.

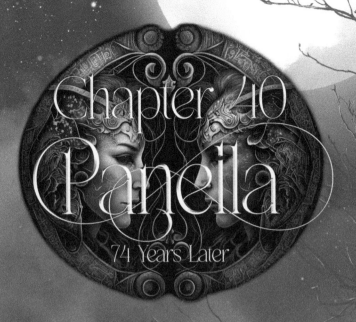

Chapter 40
Panella
74 Years Later

When she first laid eyes on the cavernous room, filled with shelves stacked with a variety of texts and artifacts, she was speechless. She had never seen so much undocumented knowledge in one place. However, after the bliss wore off, she realized what a daunting task it would be to process all of it by herself.

Thanks, Ciaran.

After spending the first several years attempting to make heads or tails of the system—whoever left all of this behind—used, only to find there *was* no system. She wasted over a decade of her life attempting to sort everything into groups. Several years into it she realized there were too many texts about things she had never heard of. How was she supposed to sort what she did not know? After almost forty years, she stepped away from the secret room.

Panella still had yet to process the information on the Great Battle they *borrowed* from the Day Court. She had barely looked at any of it in decades. Taking in the amount of scrolls and tombs they acquired, she knew processing all of it was going to take years.

Which it had.

Nearly a quarter of a century.

It was finally done, and yet it left them with more questions than answers. Frustration did not even come close to describing the way she felt. She spent so much of her life on one project, and in the end, it did not unveil what they needed most. It had all been for nothing.

There *was* a way to protect against blood magic. Unfortunately, the pages containing the information were always missing. She was willing to bet it was the queen who tore them from all the texts she could get her hands on. It was smart. If the pages no longer existed, the information could not be used against her. Panella cursed her for having the forethought.

When she came across something written about moonlight, her pulse pounded in her ears and she shook with anticipation, only to look to the next page and find that one was missing as well. She nearly threw the book across the room. She had been so angry. In the end, she was happy to have found even that one mention of moonlight. If it had not been within the very last paragraph before the torn-out page, there would have been no mention of it at all. There seemed to be a connection between whatever combated blood magic and whatever the moonlight was. At the very least, it was something to show Kes. Finally, he had proof that the goddess had not given him an impossible task.

She knew she needed to get back to processing the never-ending texts hidden below the archives. Yet, every time she thought about it, a heavy cloak of dread weighed her down. It was an impossible task to complete on her own. She thought Ciaran was being absurd, but she was not going to be the one to say anything about it. He had not seemed particularly stable the last few times she saw him. She was only hoping he would not decide she and Lyra knew too much and killed them. No, she was definitely not going to be the one to say something.

Panella had a problem. She was far too optimistic when it came to toting whatever work she was planning to take home. She never tied any of it to herself, like any witch with common sense would. No, instead she carried everything—regretting her choice every time. Although she might have really overdone it this time, she could barely see the hall in front of her.

It did not help that Nightfell's halls were always dark. Torches and moonlight only illuminated so much. Both cast exaggerated shadows in every corner and around every bend, making it impossible for her to tell at a glance if someone was coming. She never seemed to guess right and bumped into others while stepping out of the way for shadows. She stared into the shadows at the end of the hall as she made her way towards it.

Did it just move—

Her feet were knocked out from under her, and everything stacked in her arms went flying everywhere. Landing hard on her butt, the air whooshed out of her while she tried to comprehend what in the stars had just happened. She could have sworn she had been the only one in the hall just a few moments ago.

"Uh oh, momma is not gunna to be happy with me," a little voice said, sprawled out next to Panella while loose sheets of parchment slowly drifted to the ground around them.

"Why?" Panella asked, truly confused. Their run-in had been a simple accident.

"Because she told me not to go running around the corners of the hallway and to watch where I was going," she said, shaking her head at herself. She sounded so serious Panella had to fight to hold back her laughter.

"Ah, I see, and that was not what you were just doing?"

"Nope," she said with a little pop on the 'p' sound. "She's probably going to take away my dessert," she groaned.

"Not dessert!! That's the worst!" Panella loved sweets. Her sister loved food in general, but for her it was all the sweet treats. Having her dessert taken as a youngling was the absolute worst punishment.

"Right! I would rath—"

"Oh! Oh, my goddess, I am so sorry. I have been trying to teach her not to run in the halls and to watch where she's going. Tyne, what am I going to do with you?" asked a melodic voice that belonged to the ethereal witch running towards them. The wind was knocked out of Panella for a second time.

"Sorry, momma," she said in that sad, sing-song way all younglings adopt when trouble finds them.

"It's not me you should apologize to," her mother admonished her.

"Sorry...what's your name anyway?" the girl asked.

On some level, Panella heard the question, but she was dumbstruck by the younglings mother. Long black silky hair and green eyes—that looked more feline than witch—complemented golden bronzed skin that she bet glowed in the sun. She was the most enchanting being Panella had ever seen. She could have stared at her all night. That was until a small finger tapped her on the shoulder.

"Oh, sorry, what? My name is Panella."

"Pah-nelya," the youngling said with all the confidence of youth.

"Not quite, but it's good enough," Panella said, smiling at the young witch. A voice cleared and the girl, Tyne, apologized again.

"It is completely fine," Panella said, meaning it. It did not bother her when younglings acted like younglings. She herself had been a terror, so who was she to judge?

Picking herself up, she offered her hand to the youngling, who took it and smiled at her. One of her front teeth was missing, making her even more adorable. She helped the young witch to her feet before picking up her scattered belongings—things she should have tied to herself in the first place. Although, if it meant running into Tyne's mother again, she would do it every night.

"Oh! Here, let me help you," Tyne's mother said, and stooped down next to Panella, allowing her to catch her scent of bergamot and something smokey. She was so entranced by the female she missed another question from Tyne.

"What was that?" Panella asked, slightly dazed.

"I said…" Tyne drew out the word with a little eye roll, disbelieving Panella would have the audacity not to hear her. "Do you have a youngling?"

She felt a little pang at the question. It was something she had always wanted; however, it was not something the goddess chose to bless her with, and she had come to terms with that a long time ago.

"No, I do not."

"Oh. That's my mom. She's the one I was telling you about that likes to take my dessert away as punishment," she said. Leaning in conspiratorially and speaking in that whiny voice all younglings do so well.

"That's a true travesty," Panella said, sounding forlorn while giving the youngling a sorrowful look.

"What's a travesty?" the little witch asked, a furrow forming between her brows. That's something Panella admired about younglings. They want to know *everything*—a trait Panella never grew out of.

"Tyne…"

"Oh, it's alright, I do not mind. A travesty is like a super big sad thing."

"Yes! A travesty! Want to see the new spell I learned, Miss Panella?" she asked, jumping from one thought to another chaotically.

"Just Panella is fine, and of course." It took every ounce of control Panella had not to laugh as the youngling stuck her tongue through her missing tooth in concentration. She was attempting to animate the paper frog she pulled out of her pocket, but one of her hand motions was not quite right.

"Can I show you a special way to do that?" Panella asked the young witch. She looked both ways down the hall, as if making sure there was no one near to overhear the special instructions.

"There's a special way?" Tyne asked in wonder.

"Oh yes, and it's much easier," Panella said as seriously as she could. Tyne nodded her head vigorously while trying—and failing —not to bounce with excitement. "First, you have to go like this," she said, touching the tip of her thumb to the tip of her middle finger. "Then you have to stick your little finger out like this. Now, this is the special part. Are you ready?"

"Yes," she said in a near whisper.

"You have to tap the object three times with the tips of your thumb and middle finger," she said, tapping the paper frog three times. "Then you sweep your pinkie over it in a big U as you say the chant." Tyne tried the spell the way Panella showed her. She got it just right on her second try before jumping up and down and squealing with delight.

"Oh!" Tyne said, chasing after the now animated paper frog hopping down the hall.

"Thank you. You did not have to be so kind and patient with her. Few are. I am truly grateful, and I cannot apologize enough," she said, looking directly into Panella's eyes. She could have sworn the green in the witch's eyes glowed.

"No, it's completely fine. I love younglings. Conversations with them are never dull, and the things we all take for granted amaze them," Panella said, and the beautiful witch smiled at her warmly. Panella had to remind herself not to gape at the female and nearly lost the battle when she smiled. Her entire face lit up as if the sun shone from within her.

"Well, I hope you understand you have now gained a little shadow for life," she said, laughing as her daughter hopped like the paper frog she was chasing.

"That sounds perfect to me. Does that mean I have also gained your presence for life as well?" Panella asked boldly. She was rewarded when a blush crept across the female's face.

"You do not even know my name," she said with a nervous little laugh.

"I would like to," Panella said with a smile.

"Ravyn."

With that one name, Panella knew her life had forever changed.

Chapter 41
Tatiana
78 Years Later

"L et's go hunting!" Tatiana exclaimed with all the enthusiasm of a youngling. A few decades ago, she finally told Raindal about the blood magic and it was the best decision she ever made. He loved hunting down high fae almost more than she did, and he always knew which fae to go after. She did not care who they were as long as their well ran deep.

She still craved the raw power of a witch and continued to search the abandoned covens for any sign of activity. She knew they had returned at some point. Their libraries, along with all the portraits they had scattered around in their peculiar ways, had all vanished. It angered her that she listened to the whispers when they told her not to waste her time. If she had ignored them and checked the covens daily as she had wanted to, she would have caught a witch or two. Perhaps she would have gotten truly lucky and been able to grab twenty witches, or even more! Then she could have rationed them out over the next several years.

"*You have no self control,*" the *whispers* said while laughing in their eerie way. *"They would have all been gone before the day was finished."*

"No! I could have controlled myself if I wanted to."

"What about the thirteen you captured all of those years ago with that exact thought in mind, and then you devoured them all in one eclipse night?" She swore the *whispers* loved nothing more than to taunt her.

"Not all of them." She had tried to complete a very specific ritual that night. It required all thirteen witches, so the *whispers* point was moot. It still enraged her. She took it out on the creature whenever she recalled the way she stole the final witch's life force all these years later.

"Ah yes, your sister did something to the last one," the *whispers* said, interrupting her thoughts. She could hear the laughter hiding behind each of their echoing words. There was no way to know how she did it. Although she eventually admitted to it, she would not admit to how she did it, no matter how painfully they tortured her. The rows of wings mounted on the stone walls could attest. She had recently placed the final set to fill the entire wall. If only they did not take so long to grow back, she could have filled the entire room at this point.

"Do not call her that!" she screamed at them.

"Why? Is that not what she is?" they asked, mocking her.

"No, she is a half rotted creature," she replied with a sneer.

"That she may be, but that does not change the fact that you both share a father, therefore making you sisters," the *whispers* replied. They were being too literal, and they knew it. They enjoyed saying things just to irritate her.

"Shut. Up!" she screamed, this time out loud. Raindal glanced at her, but his expression remained neutral. He never judged her for her outbursts. He was such a good little pet.

"My queen, I had not realized you were already engaged in a conversation. I apologize," Raindal said.

"It's fine, Raindal, you will learn eventually." She knew if there were anyone who could discern when she was having a conversation with the *whispers*, it would be him. She never regretted choosing him. He was always attentive to her every move and even learned how to anticipate her every need.

She loved that about him. She also loved that he would pleasure her anywhere, in any situation, every time she ordered it. She never considered feeling anything negative about demanding he pleasures her since it led to his pleasure as well. Just thinking about the many ways he had taken care of her needs made her desire grow as she stared at him. He was saying something, but she was not listening. She imagined him thrusting inside of her.

He was larger than Reminold. At least as far as she could remember. She did not recall him stretching her the same way Raindal did. Heat flooded her core, thinking about the way he filled her. It would have been so fun to have had both of them inside her at the same time, loving her. However, because of that creature rotting in the depths of the palace, she would never have the opportunity to feel such satisfaction.

Thinking of *her* always made Tatiana's temper flair. Hate did not begin to describe the way she felt about the creature. She tried to kill her in every way she could imagine—even setting her on fire. Unfortunately, the stupid Land was faster than the flames and healed her before she could burn away to dust.

Tatiana hated the Land as well. She was glad it was rotting away. Raindal did not think she paid attention at the council meetings, but she did. Sometimes. She was highly suspicious of two of the members, but the lone female was firmly in support of her. If she had enjoyed the touch of a female, she would have kept her in the same way she kept Raindal. He was her loyal, little pet. Well, perhaps little was not the correct term when it came to Raindal. She giggled at the thought.

She wanted him inside her now. Wanted to be loved and he

would be the one to make her feel so. She smiled at him coquettishly and nearly laughed when he snapped his mouth shut, cutting off whatever he had been saying.

"Raindal," she said in a youngling-like, sing-song voice as she sauntered towards him. "I am in need of your special services."

"My queen, let's go hunting—"

"I do not wish to go hunting. I want to be pleasured!" she screamed while stomping her feet to emphasize her annoyance, in much the same way a youngling would.

"My queen, I only me—"

"Yes. I am your queen, and you will do as you are told," she demanded. She could not stand it when anyone opposed her, even if she *did* go from one idea to the next quickly. The answer should always be, "yes, my queen," and nothing more.

"Would you not rather make a sa—"

"No! I told you what I want and I want it now! You would dare deny your queen? After everything I have done for you? You ungrateful wretch!" she screamed. She picked up the closest thing to her, a glass vase, and threw it at him. She screeched in anger when he stepped out of the trajectory and it shattered against the wall. She picked up every object she could reach one by one, lobbing each of them at his head. Her rage only increased with each miss. She finally exploded and swiped everything off of every surface around her lounge, sending them crashing to the ground. No shelf was left occupied and no object was left intact.

When she finally turned back to look at him, it further enraged her to see he had zero reaction. She reached out with her blood magic and took control of him. It was not the first time he forced her to do so, and each time his reaction was always the same. His eyes flared wide the moment he felt his body no longer belonged to him—it belonged to her. She loved that expression. It was the only time he wore any expression around her besides indifference.

"Tisk, tisk, Raindal," she said. "I told you to never deny me or it would force me to do this again. I would say I hate doing it, but that would be a lie. The face you make each time brings me so much joy."

She walked in circles around his frozen body, dragging her hands across him along the way. When she stood in front of him again, she cupped his flaccid length in her hand.

"Well, this just will *not* do," she said, making him harden with her magic. "There, that's better. Now, Raindal, what will it be? Will you decide to give me what I want, or will you give me no choice but to take it?" Turning from him, she released her hold.

Other rulers would not be so kind. They would never give a choice to their subjects like she did. He should be grateful. Not only did she let him pleasure her, but she also allowed him to make choices. She truly was a kind ruler. The sound of the *whispers* laughing at her were drowned out by Raindal's voice.

"My queen, you misunderstood my intentions. You sounded rather excited to go hunting," he said, walking up behind her to slide his arms around her. Leaving a trail of kisses down her neck, he slipped the strap of her gown off her shoulder for better access to her body.

He drags his hand up her stomach until he reaches her breasts. Grabbing one in his hand, he gives her a squeeze, and she arches into him. When his other hand makes its way to her core, she sighs—happy again. Now that she is getting what she wants. As she let herself fall fully into the pleasure she demanded, she said, "You really are quite lucky, Raindal."

"Yes, my queen."

She smiles at his correct response. Like every pet, he was trainable. She moaned as his fingers found the bundle of nerves her pleasure radiated from.

Tatiana was loved.

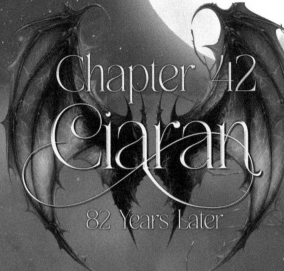

Chapter 42
Ciaran
82 Years Later

"It must be here somewhere," he said to himself. Running his sweaty hand through his tangled hair; he grips it at the root. His father always had this one journal on his desk. He saw it every time he was there as a youngling. It was the only journal he had not located. It had to be there.

It had to be.

He paced his study, swinging the bottle in his hands as he traveled the tight circle he had walked an unknown amount of times, wearing a path into the flooring. If he did not find it soon, he was not sure what he was going to do. His failure to find a way to be able to protect her against the queen's blood magic had been breathing down his neck.

"Ciaran?" a being called from behind him. He whipped his head toward the voice. He saw Kes standing there, but he could not be sure it was truly him. It could be a new spectral coming to haunt him.

"Are you real?" he asked, no longer trusting his eyes.

"Of course, I am. Do you think anything this great could ever be replicated?" his cousin said. It was definitely him.

351

"What are you doing here, Kes?" he asked. Now that he knew he was real, the interruption annoyed him.

"What? Do I need a reason to visit my favorite cousin?" Kes asked, attempting to sound innocent.

"I am your only cousin," Ciaran said, rolling his eyes at him.

"Same thing."

"What do you want, Kes?" he demands. Kes sighed as he navigated around books, bottles, and random broken furniture on his way to one of the chairs. When he got to the chair, he looked up at Ciaran and raised one of his downy brows before picking up a discarded pair of pants and tossing them into the other chair.

"We need to talk, cousin. Gods, it's dark in here. Do you ever open the curtains?"

"No."

"I should have expected as much, considering you smell as though you have only bathed in a vat of wine for the last several years," he said, waving his hand under his nose. He was not far off from the truth.

"I have nothing to talk about," Ciaran said, not only confused by Kes's sudden appearance but also by his sudden desire to talk. They had not said more than two words to each other since the night he came down the stairs of the secret room and found him and Etain down there. He could not imagine what there could possibly be to talk about.

"Ciaran, you are reminding me of someone."

Ciaran waited for Kes to elaborate and when he did not, he threw his hands up in annoyance, the liquid sloshing out of the bottle with his movement.

"Alright Kes, I will play your little game," he said, resuming his pacing. "Who is it I am reminding you of?" He knew who Kes was going to say.

"Your father." It was just as he suspected. "Ciaran, you are not well. What is going on with you?"

"Nothing is wrong with me. I assure you, your worries are unwarranted," he said, waving his hands dismissively.

"When was the last time you saw Etain?"

The question stopped Ciaran in his tracks and he whipped his head back to glare at his cousin. "Leave Etain out of this," he seethed.

"If I could, I would, cousin. I see her almost nightly. While she looks better than you, she still looks miserable. She fills every moment of every night and is running herself ragged in an attempt to distract herself from you."

Ciaran turned his attention away from his cousin and attempted to feel his way down the bond, something he had not done in—he could not truly recall the last time he tried. He was met with the same barrier as the last time he tried, remembering why he had stopped in the first place.

"I would hate for her to fall into the same state as your mother. However, with the amount you are drinking, it looks like it is you I should be afraid for," Kes said with a grin. It shocked Ciaran that his cousin thought it was acceptable to *ever* use the threat of Etain becoming like his mother as anything resembling a joke.

"Get the fuck out," Ciaran snarled in a low voice, shadows pulling in tightly around him. Kes raised his hands in surrender.

"I meant nothing by it cousin, but I—"

"I said get the fuck out!" he roared as his shadows went barreling towards a shocked Kes. He ported away before they could touch him. Laughter bubbled up from deep within his gut and came pouring out of him. It sounded wild, even to his own ears, and he could not understand what he's even laughing about.

His one and only priority had not changed in all these years. He was still trying to find a way to protect himself and Etain from the effects of blood magic. If the queen were to come to the palace right now, there would be nothing he could do to keep Etain safe.

Kes's concern was one he had been having himself. There was

no denying he was behaving just as his own father had, and laughter ripped out of him again. He should have known he was always fated to become the being he despised most. The *whispers* were a constant battle to ignore. He was having a hard time distinguishing which thoughts were his own, and which were the ones the diseased part of his mind was trying to convince him were.

When he looked up again, his mother sat in the same chair Kes just vacated. He glared at her. She gave no reaction, just the same bland smile and constant glass of wine.

"What do you want? Are you here to tell me about my own mate as well?" he asked the mirage before him. "You cannot say anything! You were not there when I needed you most! You do not get to have an opinion!" he screamed while throwing the bottle at the chair, wine splattering all over it. At least the image of his mother was gone.

Fear was not something he was used to experiencing, but what Kes told him about Etain made him terrified he was going to lose her. He knew it was possible for mates to reject each other and live separate lives, although he had never heard of two fully bonded being able to. Then again, if he were honest, he knew little about true mates. He knew what he felt, and he knew one could not live without the other for long. Perhaps the fact she was a witch changed the rules. That terrified him even more.

If the mate bond rules were not the same for them, did that mean she could sever the bond and leave him? Would the same rules still apply to him? If she left, how would he ever be able to protect her from being enslaved by the queen and her blood magic?

No, that was not an option. He needed to find a way to protect her, and soon. In the meantime, he did not know what to do about their current situation. He called another bottle to him and drank from it deeply. Maybe he could find the answer he needed at the bottom. At the very least, it might give him clarity.

If these damn ghosts from his past would leave him alone, he could think clearer. He needed to find that journal. It had all of his father's notes on his experiments, and maybe there would be something within the pages he could use.

It did not matter that Etain forbade him from stealing the power from the surrounding beings. He would do whatever he needed to in order to secure her safety. Everything else could be dealt with later.

He felt eyes upon him again and spun around, expecting his cousin to have returned for round two. He never knew how to leave anything alone. Instead, he found nothing. He felt them behind him again and spun with his unnatural speed, determined to catch whoever it was. Again, he found no one.

"Who's there?" he demanded, certain he was not alone. If he were thinking clearly, he would have recalled the only beings that could enter his tower were Kes and Etain, but he was not in his right mind. He opened the curtains to check behind them, only to immediately shut them again. The moon was too bright, and he was convinced it had gotten even brighter in the last...however many nights it had been since he last let in any light.

He opened every cabinet and looked behind every possible hiding spot in his study. Still, he found no one. He shook his head, trying to clear the confusion. He had just been doing something. For the life of him, he could not remember what it was.

He called another bottle to himself, surprised to find the one in his hand empty already. Considering the amount of wine soaking his shirt, he thought most of it never made it to his mouth. He put the fresh bottle to his lips and drank half of it at once. When he looked back up, everything appeared as hazy as his thoughts. He preferred it like that. Perhaps it would help him think if his surroundings matched his mind.

He needed to find that journal. At this point, he was growing desperate. Etain would leave him if he could not protect her. What good was he to her if he could not do the simplest of things and keep her safe? The journal would have answers, he knew it. He just had to find it.

"I know where one of your father's hidden journals is. Perhaps it is the one you are searching for," the echoing sound of the *whispers* said. He had tried, he really had, to ignore them. Yet what was a little more madness if it meant Etain was safe?

"Where?"

Chapter 43
Anin
87 Years Later

t's been a long time since she was made to watch one of her
sister's sick ritual sacrifices. When she first came to and realized she had been moved to the larger cage in the run-down
temple, she feared she was about to witness the death of more
witches. She tried to look into the other cage across the room, but
the combination of the eclipse sun, stone pillars, and half-walls
draped everything in shadows.

Voices came from across the room, yet there was no sight of
the queen or her pet. That did not mean they were not close by.
She did not want to risk calling out to the other cage and drawing
attention, bringing their end even sooner. The thought had barely
crossed her mind when she heard the sound of the two sets of
footsteps she knew all too well growing closer. Her body always
reacted to that sound before her mind could catch up. Anin
wondered if even when she got out of here—*if* she ever got out of
here—would she always have nightmares filled with the echoes of
these specific footfalls?

"My queen, the creature is awake."

"Wonderful. I *so* do love an audience. Oh, Raindal," she said, laughing, "look at how she drags herself around. She really does look like a creature now." Tatiana cackled, and the sound was terrifying.

She was certain Tatiana did not always sound that insane. Had she been crazy the entire time Anin was in her 'care'? Absolutely. However, within the past several years, she seemed to reach a whole new level of derangement. She sounded more like a youngling every day, and her paranoia made her unpredictable. She saw and heard things that were not there. Many times, Anin witnessed her stop mid-action and remain frozen for several minutes. When she finally came to, she picked up right where she left off, as if nothing happened.

She stopped being shamed by Tatiana's words a long time ago. Was she dragging herself around like a creature? Yes. Did she care? No. She was only happy to have the freedom to move her limbs and was working hard to get the feeling back into them so she could finally stand on her own. The last time she had a chance to move was so long ago now she could not even recall when it had been. Typically, she was dropped out of her cell and then dragged across the floor to be put into whatever position they wished to torture her in. The more time that passed, the less often they came to "play," as Tatiana liked to call it.

On the one hand, she was happy. It was a relief to be left alone for long stretches at a time. The only pain coming from not being able to move her body—painful, yet bearable. On the other hand, being left alone with only the images she and Kes projected to each other, she feared, was driving her into insanity. She had to be insane because who in their right mind would ever be uncertain over which was worse, being left alone or tortured?

"She does look like a creature, my queen," he agreed, lip lifting in disgust.

"I think it's time for us to get started," Tatiana said, hopping up and down as she clapped her hands. "Are you excited, Raindal?

You must be. I know how much you love these and...other things."
She giggled.

Anin noticed Tatiana spoke for Raindal more often than not.
The more Tatiana treated him like an object, the better. He
deserved a life of nothing but pain for everything he did to her.
She had to find joy where she could.

"Of course, my queen," he said robotically.

She had recently reconsidered her earlier assessment, and
thought it was possible for him to be under the control of her
blood magic after all. He seemed to be in a constant daze; that
only lasted for a few visits. It quickly became clear he was in full
control of his body. Between the two of them, she was not certain
who was the most insidious.

"I can feel the power coursing through me already! I cannot
wait! Open the door, Raindal. Let's see the beings we have to play
with today." He walked to the cage and paused for a minute.

"These are not the fae I picked out," he said, confused. His
brows scrunched as he peered into the cage of sacrifices. He said
'fae' and Anin sighed with relief. She felt horrible for being happy
it was fae over witches. Technically, the fae were her kind, but they
had chased her all over the court until she finally left. The witches
had taken her in without a second thought and raised her as if she
were one of them. They would forever be her kind no matter what
happened with the Day Court.

"My queen, what is happening?" a wary voice asked from
behind the bars.

"You dare ask questions of your queen? For that, you will go
last." Tatiana glared at the female Anin could not see for daring to
ask a question that anyone would in their situation. "Do any of the
rest of you want to ask something of your queen like I am nothing
more than a servant?" No one else made a single sound.

"Who would you like to start with, my queen?" Raindal asked,
his earlier confusion gone. He was a being she could never figure

out. He was depraved, and yet seemed to be checked out more than living in the moment these days. She wondered if something happened between them. A smile crested her face, thinking about how there was possibly trouble in paradise.

"Hmm, I think...that one!" she declared, sounding like she just won a prize. Anin watched a male fae walk out of the cage in that stilted way beings do when taken by Tatiana's blood magic.

Once on the altar, she wasted no time and sliced into the male's neck. Golden blood poured from him and coated the emblem the queen stood on to absorb his power. When had she stooped so low as to sacrifice her own court members? While Anin was relieved it was not any of the witches, she was still horrified watching any being lose its life so senselessly. The queen's addiction to power was uncontrollable.

Tatiana sagged after absorbing the first fae's power and sighed. "It is just not the same," she said. "There is nothing like a witch's raw power. A fae's well is like the memory of what a witch felt like. I need to find them. They have to come out from hiding at some point."

She wondered if that meant the witches went to seek refuge with their queen in the Night Court. The idea of Tatiana not being able to get what she craved most made her chuckle. The queen's head whipped towards Anin's.

"Is something funny, creature?" she asked, but not even her insult could lessen the smile stretching Anin's face. It was always strange to smile after an extended period. The muscles felt uncertain and ached quickly.

"Oh, no, of course not, dear sister," she replied, infusing her words with sarcasm. "How could I ever find your suffering amusing? That would be insensitive."

"Shut up creature, or I will—"

"You will what? After all of these years, sister, is there anything you have not done?" As soon as the words spilled from her lips, she regretted them. She knew her sister would find something new for her just to prove a point.

"I'm sure I can think of something." The smile she gave Anin confirmed her fears.

Why could she not just keep her mouth shut? Something about this place always made her feel emboldened, as if it was the end of the line, and she might as well say and do whatever she wanted. How could she forget there was no end of the road for her? Only her sister's talent for making her wish there was.

The next fae stepped out from the cage and was quickly strapped down. With her craving lessened from the first murder, Tatiana's blood lust made an appearance. She was constantly arguing with whoever spoke to her inside her head. Lately, she had been vehemently denying the name "Blood Queen." However, Anin thought the name was perfect for her demented sister.

Her thoughts were proven as she sliced into the fae male on the altar. His screams echoed throughout the cavernous space of the crumbling temple. The joy she had just felt over her sister's desires being denied was dashed by the sound. She might not feel like one of the Day fae, but in this, they were kindred. She knew the pain he was experiencing and felt tears dampen her skin. No one should ever be forced to go through something so heinous. She was not sure if she was lucky her sister had never been able to kill her or if the male currently in the throes of death was the lucky one.

It was getting harder, nearly impossible, to deny that part of her mind that wanted to pull her in and keep her there for an eternity. It would be the only sort of death she could have. Kes must have felt it whenever she began to slide down that dark and slippery slope into the promise of freedom her mind offered her. He pulled her away from it every time, yet lately, it was not as easy as it had once been.

As the male reached the edge of his life, Tatiana finally

ended his suffering by dragging the same obsidian blade over his throat. The same one that had once severed her own. Her sister stumbled slightly after absorbing the male's power.

"Raindal, get rid of the body. It's time for the real party to begin," the Blood Queen said. They both watch him approach the body and incinerate it. He had done that to her once. It was something she would never forget.

The final fae, the one who dared ask for information, came out of the cage. While her limbs were stiff in the way all beings were when controlled by blood magic, she still had tracks of tears marking her face. Something about the sight loosened Anin's tongue.

"How can you do this to your own subjects?" she said, sneering at the queen.

"As you just said, they are *mine*, and I can do what I want with them. Right, Raindal?" she asked in a sickly-sweet voice.

"Yes, my queen," Raindal said automatically.

"Oh, yes! Your pet will definitely *not* only tell you what he knows you want to hear. For all you know, he might hate everything about this and you while he pretends to be everything you want him to be."

"Well, that's a bit of a reach, princess," he said and laughed. He crossed his arms and leaned casually against the half wall with an easy smirk, looking entirely too comfortable with everything happening.

"Well, of course. I am only saying you would never tell her if you ever actually disagree with her. Even if you did, she would likely use her blood magic on you." The grin slipped from his face and his expression soured. "Oh," Anin started laughing. "She already has."

He glared at her, and she did not care if that look promised an abundance of pain. She won this time, and they both knew it.

"It does not matter either way. I am not asking for opinions," Tatiana said, shrugging.

"Right. Why would the Blood Queen of the Day Court ever ask for an opinion that might confirm how insane you actually are?" she asked, rolling her eyes.

"Do. Not. Call me that!" Tatiana raged. Anin just smiled at her.

"What? Is that not what you are?" she asked. Tatiana ignored her and instead focused on the poor fae female who was likely about to get the brunt of the anger Anin had just fanned the flames of. "You are not the Queen of the Day Court, that is for sure. No true queen would ever sacrifice their own members."

"Shut. Up!" She spun on her heel to yell at her, but Anin was not looking at her sister. Her eyes locked with the Day fae's. She opened her mouth to speak, and while she spoke in a whisper, Anin heard every word.

"I should have believed in the true queen when the rumors began. Forgive me, my queen."

There was no mistaking that her words were for Anin and not for Tatiana. A tear slid down Anin's face, knowing the brave female was in for a realm of pain. The smile she gave Anin as Tatiana screamed told Anin the female had known exactly what would happen, and she did it anyway.

Her screams pierced holes in Anin's heart as the knife entered her again and again. She wished she could summon whatever had spared Tallon. It did not matter how hard she tried or how desperately she wished for it; nothing happened. No power emerged again. Eventually, her screams turned into weak moans. She thought that would be the end, but Tatiana reached a level of depravity not even Anin thought she was capable of.

"Raindal," she whined. "I have a need." At first nothing happened, and Anin was not sure what that meant. It quickly became clear when she glared at him before he sauntered up to her and caressed her body.

No—oh gods, she cannot be serious.

He flipped her skirts up, freed himself, and was buried inside her in one swift movement. The sound of her moans mixed with those of the dying fae made Anin feel like she was going to vomit. It was even worse when Tatiana continued carving into the female while Raindal thrust into her. The fae was too close to death, so Tatiana was forced to slice her throat. The combination of power coursing through her and Raindal's movements made her scream out her release and fall on top of the now-dead fae.

Anin was appalled—shocked, even. She was staring wide-eyed at the disgusting scene before her. She could not believe what had just happened. However, she should not be so surprised based on the activities that happened regularly after they visited her cell. That was just not something she had ever thought of as a possibility for either of them.

Movement shook her out of her shocked daze as she watched as Tatiana lifted herself off the dead body and stumbled with her eyes glazed. She was drenched in the proof of her actions, looking every bit the Blood Queen she was.

Chapter 44
Council Member

92 Years Later

The influx of lesser fae into the city was reaching an extreme capacity. The high fae making deals with the lesser fae could not even keep up with the amount of bodies that passed through their gate each day. They had resorted to closing off the city for periods of time while they processed the masses of lesser fae.

The council member was once again down at the gates, getting a firsthand look at the issue. He has argued for decades now to increase housing for the lesser fae. It always amazed him how his fellow council members could ignore the issue at hand. Some of them did not even consider it an issue. Then there were the ones who seemed to think living in filth was exactly what the lesser fae deserved, particularly the queen's new favorite council member.

Shockingly, the queen began regularly making appearances at the council meetings. Each time, she seemed to have fallen even further into madness. He was beginning to truly fear for the security of the Day Court. Between the Land and the queen, both seemed to rot away while their city became overrun with bodies; he did not think the court could survive much more.

The high fae forcing the lesser fae into dealing with them—more like slavery—had become far too extreme. They started requiring families to hand over the most beautiful amongst them and then made those fae agree to a life of prostitution. If they refused, then the entire family would be executed. He tried to deter the council from approving such barbaric deals. It was difficult to argue against the majority without drawing attention. He tried making them think it was disgusting and reminded them that their laws clearly state there are to be no relations with the lesser fae.

Unfortunately, he lost that argument when one merchant making these deals suggested it was an exchange of goods and that it was in no way a relationship. The majority of the council sided with him and decided that lesser fae were goods and not beings. They drove their point home when they said it was that or they would start exterminating entire families.

Not a single one of the lesser fae wanted to be there. Coming to Daybreak City was entirely against their will. There was only one other council member who also saw how depraved it was. He reminded them that the fae do not take a body against their will—ever. The merchant smiled maliciously and reminded the council member that the lesser fae entered the agreement out of their own free will, and that was the end of the discussion. It did not matter that the options they were given were not truly choices. If they did not agree to the deal, they chose death—what kind of free will was that?

The queen still thought the solution was easy. She wanted to exterminate them and was annoyed her wishes had not been carried out to begin with. It took all of them arguing for various reasons to continue allowing the lesser fae to enter the city, and then agreeing to extermination once they reached true capacity. That seemed to appease her enough to drop the subject.

After that meeting, the queen looked suspiciously at anyone who spoke in favor of the lesser fae. It did not matter whether it was within the gates of Daybreak or any ideas to reroute them to other cities. To her, they were less than nothing—goods to be traded.

"They have no power, therefore they are worthless. I will not allow city resources to go to maintaining the little shanty town they have created," she said disgustedly. She would eliminate all of them if she were willing to lower herself and actually step foot into the city.

"My queen, if we do not help them create enough housing, they will seep into the rest of the city. We do not want them spreading their filth," he said, trying to appeal to her need for cleanliness and order.

"Then kill them," she said with a shrug. "Any lesser fae found dwelling anywhere outside of their shit hole will be put to death immediately. Make sure not to announce it either. It will help thin the herd if they do not know." The laugh she let out was chilling, and the smile that followed made the hairs on the back of his neck rise.

"Yes, my queen," Agrona said. She was the only female on the council and did everything she could to be the queen's next favorite. It was disgusting.

"I still think we should exterminate them," the queen said, sounding bored.

"My queen, they are the ones that do all the labor throughout the city. Making it so we never have to lift a finger," Wyndor said. He had deals with more lesser fae than any of the other high fae. It was not a surprise he would want to keep them. In this instance, the male's selfishness worked in the council member's favor.

"Hmmm..." she hummed, looking at him through narrowed eyes.

"It's better to allow them in so they can do all the things no high fae should be expected to do."

She nodded once, apparently placated.

"What of the destruction these rebels are wreaking on my city? And who is spreading lies about a false queen? I want this dealt with. Find out who is responsible. Kill the lesser fae's young. That will get them to talk," she said. You could feel the rage rolling off her in waves each time the true queen came up. It always made the council member laugh on the inside. He knew she reacted with rage to disguise her fear.

"My queen, have you considered what that would look like?" he asked, hoping she would not immediately shut him down.

"What do you mean? Of course, I have. If their young are being killed, that should put an end to the rumors," she said, looking at him as if he had grown a second head.

It was a risk the council member took not immediately agreeing with her—again. He feared she might look too closely if he did not make this convincing.

"Perhaps, or it will legitimize the rumors. By reacting that strongly, you make it seem like the lies are true, and that is why you want them to be silenced," he said.

The queen stared at him longer than was comfortable before she sighed and sat back hard in her chair, pouting. "Fine."

In the following meeting she attended, the council member remained quiet and only spoke when necessary. He did not want to draw any more attention to himself, so he adopted an expression of indifference. When talk of the lesser fae came up, he sat there and looked bored. The queen continued to glance at him throughout the entire meeting, but by the time the next one came around, she paid him no more attention than was normal.

There were times when she attended the meeting, and physically she was there, but mentally she was somewhere else. She stared off for long moments, wearing a blank expression that he always found particularly terrifying. When she finally came to, she would go into a fit of rage if anyone even batted an eye at her.

The council member was desperate to find a solution to the immigration issue. His plan was taking much longer than he originally thought it would. He needed something to temporarily relieve the pressure caused by the sheer amount of bodies the city took in daily. The only solution the council member saw was to send them further north. It was dangerous, but the city meant a death sentence or slavery for the lesser fae.

"It will all work out," a quiet voice said from behind him. He turned to find his mate's mother smiling at him kindly.

"What are you doing here?" he asked. The gate was not a safe place for any of the lesser fae who have already made deals. It might activate the consequences of their deal if it thought she was trying to leave.

"I am working, do not worry," she said gently. "I know what you are doing, and I know how my son feels about it."

"I am sorry—"

"Whatever for? I think what you are doing is admirable. While I understand why my son hates it, I also understand that you are only trying to create a safe and happy future for him. For all the lesser fae, really," she said, keeping her voice low to prevent them from being overheard. That was the last thing he needed.

"I only wish Balthier saw it that way."

"On some level, he does. My son is hot-tempered—I am sure you might have noticed. He's quick to react, and when he's hurt, he lashes out to harm the one he blames for his pain. Then he pushes them away so they cannot hurt him again."

He had noticed, and that's why he was trying to give Balthier the space he needed.

"I hope so," he said softly, trying to keep the emotion out of his voice. He missed his mate. The past several times he sent a scroll asking him to meet at their secret place, he had not shown. He knew he was mad at him but thought he would come around after a little space. Apparently, he needed a lot of space.

"Hang in there. Everything will work out, however fate decides. We can pretend to have control over our lives, but everything we do has been decided by fate. It always gets what it wants."

He knew she was right. He also knew fate brought them together to create the catalyst needed to spark the change fate demanded.

"I trust that fate has a happy ending for us."

"As do I. There will be a happier future for all of us," she said. She placed her hand on his arm and gave it a gentle squeeze as she turned and walked back to whatever job she had been assigned for the day.

They would get their happily ever after. He was unwilling to accept anything less.

Kindness saw everything. They knew what was taking the high fae of the palace. They also knew the golden queen was not alone within herself.

Kindness knew the little queen's light was becoming nothing

more than a memory, but they could not find fault within her. The rebellion was taking longer than even Kindness had expected. They feared the little queen would not last for much longer.

Kindness knew fate would get what fate wanted, and there was nothing any of them could do about it. Fate and the Land chose the little queen. Therefore, Kindness knew she would survive.

She had to. Fate demanded it.

Chapter 45

Kes

97 Years Later

From the moment Panella mentioned finding the word "moonlight" in a text about the Great Battle, he finally felt like he had direction. Kes knew whatever information had been torn from the book was exactly what the Many Faced Goddess intended him to discover. He spent every waking moment either training or down in the hidden room helping to siphon through all of the text, searching for anything on the Great Battle. They spent hours every night looking and barely made a dent.

He was losing his mind. It was taking too long, and no matter how many times he tried to rescue his mate, he always failed long before he came close enough. It was the worst feeling to be that close and yet still unable to do anything for her. If he did not figure this moonlight shit out soon, he was going to do something stupid.

He knew they were running out of time as they hurtled toward the edge of a cliff from which there would be no return. He did not know what it was or what it meant, only the foreboding he wore like a second skin. Between Anin's slow decline into despair and his own anxiety, he grew more on edge with each passing night.

"Here, look. I found another mention," Panella said, walking over to where he sat, carrying a large tomb in her hands. "If you look right here... I have no idea what it's talking about. Do you?"

The power of the moonlight might be the most powerful source in the realm. When it is used correctly with the appropriate spells and stones, it can be unstoppable. Although rare, once converted, the effects are permanent. This is particularly helpful for those spells with an expiration date. It is responsible for turning the Great Battle in favor of the realm.

"I have no clue. Did the Many Faced Goddess write this? Because it's nearly as vague as the information she gives," he replied. His words were never kind when he spoke of the goddess.

"You know what? I am not entirely sure. Let me see if I can find out who authored this book...ah, I found it. It says it was written by The Many Faced Goddess just to annoy the shit out of Kes of the Night Court."

"Ha. Ha. You are so funny Panpan," she hated the nickname. He gave it to her several decades ago. The look on her face had made him laugh—a true laugh. It was for that reason alone he was certain she tolerated it.

"Says the walking pillow," she deadpanned. He laughed knowing Anin would have approved of that one. He missed the threats of being turned into random inanimate objects—like an extravagant hat. Gods he would give everything for her to call him feather duster again to his face.

"This makes it sound like a form of power," she said, returning her attention to the page. "I thought it might have been a type of magic that was used to blind one's opponent. However, based on this, I find that unlikely."

"Maybe it's something that recharges your well faster? However, that does not explain the use of it with spells and stones. Do you know of any spells that mention moonlight power?"

"No, but that does not mean they do not exist. I can search the coven libraries and see what turns up." She made a note on her scroll to not forget.

"Either way, it's pointless speculating. It's not like it brings me any closer to freeing Anin."

"Well," she said, "that might not be entirely true."

"Which part?"

"Both. Sometimes all you need is to talk out your thoughts. Hearing them aloud can spark a thought you might not have had otherwise. If speculating made one of us make a discovery, then it could mean Anin's return." She had a point.

"I still do not understand why the Many Faced Goddess could not give me the answer she obviously knows," he said. All these years later, thinking about the last time he found himself in the mushroom hut still made him angry.

"I understand it's difficult not finding the answers you desperately need. I myself did not think this would take even a fraction of the time it's taking to get her back. However, you need to focus on the fact that the Many Faced Goddess said there were things that needed to happen before she could be rescued," Panella said calmly. Everything she just said and the way she said it irritated him.

"Yeah, I know there are things that have to happen. Why do you—"

"No, Kes, *before* she could be rescued. She said Anin *would* be rescued, which means she will be. It might not be on the timeline any of us would prefer, but at some point she will be home, and we will all be together again."

He was silent for several moments. He had never thought about everything the Many Faced Goddess had said and only focused on what he needed to do.

"Panpan, you are too smart. You are making me look bad," he said, placing a hand over his heart and exaggerating his words.

"You say that like it's hard," she said, raising an eyebrow at him.

"Ouch, Panpan, ouch."

The time spent alone in his quarters was the hardest for Kes. When he's around the others, he can distract himself with their company, or throw himself into training to quiet his mind. When he's alone and surrounded by silence, all he can do is think of her. Everywhere he looks he sees the echoes of her. Although, even they are starting to fade. He sleeps in her bed more than his own even though it smells more like him than her now. Every so often he catches a whiff of the memory of her scent. He did not want to admit to no longer being able to recall it.

Her scent was not the first memory to fade. The way her hair sifted through his fingers holds that honor. He was desperately holding on to the sound of her voice. Every so often he would panic when her voice was slow to surface in his mind.

The few nights they had were a mere blip compared to the rest of their long lives, yet that time has made the biggest impact. The moment he tackled her in the woods of the Human Realm, he knew his life had changed forever.

There had been a small part of him that wished he could forget her when she had first been taken. It was one of the more stupid wishes he had ever made. It was right up there with wishing for a—well, it was better not to wish at all. Beyond that, he knew it was impossible. He would rather have the few nights they had together with a lifetime of trying to rescue her than never to have known her.

He missed her. It felt like he walked around with an Anin-sized hole within him. While he might no longer be certain of his memories, his body knew he was missing something integral.

When he sent Anin the image of him waving ridiculously, he was not surprised when there was no response. She barely responded to him in general, and when she did, he could tell she was trying to pretend like she was better than she was, even though it was clear she was not. He tried again when he could at last feel her presence—finally. She might not respond, but at least she was listening.

He can feel her slipping further away, her mind placing more than physical space between them. Now, whenever they speak, he's torn between telling her whatever she needs to hear to survive or the truth. How much is too much? Too little? There was one thing he knew for certain—he was failing her. There was nothing he could do but watch her slip through his fingers. Much like the memory of her hair doing the same.

"Panella said something tonight that had never occurred to me. The Many Faced Goddess said there were things we both had to do before rescuing you. She said we *will* rescue you. You will get out of there, Anin. I promise," he said, hoping that his images conveyed how sure he was that they would be together again.

She sent him an image of her trying to form a smile—at least she was trying.

"If you say so."

Chapter 46
Etain
103 years later

"I grow tired of having the same argument with you, Syndari," Etain sighed as she listened to the fae complain about the witches once more.

"Well, perhaps you should do something about the infestation," the Night fae sneered.

"Syndari..." Georden admonished.

"No, Georden. It's fine. I do so wish to hear more about what Syndari thinks their queen should and should not do." Etain was getting closer every night to ridding the council of one less member. She knew Ciaran would not care one way or the other. If he had been to any of the past several council meetings, he would have likely removed them himself; however, she was not her mate. That much was painfully obvious. She would not resort to violence, but she was not above a display of power. The only issue was she wondered how long her little performances would work until they required actual action.

"Yes, Syndari. Why not enlighten us all with your thoughts on our queen?" Kes said.

She was grateful he continued to show for most of the meetings, even when his king did not. A barely controlled rage festered just beneath his skin, and she thought perhaps she would not have to sink to violence after all. He just might handle it for her—not that she wanted that exactly, either.

She needed them all to respect her—not her mate, not Kes, not even her power. She needed them to respect *her*—their queen. Syndari was the last one to hold out from within the council. She thought by now, with all the good she had done for the court, she would have had all three of them on her side. They were the ones that knew how tirelessly she worked for the Night fae and the witches. Although, it seemed it would not be enough for all of them. Her being a witch would always cloud some beings' view of her.

"I only meant..."

"You only meant to tell your queen what she should do." Etain was so tired of listening to the creature's voice. Their words seemed to slither over her, leaving her feeling like she needed to bathe immediately.

"If the king were here..." they started.

"If Ciaran were here, you would likely be down a head. Consider yourself lucky that I am the one here and not the king. I must warn you, Syndari, my patience seems to have a limit and you are determined to find it. I do not want to hear your voice or even see your mouth open to spew out any more of your vitriol when it comes to my kin. While I might not take your head, I do not take issue with locking you away in the borderlands for an interminable amount of time." She did have an issue with doing something like that, but Syndari did not need to know. "Do not test me," she said, letting her raw power out.

She would not say she had control over her raw power, but she had learned to work with it and direct it to best serve her needs. In this moment, she used it to fling the fae's chair hard into the wall behind it while everything sharp within the room embedded itself around their head in the wooden paneling. The fae blessedly had nothing to say and only shook their head in acknowledgment.

"You are all excused."

"Well, as always, it's a pleasure to see you, my queen," Georden said before bowing and walking over to have a private conversation with Galetia. The Night fae had wormed his way into Etain's good graces early on when he quickly saw the benefit of having the witches within their borders. She could accredit most of the assimilation between the witches and Night fae with the work he and Galetia spent decades building.

She liked to walk the halls of Nightfell. She did not enjoy it the same way she did walking the streets of Witch City, but she liked it well enough. Over the years, the number of sneers had lessened a fraction, yet the few tight smiles she received from more and more Night fae was the measurement of success she chose to go off of. Expecting the same warm welcome the witches gave from the Night fae was like expecting a pig to fly, which she supposed in this realm anything was possible.

The sneers would never go away entirely unless she were willing to compromise who she was at her core and make the court fear her the way they did Ciaran and Kes. She was less than willing to compromise any part of her these nights. The slightest movement toward that direction felt like a slippery slope that she was unsure did not end with her compromising everything. It would become easier with each slide down that dark path to find her way back to Ciaran and yet lose herself entirely along the way.

No. She would not compromise, and she would continue to seek more tight smiles and nearly friendly nods.

W itch City was abuzz with the chaotic movements of too many witches rushing about. The preparations for the Samhain celebration in two nights' time were well on their way. Etain worked with the head witches to learn all the steps so she could lead the ceremony. The last time Samhain came around, she had been queen for just over three years. She had not felt prepared to lead the ritual then, but over the last one hundred years, she had gained confidence.

Samhain comes just once every century. It's the celebration of the natural ebb and flow between the two courts. The sky illuminated by the sun recedes and the sky illuminated with the moon expands, only to exchange a century later. Witches celebrate all the changes that happen within the realm which are few and far between, unlike in the Human Realm. They loved hearing her stories about the changing of seasons and the different ways she and her mother used to celebrate.

Most witches never cross the veil, even though the most thinnings happen in the Borderlands. With the Night and Day fae using the veil at the same time, they never felt it was safe enough to visit the veils, let alone cross. When the two courts were in the same location at any time, violence was common. Witches preferred to stay out of the drama. It was bad enough living between the two courts and their massive egos. The addition of being the first to deal with either court when one decided to go rogue only made it worse. Nothing like that had happened in a long time, but the threat was always there.

She smiled at a group of younglings who came very close to colliding with her as they excitedly ran across the intersection of a bridge with abandon. Dark wings sprouted from her and immediately flew her out of their path. They stared with open mouths before stumbling over themselves to apologize. Laughing, she waved them on. Life has a way of slowly carving that carefree spirit out of younglings bit by bit each year. She did not feel the need to speed that process along, and something about watching the way they ran off, giggling to each other, lifted a weight off her shoulders—even if it was temporary.

Etain was on her way to meet with Seraphina. The head witch had been helping her the best she could with her dark shade power. The amulet became a much larger help than she originally thought once Seraphina found a passage explaining how to utilize it. Etain could have kicked herself for thinking all she had to do was wear it.

She still had yet to have another vision, but at least she could access her strange inkblot wings when she reached in for them— most of the time. The tricky part was making sure they did not decide to disappear mid flight. She had taken to bringing a broom with her just in case, but she loved flying. The first time she ever flew was with Ciaran, and she had fallen in love with the act right alongside him. Anytime thoughts of her mate came up, there was a sharp pang in her chest where the mate bond still connected them.

When she entered Seraphina's study, the head witch jumped and made a surprised giggle. For a moment Etain wondered if she had gotten her nights mixed up. She spent one night every week meeting with each one of the head witches.

"Oh, I am so sorry! I thought you would be expecting me," Etain said, still standing in the doorway in case she did, in fact, have her dates wrong.

"Yes! Yes, of course. I guess my research pulled me in deeper than I thought it had. For a moment, I felt like I did not even exist. I was so engrossed in the story," she said, flustered.

"What are you reading?" Etain wanted to get lost like that in a book. It sounded like a wonderful escape.

"That's the thing. I am not sure yet. This is what I am working on," she said, closing the small red leather-bound book. "It's an ancient text from our library that has not been touched in at least a millennium. The head witches of the Coven of Remembrance go through all the obscure books to prevent the knowledge from being forgotten, hence the name of our coven." She pushed the text off to the side and let her hand linger on it before tearing her eyes away and giving Etain her full attention. "Come, have a seat."

"Are you sure? I can come back if you are busy. I do not mind."

"Nonsense, and besides," she said, pulling a small black book from a stack on the side of her desk, "I have a new old book for you. It looked so much like the one I gave you originally. I thought it might be a duplicate, but it looks like it is a companion to the first." Seraphina slid the book across her desk as Etain took a seat in one of the large chairs on the opposite side of the head witch.

"This is wonderful! Hopefully, it contains at least some answers to the questions the first book created." Etain began flipping through the pages and glancing at its contents.

"I hope so. I am only confused as to why it did not appear when I first made a request. It should have arrived when the library sent me the original text." She seemed troubled that the spell on the library had not worked the way it was intended to.

"If there is anything I have learned since coming to live on this side of the veil, it's that fate works exactly the way it intends to. I imagine the library presented it when fate had determined it would," Etain said, believing every single word.

"So you do not think we have any say in the way our lives unfold? Is it all up to fate?" she asked Etain, sounding surprised.

"Yes, and no. I believe fate has many paths, and each time we make a choice it can lead us on a unique journey. I simply believe the end result will always be the same. You can decide how you get to your destination, but your destination has already been determined," Etain said.

Fate had been heavy on her mind over the past few decades. It brought her comfort when she thought about Ciaran. Fate brought them together, and they had made choices leading them in opposite directions from each other. She fully believed fate intended for them to be together when it paired them as mates. Therefore, she just needed to be patient and they would be together again. Or so she hoped.

"Hmm," Seraphina mused. "I can see that. You could even argue that history has proven that to be true. Every time the balance of the Land is thrown off, it always comes back into the balance required for the realm to exist."

"Sometimes, I think fate only meddles when it sees something coming in the future that forces their hand to create different fates for all that will be involved."

"That would also make sense in regards to history. Most major conflicts are created over multiple generations before they come to a head. You could even say the ones that end up having to deal with it were fated. They always seem to have everything they will need to succeed," the head witch said thoughtfully.

"I think it's comforting."

"In a way, it's also terrifying. If you are fated to be the one to end a conflict, life is never an easy path," Seraphina said, and a little tremor made its way down her body.

"Maybe not, but ultimately it is not a punishment to walk whatever path fate has determined for you. It spends generations molding you into the exact being to face whatever the issue is head on."

"History has also shown us that everyone forced to deal with these conflicts never survives them and remains completely whole," the head witch said.

"Perhaps fate gives them more to begin with, so when forced to give so much of themselves they are not left with an empty shell of a being in the end." She hoped that was the case at least.

"That's definitely an intriguing way to think of fate."

They were both quiet for a few moments, processing, when the door flew open. Both females jumped halfway out of their seats.

"Cordelia, is everything alright?" Seraphina asked.

"Oh. What? Oh, yes. Fine. Everything is fine." The head witch of the Mystic Fates Coven did not seem well.

"Was there something either of us could help you with?" Etain asked the disoriented witch.

"Oh, no. No. I was not expecting either of you to be here. I was looking for...something," she said before turning to leave and closing the door behind her. Etain and Seraphina looked at each other for a few moments, as if neither of them were certain of what they had just witnessed.

Hours later, after they looked over the contents of the new book, Etain left and went back to her apartment. She lived there full time now, ever since the lunar ball so many years ago. She fell into a routine and that brought her comfort.

Her aunt would come for a visit in a few hours and they would talk long into second night. Then she would get up and spend the night at one of the seven covens. What had started as lessons with each head witch had now become time spent with her closest friends while they planned the future of each coven together. The difference between the acceptance of the witches versus the Night fae was...well, night and day.

The witches accepted her not only as a fellow witch, but also as their queen—with no complaints. Not even when she had little control or knowledge over her powers. The Night fae were far more complicated. She had the support of some, but the majority were still a long way off. Ciaran's absence was not helping her cause. She wished she could say she enjoyed her time with the Night fae as much as she did the witches, but that would be a lie. She tolerated the Night fae at best, and they her. However, the witches were her family and she would look after them as such.

She made a mental note to check on Cordelia. Her behavior earlier had been highly unusual for the witch she knew.

She was happy enough with the life she was living. It was not the one she wanted most of all, but it was not a terrible existence. She was used to being independent long before she came to the Fae Realm, and she easily fell back into it. At least in Witch City she was loved and not shunned, like she had been back in her little town in the Human Realm.

She thought if she kept telling herself that her current life was enough, she would believe it. She hoped she would...eventually.

Chapter 47
Lyra
107 Years Later

"Happy birthday, sister," the twins said at the same time as Lyra stepped out onto the rooftop they often sat on when they wanted to get away. Birthdays used to be a big event for them. Witches love celebrating the moment a new power is born. For the first 229 years of their lives, the coven would make a big event out of their birthdays. Twins were such a rarity that sometimes witches from other covens would come to celebrate with them as well.

For the past 107 birthdays, neither witch felt like celebrating. The coven tried the first couple of years after Anin was taken, but it did not take long for them to give up. The idea of celebrating anything without their other sister left an unpleasant taste in their mouths.

"I miss her," Panella said, looking out over the wild irregularity of Witch City.

"I do, too." Lyra took her seat next to her sister, their feet dangling over the edge.

"I feel we have failed her, leaving her for so long in that place."

393

"We only fail if we give up," Lyra responded. "Though, every year she is left to the queen's madness, my soul cracks a little deeper."

"I know we will get her back at some point. I only worry about what will be left of her when we do."

"As long as there is something left, that's all that matters. If there is even the smallest glimpse of our sister, we will do whatever is necessary to pull her further from the recesses of her mind until we have her back," Lyra said, voice full of conviction.

"We have done it once before—"

"We can do it again," Lyra said, finishing Panella's thought.

When Anin first arrived at the Silver Moon Coven, she never spoke and was startled easily. Losing her mother and being forced to flee her home while being hunted for years left its mark. It was not until she finally stumbled across the coven's front gates and Galetia accepted her as one of them that she felt comfortable enough to finally breathe.

There had been no discussion between the two sisters about adopting the silent nymph, they just decided collectively the moment they saw her. The twins had never once been quiet in their lives, and their chatter seemed to compensate for her lack of noise. It took a few months until she said her first words to them. Until then, she would only speak to Galetia, always in as few syllables as possible and never in front of anyone else.

They were having a conversation in their silent way, and Anin had been around them long enough to know what they were doing. She finally had enough and yelled at them to stop doing that in front of her. Her outburst shocked all three of them. She clapped a hand over her mouth and looked instantly regretful. The twins burst out laughing, which only stoked Anin's anger more.

They had to reassure her they were not laughing at her. They had communicated that way for so long they did not even notice when they were doing it anymore. Her anger immediately fell away and was replaced by embarrassment. The twins did not acknowledge her dark green flush and included her in the conversation from there on.

It was slow progress, but they learned one important fact about their adopted sister: her anger was the key to pulling her out of the depths of her mental isolation. They had to poke at her repeatedly over the following year until she began conversing with them easily. It took her several more years to open up to the rest of the coven, even when they all loved her as if she were one of them. In all the ways that mattered, she was a witch. Even the Many Faced Goddess claimed Anin as one of her own.

"Do you remember that time we were in the library after hours looking through the text forbidden for younglings?" Panella asked, sparking the memory.

"How could I not?" Lyra asked, laughing. "We had her convinced the section was monitored by not only the witches she saw during the day, but after hours, by the witches who had passed on and remained bound to the library."

"I still cannot believe she actually believed us!"

"We did make it feel believable."

"We did," Panella said, nodding her head in agreement. "With the way we made a book open and close or flip through pages, only to ask, 'What was that?' Every time we pretended to be more afraid, she became so, too."

"The best was the chair sliding across the floor. I can still remember how pale yellow she turned!"

"Oh, but nothing can top when you suddenly 'disappeared', taken by the witches haunting the library."

"Well, you played your part perfectly," Lyra said, bumping her shoulder into her sisters. "Pretending to panic because you did not know where I went and you could no longer hear me in your mind."

"I almost felt bad when tears began to track down her cheeks," Panella said. "Until you jumped out and yelled 'gotcha!' I thought I was going to die from laughter."

"The way her vines just exploded from every little crevice with her scream of terror!" Lyra said, holding her stomach as more laughter ripped from her.

"I will never forget the way she raged at us afterwards when she realized the whole thing was nothing but a prank."

"Nor will I," Lyra said, wiping the tears that formed from laughing so hard. "We paid for it in the end, though."

"That we did," Panella said. "When Galetia came in and found all three of us in the library, I thought for sure Anin was going to tell her what we did."

"I thought she was going to be livid about the vines now decorating every square inch of the library!"

"Me, too! Instead, she said, 'Anin, I love the greenery you have created here. It makes the library feel alive!'" Panella said in her best imitation of the head witch. "I sighed in relief because I was not going to let Anin get in trouble for the prank we played on her."

"Oh, of course not. Although, when Galetia asked what we were doing there and Anin remained silent alongside us, I knew she officially claimed us as her sisters, too." Lyra smiled. It was one of her happiest memories.

"Somehow Galetia knew we were to blame. We were on floor duty for the next three rounds of chores assignments!"

"Even with magic, the floors take forever," Lyra groaned, recalling the way her knees were bruised by the end of the first week.

"Yes, and those three weeks she assigned Anin to tend to her vines in the Library! It was worth it though," Panella recalled. "I'll never forget the way the vines quite literally exploded everywhere and the immediate embarrassment written all over her face." The two laughed, reliving the memory.

"We were always getting her into trouble or playing pranks on her, and for some reason, it seemed to make her love us more."

"Well, we have also been fiercely protective of her," her sister said. "I think that won us several points in our favor."

"True, and it's not like she and I did not play pranks on you, or you both on me. It was just in our mischievous nature."

"I can think of only one time she stood her ground and refused to go along with our shenanigans any longer."

"Ohhh—when we snuck out and found that Day fae creeping across the Borderlands?" The memory instantly resurfacing in Lyra's mind.

"Yes!" Panella exclaimed. "We made up so many ridiculous stories about what he was doing. Remember we collectively decided he was a thief sneaking around looking for unsuspecting witches?"

"That worked until we grew closer to the border."

"And with every step closer to it, Anin became more anxious."

"We changed the story. He was still a thief, but he was sneaking into the night to steal the moon. We thought the ridiculousness of the story was hilarious, and it distracted Anin enough to keep her going," Lyra said. She chuckled, shaking her head at the absurdity.

"That was until we approached the actual border and she stopped dead in her tracks while we kept going."

"It took us several more steps to notice she was no longer beside us."

"We tried to get her to hurry, so we did not lose the Day fae."

"She refused and we could not sway her, for once."

"Yes, she said we could not understand and that the male they were following was insane. Day fae do not cross into the Night Court if they wish to keep their lives. She mentioned some story about how Day fae believed there was some land across the water on the other side of the Night Court and how absurd that was," Panella started.

"Her mother told her about another nymph she spoke to before she was born who made it her mission to tell every lesser fae community she came across that it did not exist and any Day fae who crossed the border only had a painfully drawn out death awaiting them," Lyra finished.

"We promised we would protect her, and she just laughed at us. She said, 'The fae warriors patrolling the border were no match for our youngling witch skills'," Panella said in her best Anin voice.

"Oh! She was so snarky! By that point, there was no sight of the Day fae any longer and we relented, returning to the coven," Lyra said, her body shaking with laughter.

"We never tried to convince her to cross the border again." They were both quiet for a few moments, each of them lost in the past.

"There's something I have wondered about from the moment we found out Kes was her mate. What if fate had been trying to get her to Kes that night? If we had crossed the border, would it have been him that found us? Would things have turned out differently?" She knew it was pointless to think about the what-ifs, but this was more her wondering if fate had tried to intervene earlier.

"I had not thought about it, but it's possible. It was not that we never tried to get her to cross it again, the opportunity simply never presented itself again."

"That's exactly what I was thinking. Then the time she crossed, thinking there was no other option for her, just happened to be during the blood moon. The one night when there would be the most Night fae out hunting the realm that she tried to escape within," Lyra said. She had spent a long time thinking about the past and fate over the last hundred odd years.

"What are the odds her mate would find her?"

"Right? The only other time she came close to crossing was that night. I do not know if you remember, but we had an uncontrollable need to follow that fae. It felt like we had to keep going and danger did not matter." It was the strangest sensation, as if Lyra were being pushed by the hand of fate itself.

"That is so true. I remember that well."

"Fate has a funny way of getting what it wants and seemed to place her in his path eventually, anyway. It might have changed the outcome of the future we are now living, yet it does us no good to dwell on what might have been. Neither of us has the power to do anything to change the past," Lyra said. She had wished for the power to do just that for several years after Anin was taken. It took her a long time to realize no one should have that kind of power.

"Yes, I know. It's just hard not to think about the possibilities of what could have been."

"Perhaps if things were different, you would never have met Ravyn and her daughter." Lyra was positive that if anything in the past had gone differently, their futures would have looked entirely different.

"I suppose that could be true, although I do believe we were fated to find each other," Panella said, a small smile stretching across her face. Her eyes always lit up whenever she talked about Ravyn.

"And yet, if you found each other too soon, Tyne would not exist."

"You are right, and there is nothing worth her never existing."

"You truly love them, then?" Lyra asked, but she knew the answer.

"With all of my heart," Panella said without hesitation.

Lyra wrapped her arms around her sister and held her for a few moments before saying, "I am happy for you, sister. You deserve happiness, and even while we are surrounded by the obvious absence of our sister, you are allowed to find joy and you are allowed to feel it."

"I feel guilty. Our sister is miserable, and yet I am happier than I have ever been. I do not want anyone to think the return of Anin is still not my top priority," Panella said quietly, finally voicing her greatest fear.

"Panella, both can be true. You can find what or, in this case, *who* brings you the most joy while also missing our sister. It's not a wound that will heal until she is back with us, but it does not mean there is not more room in your heart."

"It's the strangest feeling. I did not know I could be so happy and fulfilled while being so incredibly sad and empty. How can two completely opposing feelings reside in my heart at the same time?" Panella asked. It was a good question, and it was one Lyra was certain there was no correct answer to.

"I am not sure, but I am of the mind that we have different hearts for different loved ones. One of your hearts can be completely shattered while another thrives. My Anin-shaped heart is decimated while my Panella-shaped heart is soaring knowing you have found someone who makes you feel complete. One does not change how the other feels, and they both reside within me simultaneously. You should not feel guilty for being happy, sister," Lyra said, verbalizing her feelings as best as she could while also showing her sister what she saw.

"What if when she gets back she thinks because I have been happy while she was suffering, I did not care?" Panella asked as she picked at a pinprick hole in her pants.

"Do you really think she would ever want anything other than happiness for you? Knowing her, the way we do, I imagine she has been hoping we have forgotten about her and moved on completely. Yet she also knows us, and knows we would never give up or forget about her."

"I just do not want her to resent me or shun them. I know it's irrational, because while I worry about things like that, I also know I am creating false scenarios," Panella said, a slight warble to her voice.

"Panella, Anin will love them instantly because you love them. It will not be long after she meets them until she loves them for herself as well. I love them because you love them, and I love them because they are now my family. Anin will be the same." Lyra was certain if Anin knew of their existence, she would already love them.

"You love them?" Panella turned to look at her sister, amazed by her declaration.

"Of course I do. How could anyone not love Tyne?" Lyra softly elbowed her sister's ribs.

"It's true," Panella laughed, "she has a way of quickly worming her way into your heart."

"Exactly. It will be love at first sight between her and Anin. Can you imagine Tyne's reaction to her wings? She adores the bird's wings and they are nothing but black feathers. Anin's are vibrant and shimmer in the sun."

"She will idolize her. It's already troubling how much she adores Kes. She has even started adapting his theatrics. Imagine how bad it will be when Anin is back and the weight of her absence is no longer keeping his dramatic nature pinned down," Panella said, trying to keep from laughing.

"Goddess, help us all!" They both burst out into laughter. There was a long silence between them as they both imagined what that would look like. "It will be the best kind of madness," Lyra whispered.

"I cannot wait."

Rebel Leader

The rebel leader's frustration was reaching an all-time high. For decades, high fae had been disappearing, but over the last several years, the frequency had increased. The rebel did not care, but they *did* care about how the high fae were more concerned with that than the destruction the Day Court rebels and the Night Court's Silent Shadows were enacting. The rebel also cared that the high fae who had joined the cause had to tread lightly because of the paranoia gripping the fae within the palace walls.

The work the rebels were doing seemed like nothing more than youngling's play after the killings began. The city was bursting at the seams with most of the southern half of the court now residing within its walls. The Dayless Quarter was well past capacity and newcomers had begun to overflow into the streets of the city proper.

The first to be massacred was an entire family—younglings included. They had only just arrived and were only looking for a clean place to rest before they attempted to find room within the Dayless Quarter. The screams could be heard for miles and blood stained the location for weeks.

The second was another family. They had been forced to hand their youngest daughter off to one of the disgusting high fae running the pleasure houses. She had fought against it and only surrendered when her options were to make the deal or her entire family would be slaughtered. It did not matter in the end, for not more than half a day later, they were butchered in the streets.

Sirens were rare and were typically only born to high fae, but occasionally two lesser fae would create one. Her beauty made her popular. She tried to mutilate herself, multiple times, only to be healed before any mark remained. Killia had been nothing but a shell of the siren she had once been when they first met. The rebel leader gave her a purpose and a way to seek her revenge.

"You are late. I have little time," the rebel said in a hushed voice to the siren.

"It could not be helped. I was *gifted* another call." Her eyes were quick to go vacant whenever she mentioned her circumstances. The rebel knew better than to pity her and never commented on the rare occasions she spoke about it.

"Were you able to get it?"

"Yes," she said, pulling out the rolled up plans to the pleasure house. The gleam in her eyes as she passed them to the rebel gave away her excitement. "I will do my best to get everyone out, but do not worry about us. We would all rather be dead."

"Very well," the rebel leader said, nodding. The siren turned to leave, but before she could get more than a few steps away, they called out to her. "Killia?" She paused and looked over her shoulder, waiting for them to continue. "Survive. You have so much more vengeance to seek."

She gave the rebel a wicked grin before rushing off in a flurry of gossamer silkane.

Chapter 48
Etain

110 years later

S he wondered if Ciaran even remembered what tonight was. She had not seen him in...a month? Two months? She truly could not recall. Whenever they had seen each other, it was awkward and uncomfortable. She could tell he was frustrated with her distance and did not think she was being reasonable. Meanwhile, Etain could not stomach how selfish he truly was and often wondered if she had been blinded to it in the beginning, or if he had just been that good at hiding his true nature for a short time.

One hundred years ago, within a few nights of listening to his grand proclamations, she allowed her life to be tied to his without any true thought. Part of her thought he must have lied to her the entire time, and yet the larger part of her knew that was not true. He had never tried to hide who he was from her. Their desires had just aligned perfectly in the beginning. Her desperate need to be loved and belong to someone, while he was desperate to end his curse to take the throne as the true king and all the power that came with it.

His attention and the love he gave her—only her—so freely had been addictive. She had craved him, *still* craved him even, and she knew his love was not a lie. The bond told her as much. However, is keeping part of yourself hidden a lie of omission? Had he even kept it from her? She thought it unlikely. There had simply not been enough time for her to see it. Their first few nights together were filled with chaos and never-ending mayhem that when life slowed down even a fraction, their truest selves had time to make an appearance.

She loves him. She tried not to and found it impossible, and not only because of the bond. One hundred years ago, she freely gave him her heart and, for better or worse, it was his for as long as they both held breath. Even if she were to spend the next several hundred years alone.

She was never truly alone. Living in Witch City made it impossible for that ever to be the case. While never asking her about it directly, the entire community of witches knew there was something wrong between the mates. They silently offered their support and constantly stopped by to offer their company as well. The small bedroom she created for herself decades ago, when she still thought the arrangement would be temporary and her mate would come to his senses soon enough, had turned into another guest room.

Now she had a room fit for the queen she was meant to be. A large, four-posted canopied bed sat in the center of the rounded room. The majority of her walls were spelled to mimic the view from outside Ciaran's windows, and her ceiling had been spelled to reflect the night sky. She found peace every time she entered her room.

Her bathing chambers were similar to the one she loved so much in his chambers. The differences being where his was black, hers was a deep emerald green. She had smoothed and curved the harsh masculine lines and raw looking stone into a softer feminine appearance. As she looked around the space, she thought she might just love her creation more than Ciaran's.

Sighing, she turned on the tap and the hot water rushed to fill the tub. She danced her fingers along the surface of the falling water and, like every time she went to enjoy any luxury, she thought of her friend. She wondered if she was being afforded something as simple as water to bathe in.

She missed Anin. They only had those first few nights together, yet it had been enough for Etain to become attached. She instantly felt a connection to her; one she had never before had with another female and not had since. The promise of a deep friendship was something she had longed for her entire life—a connection to another without the nuances of romance. Ciaran might be her fated mate, but her soul craved a mate as well. She had a feeling deep within telling her it was Anin. She wondered what Anin would have to say about the current state of Etain and Ciaran's relationship.

Turning off the tap, she shed the wrap she wore and slid into the warm embrace of the water. She had to laugh when the memory flitted across her mind of Anin fixing the hideous gown the Night fae had dressed her in. The looks of horror they both wore when all the other beings had fled from the Queen's Suite was now a funny memory for her. It took her a long time to gain the love and respect of the Night fae, and even now she was not sure she had that from more than half of the court.

She had been so nervous that day, so afraid to speak up and direct the fae preparing her. Now, she had no issues making demands for whatever she desired and commanding the council to do her bidding. The only difference between the way she ruled and the way Ciaran ruled was she did so with kindness first. She learned she can be both stern and kind, unwavering and yet soft all at the same time.

At the time of their mating ceremony, she had only been in the Fae Realm for a few short nights and was still reeling from the sudden change in her life. Had it not been for the certainty she felt coming from Ciaran, her nervousness might have been her undoing. If he had not shown up in the Queen's Suite—a room she had not been to since—when he did, she might have torn it apart to keep her mind off the insanity her life had become.

Snooping when she was anxious was something she had done since she was a small child. There was something about finding hidden treasures and secrets that took her mind off of whatever was impending. Her mother often found her looking through her things and would laugh, asking her where she thought she could hide anything from her in their small two-room home.

Sometimes she missed the simplicity of that small home and it saddened her she could no longer recall the smell it once carried of drying herbs and that something else that was distinct only to her home. Something only time and several generations of witches living in the same small home could create.

The journal!

Jerking forward to sit up, causing water to slosh over the side of the tub, she could not believe she had completely forgotten about the journal. She found it hidden in the secret compartment of the bedside table the night of her mating ceremony. Perhaps she should not be surprised to have forgotten about it. Given the way that night had gone, and the subsequent decades after that, had kept her mind busy with far more important things. Like her stolen friend, who they had not been able to do anything for since her mad sister showed up and snatched her away. Not that Ciaran was any help, being more concerned with his wants than returning his own cousin's mate.

She sighed, pulling the book to her with the magical tether she had created over a century ago. At least now, it could serve as a distraction to her tumultuous relationship and the choices she would need to make for her future if she no longer wished to be this miserable. That, however, was not something she wished to contemplate at that moment—if ever.

It was smaller than she remembered and the dark leather was soft, not hard like most books, making it easy to open. She ran the pages across her thumb. As they flipped quickly from one side of the book to the other, she chose a random page to open to. The words were written in an elegant calligraphy she thought might put Ciaran's to shame.

Father says I have no choice. The crowned prince has demanded my hand in bonding and there is no denying the prince. It does not matter to the prince I had already promised my heart to another. He did not even ask me. He simply told my father he chose me as his queen. It does not matter that my family is of low standing. Apparently, his decision was solely based on the depth of my well of power. He did not even care to know my name.

Larksaud suggested we run away together, but where would we go? The realm is not so large, and the court is even smaller. There is nowhere we could go where the prince would not find us. Then what would happen? I would still be in the same position. Only then, Larksaud would likely be dead, and possibly my parents as well.

I could not survive the life that waited for me if the life I sacrificed was in vain. When I told him as much, he raged and shattered everything within reach. I was only happy he did not also burn the entire city down.

I could never have prepared for my life to take such a horrific turn. The prince is cruel – even more so than his father. I fear what the future holds for me. Will I be able to see my family? Larksaud? Will we be bonded only in name, and will I still be afforded a relationship with my love? Would he even still want me if I were forced to bed the prince?

I cry and beg fate to please right this wrong, for this simply cannot be the path I'm meant to be on. My pleas and tears have not been enough to cause any change in my circumstances.

Etain wonders what queen this was and when she lived. She feels her own tears stream down her face as she reads the devastation clear within the queen of the past's words. Is sorrow a curse the queens of the Night Court are all subjected to?

I will become Queen tomorrow, and the fae I am before that moment will be lost forever. As much as I hope I will be able to still see my loved ones, I have this feeling tomorrow will also be the last time I am to see any of them. I wonder how long it will take Larksaud to move on. Maybe fate will be kinder to him and he will meet his fated mate. I hope he does. I hope one of us gets to have a happily ever after.

Father said to look at it as a new beginning, yet I cannot help but think I will walk to my death tomor-

row. The moment I am bonded to the prince and declared queen will be the beginning of my slow demise. Maybe I will be lucky and the prince will accidentally kill me. He has been known to go into fits of rage and any fae unlucky enough to be nearby do not survive.

I can only hope.

Tomorrow Dealla dies and a stranger takes my place. I understand how dramatic this all sounds, and yet it is the truth of it. I only found out yesternight I was to wed the prince in two nights' time. I have had two nights to try to come to terms with the reality of my new future. Two nights in which to mourn the death of the future I envisioned for myself. Two nights to say goodbye to all that I hold dear, and two nights to prepare for the unimaginable.

I have never desired to be Queen. I only ever wanted to be bonded to Larksaud and have a family with him. I wanted to be a mother and have younglings to show the same love and affection my parents gave to me. It is not something common in the fae, particularly the Night fae, but it should be.

I do not think cruelty is in our nature. Mischief for sure, and perhaps even some wickedness. However, wicked does not necessarily mean cruel. You can be wicked while also carrying the love for the ones dearest to you. It is not a weakness, and my family is a testament to that.

This is my last entry as the fae I chose to be.

Tomorrow I will become someone I am forced to be.
Farewell,
Dealla

Etain recognized that name. Ciaran did not talk about his parents, and even made a point not to acknowledge their existence. While looking for the exact date of Ciaran's birthday—he was not sure he had ever known the date—she stumbled across the names of his parents. Dealla was his mother. The water had grown cold, prompting her to get out of the tub. She got dressed and sat down in her overstuffed chair and flipped to the beginning.

E tain sobbed as she shut the small journal in her lap. She not only cried for the life this poor female was forced to endure, but also for Ciaran. He was robbed of having at least one loving parent. Perhaps if he had known love from a young age, he would have at least a hint of morality; possibly even a small amount of compassion. She knew based on the one time he spoke to her about his parents that he did not know his mother's story. It was something he deserved to know.

Ciaran needed to read this and discover for himself the fae his mother had been. At the same time, she knew it was unlikely he ever would. He did nothing unless he wanted to. She used to be able to get him to do things for her sake occasionally; however, those times have become fewer and further between over the years. Still, she would at least try.

She had not ported to his study in so long she was suddenly nervous about going there now. Would she be welcomed? Had he changed the wards to keep her out? There was only one way to find out. She took several steadying deep breaths, closed her eyes, and opened them inside Ciaran's study to find him sitting at his desk, looking at her in surprise.

They stared at each other for a long moment, neither of them saying anything. She walked over to the desk, presented the small journal, and placed it on the corner of his desk. Her fingertips brushed across the soft leather once more, wishing she could comfort the female she now felt connected to. Part of her did not wish to leave it with Ciaran, knowing how destructive he could be; she worried it might not survive. Ultimately, she knew fate had already decided, and whatever would come of it was not in her control.

"You should read this," she said, pulling her hand away and meeting his gaze with her own.

"Oh? What is it?" he asked without glancing at the book. He had yet to take his eyes off her.

"A journal."

His eyes flicked to the object with her answer.

"Whose journal?"

Etain paused. She almost feared his reaction, and with neither of them allowing the other to feel their emotions through the bond, it was impossible to know how he would react. "Your mother's," she replied cautiously.

He stared at her, saying nothing, while the muscle in his jaw ticked. Deep down she had known exactly how this was going to go and she should not have allowed herself to hope for anything different. She turned away and was about to port back to her apartment when she felt his hand lace with hers and gently pull her towards him.

"I miss you, little witch," he said softly.

"And I you." Her heart sang and filled with joy over the simple touch. She knew it would shatter her the moment she left.

"Are you well?"

She was not sure she knew how to answer that. Was she healthy? Yes. Was she happy? No.

She gave him a small, sad smile and said, "Sure, Ciaran."

Releasing his hand, she took one step away as she watched his hand fall to his side. She ported back to her apartment before either of them could say anything else. What else was there to say that they had not said to each other already? She had to protect the wellbeing of her mind, since she could no longer shield her heart from him.

The small moment of physical connection made her loneliness that much more apparent now. That emptiness inside her she had gotten so good at ignoring felt like a brand new wound all over again. She clutched at her chest as she fell gasping to her knees, sobs wracking her body.

She could never hate him, and she would always love him. Even if he was slowly killing her, breaking her piece by piece until the only thing remaining was a husk of the girl she had once been. She begged Hecate and fate to please take this pain from her. She did not know how much more of it she could survive.

Happy anniversary, Ciaran.

Chapter 49
Council Member
116 Years Later

Chaos was taking over the Day Court and not in the way he had been manufacturing for the past hundred years. The missing high fae were making his job more difficult. With everyone's growing suspicions, they paid closer attention to everyone else's actions. This made it difficult for him to continue spreading propaganda and waging his political warfare without drawing attention to himself.

To make matters worse, Daybreak's palace and city were near to bursting with the arrival of even more lesser fae by the day. Even with the magic and powers available, it was difficult keeping the section of ramshackle huts in the city designated to the immigrants hygienic. They called the ever-growing hut city "Dayless", but he thought a more appropriate name would be "Hopeless".

The stories the lesser fae brought with them were becoming harder not to take seriously. When the lesser fae began their migration into the northern part of the Day Court, they brought with them stories of a slow-moving rot. They said it ate away the land and eventually it began to consume their towns. Now, the stories were growing even more graphic.

Not even an hour ago, he heard from a new arrival about a quickly growing viscous substance that not only consumed the land and buildings, but had also consumed the slower moving fae among them, leaving no trace of the being they had once been behind. It reduced everything it consumed to nothing more than black dust. Many were mourning the loss of their elderly loved ones and, even worse, there were some devastated by the loss of their younglings.

It was not common for him to have a few hours to himself before anyone would note his absence these days. Deciding it was the perfect opportunity to investigate the claims of the lesser fae, he ported south. He moved from one southern town after another until he reached one that was showing signs of the rot they spoke of.

The town was abandoned. And recently, by the looks of it, meaning more immigrants would be descending upon the city soon. He wished he could tell them all not to come, for a new horror awaited them there. Predatory high fae were always looking for new lesser fae to force into impossible bargains.

As he watched the tar-like substance creep its way up the side of the next home in its path, he knew the lesser fae had no other options. They could try to make a living in the Borderlands, although the rumors were the witches abandoned it. No one knows why, but many stories have been created. Some of them were entirely too far-fetched, like a monster accidentally created by witches was hunting them in revenge for them trying to enslave it. He had to roll his eyes at that one.

The "rot" quickly engulfed half of the building, causing the entire structure to fall in on itself, no longer having the support of one side. It was terrifying how everything behind the substance turned to the black ash that had been described to him and fell to the ground like dust in the wind. What was once a hearty structure was reduced to small particles of nothing. Even more terrifying was the speed at which it moved.

He did not want to linger in the path of destruction much longer, yet he could not look away. He was tempted to use his elemental magic on the substance to see what would happen, and then thought better of it. There was no way to know if it was capable of retaliation or if it was a mindless disease on the land.

Now that he saw with his own eyes the devastation left in the wake of the "rot" and the speed at which it moved, he feared for the future of Daybreak. It would not reach them anytime soon, but if they did not do something, it would reach them eventually. The major issue facing him now was how to get the high fae of the court to take it seriously. He knew none of them would lower themselves to step foot into lesser fae territory to see it with their own eyes.

Time was quickly escaping him, and he was desperate to see his mate again. It had already been far too long. He sent Balthier a message with his spelled scroll asking him to meet at their secret place before porting to it himself. He waited for several minutes, fearing Balthier would not be able to get away, when the door opened and his mate walked in.

It never ceased to amaze him how after all of these years, Balthier still managed to take his breath away each time their eyes met. He quickly approached his satyr and held him for a long while before finally releasing him.

"Are you well?" he asked while looking him over for himself.

"Stop, I am fine," he said while swatting his hands away.

"That bruise on your cheek says otherwise, my love." It took everything within him to control the rage the dark green mark fueled within him.

"Hazard of being a lesser fae in high fae territory." Balthier always did that—tried to make light of the violence against him as if the pain he endured was nothing.

"Who was it?" He wanted nothing more than to hunt the fae down and make them disappear alongside the rest of the missing high fae.

"Stop. You know you cannot do anything to bring attention to you or to us." He knew his mate was right, but that did not mean he always did what was right.

"I will find a way," he said, knowing exactly how he could make it happen.

"No—what if someone catches you and then you get blamed for all the other missing high fae?"

That was also true, yet if he learned anything over the past hundred years it was that he could do anything undetected if he tried hard enough.

"Perhaps, but am I supposed to do nothing when my mate shows up with new injuries? How am I to protect you if I do nothing?"

"Who says I need you to protect me?"

"The bruises you wear," he said deadpan, making Balthier roll his eyes at him again.

"You know it does not bother me half as much as it bothers you." He crossed his arms and leaned casually against the wall behind him.

"Balthier—"

"Now, what is it you need to tell me? While I always enjoy our surprise meets, I know there is always something you either need or wish to tell me. Which is it this time?" The sharpness in Balthier's voice made his brows scrunch in concern.

"I finally went to investigate the stories the new immigrants have been telling." This made his mate stand to attention.

"You saw the rot? Why would you put yourself in harm's way to investigate something I could have easily told you about? You know that is why mother and I fled our home in the far south all of those years ago," he said, voice raising.

"I know, and it is not that I did not believe you. I only wished to see for myself the destruction and the speed at which the substance moved." If he had not gone to see for himself, he would never have truly understood how serious the threat looming was.

"The rot. That is what we call it." He almost sounded angry.

"Yes, yes, the rot."

"And?" He was definitely irritated.

"It's moving rapidly, no longer the slow spreading substance you told me about when we first met decades ago."

"Where is it now?"

"There are seven more towns between it and the border of the high fae territory."

"Ah, so it will soon become everyone's problem."

"I fear they will not take it seriously until it reaches the city's limits, and by then it will be far too late." A chill made its way down his spine, thinking about the swiftness he watched it consume what had once been someone's home.

"What will you do about it?"

"I am not certain yet. I do not think there is anything I can do until the high fae stop disappearing and the new queen sits upon the throne." He knew that still had to be his priority.

"You have put a lot of faith into this unknown queen. What if she is just as bad as her sister?" Another good question, and one he thought about as well.

"She is half lesser fae and spent most of her time with the witches. She knows what it is to be seen as lesser *and* what it is to be seen as an equal. That has to count for something." He would keep believing that unless she gave him reason to believe otherwise.

"Well, I guess only time will tell." His mate was always skeptical. It was likely the outcome of decades of disappointment. He refused to be one of those in the long string of disappointments in Balthier's life.

"Speaking of time—"

"Yes, run along back to the palace and see to your duties." He waved his hands, shooing him dismissively.

"You know I would never leave your side if it were an option. How am I to protect you if I cannot even freely be with you?" He took a step toward his mate, needing to close the distance between them.

"Right, you do all of this for me," Balthier said, rolling his eyes.

"Of course I do. I will do whatever I must to ensure we have a future together, Balthier. Anything." He would do, and he had done, whatever it took to reach the future he promised his mate.

"I know," he sighed, running his hands through his moss green hair. "You are doing everything you can for not only us, but for all the lesser fae."

"I am doing everything I can for you. Everyone else will merely benefit if I am to succeed."

"You will. I know it."

Balthier took his hand and gave it a gentle squeeze before pulling him in for a kiss. Before the heat between them could become the blazing inferno they often fell into, the council member pulled away and dropped his forehead to Balthier's.

"You have to go." It was not a question. Balthier knew their time had been limited.

"I have to go," he said, lingering. "I do not want to, though. I never want to."

"I know, but you have to save the court. If you do not, who

will?" Balthier asked, giving him a small, sad smile that tore at his heart.

"One day, I will never be forced to leave your side again," he vowed.

"I will hold you to that. I better get back anyway before this bruise has a matching one," he said, flicking his hand in the air like he had not just verbally stabbed the council member in the heart. A growl slipped out of him that made Balthier chuckle. "Go, before you do something stupid and jeopardize all of us."

"I love you, satyr." Every time he left his mate, it became harder to do so.

"I love you, too." Balthier turned and walked out the door that he had just entered through what felt like seconds earlier.

* * *

Hours later, he found a pocket of time to sneak away once more and went to the kitchens, finding them empty at this hour of the day. He moved the sack of grain next to the oven primarily used for baking bread and lifted the stone beneath it. He pulled out the clothing he hid there and changed into them before donning the heavy black cloak. Grabbing fresh bread, fruit, and a water vessel meant for travel, he filled the satchel that had become as much a part of his costume as everything else he wore.

Contorting his body and voice into the persona he created just for this task was never easy. Hunching the way he did and twisting to the side to give himself the appearance of a much older lesser fae was painful, and the voice scraped at his vocal cords. He did not have the opportunity to become this creature often, so he could tolerate it for a short period of time. It was worth it.

He took a few steps to make sure his gait was correct before he turned and took the stairs that descended into the dungeons. Whenever he had the opportunity, he went to check on the queen's prisoner. Lately, she had not been doing well, and he was growing increasingly worried her mental state might not recover. He was doing everything he could to convince her to hold on just a little longer.

He hoped for all of their sakes it was not much longer.

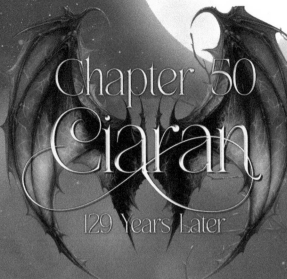

Chapter 50
Ciaran

129 Years Later

He stared at the little leather-bound book that still sat on the corner of his desk where Etain placed it years ago. It taunted him ever since, yet he refused to touch it. Part of him wanted to know what was in there that she thought he should know; the other part wanted nothing to do with anything dealing with either of his parents. So many times he nearly tossed it into the constantly raging fire burning in his hearth. Every time he thought about it, the *whispers* encouraged it, which made him think twice. Then he would think about how it would hurt Etain, and that alone is the reason it still sat on the corner of his desk, untouched. He was afraid of what he would do the second his fingers made contact, but he could not decide if he was more afraid of destroying it or reading it.

Something happened tonight to cause her to drop the tightly woven shield she constructed around their bond, which prevents him from feeling what she does. The misery and despair struck him harder than any physical blow ever could. He was shocked. He knew things were far from where they started over a hundred years ago, but he was unaware it had gotten that bad. He had been staring at his mother's journal ever since.

"You do not want to read it, so do not read it," the *whispers* said.

They sounded like many beings speaking with one mind, and he made it a point to do the opposite of whatever they told him to do. Although lately it was becoming harder not to listen to them. He knew he was sliding deeper into his madness, because the *whispers* had begun to make sense.

He lived in a constant state of fog. Sometimes he would remember he was a real being and reality would hit him, waking him from his dreamlike state and leaving him filled with anxiety. He was never certain if it was because he wished to go back to the foggy haze, or because he could never remember what he was doing while living in a waking dream. The confusion of having so many voices in his head at one time and the constant effort to ignore them had taken its toll on him. He could not even remember the last time he left his tower.

The discoveries the *whispers* led him to find, whenever he listened to them, were a major part of what was making it increasingly difficult to ignore them. If they had not reminded him of his father, it would be even more difficult to do the opposite of what they suggested; he mostly did that out of spite. They led him to several journals he never would have found otherwise. Each of these journals contained more pieces to a puzzle he was beginning to understand would lead him to an insane amount of power. He wondered if it would be enough to no longer worry about the Day Queen and her blood magic. If it were enough to protect Etain and himself from her, he would do whatever it took.

It was the shock of her emotional state that ripped him out of his current fog. Perhaps if he read the damned thing, it would bring Etain a small amount of joy and lift her out of the anguish he felt she was under for a brief moment. Was it his fault she felt like that? Had he been lost in his need to protect her from ever feeling the way he had as a youngling, that he failed to see the harm he was doing to his mate? He promised to never hurt her and yet she was hurting, and he knew it was because of him.

He stood up from the desk chair for the first time in...he could not remember how long. He took the few steps required to get around his desk and stared down at the dark leather journal. He ran his fingertips softly across it, the same way she had when she placed it there. The protective way she had gazed at it was the main reason it still existed.

He would never forget the shock of her suddenly appearing in his study. He had been in one of his fogs and she was like a bright light chasing it away. Every time he saw her, he was in awe of her beauty, and with sightings of his mate becoming sparse, he took his time drinking her in.

Every word she spoke sounded like music to his ears, and he realized he had been starved of her voice. When he grabbed her hand, his body immediately came to life, and the mate bond warmed and radiated heat throughout him. It was not only Etain's voice he was starved of; he hungered for her touch as well. The moment was gone a half second later, and she left him standing alone in his study with the *whispers* laughing at him.

"We can show you where to go for the final piece of the puzzle," the *whispers* taunted him.

The offer was tempting, but more than anything, he wanted to ease Etain's pain. He picked up the journal and crossed to one of the large wingback chairs by the fireplace and sat. He flipped open the page and was surprised to find a script so similar to his own. If it had not been for his mother's name decorating the first page, he would have thought he confused the book with one he had written.

I, Dealla of the Night Court, have fallen in love this

very night. I do not think he even knows who I am, and yet his kindness made me immediately head over heels in love.

It cannot be his father she speaks of then.

The way he was with the younglings at the festival made me feel a strange tingling inside, while everything seemed to melt within me at the same time. If that is not love, I do not know what is.

His name is Larksaud and he sells fresh baked goods at the market every day. He brought a sweet treat for all the younglings tonight and asked for nothing in return. Imagine! A Night fae doing something as pure as that! I wonder what he would think if I told him how I felt? Does he already have someone he's promised to? Perhaps he will think me too young at ninety-eight years of life, just as my father does.

I told mother and father I found the being I wish to be bonded to and they both laughed at me! I could not believe them! For all of their talk about finding a kind male and raising our younglings with love and kindness if we ever wish to enact actual change in the court, they laughed at me! They did say it was not because of the male I chose, but for doing so without even exchanging a single word. I have to admit they might be right about that.

So tomorrow I will go to his bakery, and I will go there every day until he declares his love for me!

However, knowing me, I will be too impatient and blurt it out sooner than intended. I cannot help it. When I set my mind on something, I become rather obsessive over it. I hope it does not scare him away. Oh! What if I frighten him!? I suddenly find myself nervous...

This proved his mother was not always the empty shell of a creature she had been in his youngest years. He tried to remember her. She was beautiful, as far as he could recall. Her eyes were the same as his own, everything else he got from his father. Well, perhaps not everything. It seems he inherited some personality traits and possibly even his penmanship from her.

It was hard to remember the details of her. The things that stick out to younglings are often not the same things that hundreds of years old fae notice. He remembered the style of gowns she wore and that constant cup of wine, or at least what he assumed was wine, in her hand. She always had a faraway look with an empty smile upon her face. He could not remember the color of her hair or her skin, and he was not sure he ever actually heard her true voice.

After reading just these few paragraphs, it was clear she had once been a lively fae with a strong will. He could only imagine how much that enraged his father. What happened between this journal entry and his birth to make her a shell of the creature who wrote this?

Perhaps that is what Etain thought he deserved to know. He was tempted to throw the book in the fire once again. Did he even want to know what had turned his mother into the uncaring, horrible mother she had become? Would he feel sorry for her? Did he want that?

"Do it, throw it into the fire," the *whispers* dared. That was enough to make him look back down at the page to keep reading.

Entry after entry—once he got started he could not stop. He found himself liking the female his mother had been and wishing he could have known *her*. He grew angry with each entry after she found out she was to be queen, until he reached the very last one.

Dearest Ciaran,

I hope someday you find this journal and read this letter. I will have to hide it well enough to keep your father from finding it, but perhaps you will become even more curious with age. I do hope so. It's the most joy I have ever felt watching you discover things for the very first time. You are already so smart and delightfully cunning. I hope this place never takes that away from you. My biggest regret in life is not being able to watch you become the male I know you will be. However, I suppose I cannot truly regret it, knowing my sacrifice will save you.

Your father is a horrible fae and a horrible ruler. His father was terrible, but he is the worst kind of being imaginable. He stole me from a life I loved and has beaten me down every night since trying to get me to relinquish my power to him. I have refused for hundreds of years and knowing I could dig at him by refusing every time has sustained me in this miserable existence.

That all changed the second I knew I was no longer alone. I was no longer my priority. You were. The way your father regarded my rounding belly made the hairs prickle along the back of my neck. I should have suspected something and denied him when he came demanding his rights as my bonded mate and reminding me of my duty to create an heir.

I will be honest, as disgusted as I was to lie with him, a part of me was hoping something would come from it. He wanted an heir, and I did not wish to be alone any longer. I thought you would be my opportunity to create the change I had always wished for by nurturing you with the love and affection I grew up with. You could be the new beginning the court needed.

The moment I held your little winged blue body, I learned it was possible to live with your heart no longer residing within your own body. The moment you were born was the moment my heart was no longer my own. It belonged and will always belong to you, my son.

I remember how I foolishly thought myself in love with Larksaud as a young fae. I did not know what love truly was until the moment I first touched you. The pain I had endured only moments prior was forgotten as I stared down in wonder into a pair of eyes matching my own.

You did not cry, as most youngling babes do. You opened your eyes and you stared into my own with an uncanny amount of intelligence. I was sure you were returned to this realm remembering who you had been the last time you were here. You were already taking stock of your environment and figuring out the hows and whys of the realm around you.

The past three years have made the hundreds of torturous ones worth every moment of them. I would live thousands of more years like that if it meant I could have another three with you now. Unfortunately, your father had been scheming the entire time my life was consumed by you.

He snuck into my room one night while we both slept and tried to take you from me. He almost got away with you except you cried out for the first time in your life, and I jerked awake right as your father scooped you into his treacherous arms.

He tried to convince me to let him have you. He told me we could create more younglings if I let him have just this one. Your well of power was incredible even as a small youngling and he wanted it. He wanted to steal it from you and in the process, he would steal your life as well. I would not hear of it.

You must know, by that time, your father's power had diminished to such an extent I was far more powerful than he was. The second I tapped into my power, he pulled out an obsidian blade and held it to your little throat, and everything disappeared except you and the blade your father held against you.

I will spare you the details of the deal he offered in exchange for your life. Just know, I would make the deal over and over again and regret nothing if it means you get to keep your life. That was the promise he had to make. He is never going to be able to take your life. My life as the price for yours was the easiest choice I have ever made.

I hope it does not take you long to grow strong

enough to protect yourself from his vile, wicked ways since I can no longer protect you myself. I do fear for you, and I can only hope the few years of love I have showered upon you were enough to break the cycle. I know your aunt and uncle will do the best they can to help you. They already care for you nearly as much as they do their own son.

I wish we could have had all the time together that I thought we were promised, and I am so sorry I will not be there for you the next time you need me and every time after that. I wanted nothing more than to be there for everything. I wanted to watch you discover all the wonders the Night Court has to offer. Teach you how to use your shadows—another thing you got from me—and watch you turn into the ruler I know you will be. I wish I could know the being you choose to love, or perhaps you will be lucky enough to find your fated mate. Gods know you deserve something good like that.

I am sad I will not get to know the being that is lucky enough to get to love you. Just know I already love them as if they were my own youngling because they make you happy. There is nothing a mother should want more for their child than a happy life.

I know your youngling years will be difficult, likely even tortuous. If there was a way to spare you from that, I would make that deal, too. Please do not let your father win in the end. When you find the one who makes you feel alive and lights up your darkness, hang on tight and do everything you must to never lose that happiness.

I can only imagine the effect your father will have on you, but know you have already been loved and you are not a monster. You were born and you were loved. I just know when your essence returns to the realm you will go to the beyond being loved then as well.

Perhaps in another life I will get to be your mother again and then we will have the time that was stolen from us. Until then, never forget how much I love you.

With all my love,

Mother

Ciaran stared at the fire for a long time processing the words of his mother. Everything he had always assumed to be true about her was not. She had loved him and he left her here to rot. He wanted to rage and destroy the entire realm, but the last words she wrote rang loudest in his head. Etain lit up his darkness, and he was going to do whatever it took to hang on to her.

There was only one option—one he carried with him nearly all of his life. He reached into his pocket and pulled out a ring of white metal. It had once been the greatest weapon ever used against him. Was it possible it could now be his salvation? A failsafe?

He understood he lacks morality, so if he wants to not only keep his mate but also make sure she lives a happy and fulfilled life, he would need to acquire some. That was not exactly an option, yet this ring might give the same results if the right being held the power. He would trust Etain with his life, and he knew he could trust her with control as well.

"Do not be stupid. Giving someone control over you is giving your power away. She will use it to control you just as your father did," the *whispers* hissed at him.

He had to chuckle. They would say anything to convince him to do what they wanted, and even though they were of his mind, they did not know Etain. She would never take advantage of anyone. Not even her greatest enemy.

He knew exactly what he had to do, and he did not imagine it was going to be easy to convince her; he would though. It was either convince her or lose her, and only one of those was an option. He trusted her, but he still feared wearing this ring ever again. He needed time to plan and time to gain some control over his mind once more. The voices in his mind raged at his thoughts, which only made him smile one of his too-wide, wicked smiles.

He would do whatever it took.

Chapter 51
Etaín
130 years later

"Hello, little witch," Ciaran said in a soft voice, startling her. She turned quickly, surprised to see him standing in the center of her lounge. She did not know he knew where her apartment was; although she guessed it would not be too hard to find if he truly wanted to.

"Ciaran!" She nervously wiped her suddenly dampened palms down her dress. "What are you doing here?"

She could not decide if she was happy to see him or not. On one hand, she had not seen him in far too long, and every time she saw him, it made her heart soar. On the other hand, their interactions had been the equivalent of two strangers passing over the last few years.

"I read it."

She finally looked into his eyes, taken aback by the raw emotion clear across his face, something she had never seen him wear before. She softened toward him at those three brief words, understanding the devastation swimming in his eyes.

Neither of them spoke as she waited patiently for him to say whatever it was he came to tell her. He raked his fingers through his hair and looked away from her. She could not decide if he was nervous, or if he simply did not know how to handle the emotions he was experiencing. Perhaps both.

"Would you like to go to the falls with me?" he asked, turning back to look at her. She hesitated, which caused his face to tighten, and he looked away again. Before he could port away, she walked towards him, the movement bringing his gaze back to hers.

"Yes." She did not know a single word could light his face up so beautifully, but then he had always been beautiful to her.

He gazed down at her and reached out to grasp a lock of her hair and tucked it gently behind her ear. She closed her eyes at the soft touch of her mate. She could not remember when he had last touched her. When she opened them again, they were standing on the top of his tower. It was his tower now—not theirs. She had barely stepped foot inside it over the past few decades.

Neither of them said anything as they each braided their hair and prepared for flight. He made to pick her up before he stopped, remembering she had her own wings. The clumsiness between them reminded her of their first few hours together.

"My wings are still unreliable," she lied, recalling the way he used to carry her there in the beginning. The constant touch helped them relax and become comfortable with each other. They needed that again. He looked at her suspiciously for a few seconds until the side of his mouth ticked up for just a moment before he grabbed her and shot them into the sky.

They said nothing along the way, each of them reacquainting themselves with the other. The closeness throughout the flight did exactly what she had hoped. The hold they had each kept on their bonds, which blocked each other out for nearly a hundred years, loosened until it eventually opened fully to the other.

It was dizzying adjusting to having more than one being's emotions flowing through her again. He was nervous; whether it was her presence or something else, she was not sure. Every time he looked at her, hope filled him; it was breathtaking which made it hard to keep from allowing herself to hope as well. More than anything, she felt the devastation and anger she knew was from reading his mother's journal. A few years may have passed, but she still remembered clearly the horrors his mother faced from his father.

The sound of the crashing water in the distance grew closer with each flap of Ciaran's wings. She cannot remember the last time she had visited the falls. They had not been in decades at least, and she did not feel right about going there without Ciaran.

He landed softly on their rock that stuck far out over the falls then set her down on her feet. His hands lingered around her as if he were afraid she would disappear if he let go. She slid her hand under his and grasped his fingers with her own to reassure him she was not going anywhere. He led them to the ledge and shielded them from the mist with his wings while they gazed out over the inky black water. A perfect image of the full moon in the sky reflected at them. She had forgotten how beautiful it was there.

"I understand now why you wanted me to read it. I only wish I had listened to you sooner," he confessed while still looking out over the water. He looked so vulnerable at that moment.

"I wish I could have met your mother."

"She was not the female that wrote those words by the time I was old enough to have any memory of her. I am not convinced she was even truly alive. I would not put it past my father to somehow keep her body animated while what made her who she was returned to the realm." He finally turned to look at her and a tear rolled down her face as she watched her mate crack open before her. "At least, I hope that's what happened. I am afraid, little witch. I am becoming a near replica of my father. I promised myself it was something I would never do. I would become a monster of my own making, not a shadow of his. Somewhere along the way I got wrapped up in the need for more power. I thought if I were strong enough, I could keep what my father did to me from happening to you at the hands of the Day Queen."

"What do you mean? What did your father do to you?" she asked, giving his hand a squeeze. He stared back out over the water. Whatever he was about to say was too difficult to do while looking at her. She leaned into him and rested her head against his chest.

"When I was nearly ten, my father gave me a gift, or what I thought was a gift. I should have been suspicious, because my father had never once given me anything. However, I was just a small youngling craving his father's attention. I eagerly took the dark red ring he presented to me. He even offered to put it on me himself."

He took a few moments to gather his thoughts.

"When he placed the ring on my finger, the pain that engulfed me is something I have never forgotten, no matter how much I try to tell myself that I remember nothing from that time of my life. The gift my father gave me was a conduit for him to access my well of power and block me from using it."

"Oh, Ciaran... I am so sorry." She already hated the creature that had the privilege of being his father, and now she wanted to physically harm him. Violence was not something she embraced, yet for him she would make an exception. What kind of father harms their own child in such a way?

"That was not even the worst of it. The ring also gave him complete control over my body. For ten years, my body was not my own beyond the random night here and there when he used my well completely and forced me to sleep. I learned early on not to tell him when he was getting close to the bottom. At least then he could not use me or my well for the couple of nights it took for me to wake."

She did not know what to say. She knew his childhood had not been great, but she did not know it was so traumatic. No wonder the idea of the Day Queen having magic she could use to control him created such a manic desire for more power.

"He made me the executioner to both of Kes's parents," he said in a near whisper.

"He did what?" she tried to ask as gently as she could. There was no way she heard him correctly.

"I killed Kes's mother and father. He was there to witness both." He looked back at her and his eyes searched hers frantically. The bond filled with fear, and she realized he was scared of her reaction.

"Ciaran, you did not kill them. Your father did while making it even more traumatic for both you and Kes. I am so sorry you were forced to go through unimaginable horrors. He was not a father to you, he was your tormentor."

He visibly relaxed with her words. It looked like a weight had been removed from his shoulders.

"Please understand you cannot be held responsible for anything he made you do. You know this, right? You were a youngling with no control over your own actions. You were as much a victim as Kes and his parents were. You do not have to tell me all the things he made you do, but if you want to, I am here to listen and I would never hold any of it against you. You are not a monster." She believed every word she said to him.

He laughed and removed his hand from hers to wrap his arm around her and bring her in even closer.

"Little witch, I promise you I am a monster. I do not care what happens to anyone beyond you and myself. Not that I wish anything malicious to happen to my cousin, yet I would let him burn if it meant one of us had to sacrifice. I am selfish. I know I am and I do not care. It does not bother me, I think nothing of it.

The only time I ever stop to think about my actions is when I think I have hurt you. If it is for your protection and it causes you pain...well, I think that is a small price to pay to keep you safe. I do not know how to think any other way, Etain. Believe me, these years with the distance growing further between us have made me wish to be the kind of male who had a moral compass."

She opened her mouth to protest, but found she could not disagree with what he was saying. His lack of morality had been the primary cause of the distance gaping between them. She could not accept his complete disregard for anyone else.

"Do not worry, little witch, I am not trying to get you to reassure me. I know all of this is fact. After I finished my mother's journal, I sat for a while and contemplated a solution. I am unwilling to lose you, my love.

When I was around twenty years of age, I was able to escape the palace through a window from my room in the tower. I ran away to the mountains where I met a strange fae who, by some luck of fate, had a sword that could cut through all magic, including the magic from the ring I had never been able to rid myself of. He sliced my hand off." She gasped. "He took the ring and somehow removed the unnatural magic from it, returning it to its original state."

Reaching into his pocket, he revealed a white metal ring sitting in the palm of his large hand.

"It still contains a spell that is similar to the one my father used on me. The only difference is now it can only freeze the wearer in place and immediately cut off their power. The effects last for about an hour before everything is returned to normal."

He held the ring between two fingers and turned it, glinting in the moonlight.

"I had every intention of making my father wear it so I could give him some idea of the pain he caused me. However, by the time I returned, he was bound to his bed and a slave to his rapidly aging body. It did not take long for him to become ash, and I left him to die alone. His thoughts were the only company he had, and even they had abandoned him.

I have carried this ring with me every night since it was cut from me several hundred years ago. It has become a reminder of what can happen if you trust too easily. Now, I think it might serve a different purpose."

He snatched the ring back into the palm of his hand and quickly moved in front of her face before he opened his palm again, presenting it to her. She looked at it, scrunching her brows in confusion.

"What do you want me to do with it?" He could not possibly expect her to wear such a thing.

"I want you to put it on me."

She jumped up quickly and backed away, shaking her head.

"No, I could never! Why would you want me to do the same thing your father did to you?" She thought he must be mad. There was no way she would ever want to control another being. "I could never be the one responsible for taking your body away from you, even if only temporary."

He stood and took a large step forward for every step she took back, closing the distance quickly. He dropped to his knees in front of her, making him only a head shorter than her.

"Please, little witch. I know what the problem is between us. You are good and kind—selfless, even. I am wicked, cruel, and selfish to the core. I am aware I am this way, and I have no problem with the way I am, except for being responsible for the misery we have fallen into over the last few decades."

"Ciaran..." she said, shaking her head. She did not know what to say, but enslaving another went against the very fabric of her being.

"I have no moral compass. I need you to be my compass for me, little witch. You would never use it unless I forced your hand because you are pure of heart. I want—no, I need you to use it whenever I am doing something that pushes you away."

"I cannot..." she started before he leaned forward to rest his forehead against the place where she felt the bond in her chest and wrapped his arms around her hips.

"Please, Etain. Do you not understand I would rather live the rest of eternity frozen in place and locked away in my mind if it meant I got to hear the sound of your voice every night? I cannot go another night without seeing your face everywhere I turn and being surrounded by your scent. It has been a far worse torture not being able to be the mate you need me to be."

She was speechless. She opened her mouth to respond, but nothing came out.

"If I were to lose you because of my own actions, it would kill me. I would be a walking corpse, living only to make sure you survived. I cannot go another moment back the way we were. I love you, little witch. I miss you." He looked up into her eyes while she gazed down in shock at the single tear rolling down his cheek. "Please."

Her own tears fell with abandon. How could she deny him and herself the future they deserved?

"I once thought my greatest fear was having my control taken from me again, yet now I know my biggest fear is losing you."

"Alright," she sighed out on a silent sob.

"Thank you, little witch," he said with relief.

"However, if you ever want it off, I will gladly remove it, and I will never use it unless it is completely necessary. Please do your best to make it so that I never have to use it."

"I will do my best, although even my best is questionable," he said with one of his too-wide grins. He held the ring up to her again, and this time she took it from his palm.

"Do I have to do anything?"

"No, when you put it on me, you will feel the connection to it." He held a hand out, waiting for her to place it on his finger.

"Are you sure?" She looked deep into his golden eyes, looking for any hint of uncertainty.

"Entirely."

She took a deep breath and slowly let it out as she slipped the ring onto his finger. Just like he said it would, a connection formed between her and the ring the moment it settled into place. It waited for a command she hoped she would never have to give.

He pulled her to him and gently kissed her. "Thank you, little witch," he said, a breath away from her mouth.

When he kissed her again, she kissed him back. When was the last time they kissed? She was uncertain, yet she was also certain she desired nothing more in that moment.

He sat back on his heels and pulled her into his lap, deepening their kiss. Her body was screaming for his touch while the mate bond sang between them. They each became ravenous for the other and began impatiently pushing off the fabric that kept them from each other. He lifted her to remove her dress while leaving a trail of kisses down her neck and in between the valley of her breasts and moved to pull one of her hardened tips into his mouth. She arched into him, his mouth scorching her, transforming the fire burning inside her into an inferno.

"Ciaran... I..." She tried to make words form, but all that came out was nonsense.

"You what, little witch?" He sounded far too pleased with himself just before he shifted his attention to the other breast and a hand began slowly trailing up her leg until finding its way to her already drenched core. He growled out his approval and entered her with two of his thick fingers.

"Oh, gods... Ciaran..."

"How I have missed hearing those words slip from between your lips, little witch." He freed himself and pulled his fingers from her, causing her to cry out from the absence of him. "So needy," he said as he sat her down and fully fit his cock inside her. Both of them paused and sighed with relief.

Staring deeply into each other's eyes, they began slowly moving. It was a leisurely climb to the top of her pleasure, each of them wanting this to last for an eternity. They were both nearing their peak and could no longer keep the slow pace. He held her in place as he drove into her. A moment later, they both fell over the edge of ecstasy before she collapsed onto him. He held her for several moments before porting them back to his chambers. Perhaps even *their* chambers once more. Now that she had him back, she was never letting go.

They spent the rest of the night re-exploring each other's bodies and coming together several more times. The empty feeling she had carried with her for decades was gone, and she once again felt full. She was still worried about the ring and the consequences if she ever had to use it. She could only hope that night never arrived.

For now, she was only grateful to be back in her mate's arms again.

Chapter 52
Kes
134 Years Later

K es arrived at the ruins in the middle of the Borderlands
early. He always got there early. Being physically closer
to Anin strengthened the spell on their bond and made
it easier for them to communicate.

An image formed in his mind of them standing in the moonlit
woods of the Night Court. He sent it to her before he reached out
to caress her cheek in greeting. He waited for her response, but
one never came. Concerned, he created an image of himself
reaching out to her, his way of saying he missed her.

Finally, he got a response—an image of just her hand reaching
for him. It's not much of a response, but these nights he's happy to
get anything from her. He compiled quick images from his
memory of him and Lyra training and the mountain of information Panella was searching through in the secret room under the
archives. The only thing he did not show her were the times that
he got close enough and tried to make it down the hall to her. He
knew she could feel it each time. She did not need to see it as well.

Her responding image was her wearing a small smile. The

image she projected of herself was becoming more distorted by the night. He could not decide if she was forgetting what she looked like or if it was how she saw herself now. Either way, it was troubling.

"I am coming for you." He waited several moments for a reply, but one never arrived. Her responses to him have been coming less frequently, and after this most recent failed attempt at rescue, she pulled even further into herself.

He always worried about her, more now so than ever. She was losing her will to live. He could feel it. What would be left of his mate to rescue by the time the moonlight decided to let him in on its secrets? The goddess might have told him to wait, but there was no realm where he ceased trying, even if it felt like throwing himself against a stone wall. The moon needed to stop being so elusive and relinquish her secrets to him.

"Yes, I am talking about you. Normally, I would applaud any theatrics with your stupid little secrets. However, your timing is complete shit," he said, staring out at the glowing white orb in the distant sky. It was always strange being this far from the Night Court and not being able to look up to see the moon. At this distance, she looked rather small.

"Are *you,* of all beings, scolding the moon for being dramatic?" The Day fae asked from the shadows.

"Maybe. Were you watching me scold the moon?"

"Maybe," the fae admitted.

"Well, I imagine there are far better uses of your time than staring at my beautiful face. While normally I could not blame you for it, there is too much to do. What is taking so long? I can feel her crumbling away like these ruins around us, reduced to nothing but a mere suggestion of the vibrant being she used to be."

"I understand. There are many working together to get your nymph on the throne."

"I told you already, I will support whatever she wants. If she wishes to take the throne, then I will support her. If she does not, I will stand between her and any other being who thinks to demand it of her."

He would never push to do something she did not want or did not desire to do. He hoped she wanted nothing to do with the Day Court again once he had her back. Although, knowing her, there was no way she would leave anyone to suffer. If what he had heard about the treatment of the lesser fae were true, she would consider them her responsibility, while she was his.

"Admirable, if not short sighted. The entire realm will depend on her becoming the queen," he said, rolling his eyes.

"How so? The Night Court does not care who sits upon the Day throne."

"Does it not? The entire realm depends on balance. Without it, the realm will perish. What do you think will happen to the Night Court if the Day Court no longer exists?"

"How would the Day Court not exist? I thought I was supposed to be the dramatic one." He cocked a downy brow at the Day fae.

"There is a disease on the land—"

"Yes, we know. It's not something that plagues the Night Court, therefore it is not our problem."

"It's nearing the border that separates the lesser fae territory from the higher fae," they said, genuine concern in their voice.

"Of all the idiotic things your court does, separating the fae into territories is possibly the most ridiculous of them all."

"It's one of them, that's for sure. Now, as I was saying, the substance is picking up speed and it will reach the border within the next hundred years easily. How many more hundred years until it consumes the entire Day Court? Where do you think it will go next?" The Day fae made a solid point.

"What I do not understand is why your court does nothing about it. Do you even know how to combat it?"

They should have already begun attempting to figure out how to rid their land of the disease.

"I never said the high Day fae were smart. They would never dare lower themselves and enter the lesser fae territory. They fear appearances more than they fear some unknown entity they can convince themselves does not exist," he scoffed.

Kes did not want to admit it, but he did not entirely despise the fae.

Kes laughed loudly before saying, "You must be joking. How could any fae be that preposterous?"

"I ask myself that daily. Do you now understand why I am working as hard as I can to get your mate on the throne? Even if it means a Night Court prince as our king."

"The disease plaguing your land aside, why do you care?" He could not understand what was driving the rebel leader to risk everything. If they were discovered to be working with the Night Court, it would be the end for them.

"The rot is reason enough. It has been plaguing us for hundreds of years already. Many of the elders, goddess love them, had a wild idea about some secret island—"

"There were so many Day fae who went chasing that ridiculous notion. I heard it so often on patrol I finally went to investigate for myself. There is no island, only open water for as far as I could fly." He almost forgot about that.

"One elder I know had been told that by whoever found her and her youngling son trying to cross into the Night Court. The being that escorted them to the border told them never to cross again. The first few decades of the babes life she spent visiting all the southern villages telling all who would listen, there was no island. She told them it was not worth risking their lives over it and to *never* bring their younglings across the border," the Day fae said.

Kes was stunned. What were the odds they spoke of the same nymph and her youngling son that he spared so long ago?

"Beyond that, the treatment of the lesser fae has only become worse. There is no choice for those fleeing their homes to avoid the rot. They must go north. Upon arrival at the gates of Daybreak City, all lesser fae are forced to make impossible bargains. Many of the young and beautiful are forced into the unimaginable. They are being sold by high fae to other high fae that wish to...take."

"Just when I think it is not possible for your court to become even more asinine, it proves me wrong. No fae takes another's body. How would they even justify something so barbaric?" Kes asked. It was so much worse than he thought.

"They claim lesser fae are nothing but goods, no longer considered living beings. They design the bargains in such a way that they can claim each lesser fae does so of their own free will."

"Why would the lesser fae ever agree?"

"There is no choice. You make the bargain or you die. Lately it's not just the individual threatened with death, but the entire family, since the city is well over capacity. This is why I have been working to create chaos for the high fae of Daybreak. The more painful the rebellion makes their lives, the more pressure they will apply on the queen and her council. To be honest, I thought the movement would be further along by now."

"That makes two of us. We are running out of time. What's the holdup?"

"Things were going well for a while until powerful fae started disappearing."

"What does that have to do with anything?"

"The high fae are more focused on their missing loved ones than anything else. It has made them more suspicious, so those working for the rebellion within the palace have had to be extra prudent. We just need the right fae to say the right thing to the Queen at the right time and then all should align for the rescue. In order to get there, we are going to have to become a larger threat than whoever is taking the high fae."

"The rebellion is not responsible for the disappearances?"

"No. I wish we had the skills to pull something like that off, but most of us are untrained and have minor power. The high fae amongst us are more valuable inside palace walls than causing destruction outside of them."

"You have high fae joining you?" Kes was not sure that was a good thing. He did not trust Day fae in general, but he trusted their high fae even less.

"Yes—more every day. It is not as many as I would hope, but the ones that have joined us all have their own reasons. Many come to us, no longer able to stomach the treatment of the lesser fae. Some secretly have lesser fae mates and will do whatever it takes to have a future with them, while others despise the queen."

"How do you plan to become a larger threat?"

"That's where you come in. I need you to train the rebels like you do the Silent Shadows." Kes barked out a laugh. The rebel leader could not be serious.

"You want me to train Day fae? Did you not say most of you have little to no power?"

This was madness. There was no way he was going to train a bunch of useless Day fae. Ciaran would take his head just like he had his parents if he ever found out.

"Yes, but they are the best at sneaking around. You want to speed this up? This is how you help do so." There was nothing he would not do to get Anin back even a minute earlier.

"Fuck."

"Is that a yes?" The Day fae had the nerve to laugh.

"No one—and I mean no one—is ever to know about this. Except for Anin's adoptive sisters, the twins, Lyra and Panella. My cousin would not take it...well." That was an understatement.

"Deal. When I tell you it is time, it is time, and you need to be ready to act one hour later. I cannot promise the window of opportunity will be perfect, but the queen at least will not be a problem. Unless the distraction fails miserably, yet I think the queen's pride will get the better of her."

The confidence the rebel had in their plan was palpable. Kes only hoped it was not misplaced.

"I will be ready for anything. Take care of the queen and nothing will stand in my way."

"Good, be ready," the Day fae said, reaching out.

Kes grasped the shadowed figure with his own in an unspoken agreement. It was strange for a Day fae and a Night fae to get along; it was unheard of to work together towards the same goal.

"Always."

Chapter 53
Anin

136 Years Later

I t was a special kind of torture to be within the Day Court and yet forget what the sun feels like on your skin. Time has no meaning down in the damp stone room with no accurate way to tell how much has passed. She knew it had been at least days, possibly weeks, since she had any company. How pathetic must she be to crave the company of her tormentors, but at least then she would have something to break up the monotony of her life.

The grate of her cage felt like it had begun to embed into her skin again. There was not enough room for her to roll over and she could barely move her arms a few inches. She would almost prefer the pain of lying on her bloodied back than slowly fuse to her cage, even with her wings growing back. Again.

The smell, she no longer noticed, but she knew it must be unbearable. The rows of wings lining the wall gave her some idea of how much time had passed. The first set Tatiana had removed from her were nothing more than rotten husks while the most recent ones were still vibrant, although they had started to wilt. All of the sets in between were in various stages of decomposition.

She was not sure how long it took for them to regrow, but it was not long enough and excruciatingly slow at the same time.

She used to not be able to look at them; they were a reminder of what she did not have any more. Now she passed the little time she spent awake studying them. They all had the same color pallet, though they were each unique. She would never have any exactly like them ever again. She doubted anyone else would be able to pick up on the minor differences if they had not spent what felt like an eternity staring at them.

She could turn her head and look in the other direction, but that was worse. The mirror still hung on the wall giving her a perfect view of herself with the rows of rotting wings in the background. She looked everywhere other than at the creature she had become; she could not face her. On the rare occasions she let her head switch positions and her eyes accidentally collided with their reflection, she did not recognize the female she saw. Nor did she truly remember what she looked like before.

The mental images Kes sent were enough to remind her, although she had lost the will to respond to him a while ago now. She spent most of her time locked away in the smallest recess of her mind, where she was safe from the reality of her existence. Every time it became harder to leave that place and acknowledge anything, even Kes.

When she let herself out of that little protective bubble, she was forced to endure the pain being inflicted upon her, Kes's hope, or the rotting of her wings and self. She did not know how much longer she could keep pulling herself out. Soon she would never reemerge.

While the thought of never resurfacing sounded like finally finding peace in her own way, it also meant Tatiana would win. That thought alone had kept her going longer than even Kes's hope. Now, she was not sure she wanted to fight it anymore. What did she care if her sister won? She was tired of losing. Would it not be a win for her if Tatiana could no longer torment her?

For the longest time she thought fate would make sure she made it out of the small cage at some point, yet now she believed this had been her fate from the beginning. She was never meant to leave this prison. She only hoped her sacrifice would lead to the downfall of the mad queen fate decided to give her for a sister. Something had to come out of this—something good.

She could hear the shuffling of feet coming closer. Over the years she could tell who was on their way and what kind of mood they were in based on their footfalls. Out of the three beings that came down her hall, this was the only creature she looked forward to seeing. Even if she had never actually seen them before, they were the only bit of kindness she was given.

She guessed the being was a lesser fae based on the stature and shape of the body. The voice made it impossible to tell if they were male or female or perhaps they were a shifter. Either way she did not care, she was only grateful for the company and the gifts they brought each time. Oh, she hoped they had an apple or two this time. The taste lingered for longer than anything else.

She could always hear them and smell them long before she could see them. They smelled like fresh baked bread; she guessed they worked in the kitchens. She loved the smell of fresh bread. The only problem was when he left, the smell left with him, and she could once again smell the rot and decay she was surrounded by. Not to mention the stench wafting off of her.

"Apologies for not coming sooner, little one."

They always called her "little one" which she found amusing considering she would tower over the hunched figure. It was endearing nonetheless.

"You came," she rasped. She could not remember the last time she used her voice. The sound that came out was terrifying, like she swallowed glass and then washed it down with fire.

"Of course. I am only sorry the opportunities are not easy to come by. What would you like first, little one? I have brought water, bread, some fruit—yes, even an apple," they said before she could get the question past her lips.

"Water."

Maybe she could wash away the ache in her throat. Not only did it sound like there was glass in her throat, it felt like it as well. They approached her and she turned her head as they poured water into her mouth. It embarrassed her the first few times her little savior came to visit and had to feed her by hand. Now, she had no shame left in her.

"Thank you." She still sounded like the monster she appeared to be.

She gave the cloaked figure a small smile. It felt strange to have her cheeks stretch into the now unfamiliar shape, and her lips cracked from the effort.

Breaking the bread into bite-sized pieces, they brought a piece up to her mouth and she gladly opened for it.

"There is an uprising happening," they said while continuing to feed her.

Before she could ask any questions herself, they continued, "It has been gaining momentum for decades now. I did not tell you before, because I did not wish you to get your hopes up if it went nowhere."

"An uprising? For what?" she asked between bites. She was so intrigued by the news from the outside realm that she forgot to savor each morsel.

"For a multitude of things. For the freedom of the lesser fae, the rot plaguing the land coming this way, and most of all—you."

"Me?"

"Why yes, of course, they want the true queen on the throne. Even the high fae on the side of the rebellion who know you are half nymph."

She scoffed at that, scratching her throat again in the process promoting a fit of coughing. They brought the water back up and poured it slowly for her to take small sips until the rawness left her throat again.

"I am no queen."

Sure the Land wanted her to be, but how could someone so broken ever rule a court?

"Do not be silly. You must keep your strength, both in mind and body, so that when the time comes you are ready to reach out and take your freedom for yourself. It could be tomorrow, or it could be decades longer. No one can know for sure. Prepare yourself and keep your wits about you."

She was sad to see the bread down to its last piece as they brought it to her mouth.

"I do not know how much longer I can survive here. Sure my body will live on, but my mind is near death already," she told them in a near whisper. It was the first time she voiced the words out loud, and she feared doing so might give her will the permission it had been seeking.

"You must. You have no choice," they said while pulling some berries from a pouch.

She did love berries.

"Are you bribing me with food?" she asked in an attempt at a joke.

"Is it working?"

"Let's pretend it is." She did not want to lie to her only friend in this place.

"Little queen, do whatever you must to hold onto yourself. If that means you must lock yourself away, do it. Just do not forget how to come back out."

She felt moisture on her face and it took her a moment to realize there were tears rolling across her cheeks. At this angle, tears pooled on one side before finally tipping over the bridge of her nose. She had not cried in so long that she forgot what it felt like. The kindness this creature showed her was not something she would ever forget.

"I will try," she whispered.

"Very good little queen. Just keep trying."

"I do have one condition though."

"And what is it the little queen requires?"

She could not be certain since she could not see their face, but it sounded like they were smiling.

"Only if you bring me more apples."

"It's a deal. The little queen will get her apples," they said laughing as they cut the apple they brought her and fed her a piece.

She nearly moaned in pleasure with the first juicy crunch. She did love apples, but of course they were not reason enough to keep going, although she would do her best—for her loved ones, for the memory of the witches Tatiana murdered, and the future she and Kes were owed.

For all of them, she could try. For her throne, she would try.

-Inara Gage

PART THREE

Through corridors of years and
an empty existence,

Of mountains, Ill move to erase
the distance.

Ill battle the sun and go to war
with the moon

I'd lay waste to the realm if it
kept me from you.

— Inara Gage

Chapter 54
Etain
137 years later

"Well, my favorite Lunar Ball was one hundred thirty-eight years ago before *she* showed up..."

Etain could clearly hear Leona talking to the female fae that followed her every move and tried to emulate them. She had to roll her eyes. The poor wretch had yet to move into the present and still lived in the past.

"...I say I was full. I mean, I had never been stuffed with so much cock in my life! I could not decide if I was going to die of pain or pleasure from the way he was..."

Ciaran growled. It seemed she was not the only one who could hear the walk down memory lane happening.

"Ciaran, do not let it bother you. It does not bother me. If anything, it makes me feel sad for her. Imagine the highlight of your life being so long ago only for the other being involved to have no recollection of the event, never thinking of you," Etain said, her pity for the female apparent.

"Little witch, she's purposely attempting to disrespect you. I had no idea she was even still here. I thought she left after her father lost his head," Ciaran growled out. He sounded more agitated than she thought he should for the circumstances. He was not one to let something so trivial bother him.

"...I could not sit for an entire night without being reminded of the way he..." Whatever Leona said was drowned out by the laughter that erupted from her minions who were hanging on her every word.

Or maybe he was.

Etain glanced worriedly at Ciaran, who squeezed his eyes shut and clenched his fist. The muscles in his jaw bulged from the force of clenching it. He looked like he was fighting not only anger but pain, too, and shook his head as if he were trying to clear it.

"My love? What is it?" she asked as she gently placed her hand on top of his. She felt him relax for just a moment before his body went even more rigid. "Ciaran?" she called to him. This time, fear and concern coated her voice.

"She does not deserve to breathe the same air as you," he seethed. While she was pleased that he was even more annoyed than she was at the female, his fervor worried her.

"Well, that is a bit dramatic, do you not think?" she asked, hoping to lighten his mood.

"I will rip her lungs out of her offending mouth," he said through clenched teeth.

"That is entirely unnecessary," she said with nervous laughter. She could not decide if he was joking or was serious. His eyes were still clenched shut, and she brushed her fingertips over them. "Ciaran, you are frightening me. Please, tell me what is happening to you."

His eyes flew open so suddenly she jerked her hand away from his face with a startled gasp. When he turned to her and they locked eyes, his were molten gold and the shadows from around the room seeped towards him. For a fraction of a second, she could see fear behind his eyes before they went wild again and there was no sign of her mate anywhere within them.

Something was not right.

"Ciaran!" she called to him again, this time louder, while trying desperately not to draw attention to them. The court did not need to know that something strange was happening to their king. She was about to port them to their chambers when a force bore down on her, keeping her firmly seated on her throne.

Ciaran stood, and with each step he took down the dais, the shadows writhing around him grew. It was obvious to anyone watching he was making his way toward the idiotic female whose mouth unknowingly put her in the direct path of her king's wrath. He was going to kill her, and while Etain had no love for the female, she also had no desire to watch her die a pointless and gruesome death.

"Ciaran!" she screamed at him this time.

Leona, apparently misinterpreting Etain's desperate plea for his attention, thought he was going to her for a repeat of the greatest night of her life. She stared Etain in the eyes for a few moments and then gave her a sardonic and victorious smile.

"Run!" Etain tried to warn the bitch, even though she had half a mind to leave Ciaran to his rage.

Leona just rolled her eyes, again being too dense or too delusional to read the situation. Etain thought it was a little of both. She watched as Leona seemed to become an entirely new creature. Still the same Leona, but now she dripped sensuality, the idiotic siren. Etain learned a long time ago the ethereal being was only so appealing because she was quite literally born to be. It still baffled her how a goblin as ugly as Royad managed to father a siren. If only she had been gifted even a modicum of self preservation.

Ciaran was nearly indistinguishable from his shadows, and the rage he carried radiated off of him in waves. Finally, the danger Leona was in began to trickle in through her thick skull. Etain knew this was going to get bad, and fast, if she did not free herself from these damned shadows. Somehow, she needed to tap into her blue power without the use of her hands to form the commands.

She tunneled into her orange, searching for an unseen solution. The concept of combining colors was new to her, and she felt awkward as she mentally attempted to entwine the two colors together while still keeping her eyes on the scene before her.

Frustration morphed into a panic until blue and orange poured from her and flowed into a swirling shock of vibrancy. The two colors twisted around the shadows, holding her in place, dissipating them. She shot to her feet and ran toward the writhing mass of shadows that was her mate.

"You dare disrespect your queen?" Ciaran roared at Leona who stood frozen in place with her mouth opening and closing like a fish, while attempting to form a coherent thought—any thought even.

Her survival instincts finally kicked in, but it was too late. A hand of shadows reached out and latched on to the siren's arm. A terrified shriek morphed into an agonizing scream within the span of a breath as her arm was ripped from her body. It was a sound Etain could feel in her teeth.

She really did not want to be the reason anyone was killed, even one as annoying as Leona. If the scene in front of her were not so gruesome, she might have laughed at how she once thought Leona a threat to her relationship. Losing an arm was punishment enough for her disrespect. You would think she would have learned her lesson the last time Ciaran divested her of a limb.

Just as she was about to reach Ciaran, shadows shot out of him toward the crowd of onlookers. Etain did not think twice. She sent her colors streaming toward them, instinctively knowing they were meant to cause harm. Within a moment, the shadows were contained within a vivid orange and blue web, stopping their trajectory. The shadows were placing too much strain on her power. His power felt feral and full of rage. This had to stop. Now.

She let out a cry of anguish as she connected to the ring and activated the failsafe Ciaran had given to her. It was something she hoped she would never need, yet there was no other choice at this moment. Ciaran was about to explode, and there would be far too many casualties. She knew it would not bother him, however, she would never be the same.

Ciaran froze just as she reached him and ported them to their chambers. With his shadows gone, she could see him and was devastated by the sight he made. His face was contorted into a rage so primal it looked agonizing. Gods, she hoped he would forgive her.

"Oh Ciaran, please...please forgive me," she sobbed, as she fell to her knees in front of him. "I am s-sorry, there were too many. There were too many fae and witches in your warpath. I could not let you harm them. Oh gods, am I any better than your father now? I have enslaved your body and trapped your mind within in it, just as he did."

She wanted to be mad at him for forcing her to make such a choice, although she was finding it difficult. Had he not told her this was the exact thing he was capable of? Something he knew she could never forgive him for and was the exact reason for giving her a way to prevent it? She knew this was true, and yet it did not make it any easier on her conscience. Even more so now that she knew what his father did to him as a small youngling.

For what felt like an eternity, Etain waited for the ring's spell to wear off. The entire time she went between begging him for forgiveness and chiding him for giving her no real choice. The ring's spell also cut their bond off from each other, making her unable to feel him. Her anxiety amplified as the minutes passed, dreading his response. How could he be anything but disgusted with her? He would look at her and see his father, and all the heartbreak they overcame would be for nothing.

"Little witch."

Etain cried with relief when she was flooded with love and gratitude through the bond. The spell had finally worn off. She leaped up off the ground and shot into his waiting embrace.

"I am so sorry. Please, please forgive me," she sobbed into his chest.

"There's nothing to forgive, little witch. I gave you control because I have none, and you used it. There is something I have not told you. I did not think it was important at the time and thought it would only make you want to run even faster from me," he said, uncharacteristically nervous.

"What is it?" she asked.

He picked her up and carried them to the edge of the bed, sitting her across his lap. She could feel his anxiety as if it were her own through the bond. It was something she had only felt from him one other time, and that had been the night he gave her the ring.

"There's a disease of the mind that has plagued every male in my line since my great grandfather. Or, at least, that is what I thought it was. I have been hearing these *whispers* in my head for the past several decades. I thought it was the disease I watched control my father when I was a youngling. I ignored them for so long, determined not to rot away like he did. Yet over the years it became impossible, and they seemed to get louder whenever my anger flared.

When you activated the ring, it not only cut me off from my power and magic, but it seemed to have cut *me* off from others as well. *You* and the *whispers*," he said quietly, locking eyes with her. "They are gone, the *whispers* are gone. The hold they had on my mind is gone. I am free of them. I can feel it."

"What are they then? No disease would be cured by cutting off the access to your power," she asked. She had never heard of any disease or illness being connected to a being's power or magic.

"No, not a disease, after all. I had some time to think about it while frozen. When my father was on his deathbed, he said the *whispers* had left him because he was no longer useful. At the time, I thought he was just a mad king speaking nonsense. Now I think he might have been telling the truth. Perhaps the *whispers* are not a what, but a *who*," he explained.

"Who has that kind of power? Is that something blood magic can do? You do not think it was the Queen of the Day Court, do you?" Etain rapidly asked question after question.

"I do not think so, considering how many generations they have plagued. Although, I do not know for certain. Nor do I know who else it could be. Either way, I am glad to be free of them and I have you to thank for it, little witch," he said, as a sly grin cut across his face. "I think I might need to show you just how appreciative I am." He picked her up and tossed her across the bed, eliciting a squeal from her.

"Ciaran!" she exclaimed, as he worked his way up her body, kissing and nuzzling her in all of her most sensitive places. Heat bloomed within her core and radiated out through her body, causing her breaths to come heavier and more rapidly.

"Little witch...little witch...come out and play," he said in between kisses before nipping at the inside of her thighs, pulling a moan from her. "Where's that power of yours with very specific... desires?"

It was not surprising when her red power surfaced in response, enticing her to use it. However, what was surprising was when, just like in the throne room earlier, vibrant red poured from her. It flowed around them, and Etain felt a new potential open up inside her. She tested her control over the river of red surrounding them by moving it to swirl in different directions. She felt awkward and sometimes the flowing power jerked clumsily, but she controlled it.

A sly grin of hers emerged as she directed her power to wrap around each of his wrists and ankles before flipping him onto his back and pinning him to the bed. She climbed on top of him, settling across his hardened length bulging against his laces. She rocked against him without thinking.

"What do we have here? Little witch has some new tricks," he said with a heated laugh before he thrust up against her, both of them seeking each other through the fabric barriers between them.

"Apparently. This is all very new to me. It happened for the first time earlier in the throne room," she said, moaning as the friction between them built.

She resisted the urge to rip their clothing off and come together quickly. Instead, she leaned over him and moved up to his lips, grazing hers over his, not quite touching. He chased her mouth with his own, yet she denied him only to lick a trail down his neck. Opening his shirt, she continued to lick a trail down his chest. She swirled her tongue around each of his hardened nipples before biting down on one. She was rewarded with a hiss followed by a low growl, heavy with desire.

"I am supposed to be the one showing you my gratitude. Two can play this game, little witch," he said.

Darkness solidified into two shadowy replicas of himself. They picked her up and ripped the dress off of her in one quick pull, tearing it down the center before doing the same with the scrap of fabric the Night Court called undergarments.

Within a single breath, she was naked and placed directly on his face. One of the shadows held her hands behind her back while the other held her hips in place so she could not squirm away from Ciaran's feasting mouth. He sucked on her while the shadow holding her hips lavished her breasts. The one holding her hands snaked its other shadowy hand up into her hair to grip it hard at the nape, just as he knew she liked. It forced her to look at the ceiling and not at the way her body was being worshiped.

"Oh gods, Ciaran...oh gods..." Her ascent went higher and faster with each sensation. "I... I... Ciaran!" she screamed, as she came crashing over the edge in an explosion of pleasure. The shadows holding her disappeared and she collapsed on top of him, panting for breath.

"You see, little witch," he said. "I could never compare you to my father, for I would die a happy male even if I was nothing more than your slave for the rest of my life. It would not matter, as long as I had you."

Chapter 55
Lyra

Lyra knew she had to trust fate and do as the Many Faced Goddess instructed, but she had a difficult time waiting for all the necessary events to fall into place. Each birthday that passed felt like a hopeless tally of loss. One hundred thirty-seven birthdays without Anin.

At least once per year Kes concocted a new wild rescue plan, and no matter how far-fetched it sounded, Lyra was always the first to offer assistance. Each time they were thwarted before they could even get remotely close to Anin's location. Every time they showed up in the Palace, the queen seemed to always be where they ported. They have been lucky she has not noticed them lurking. Or perhaps she had, and that was what prompted her to add the spell to the hall that led to Anin.

The only thing they could do was to continue to prepare for the inevitable war that would commence the moment they recovered her sister. This current group of Silent Shadows in training was not filling her with confidence. What started out as a group of ten was now down to seven, and she would not be surprised if only a few of them made it to the very end.

"Brucie, stop being so worried about falling! Even if you fall, it will not kill you. Get control of your fear or you will not make it through next week's cut!" She yelled at the fae while shaking her head.

He was larger than most, and while that might help him in combat, it did nothing but hinder his stealth. She had the recruits running laps around the edge of the opening to the sky in the training room. It's only a few stories of a drop and him being a fae meant he would heal in less than a night.

What the fuck kind of name was Brucie, anyway?

The smallest were the lithest, yet where they excelled at stealth, they failed in combat. In order to make it as a Shadow, you needed to be just as good at remaining unseen as you were at fighting off foes. While one or two of them showed promise, they all had a long way to go.

"That's enough, line up!" she shouted up at them. It never ceased to blow her mind how many of them plopped down, making as much noise as possible. Had they forgotten they were training to become a spy. She assumed it would be obvious that from the moment they stepped foot into the training room, they should do their best to be the Shadows they all wanted to become.

"Pair off—"

"I would like to suggest we work on hand to hand combat," Zandar said.

She was sick of his constant interruptions. "Oh? Would you like to train the class? I think you would be great at showing them all exactly what not to do."

The fae bristled. "I can take anyone in combat," he said, full of misplaced arrogance.

"Fine, show us all how amazing you are. If you can land a single blow on me, I will eat my words."

A malicious grin stretched across his face as he advanced. There were always a few of the Night fae who assumed they were stronger and better qualified than her because she was a witch.

She did not move an inch as he waltzed up to her, his intent at intimidation clear. She cocked her head to the side, and his confidence faltered slightly. Not enough to make him back down.

Good.

On his first swing, she reached out with one hand and grabbed him by the wrist, pulling it unnaturally and using his momentum to flip him. The air whooshed from him as he landed hard on his back. The only movement she made the entire time was with her one arm. It was such a simple move and yet he had walked right into it.

She smiled down at him before asking, "Are you finished, or would you like to pull your dick out next to measure it? Something tells me you are just as overly confident when it comes to judging size."

The fae's gray skin flushed a dark charcoal. This was not the first time she had to hand someone's ass to them, but sometimes she had to do it a few times in a row before their minds caught up with their pride. She could not tell if he was going to be one of them or not.

He sat up and said something under his breath.

"What was that?" she asked, cocking her head to the other side when he glared at her. "There is no room for cowardice here. If you wish to say something, say it. I will warn you though, you better be prepared to back up whatever trouble your mouth gets you into. I was nice the first time, but I will not be again."

"Nothing," he growled out.

"That does not sound like nothing, little fae-fae," she said in a sing-song voice, eliciting snickers from the remaining trainees. Zandar—or "fae-fae," as she was now going to call him—was obviously mad; more like his ego was in tatters. However, he got himself up without any further grumblings and took his place in line, glaring at anyone who was still attempting to choke back laughter.

Movement caught her attention out of the corner of her eye and she saw Panella standing in the doorway to the training room. Over the past several decades, it became their birthday tradition to spend a good portion of the night catching up on each other's lives, since fate had taken them in different directions.

"Change of plans. There are seven of you and seven head witches. Each of you will take one and follow them. If you are discovered, you are cut from the Shadows. Decide amongst yourselves who you will follow."

They immediately broke off into a group and she heard them bickering already over who would get who. She rolled her eyes as she approached her sister.

"I see this group is particularly annoying," Panella said.

"'Annoying' is not the word I would use, but yes. You just missed the show me and fae-fae put on." Panella's brows scrunched as she looked over at the group of fae trying to decipher who Lyra was talking about. "The overly confident looking one."

"Ahhh," she said, nodding. "You will have to tell me how he came to earn that name. Shall we?"

"We shall."

The two sisters left the training room with the bickering trainees behind to go find their current favorite rooftop in Witch City.

"Of course, you should. You love each other—why would you not?" Lyra asked.

They had been talking for hours and she finally got out of her sister what had clearly been weighing on her mind. She had seemed distracted the entire time.

"Witches do not have bonding ceremonies."

"It does not mean we cannot. It just means it has never been done."

Lyra thought it was obvious and could not understand why her sister was so uncertain.

"True."

"You love her?" she asked Lyra.

"With all that I am," Panella said. Her eyes held a smile, and it was as if something within her glowed at her declaration.

"You love her daughter?"

"As if I birthed her myself."

"That sounds like you were fated to me. They are your family, with or without the ceremony. Might as well have it," Lyra said again, thinking the answer was obvious.

"What if a Chronicler does not show?"

"Why would they not come to document the first ever bonding ceremony between witches?" Lyra asked, her brows furrowing. That seemed like history in the making to her.

"They would not come if they did not recognize the ceremony," her sister said, pulling on a thread unraveling from the seam of her shirt.

"Panella, you are being ridiculous. They are impartial and are only present to preside over and document events. Would this not be an event?" Lyra threw her hands up and sighed. She could not understand what her sister's problem was.

"It would," Panella said.

"Then stop being silly," Lyra said, knocking her in the shoulder. "Or could it be that the Great Panella is afraid to ask her love to join with her for life?"

"What? No... I..." Panella tripped over her own words.

"You *are* scared!"

"I am not!" She most certainly was. She let her emotions slip through accidentally.

"Yes, you are! I can feel it now! Panella, why are you afraid?"

"What if she rejects me?" Panella asked softly.

"Oh, dear goddess, you cannot possibly believe that! Please provide one logical reason why she would ever reject you." Of all the ridiculous things she could have predicted to come out of her sister's mouth, that was not one of them.

"What if she does not believe witches should have bonding ceremonies?"

"What if, what if, what if! Sister, stop being so obtuse. What has she ever done or said to make that a logical question?" Lyra was not sure if Panella was just trying to talk herself out of it or if she truly believed the drivel spewing from her own lips.

"Nothing," Panella sighed. "I just could not take it if she said no. I do not even wish to do it until our sister is back."

"Panella," Lyra said gently. "You cannot place your life on hold for Anin. She would be so angry if you wasted time on some misguided attempt to not offend her."

"You truly think she would not be upset?"

"Of course she would be upset. Not because you and Ravyn decided to tie your lives together, but because she missed it. However, to wait for her return would make her feel guilty, like she stole away your life, and you know that is exactly how she would feel," Lyra said, finally understanding her sister's hesitation.

"We could always have a celebration when she returns."

"Yes, we should have a celebration for all the events we were not able to spend together. Assuming she is well enough. I do not think she will be able to handle much for a while. All the more reason not to wait for her."

That was a big concern she had for their adoptive sister, that she would return home and everyone would expect her to be the same Anin from before. There was no way her sister came back unchanged.

Panella nodded her head while staring out at the city below them. Neither said anything for a while as they watched the witches rushing about the chaotic streets of their home. She already thought of Ravyn as her sister and Tyne as her niece. The bonding ceremony would only make it official. Why her sister was nervous about it was beyond her. They would likely start a new tradition witches would adopt from here on out simply because it had been done before. She supposed being the first for anything was always intimidating.

"I will ask her," Panella said, letting out a deep sigh.

"Oh, finally seeing sense, dear sis—"

"I have been looking for you everywhere," Zandar said, attempting to catch his breath as Lyra jumped up from her seated position. He stepped further onto the rooftop and into the light, his skin shining from exertion.

"I am impressed you found us here at all, and even more so that I did not hear your clumsy footsteps coming. Good job fae-fae."

The male groaned at the use of his new nickname.

"Please tell me you do not plan on calling me that forever."

"Only time will tell fae-fae. Now why have you interrupted our sister time?"

He looked at Panella, uncertain if he could divulge the information to her or not.

"You can tell her anything. What I know, she knows and what she knows, I know. Out with it."

"I was following the head witch like you instructed, right?" he began, his hands animated with his speech. Whatever he was there to tell her had him excited.

"I do not know, were you?" Lyra crossed her arms.

"Yes," he said, rolling his eyes at her. "I assumed it was going to be an easy enough assignment, and it was up to a point." The fae paused, still trying to catch his breath, making her more impatient.

"And..." She gestured with her hands for him to get on with his story.

"She started sneaking around nearly as much as I was, and I thought that was strange. Why would a head witch sneak around Witch City? I almost lost her, but luckily I was close enough to her so that when she did whatever spell you witches have to port—"

"There is no spell that allows witches to port," Lyra said. She was going to be very annoyed if he interrupted her time with her sister to tell some tall tale trying to get into her good graces.

"Hate to be the one to break it to you, little terror—"

"What the fuck did you just call me?" The audacity of this male made her want to reacquaint him with the ground.

"Little terror," he said with a grin. "You know, since we are giving nicknames out and all."

"Oh, I like him." Panella said, laughing.

"Oh, hush Miss I am too afraid to ask—"

"Okay, okay. Lips are sealed, but my sister is right. There is no spell that allows witches to port."

"As I was saying before the little terror interrupted me..." Lyra growled at him, which only made his grin grow. This male was entirely too full of himself. "I was lucky enough to be close enough, so the spell took me with her as well."

"You cannot be serious." It was impossible. There was no spell known to them like that.

"I am. We went to this run down temple in the Day Court, of all places. She was rummaging through hidden compartments in a strange stone wall that surrounded an altar. She did not seem to find whatever it was she was searching for," he said.

"That is bizarre. Panella, do you know of any witch temple in the Day Court?" Lyra asked.

"None. Are you sure it was not the borderlands?"

"Positive. I was half blinded by the ridiculous fireball directly above us, and it was their second day with the eclipsed sun. The temple had a hole in the ceiling that framed it perfectly—Oh, that was possibly not even the strangest of her activities. She was talking to herself. Not in a normal way. It was like she was having a conversation with someone who was not there."

"Who did you say you were following?"

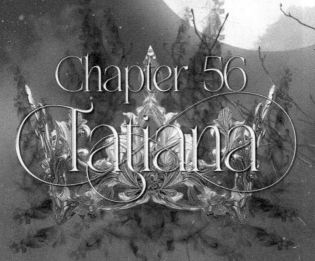

Chapter 56
Tatiana

The throng of fae waiting to speak to her was astronomical. There was no greater waste of time to her than listening to the woes of the Day fae. She had far more important things to do. The only valuable purpose these sessions served was providing her a prime opportunity to search for a powerful fae, or two, to satisfy her cravings. It had been too long since she felt the hit of fresh power surge through her veins. She started to feel the crawling sensation she got when she went too long without a sacrifice. It made it even harder to sit on her throne and plaster a kind smile on her face while pretending to care.

She gave the appearance of listening to the issues brought before her without truly doing so. Apparently it had become obvious a few times when her response was not appropriate to the situation and caused a ripple of confused murmurs. There was nothing to be done about it. She was too busy conversing with the *whispers* inside her mind.

"That one," the *whispers* declared of a smaller fae with a sizable amount of power.

"That one would be missed," she replied in her mind. She recognized the female. It was someone who had her hands in too many things for her to disappear silently.

"Who cares? What are they going to do about it? Besides, no one would ever suspect their queen," the *whispers* said.

They made a good point. Who *would* ever suspect her?

"Perhaps not. What about that one?"

The fae she looked at was a large male she had never seen before. He held a decent amount of power and stood alone. Poor pathetic male was trying so hard to find his way into the group of the highest esteemed fae of the court. Not a single one of them paid him any mind. They would likely rejoice at his sudden absence.

"Too weak."

She had known that was exactly what they would say, so her eyes had already begun to search for another.

"That one and..." she said as she scanned the room. *"Ah! That one!"* She was another fae standing on the outside of the elite, looking in. None would miss her.

"They would suffice. You are a rather bloodthirsty queen," the *whispers* said menacingly.

She would never admit to enjoying the killing, even if there was nothing more invigorating than slicing across a being's throat and watching them choke to death as she absorbed their power. She loved making them each walk to their own death, yet she would still not let herself believe she had any other motives than that of the greater good.

"No, I take no joy in the necessary killing," she lied to the *whispers* —and herself.

"Why lie, Tatiana? You cannot lie to yourself or us. We know the truth of your essence." The *whispers* chided her like one would do

a youngling fae with only a couple of decades of life under them.

She despised them when they spoke to her in such a way. *"I am not a bloodthirsty queen. Everything I have done and continue to do is for the greater good of the realm,"* she said with conviction.

The *whispers* laughed at her. The sound always set her on edge. They sounded like one being with many voices, all saying the same thing at the same time. When they laughed, it was like a ghastly echo. She shivered, and they laughed again.

"Listen to the funny little lies you tell to yourself. What is the greater good you seek, Tatiana? It cannot be the drivel you told that creature you keep in the bowels of the palace. Who would you not sacrifice for another rush of power speeding through your body, giving you that momentary euphoria? From the very first sacrifice there was never any going back for you, Blood Queen," they said, sounding like they believed she had no control over her own desires.

"I am no Blood Queen!" she raged at the *whispers*.

"Keep lying to yourself, Tatiana, however, you cannot lie to us. Keep trying though, it's rather amusing," they said before another eerie laugh.

She heard soft murmurings again and looked up to see a fae with the unfortunate fate of having a head of a fish, webbed fingers, and fins for feet. He was incredibly ugly. Even worse was the stench that followed him.

Disgusting.

She glanced at Raindal, giving him the silent command to inform her of whatever it was she missed. The murmurs picked up as he bent down to whisper into her ear. The confusion of the crowd was taking on an agitated tone, which angered Tatiana.

How dare they!

"My queen, the fae before you has asked for your help in the matter of a disagreement between himself and one of the more wealthy merchants. He claims the merchant is draining the lake he and his family live in to water his crops. He has asked for you to intervene on his behalf. Apparently, his offspring and spouse are more fish than he is and cannot live without the water," Raindal explained.

"This is quite the situation you find yourself in. What is growing in the fields?" she asked the disgusting fish fae.

"He grows silkinae, and then turns it into the fine fabric many of the wealthier fae wear. You yourself wear it right now," he said, as if she did not know something so simple. Does he think she's a simpleton?

"You seem to have become an expert on fabrics rather quickly," she snapped.

"Apologies, my queen, I meant nothing by it. I simply wished to inform you what he grows and sells," he said nervously.

"You think I do not know what silkinae is used for?" she asked, the pleasant facade she wore slipped as she sneered at him. "Why should I care what happens to one fish family? Your appearance is a blight upon the high fae of the Day Court. It would be a mercy to the rest of the realm if you no longer existed. Now be gone, and either try to find a new lake or perish. I care not."

The shocked gasps throughout the crowd brought her back to herself and she immediately wished she could return the words to her mouth and never let them pass her lips.

"Why do you care? Be the Blood Queen and show them who you really are," the *whispers* crooned to her.

"I am not a Blood Queen!" she declared. She would never admit it, never.

"Whatever you say," the *whispers* said, sounding entirely too condescending.

The murmurs around the room took on the shape of discernible words. Tatiana's rage grew as she listened to the conversations happening right in front of her. They all spoke of a hidden queen of the court, one the Land approved of. They thought the shell of a fae rotting away under their feet at this moment would be a better option? She wanted to laugh at them all. That wretch could not even stand on her own, let alone rule a court!

"My queen." She startled at the sound of Raindal's voice in her ear. She had not felt him get so close. "Perhaps if they were to see the *thing*, they would see the error of their thoughts."

"That is a horrible idea," the *whispers* said, their words laced with amusement.

"You could parade her in front of them all and show them what a weak and pathetic creature she is. Plus, would it not be fun to watch her wish for death and have all these beings here witness her weakness?"

He made a wonderful point. It was something she enjoyed most about him. He seemed to despise Anin nearly as much as she did. There were things she enjoyed more, however. Her eyes perused his body, heat igniting within her as a sly smirk graced his features.

"Go get her. Make it fast, and I will reward you later," she said in a sultry voice, promising pleasure for them both. He nodded and turned to swiftly disappear into the hidden entrance.

"That will not go the way you think it will, Blood Queen," the *whispers* said in a sing-song chorus of voices.

"Quit calling me that!" she screamed at them from within her mind. She was not a Blood Queen.

"Why even worry yourself with their words?" they asked.

"The last thing I feel like dealing with is an uprising of the entire court," she said exasperatedly.

"What does it matter? You could quite literally stop them in their tracks. Do you not crave to take them all within your grasp?" they asked with a taunt.

She did and craved it immensely. However, she was not certain she was strong enough to handle such a feat. She knew the moment she enslaved her entire court, she could never let them go. She feared that without the witches' raw power to sustain her, she would burn through her power too quickly.

"*You know why I cannot do that,*" she said, tired of having this conversation repeatedly.

"*Do I? Do you truly not believe you have enough power to control them all?*" they asked. This was a matter of contention for them. They seemed to think she held all the power in the realm, while she knew she did not.

"*No, but maybe I once did. The power between the fae and witches is far different. It is not as potent and it feels like a wisp of the power I used to get from them,*" she said, truthfully.

"*Well, perhaps it is time for you to make a trip into the Night Court. All the witches are in one central location and you could easily grab several at a time,*" they said, as if it were a simple task.

"*Easily! Ha! Ciaran and his witch queen have become one with the Land. They will sense my presence immediately,*" she groaned.

"*What will they do? It does not matter how much power they possess if they cannot control their bodies,*" they said.

The idea had merit. She was starved for the witches' raw power. There was nothing she would not do to feel their power ignite inside her, even just once more. The idea made her want to port away that very moment and grab the first witch she found. She salivated, remembering the way each sacrifice took her higher and further from reality. She had been chasing the feeling the first witch gave her centuries ago. Nothing had ever been as sweet as that first hit of raw power. Not even the power she consumed from her father could hold a candle to that of a witch.

Her body screamed for her to go now, but before she could do anything, someone from the crowd yelled, "You are not a queen! You are a monster!"

Her eyes whipped through the crowd of fae looking for the one who dared speak to her in such a manner. They obviously wished for death.

"Who? Who was it? Shall I begin taking lives until someone comes forward?" she demanded as she stood from her throne and glared at the crowd.

"It was me! I do not fear death. You have already allowed this court to deteriorate while a fate worse than death is nearing our doorsteps," a foolish male said from the back of the room.

"Oh, for goddess' sake! You are entirely too dramatic. Perhaps instead of a simple death, I should show you what it is to truly crave its release," she said. If he wanted a reason to wish for death, she would give it to him.

"You are not my queen. We all have heard of the true queen you keep hidden away. You fear her and what she represents, do you not? Interesting you keep her alive, or perhaps you cannot kill her. She is fated to replace you and that terrifies you," the male seethed. The crowd was becoming emboldened by the male's words and louder murmurs of agreement joined him.

He was not wrong, and that enraged her further. Although, she would never admit to any such feelings. She glared at the stupidly brave male who dared to glare back at her, never dropping his eyes from hers in challenge. She could not wait to watch the hope and conviction flee from him the moment he laid eyes upon his so-called true queen.

She threw her head back and laughed, allowing the mania to infuse it and remove the last shreds of the queen she pretended to be. Her hysteria caused half the fae in the room to take a step back in fear. She would make them all fear her. If it was a queen they wished for, she would grant them their wish.

She would give them the Blood Queen.

Chapter 57
Ciaran

"I think I found something!" Panella called from across the cavernous secret room. It was a little less secret these nights. A group of apparently trusted witches and Night fae were working under her to process, clean, and organize all the texts and objects filling the space. Even after a few years, the amount still untouched was astounding. If it were entirely up to Ciaran, this place and the secrets it held would still be a secret to everyone but him, Etain, and Kes.

"You have or you have not, which is it?" he asked, and was rewarded for his tone with a glare from the witch.

He sighed and rolled his eyes. The female was overly sensitive, in his opinion. She rose from the table she often sat at and lifted a heavy tomb once she realized he would not go to her.

"Would it kill you to be slightly more receptive?" Panella asked him, making her complaints apparent as she took the seat next to him which Etain occupied most.

"Unlikely," was all he said in response. She gaped at him before shaking her head in disbelief.

"Well, you are lucky I enjoy research and am bound to my queen, because I would not choose to help someone so ungrateful as your blue ass," she quipped.

A too-wide grin bloomed on his face. He enjoyed the way she never backed down from him, and she was impressively intelligent.

"So you have said before, witch. What have you found?" he demanded.

"If you look right here, you can see talk of a red gemstone—a bloodstone. It was often used in the production of wearable items, such as jewelry and, in some cases, armor and weapons."

"That sounds familiar," he said, looking up into the secret room Etain had discovered, still filled with the multitude of items, each containing a red glowing stone.

"It does. However, it gets even more exciting," she said, pausing for effect. He tried to not roll his eyes again, but his face seemed to give away his annoyance as she sighed at him. "Has anyone ever told you that conversing with you is akin to speaking to a stone wall? Although, I think a stonewall might have more personality than you do."

He barked out a laugh and a grin of her own made an appearance.

"Get on with it then," he said, attempting to keep from ripping the enormous book from her hands and reading it for himself.

"The bloodstones, as they are referred to here, are used in the protection against blood magic! They prevent the wearer from falling under the compulsion and maintaining control of their body," she said, her eyes sparkling with excitement.

"How do they work?" he asked. There was no way it was as simple as wearing a stone to be protected against a magic as powerful as blood magic.

"Well, that's where it gets difficult. It says you must have the stones imbued with a drop of blood from the one who wields the magic, or someone who shares their blood," she answered. The excitement faltered for a moment.

"Interesting, so Anin's blood would work."

The nymph had never been his priority and yet now she moved to the top of his list. With her back in the Night Court, she could give him what he desired most, protection for Etain and a way to never become enslaved to another again. Well, except for Etain; he would never mind being his little witch's slave. Particularly if it ended with her dripping all over his face again, like it had a few nights ago.

"It would. The problem is getting Anin without having the protection of the bloodstones. We need her in order to rescue her," she said, throwing her hands up in defeat.

"What else does it say?" he asked, changing the subject. He did not want to deal with an emotional female.

"Not much more, only that there is a spell required to be performed by a witch. I cannot find any mention of the spell itself, either. It has a passage that mentions a metal, so in the absence of color it seems to glow like the moon. I thought that sounded an awful lot like most of the armor and weapons in there," she said, pointing to the hidden room.

It did. It also sounded a lot like the ring he once again wore, only this time it was a bright white instead of a dark red. It also sounded a lot like his sword he commandeered off a long-dead Day fae centuries ago. He remembered Master Ulgridge had a name for it—something about the moon...

"They call it Moon Blessed. The book makes some wild claims about what it can be used for. The only problem is you have to have someone who can create it. It does not naturally occur. A being with the gift of the moon must craft it. The metal is used as a conduit for magic and can amplify spells, or hold specific spells that make blades unbreakable and armor impenetrable," she said, sounding like she found that hard to believe.

Ciaran did not have any issues believing it. The ring around his finger was proof enough to him. He wondered, not for the first time, about the spell it contained. He was tempted to ask Panella. Yet he did not want to give her any kind of power over him, and the knowledge of the ring could be used against him if one truly desired to.

"This is not the first time I have heard of a metal being 'Moon Blessed'," he said.

She looked at him, expecting him to continue, and when he did not, she scoffed at him and mumbled something about a stone wall under her breath.

"Do you think this Moon Blessed metal has something to do with the task the Many Faced Goddess gave to Kes?" she asked.

If he were being honest, the thought never once crossed his mind.

"Perhaps," was all he responded. If his cousin had been tasked with discovering something about the Moon Blessed metals before he could rescue Anin, he might be able to help speed that along. The sooner Anin was back, the sooner he and Etain could be protected from Tatiana's blood magic. It was unacceptable for her to have so much power over him when he was clearly the more powerful of the two. It was obvious the Land had abandoned her. Blood magic was unnatural and disrupts the delicate balance the Land requires, making it unlikely she still had its power.

Panella said something next to him he did not hear, nor did he indicate he was listening to her. She made a production he could feel next to him, as she slammed the book closed while standing. All before stomping back to her table to rejoin her lover.

Ciaran got up and walked into the room holding what he hoped were bloodstones and Moon Blessed metals. The book, as far as he knew, mentioned nothing about the way they glowed. He wondered if that meant these stones were already imbued with another's blood. Were these used in the Great Battle all those centuries ago? If so, whose blood had they used? It would be convenient if it were someone who came from Tatiana's line. Although, if the history Panella had been uncovering was anything to go off, the royal lines had worked together for the betterment of the realm. They had gone up against two beings, one from the Day Court and one from the Night Court.

None of the history books mentioned anything about who they were. History was always written by the victors, after all. He did not understand why there was never any history that was completely honest. Were all beings too full of their own self importance to need to paint themselves in a better light? They won. What better light could there be? It did not matter; however, it would have been helpful now to know something about the ones who had wielded blood magic in the past.

He pulled out a spelled scroll and demanded Kes's immediate presence. He needed to know what the witch had just discovered and then, together, they would go to the Nocturia Mountains and see if Ulgridge still resided there. When more than a moment passed and Kes had still not arrived, he sent another, indicating it had to do with Anin. A few more moments passed and a winded Kes came barreling down the steps.

"What about Anin?" Kes asked breathlessly.

"It took you long enough," Ciaran replied dryly.

"There are a ridiculous number of stairs to get down here. Now, what of Anin?" Kes asked, clearly losing patience.

"Panella has been helping me search for any information about these red gemstones..."

"I do not care what Panella has been helping you do. What of Anin?" Kes asked again, anger lacing his voice.

"I am getting there. I might have said it was about Anin to get you here faster. It has to deal with her, but in a roundabout way. Nothing time sensitive. Do not interrupt me and you might find out what all of this has to do with your nymph," Ciaran replied, his annoyance obvious.

"Do not ever use her as a means to hurry me ever again. I would never do such a thing if the tables were reversed," he seethed.

Ciaran did not doubt his cousin, but he also did not care because the tables were not reversed.

"Yes, well, as I was saying—the red gemstones hopefully are what the book referred to as bloodstones. They, when imbued with the blood of the one who wields blood magic, and a spell performed by a witch, can protect the wearer from the effects of the blood magic," Ciaran explained.

"That does nothing for us. We cannot get close to her without her knowing and enslaving us with her fucked up magic." Kes's anger was growing exponentially.

"No, however, the book also stated the blood could come from another who shared blood with the magic holder," Ciaran said, and Kes's eyes flared with understanding.

"Anin."

"Yes. Anin," Ciaran repeated.

"Again, that does nothing for us. If there were a way to get her out of that hellhole she has been locked in for the past one hundred thirty-seven years, I would have already gotten her. One hundred thirty-seven years, Ciaran!" he raged, smashing one case holding several pieces of jewelry, each showcasing a hopeful bloodstone.

Ciaran watched him as he smashed another and heaved several breaths before he screamed in frustration. The sound of several chairs scraping across the floor sounded from the main room as the beings, who had just been hard at work, quickly made for the stairs.

"Are you done?" Ciaran asked him, beginning to lose his own patience.

"Am I done? What kind of question is that? Why yes, cousin, it's only my mate who has been locked in a cage so small she is unable to even flip over for the past ONE HUNDRED THIRTY-SEVEN YEARS!" Kes screamed.

Ciaran looked at him and raised a single brow at his behavior. Ever since his mate had been taken, Kes had not been the theatrical fae Ciaran had grown used to. As much as his theatrics annoyed him, he wished for the return of the old Kes. This one was more than annoying, and he lacked the tolerance to deal with him.

"I was not finished," was all Ciaran said. Kes turned sharply to look at him.

"What do you mean, you were not finished?" Kes asked.

"What were you tasked with by the Many Faced Goddess before you could rescue your nymph?" Ciaran asked in response.

"Something ridiculous about discovering the secrets the moonlight holds. Why?" Kes asked, curiosity blooming.

"Do you see the metal the armor is made from?" Ciaran asked, again a question in response to a question. His cousin did not seem to appreciate it.

"Of course I see it. I am standing in front of the blindingly bright metal. What of it?" Kes said sarcastically. "It's like having a second moon in this small..." his voice trailed off as if something had just occurred to him.

Ciaran had no idea what he was talking about. The metal was no more bright than any other would be.

"According to the book that described the bloodstones, this metal is something called Moon Blessed," he watched as Kes took in his words, sure his cousin was thinking exactly what he was.

Moon blessed metal and a riddle from the goddess about moon light was too much of a coincidence to not explore. Particularly now that he even compared the metal to the moon herself.

"Moon blessed..." Kes said as he rolled the name around in his head. "Moon blessed? I have never once heard of any metal called Moon Blessed," Kes said doubtfully.

"I have," Ciaran said. That got Kes's attention.

"What do you mean, you have? Why did you not mention it sooner? Like–oh, I do not know—a hundred years or so ago!" Kes screamed at him again. Ciaran was losing his patience with his cousin's behavior and glared at him.

"If I am honest, it was not something I remembered hearing until Panella read it from that book," he said truthfully.

"Where have you heard it before?" Kes asked.

"Have you ever wondered where I spent those couple hundred years that I was gone when we were younglings?"

He had never asked Ciaran about that time, and Ciaran had never asked Kes either.

"I had never given it much thought, no," Kes answered.

"I was in the Nocturia Mountains. I lived in a cave with a strange fae who it's quite possible is more than fae. I have never told you about how my father could get me to do his bidding, and I will not go into it now. All you need to know is it involved this so-called 'Moon Blessed' metal, and the male in the cave seemed to know quite a bit about it. I did not believe any of the tales he told me then, yet now I think there might have been some truth to them after all," he said.

He could see the questions swimming in his cousin's eyes, yet he asked none of them. Instead, Kes asked, "What are the chances he's still in that cave?"

"Only one way to find out. Do you feel like getting away to the mountains?" Ciaran asked. He was surprised at the joy he felt at both the prospect of seeing Master Ulgridge and the hopeful grin his cousin now wore. Where he used to wear one as a constant accessory, now it was a rare event. He supposed he missed seeing his cousin happy.

"That sounds delightful," Kes said, his grin turning into a hopeful smile.

Chapter 58
Council Member

"It's about fucking time," he said under his breath as he made his way toward the dungeons.

Finally, all of his manipulations have converged, creating the perfect opportunity for the bird and his shadows to come and rescue the true queen. He could only hope she would be better than her sister. Being a lesser fae herself, he thought it likely she would want to end their deplorable treatment. If he were lucky, she would dissolve the horrific deals they had been forced to make as well.

Migration was at an all-time high and no one had gone to investigate why. No one except him. The blight on the land was devastating. Anything in its path rotted away to nothing but the decayed residue of death. What was once lush green forests and meadows teaming with life was now nothing but a black, barren landscape. The high fae reside only in the north and stupidly thought the tales the lesser fae brought with them from the south were not their problem. Clearly the influx of migrants over the past century proved it was only a matter of time until it was everyone's problem. It would be too late by then.

He refused to leave Balthier in the hands of his slaver any longer than he must. The high fae had managed to elude the many times Raindal tried to have him chosen as a sacrifice for Tatiana. He worked too long and too hard to let his plan fail now. His love would get the life he deserved, no matter the cost. It did not matter to him that his mate was a lesser fae.

Lesser fae. What a shit way to refer to living beings.

He would burn the realm down to the ground only to rebuild it into one where he was free to love who fate chose for him. Fated mates were not something many found over the course of several lives, and yet he had. He would not let the life they were meant to have slip through his fingers.

No. He did not care who he hurt or betrayed in the process. The only being he would forever remain true to was Balthier, even if he was forced to do things he knew hurt him. The end would be worth the painful road they started their life together on. Fate would not give them each other if fate did not mean for them to have each other. He trusted that it would make sure they were together in the end. They might be a little less whole than they started out, but it did not matter as long as they were together. They could fill in each other's missing pieces.

He was getting closer to the damp stone room with nothing in it beyond a cage hanging in the center containing the broken shell of a nymph. She had once contained a fire so bright he had been willing to bet not only his life but his mates on her as well. The last several decades had not been kind to her. He watched as her flame flickered until it disappeared completely. He hoped there were still embers smoldering enough to reignite her.

The stench was nearly unbearable. Between the female who had received nothing beyond buckets of cold water dumped on her every year or so, and the collection of decaying wings hanging on the wall like trophies, it was enough to make him retch. Over the decades, he learned to breathe through his mouth to lessen the impact of it each time he came down here. Somehow, it never seemed to bother the queen.

Her latest set of wings had almost grown back completely, and if everything went according to plan, she would keep this set. She used to physically respond with a slight flinch she tried to hide when someone would enter the room. Her body was preparing for the agony that was soon to follow. Now, she barely even woke.

He had always done what he could for her. It was not as much as he wanted, but he could not risk being discovered. He would drape himself in an oversized dark cloak to keep his identity a secret, not only from any random fae he might run into, but from her as well. She could never recognize him as the male who snuck her food and water. That would ruin everything he had spent nearly two centuries working towards.

"Rise and shine, princess!" he shouted as he clapped his hands together loudly, causing her to jerk awake. He felt like a piece of shit whenever he had to play this role. However, it was the only way to save them both. He would bear her anger if he got what he wanted most in the end.

She glared at him, refusing to speak. If there was one thing he learned about this female, the best way to coax life back into her was playing to her anger. He opened the cage from the bottom, causing her to free fall to the ground beneath her. A small cry of pain escaped her. It took everything in him to maintain the character he played and not help her up. Maybe one day she would forgive him. Unlikely, but he could hope.

"Get up!" he roared. She did not budge. "I said get up! Now! If you do not get up on your own, I will be forced to help you, and I do not think you will enjoy the 'help' I provide."

"Where's your master, Raindal?" she asked.

Good, there's a spark left in her yet.

"The queen awaits our presence. I would not keep her waiting if I were you."

The confusion painting her face was plain to see. She had never gone to Tatiana or moved beyond the door of her cell before. It seemed the prospect of leaving this foul room made her burn just that much brighter.

She glared at him again as she forced herself to stand. She fell a few times until she finally got her feet under her. He smirked at her the whole time he watched her struggle, which only threw fuel on the small flame he saw sparking into life behind her eyes.

"Where are we going?" she asked, her voice rough from disuse.

"And what makes you think I would tell you anything?" he asked her in return, attempting to sound as pompous as he had spent decades convincing her he was.

"Because you enjoy announcing how much knowledge you hold over me," she said.

The smirk that formed on his face from her response was not an act. It was impressive how quickly she was pulling herself together.

"Oh princess, you have been paying attention. I am flattered. You are correct, of course. We are going to the throne room," he said sarcastically.

"Why the throne room?" she asked, sounding truly baffled.

He could not blame her for her confusion. It was a stupid move for Tatiana to parade her in front of the court, allowing them to see that the true queen existed. Many of the beings in the throne room still thought her a myth.

"So many questions, princess."

She hated when he called her that, therefore he used the moniker as often as possible. She gave him one of her better glares, one he had not seen the likes of for a very long time.

He sighed out an annoyed breath before he said, "Very well.

There seems to be a rumor circulating about another with a claim to the throne hidden somewhere beneath the palace."

"I am not sure a fact can be a rumor," she said.

He did not miss the surprise that briefly flared in her eyes. She did not know that he, her mate, and her shadow sisters had been hard at work to get them to this moment for so very long.

"Oh, well, I suppose that's true," he said with a cold laugh.

"What about that makes her demand my presence?" she asked, suspicion clear in her tone.

"I believe she has some delightful plans for you to show the entire court what a disgusting little creature you are," he said with a menacing laugh.

He hoped she picked up on the fact she was about to have an audience with the Day Court. He was pleased when the wheels began to move behind her eyes. He would need to push her deeper into her anger without breaking the flicker of determination she carried within her.

She stood there, uncertain as he strode towards the only way in and out of the small room.

"Well? Are you going to walk of your own will, or will I need to drag you there? While it could be fun to see how long your hair holds up until it rips from your scalp, I truly do not want to touch you. You are filthy."

It was not a lie. He did not wish to touch her. It was not only her filth that kept his hands away, but he knew what it was to be touched against his own desires. He was loath to do that to her. Without the watchful eye of the queen, he could give her that small control over her own body back, no matter how fleeting.

She huffed out a sound that almost sounded indignant. He had to roll his eyes and sigh to keep from smiling at the small glimpse of the female she used to be making an appearance. She stumbled after him as he walked out. He watched as she took her first step past the threshold of the room that had been her prison for the last one hundred thirty-seven years. That single footstep left a print with the blood dripping from where the cage tore away from her skin—breaking the spell Tatiana had placed on the hall. He could not have planned that better if he tried.

Her breathing picked up and he could tell the small amount of freedom overwhelmed her. Making her walk to the throne room on her own, he hoped, would give her a taste of enough freedom to inspire her to rise to the challenge that awaited her. They had not made it very far before she had to take a break against the wall, her legs shaking.

"Is that all you have?" he asked as he rolled his eyes at her again. They were going to roll right out of his head, but he had to act as though he were incredibly put out by her need for rest. "You have the two steps it will take me to reach you to start walking again, otherwise I will be dragging your filthy ass the entire way."

The look she gave him would have been his demise if looks could kill.

"How does it feel to be the queen's whore? At her beck and call whenever she needs servicing? Just like a hungry puppy, you always come running. You disgust me," she said in a way that left no interpretation for just how disgusting she found him. If she only knew how closely their opinions of him aligned.

His carefully constructed facade he wore cracked just enough, and he slipped the smallest bit.

"No one gets out of life completely unscathed. Every creature to ever live will sacrifice small pieces of themselves along the way before they are returned to the realm. Some sacrifices take larger pieces than others." She gaped as the words tumbled out of his mouth. "We all have a role to play, princess, and now it is time for you to play yours."

They stared into each other's eyes for a long moment, and he let her search for whatever it was she was trying to find. Her brows scrunched in confusion and he fell back into the character he wore so well after centuries of playing him. He laughed menacingly at her attempt to figure him out.

"Let's. Go!" he roared at her. The confusion wiped away from her face in an instant and the hatred he had become accustomed to from her replaced it.

The only other time she stopped along the path to the throne room was when they passed a beam of sunlight blanketing a section of the hall. She gasped as she stepped into the light and turned her face to the sun. He watched as some of her golden glow returned and a single tear tracked down her dirty face.

He did not know when the last time she felt the sun upon her was. He thought it was likely prior to finding herself in the violent clutches of her crazed sister. She was often teased with the minimal light given off by the eclipsed sun that illuminated Tatiana's altar of death. She could see the sun while never being able to feel it upon her. He allowed her this small mercy.

"I grow tired of having to tell you to move, princess."

"Funny, I grow tired of listening to your voice," she said smartly, turning to follow him the remainder of the way to the moment that would either set both of their salvations in motion or damn the entire realm.

When they stood just inside the hidden door to the throne room, he pulled his spelled scroll to himself and sent two words to the bird. He locked eyes with her once more, allowing the silence to stretch until he gave her the same message he gave her mate.

"It's time. I promise something better than apples if you play your part, little queen."

Her eyes flared and before she could piece together her recognition, he shoved her through the door, causing her to stumble. Just as she caught herself, he shoved her again until she stood in front of her sister.

"It took you long enough."

"Apologies, my queen. I made her walk the entire way so I did not need to touch her filth more than was necessary."

His response seemed to appease Tatiana, and she focused her attention solely on the nymph that would replace her if only given the opportunity. An opportunity like the one he just presented her with.

The realm's future draped invisibly across her shoulders and she did not even know it. Everything depended on if she would rise to the occasion and take the first step toward the role she was destined to fill. He hoped that if his thoughts were loud enough, she would hear him. There was nothing more he could do, and he knew he had just relinquished any control he once had. It was in fate's hands now.

Fate always gets what fate wants.

Chapter 59
Kes

"I hate it when you do that," he admonished Ciaran, who once again ported him without warning. Which was ridiculous, because Kes was more than capable of porting himself.

"You did not know where to port. It was easier this way," he said.

Kes shook his head at his cousin before taking in their surroundings. They stood at the gaping mouth of a cave high on the razor-sharp, steep inclines of the Nocturia Mountains. Occasional gusts of icy wind blew hard against him. If he were to open his wings, the wind would take him with it.

"Are you coming?" Ciaran asked, grabbing Kes's attention. He was already well into the cave, forcing Kes to hurry in order to catch up.

Inside, the light from the moon, which had just been nearly blinding, quickly diminished after walking several feet into the darkening cave. Just as it turned pitch black, a soft glowing blue light illuminated the space. The blue got brighter with each step they went deeper into the cave.

"What are they?" Kes asked, waving his hand toward the glowing things all over the walls.

"I have not a clue. Some kind of sediment is my best guess. I suppose it could be a type of organism, yet they never move nor does their glow go out, so I am more inclined to think it's a sediment."

"This is where you lived?" he asked. He never truly thought about where his cousin had gone, yet he always assumed he was living somewhere luxurious. While beautiful, the cave was primitive at best.

"Yes, but—"

"Who is it that thinks they may enter one's home uninvited?" a voice called from deeper within the cave.

"You still use that same line?" Ciaran said, walking confidently towards the voice.

Kes could see the glow of a fire burning from within the depths. The way the light reflected off the walls of the cave made it impossible for him to locate it; however, Ciaran seemed to know the path well. They rounded a large formation of rock that nearly reached the ceiling of the cave and found... Kes was not sure what he was. He seemed more than fae and he somehow appeared to be ageless. Not in the way the fae looked one age for most of their lives until they aged rapidly before death. He looked neither old nor young, but he *felt* old.

Ancient.

"Well, now that's a face I never thought to see again," the being said in greeting.

"I cannot say I ever thought to see yours again either," his cousin said, smirking at the male.

"Who's this?" he asked.

Kes could swear it sounded as if he already knew and was

asking to be polite. How the male would know Kes, he did not know.

"This is my cousin, Kes. Kes this is Master Ulgridge. He taught me everything I know about fighting," Ciaran said.

Master? He never thought he would hear Ciaran refer to anyone by the name master.

"Ah, well then it is you I have to thank for providing me with a worthy sparring partner. Too bad he is insufferable, and I am unable to take him down a peg or two now though," he said, grinning at this Master Ulgridge.

"Ha! I like this one," Ulgridge said, laughing.

Kes had the same feeling around this male as he did around the Many Faced Goddess—a combination of wariness and awe. There was something otherworldly about him, and Kes had the sudden thought he might not even be from their realm.

"Of course you do," Ciaran said, rolling his eyes as he took a seat by the fire.

The two males sat in silence for a moment while Kes got to glimpse into the past. It was easy to see what they likely looked like every night for hundreds of years. Ciaran was comfortable—relaxed, even. There were few beings he was ever like that with—Etain, himself, and this male. It made him immediately trust Ulgridge, and he took a seat on the opposite side of the fire from his cousin.

"What is it that brings you here?" Ulgridge asked Ciaran.

"What if he just wished to visit his old Master?" Kes said, laughing at the way Ciaran glared at him.

It had been a long time since things felt this easy between them. Kes felt it deep in his gut. This was exactly where he was supposed to be at that moment. He was on the right path and closer than he had ever been to getting his nymph back. The feeling made his old self wake.

"Neither of us are particularly social," Ulgridge responded. He sounded so like Ciaran, Kes had to laugh.

"No, we have not come for a visit. I seek information," Ciaran responded.

Not only did the two sound exactly alike, they shared similar body language. It was uncanny. This male was more a father to Ciaran than the king had ever been.

"Ah, finally believing in the—what did you call them? Fairy tales?" Ulgridge asked, laughing at Ciaran.

"Something like that. I came across a hidden room filled with weapons and armor made of the metal you once told me was called Moon Blessed," Ciaran responded, unfazed by the male's laughter. That was something Kes had likely made him immune to after the last several hundred years.

"What about it?" Ulgridge asked. He was really making them work to get the information they sought.

"How did the metal become Moon Blessed, and what does it mean?" Kes asked, his impatience getting the better of him. He was so close to having Anin back in his arms. Like all he had to do was reach out and he would be able to brush her skin with his fingers.

"Moon Blessed is a process that requires a being with the power of moonlight. They can take any metal and turn it into Moon Blessed metal, giving the metal itself power. It's quite a remarkable thing to see," he responded.

How old was this male? Kes knew he had to be old. Yet the way he spoke of the long ago past as if it happened a few nights ago spoke to an unfathomable age. Much like the Many Faced Goddess.

"There is no one who can do such a thing," Ciaran declared.

"Of course there is," Ulgridge said, as a matter of fact.

"Where can I find this being?" Ciaran asked, glaring at the male.

"He's sitting right next to me," he replied.

He sounded as if it were completely obvious and the two cousins were idiots for not knowing this already. They exchanged a look, and Kes thought perhaps Ciaran's original assessment of the male was correct. He was obviously telling tales.

"Who?" Kes asked. It must be Ciaran. He would know if he had such a power. He would have to feel it or something. Right?

"You," he answered, sending Kes reeling. "I assumed you only resembled a bird and did not also have the brains of one."

Typically, something like that would make Kes laugh. He did love when beings used bird puns to insult him, although at the moment he could not move past the fact he apparently contained moonlight power. He felt nothing from within himself that would indicate he carried a dormant power.

"I have never changed any metal. How would I know I am so called 'Moon Blessed'?" Kes asked. He was convinced the male had to be mistaken.

"Of course you have not," he said. Silence followed as they waited for him to continue. When he did not, Ciaran rolled his eyes again.

"Ulgridge, enough with your riddles. Explain," he demanded.

Ulgridge was silent a moment longer as he stared at Kes. It was more like he stared *into* Kes, beyond his physical form, seeing what no one else could.

"You both really know so little. You have the capability of the power, but the Land must activate it, and it will only do so if there is a being who also has the power of sunlight. This requires all things to have a balance. If you have the capability, that means there is another with its opposite," he explained.

As odd as this whole thing was, that made complete sense. The Land always demanded balance.

"How do you know he has the power of moonlight?" Ciaran

asked. He sounded genuinely interested. Kes would have asked this same question next if his cousin had not beaten him to it.

"I can hear it. His blood sings of it," he said with a shrug.

Kes was shocked, confused, and losing hope all at the same time. He came here expecting to find the secrets of the moonlight that would lead him to finally reunite with his mate.

"If I understand you correctly, I contain the power of moonlight, yet I cannot access it until the Land unlocks it?" Kes asked. It all sounded impossible.

"That is what I said, yes."

"Say the Land decides to unlock it. How would he use it?" Ciaran asked.

It was a good question, not that it seemed like he would ever have the opportunity.

"Ah, there is a book that went missing several generations ago that would contain all the information he would need to master his power. There was a similar book for sunlight power as well. Both vanished around the same time and have never been seen since. You know, come to think of it, there were books for all the elements. Even your shadows, Prince," he said, making Kes's hopes dwindle even further.

"You are just now telling me this?" Ciaran asked, sounding offended.

"It would not have made a difference. The books will be found when fate determines it's the correct time."

That was something they all knew too well. Fate always got whatever it wanted, and it appeared fate wanted him to have all of his desires just out of reach. The phantom feeling of his mate's skin brushing across his fingertips felt out of reach now.

"I have this power and yet I cannot use it. There's a book that holds all of its secrets, but it has been lost for so long there is no record of its existence. How am I to fulfill the task given to me by the Many Faced Goddess?" he asked out loud to no one in particular. He felt like he was so close, and yet at the same time, he must be so far away from whatever he needed to discover to free Anin. They were out of time. He could not shake this feeling like something was coming, and he felt woefully unprepared. Just like he had one hundred and thirty-seven years ago.

"I would imagine finding out you have the power of moonlight and what it can do would be considered discovering its secrets, would you not?" Ulgridge replied.

Kes stared at him, slack jawed, while Ciaran did not look surprised at all.

"How did you know that's what she said to me?" Kes asked him. He had not been there. There was no way he should know what she said to him.

"I know most things," he replied, again not elaborating.

"How?" Kes asked him. Everything about his time in this cave felt like one big question mark. He came here looking for answers and yet all he got were more questions.

"I hear everything," he said, and clearly meant exactly that. Not that he hears about most things or that he hears things. He said he hears everything with such conviction Kes had to believe him.

"You hear... Are you... Are you a god?" he gave voice to the question that had been floating around the back of his mind from the moment he laid eyes on the male.

Ulgridge simply smiled at him and gave him a little wink in response. He thought he might understand why it enraged others when Kes winked at them now. Ulgridge jerked forward in his chair and tilted his head slightly, as if he were listening to something very carefully. The angle at which his head tilted parted his hair and Kes saw a hole in the side of his head where an ear should be.

What happened there?

"The storm has reached its crescendo," he blurted.

It took Kes a moment to register the words he chose were the exact same ones the Many Faced Goddess told him to wait for. The need to take action was becoming unbearable within him. He felt like he was going to crawl out of his skin if he did not do...he was not sure what.

"Wha..."

His spelled scroll appeared in front of his eyes and he unrolled it to see a message with the two words he had been waiting for over a hundred years to read.

It's time.

Chapter 60
Anin

"Is this the queen you desire? This broken, worthless creature?" Tatiana seethed.

She shook Anin at them as if to show just how broken she was. Tatiana shoved Anin down the few stairs of the dais. Too weak to catch herself, she landed hard on each step before sprawling on the floor at the bottom. Part of her wished she could just be free of this life and die on the white marbled floor beneath her. She knew that was not an option; the Land would never allow it and neither could she let *her* win. She had promises to keep.

Taking in a shaking, deep breath, she slid her hands underneath her and pushed herself up. She would not let this opportunity to be in front of such a large group of Day fae slip away. She would let them know exactly who their queen was. What a stupid idea it had been to bring her here and parade her in front of the court. Tatiana could not control her with her blood magic. That thought alone gave her the strength she needed to stand all the way up and straighten her spine for the first time in too many years to count.

"Why would they not? A broken, worthless creature is better

525

than the blight you are to this realm. Do they know, Tatiana?" she said. Her voice somehow managed not to betray just how broken she actually felt.

"Stop it," Tatiana seethed at her.

"Do they know where their missing loved ones have gone?" If this was the one chance she had with an audience, she was going to make sure they knew *everything*. There was no way high fae went missing with no one noticing.

"Silence!" Tatiana screamed.

"You cannot silence me, you cannot control me, and you cannot kill me. Do they know that, too? The Land has ensured I do not die no matter how much we both have wished for it at any given time."

The collective gasp she heard from around the room told her exactly what she already knew. She laughed at the enraged queen.

"Tell them, Tatiana, tell them where their family members have gone. Tell them how you slit each and every one of their necks to absorb their power and feed your addiction. Tell them how they begged for you to spare them as you took control of their bodies with your blood magic and made them walk to their own deaths." Anin would hear every single one of their desperate pleas for the rest of her life. **"Tell them!"**

Even though no high fae from this court had ever been anything but hostile to her, she could not help the empathy she felt. Being forced to bear witness to a being's life being ripped away steals a bit of your own life in the process. She felt like she had already died hundreds of times. In all honesty, she probably had. The only reason she still stood was because fate and the Land collectively decided she would live.

The room erupted into cries of outrage, and the wails of despair told of the many who still hoped their loved ones would return. Anin had no compassion to spare for the high fae still living. They let their queen go unchecked for far too long, and many paid the price of their negligence with their lives. What else did they let happen to the court and its inhabitants? The Day Court had never been kind to lesser fae, and it looked to only have gotten worse based on the many lesser fae around the room dressed in rags. They all paused mid task to stare open-mouthed at the wood nymph with a claim to the throne.

One of them.

She found even more strength within herself, knowing they were watching her. The possibility she represented was enough to see a different future for themselves. They were all used to being disappointed, and she could see them desperately trying to keep themselves from hoping. She added them to the list of beings fueling her determination.

"Brhget." She would say each of their names out loud. No longer a mantra to remind her who she fought for, but a promise of vengeance she would make to her sister in front of all these witnesses.

"What?" Tatiana asked, surprised by the sudden shift in conversation.

"Thistle. You might have forgotten who you slaughtered. I have not," she said. She had not asked the fae for their names, yet she saw their faces every time she closed her eyes. Hundreds of lives cut short so Tatiana could feed her addiction.

There had been a deep-rooted rage building within Anin and if she was not careful, that rage would burn hot and fast, depleting her before she truly got started. She took one shaky step up the dais.

"Enough of this. Guards!" she screamed without taking her eyes off of Anin. She was accustomed to her every whim being carried out; it took her a moment to notice no one had moved. The look of confusion she wore was comical, and Anin felt bolstered by the blatant refusal of the guards.

"Cerridwen." Her voice sounded stronger than she felt, and

her strength was quickly dissipating. She reached down the bond to where she knew Kes was always ready to lend her strength when she had none left to give. It felt like he caressed her as power flooded her, giving her the strength she needed to continue.

She stopped wishing for him to save her a long time ago. If he could have, he would have. She felt every time he came close and then his subsequent anguish when he had to leave her behind once again. Over the years, she came to understand she would need to be an active participant in her own rescue and this was the first opportunity she had to play her part. Perhaps if she could create enough chaos, Tatiana would let her guard down, giving Kes the moment he had been searching for.

"Guards!" Tatiana yelled again, this time adding a little foot stomp that made her look like a petulant youngling.

"Faith," she continued through Tatiana's fit.

"I said enough!" Her sister finally whipped her head toward the group of golden sentinels standing at one end of the room. "Seize her!" she demanded.

One of them reached up and pulled his helmet off, glaring at her before he said, "Are you going to make us? Control our bodies against our will, as you have done so many times in the past one hundred thirty-seven years. Just as you did when you stole her away from the Night Court? Not a single one of us has forgotten the first time our bodies were taken, controlled by an unseen force," the guard sneered at her.

Emboldened, several others removed their helmets. All of them wore similar expressions of rage.

"Hope." Anin managed to keep her voice from shaking as the shock of how long she had been caged like an animal in the dregs of the Day Court took hold. It took strength she did not know she still possessed to keep a sob from escaping her.

One hundred

thirty-seven years

...stolen.

"You will do as you are told! You should not be able to speak of that day! The oath should have kept your traitorous mouth shut!" Tatiana was vibrating with rage.

Anin knew she would be on the receiving end of that rage later. However, it would be worth it. She would make sure of it. There was nothing she had not already endured at the hands of her sister. She already knew she could get through the worst.

"Destiny," Anin said in the beat of silence that stretched until the guard responded.

"That's the funny thing, *my queen*." Tatiana flinched at the way the guard spat her title at her. He held almost as much hatred as she did for the bitch. "Our oaths dissolved several decades ago. Not even the magic binding us to the crown recognizes you. We have been waiting for another option to present itself."

"Josephine!" She had to yell to be heard over the cacophony of voices rising behind her.

Tatiana's rage was pulsing from her in waves. She was close to showing them the true Tatiana. Anin would make sure she pushed her right off the edge of her fragile facade she wore in front of the court.

"Lyse!"

"Enough!" her sister screamed. She was quickly spiraling out of control. Anin knew all she needed to do was give a proverbial shove, and the queen would explode.

"River!" She was close to the top of the dais now. Just two more steps to go until she was face to face with her tormentor. She would get into her sister's face like she did all those years ago after she forced her to witness the slaughter of the witches she once called friends.

"Ophila! She was nurturing and loved freely. You stole the goodness she brought to the realm the day you ripped her life from her!" Anin's rage matched Tatiana's. Where her sister's was fueled by a lack of control, hers was over a century of pain. The queen's rage was out of control and chaotic; Anin's was honed like the sharpest of blades.

"Catra, who's dying wish was for me to make you pay! I intend to do just that, no matter how many more hundreds of years it takes." She was more certain now than ever that she would be able to keep her promise. The power Kes fed to her would be just enough to make sure everyone knew exactly what their queen really was. They would see the monster festering inside her.

"Do something!" Tatiana shouted to Raindal.

It surprised both of them when he did not immediately jump to do her bidding like the little lap dog he was. He stood there and stared directly at Anin. Tatiana scoffed and looked away from him, disgust twisting her face. He gave her a conspiratorial nod, and she recalled the way he spoke of apples and called her little queen.

He had never shown her any kindness, and yet...

"Welyn!" she exclaimed as she glared back at the fae male, who had caused her nearly as much pain as Tatiana. She must have misheard or hallucinated. He was cruel and just as depraved as his queen.

She finally made it all the way up the stairs and stood before her sister. They were the same height, making it easy for her to stick her filthy face into Tatiana's, their noses nearly touching. She stared her down while calling on the dregs of strength her body had left. Even with the boost from Kes, she was too weak. Her body used the power too quickly in an attempt to heal her.

"Tallon! Little Tallon, who was just a youngling! You are not a queen, you are nothing more than a creature rotting away from the inside. You are a coward and a monster!" she screamed louder than she thought possible, tasting blood in the back of her throat.

Tatiana backhanded her, sending Anin toppling to the side. She reached out grabbing for anything to keep her from falling down the stairs again; she knew there would be no getting back up if she did. Her hand connected with something hard and she latched on.

The throne.

Power immediately filled her as a white light shot up all around her. She heard a voice—that was not really a voice—but before she could make out what it was saying, Tatiana ripped her away from the throne.

"No!" she screamed at Anin, her rage laced with fear as she grabbed her around the throat. "How dare you!"

Anin smiled at her as the grip around her throat increased. Even when her head began to swim, she felt victorious. She had won this battle and declared war on her sister. The thought did not frighten her as much as it probably should have. Perhaps it was stupid to feel confident, but she did not care. She had won, and she could do so again.

Something caused Tatiana to lessen her grip just as Anin's world began to go black. The roaring in her ears eased just enough for her to hear the three words being repeated by the surrounding fae. Anin's smile grew even larger while Tatiana's eyes grew wide with horror. Yes, Anin would definitely win again. The words whispered by so many began to take the shape of one voice, and a name she knew was hers to claim.

"Queen of Light."

Thanks!

Oh hi, you're still here?

...If you're still reading, I appreciate you! Lol! These and blurbs are always the hardest for me to write. I mean, how do you adequately say thank you to the people who always have your back?

As always, I want to thank my family, who constantly have to put up with my nonstop working and hermit like behavior. They want nothing but success for me and cheer me on without fail.

My sister friend, who not only reads everything I write as I write it but also is a wealth of knowledge. As a psychologist, she helped me out a lot with this one. Mental health is incredibly important and I think we have all suffered, suffer, or will suffer with it at some point. We all give so much of ourselves to the people around us and the career paths we choose, we sometimes forget to take care of our own needs. Take the time. It does not make you selfish.

My fellow Distracted Inklings. We lived our entire lives on TikTok live in November and I credit those sprints to finishing Queen of Light and triggering a hyper fixation that had me spitting out 140K words in a few weeks! I love that so many in the community joined us and I am looking forward to more obsessive writing sprints in the future! I feel lucky to be a part of such a kindhearted and supportive group.

Rebekah Sinclair... for a few reasons. She not only did my beautiful cover, but she also gave me a dev edit that really pushed me to reach deeper into myself. I am so grateful for that feedback even though you were terrified to give it. She has become one of my best friends and I am so happy that we have each other to share our wild plans with.

Kimmie Chonko for being such a bad ass editor. I love we get to share this journey with each other. You are a joy to work with and I am lucky to have you as my little sister friend.

My street team and chroniclers... again... I'm sorry I am chaos incarnate. Thanks for putting up with my shit anyway.

And of course, no thanks would be complete without thanking you, the reader. Without you, there would be no Realms of Lore. Thank you for choosing to pick up my books and get lost in the world I create!

Oh, special shout-out to sour patch kids and oatmeal cream pies. The real MVPs.

Happy Birthday Jamie!

About the Author

Hi! I'm Amber Thoma, the author of *Prince of Darkness, Heirs of Darkness, and Queen of Light*. I have been a reader for as long as I can remember. I blame personal-pan pizzas (IYKYK) for instilling an obsessive addiction to the many worlds books could take me to early in my life. I grew up in Northern Virginia and lived there until a few years ago, when I moved to a sleepy little college town in the mountains. I live in a 111 year old home with my dog, Lilith, and my cat, Kitten (very original, I know), and I am minutes from my family.

Like many people, lockdown made me reevaluate my life. For over a decade, I knew there was something I needed—a change. I played around with so many ideas. Like moving to a different country, going back to school, and starting a family. None of those felt right. The part of me screaming, "YOU'RE ON THE WRONG PATH," never silenced.

Listening to my intuition when the logical side of me was smashing the panic button was terrifying. That first step off the path was the most uncomfortable thing I had ever done. They say you have to get uncomfortable if you want to enact real change.

Well, I got wildly uncomfortable and uprooted my entire life, and I will never stop being grateful for taking that first step.

If I had never taken that step, I would not have had a year of time with my niece before she suddenly passed away. I would never have taken the time to address my mental health. I definitely would never have sat down and written a book, and committing to a 5 series saga that will take me ten to fifteen years to complete would have completely overwhelmed me. I would have given up before I started, like I have so many times in the past. The folder of several dusty novel plans and intros can attest to that.

What is the moral of the story? Do not let fear keep you from taking that first step off the path you know you are not meant to be on. After all,

Fate gets what fate wants.

Also by Amber Thoma
Prince of Darkness

Realms of Lore: Fae Book One

"She felt as though she were stuck between two impossible choices and almost wished fate would intervene and choose for her."

"Hello pet, you are mine now."

The Night Court's ruling line has been cursed, and a prophecy holds the key. Four beings brought together by the hands of fate must set aside their differences to break a centuries-long curse and unveil secrets that will change everything. Over just a few nights their lives are turned upside down. After all,

Fate gets what fate wants.

Also by Amber Thoma

Heirs of Darkness: A Prince of Darkness Novella

Realms of Lore: Fae Book 1.5

"You must understand, we are wicked creatures, it is our nature. It may not be right, as you have said, but we are what we are."

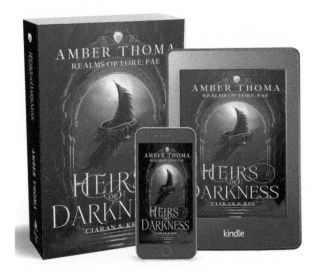

Under the corrupt rule of Ciaran's father, Nightfell Palace is no place for a youngling. Ciaran and Kes are forced to grow up quickly in order to survive the blood soaked paths and tortuous trials set before them. Ultimately, the Night Court will teach them the most important lesson of all...

Fate *always* gets what fate wants.